A
DRAGON
OF
TURICUM

C. R. BRACHER

Disclaimer:
This is a work of fiction. All characters, locations, and businesses are purely products of the author's imagination and are entirely fictitious. Any resemblance to actual people, living or dead, or to businesses, places, or events is completely coincidental.

GELU OCEANUS

RIVER BRUN

TURICUM

COPORTA

RIVER STOUR

HOBART GAP

HERCYNIAN FOREST

CALOR RIVER

REGILLIUM

BOAR'S TUSK

BERT

THE ACADEMY

EMON

HOG'S END

BATH

FINCHES FIELD

RIVER GILPIN

CAVERNS of CARCEREM

TYRUS

BELUM

PERGAMON

SINUM OCEANUS

GUARACI

TRAINING

Eldred leaned on his staff in the middle of the dirt training square, bounded by the one-story wooden barracks. He was in the first line of the hundred fifty or so squires in attendance at the Academy, with the rows growing younger and wider the further back they stretched. Proper Deirans, all of them, wiry and small, dressed in their rough woolen tunics.

Preceptor Garaint paced back and forth in front of the assembly, going on and on. "I cannot emphasize enough the importance of keeping a firm grip on your staff. Take two otherwise equal opponents, the one with a firm grip will win most of the time. Be that in a warrior taking an offensive approach to fighting and primarily seeking to strike, or be that in a defensively minded armsman looking first to avert a strike, rather than landing their own blow. I cannot emphasize enough..."

Tenny leaned over and whispered. "His lectures are more deadly than his staff."

Eldred smiled and glanced back at the children behind him, who watched with rapt attention, peeking between the gaps in the taller squires up front. They hadn't heard this same boring lecture twelve times before like he had. Probably none of them ever would.

Absently gazing out in the field beyond the square, Eldred caught sight of a bumblebee. Fifty yards away, the bee was buzzing a few feet off the ground when it caught wind of a hollyhock with five floppy flowers in bloom. Eldred focused his Mother blessed vision as the bee landed on the lowest flower and scooped up a respectable harvest of pollen. Then, it drifted up to the next flower and padded its collection even more.

What would it be like to dive into a flower bigger than yourself and full of sustenance? Eldred took a deep breath as he imagined the luxury of the experience. Suddenly, something poked him in the shoulder.

Preceptor Garaint yelled in his face. "What's wrong with you, Eldred? I called your name three times!"

"Huh?" said Eldred.

"He forgot his name, sir. Can't blame a Mercian for that," said Dreven.

The boys laughed. Eldred glared down at Dreven, the smallest and weakest member of the old-timers line, and walked up in front of the assembly.

"One foot in front of the other. You can do it, Eldred!" called Dreven with a wide smile, eliciting more mirth from the squires.

"We are going to have a demonstration of the technique from Eldred, the senior squire. I need a partner for him; any volunteers?"

Eldred towered over the preceptor as the old man looked over the crowd, choosing Eldred's victim. Tenny raised his hand; that was the right choice, the only worthy competitor in the Academy. His quickness offset Eldred's strength and reach to some degree. Dreven also raised his hand. Eldred smiled. Not a competitive match, but one he would make sure to enjoy.

Eldred's eyes widened in surprise when Preceptor Garaint chose a boy, Traden, from the second row. That was not how it usually worked. It was embarrassing enough to fight the old-timers. Traden was barely thirteen years old and was well under five feet tall.

"Traden, I want you to come in aggressively. Don't worry about hurting Eldred; he is fairly skilled."

Eldred raised an eyebrow. Fairly skilled?

"Now, Eldred. I want you to demonstrate the defensive techniques I covered today. You are stepping back, pivoting from foot to foot, blocking out, blocking out. You are not swinging at him. Check that impulse!"

"I'm always careful, Preceptor."

"Did you not club Mance in the head last week?"

Eldred glanced at the aggrieved looking squire in the front row. "He stepped into it and it was only a glancing blow."

Preceptor Garaint waved his hand dismissively. "Let's have more care today. Traden, begin."

Traden charged towards Eldred: thrusting, thrusting, thrusting. Eldred retreated at a measured pace, blocking out the attacks. The sound of clacking staves filled the air.

"That's good. Hold up, Traden. Well done." Preceptor Garaint turned towards the assembly. "What did you observe?"

"I noticed a giant Mercian fighting a little kid!" said Dreven.

"I'm not Mercian," growled Eldred.

Preceptor Garaint huffed. "Something specific—regarding the defensive work?"

"He is always blocking out, away from his body. He's blocking out," said Tenny.

"That is exactly right. I couldn't have said it better myself."

Eldred rolled his eyes. That is exactly what Preceptor Garaint usually ended up saying, as Tenny well knew. Next, Eldred would get a chance to weakly thrust his staff at Traden a few times, being careful to let his attack get blocked out, and the drill would be done. It would be time for lunch.

"Now let's have you two fight," said Preceptor Garaint.

Eldred jerked his head around to stare at the preceptor. Dreven laughed. Traden turned pale for a moment, then he tightened his grip on his staff.

"You mean really fight? Not just a little training drill?" asked Eldred.

"That's correct," said the preceptor. "Take your positions. I want a clean bout to first touch. No wild swings, Eldred. Let's begin."

The match was on.

Traden started on offense, stepping in and trying to tag Eldred's arm. Eldred batted Traden's staff away and swung for Traden's leg. Traden jumped out of reach and then stepped in on the offensive, this time swinging at Eldred's head. Eldred ducked and grimaced. You aren't supposed to swing at an opponent's head. Eldred pressed forward, driving Traden back with quick, short thrusts. One, two, three times, and there. Eldred tagged Traden lightly on the shoulder. Traden angrily threw his stick down. Eldred straightened up and smiled. Except for a few times when Tenny had been lucky, Eldred had not lost in years.

Preceptor Garaint clapped politely. "Well fought. Young Traden did quite well. When you give up size, strength and reach, you are at a significant disadvantage in one on one combat. This is a disadvantage we often face when fighting Mercians."

"I'm Deiran," muttered Eldred.

"Of course you are. Now let's adjust the contest. Noll, you come up and join with Traden. Dreven, you come up with Eldred."

"Wait. What do you mean 'with'?" asked Eldred.

"You are going to fight against each other in pairs."

"We never do that," protested Eldred.

"Today you will humor me."

Dreven and Noll went to their respective sides.

"Watch out; Traden might swing at your head," said Eldred.

"I might swing at your head," said Dreven, with an impish grin.

Preceptor Garaint walked over to Traden and Noll and clasped them each by the shoulder. "These two are standing for the trial next week. I believe they will pass. They have the Bond, or at least a taste of it."

A murmur broke out in the assembly.

"Did you know about this?" asked Eldred.

"I heard a rumor. How are we going to fight them?" asked Dreven.

"They are still only thirteen years old. Just hold off your foe while I finish mine."

"They are from the second row." Dreven pointed at his chest. "You hold off your foe while I finish off mine."

Eldred sighed and shook his head.

Meanwhile, Preceptor Garaint was whispering something to Traden and Noll while they stared into each other's eyes. After a theatrical moment, the two knocked fists and turned to face Eldred and Dreven with their staves at ready.

"Nothing excessive, Eldred. We go to first touch. Begin," said Preceptor Garaint.

Traden and Noll ran at Eldred like rabid dogs. They ignored Dreven and circled to opposite sides of Eldred, where they executed a coordinated attack, driving him back. First, Traden went high for Eldred's head while Noll tried to tag Eldred on the leg. Then Noll jabbed at Eldred's gut while Traden aimed for Eldred's foot. They pressed Eldred hard. He only had time to block and evade.

As they both went for Eldred's head, Eldred blocked Traden's attack from the right as he ducked under Noll's from the left.

"Take one!" called Eldred as he turned and crashed into Dreven. Eldred tried to keep his balance, but he toppled over, knocking Dreven down as well. Before Eldred hit the ground, he felt the slap of a staff on his calf.

"Aww," said Dreven. They had tagged him as well.

"The Bond! The Bond!" shouted the assembly while Traden and Noll held up their staves in victory.

Eldred glared down at Dreven as he got up and dusted off his pants. "Thanks for the help."

Dreven remained seated in the dirt as he contemplated the victorious boys. "If they had the Bond, we couldn't win."

"Thank you for the demonstration, squires," said Preceptor Garaint. "I wouldn't call it the Bond as yet, not till they pass the trial, but Traden and Noll appear strong. Good luck to you both. Eldred and Dreven, tough match. We are done for the morning. We will resume after lunch."

A few boys crowded around Traden and Noll, congratulating them.

Eldred walked over to Tenny, waiting for the commotion to pass. "That was a new routine."

"I didn't see it coming. Fighting in pairs now? What a pairing, too. Not even your father could beat those two with Dreven tripping him."

Eldred grinned. "My father would have killed them both, despite Preceptor Garaint's instructions."

Tenny laughed. "I suppose he might. He's killed more than a few."

"When did those two manifest the Bond?"

"Who knows? I can't be bothered to keep track of the youngsters."

"Eldred, put up your staff and come with me. The headmaster wants to see you!" called Preceptor Garaint from across the yard.

"What now?" muttered Eldred.

"At least they still talk to you," said Tenny.

COUNSEL

The headmaster lived in Bordin Hall, a handsome two-story building crafted from glossy black stone. It stood out from the other structures at the Academy, which were cheaply crafted single-story huts made with pitted lumber.

His study was well appointed with an imposing oak desk, a thick—though worn—mauve carpet and an informal sitting area off the side, with two padded chairs in front of the fire, which was burning low.

The headmaster was settled by the fire when he waved Eldred in from the door. "Come in, Eldred. Take a seat."

Once Eldred sat, the headmaster stared silently at Eldred's forehead with focused concentration. Eldred waited patiently, returning the headmaster's gaze. The headmaster was an elderly man with penetrating eyes and a face that reflected a friendly—though resolute—disposition.

Once the headmaster completed his examination, he gave Eldred a quick smile. "How pleasant to see you, Eldred. I don't visit the yard much these days, but Preceptor Grimes is always telling me about your talent with the sword. Now let's have a look at you. Hmm, you seem a bit taller. Have you grown?"

"Perhaps a little, headmaster."

"You possess a gift, Eldred, a gift from the Night Mother, who made us all. You have the strength and height of a Mercian. It's nothing to be ashamed of."

Eldred stiffened. "I'm not ashamed, headmaster."

"I am glad to hear it, Eldred. We must be the people she made us to be. Speaking on this topic, I notice your eyes in this light. The fire reflects in them oddly. They show their Maldavian nature."

Eldred shifted in his chair. "Is that so, headmaster?"

"Two blessings from the Night Mother. You must be proud."

"Yes?" answered Eldred, a bit perplexed. Deirans rarely express appreciation for the gifts that the Night Mother granted others.

"What of the Deiran gift? Will you be taking part in the upcoming trial?"

"I was just telling Preceptor Garaint on the walk over that I am aiming for the winter trial."

"The last trial offered before you turn eighteen. Is it wise to put it off to such a late date?"

Eldred turned toward the fire. "I have not found a strong pairing."

"Ah, yes," said the headmaster. "The right partner is essential. Still, I wonder, is the pairing truly the issue at hand? It can't have escaped your attention how late you are, past late, in manifesting the Bond. You are more than a year older than Tenny, and he is the next oldest."

"I remain aware, headmaster. People find ways to remind me."

"Your cousin, Harold, was in the year below you, and he ascended five years ago at one arch removed. Of course, he was graced with a Deiran stone, but then you are as well."

"Yes." Eldred reflexively reached up to touch the middle of the three stones set between his left temple and his ear. Of course, Harold's stone actually worked.

"Hamonet was the last squire remaining in your year, aside from yourself. He gave up three years ago to be a cooper, did he not?"

Eldred shrugged. "He left. I don't know whether he still makes barrels."

"And?"

"What?" said Eldred.

"Isn't it time you consider alternatives?"

"Alternatives?"

"Alternatives to being a warrior," said the headmaster with a solemn tone.

Eldred sat up straight. "I don't see what else I would be. I'm the son of the king, your king. And I am graced with a Deiran stone blessed by the Night Mother herself." Eldred brushed back the hair from his left temple to show three small stones set in his skin: Mercian red, Deiran blue and Maldavian green.

The headmaster glanced at the gems. "I know. It seems promising. It has always seemed so promising: King Alfred's blood, one of the remaining fatum lapis. But it is not enough. You will have until the winter trial if you so desire, but I can tell you now—you shall not pass."

"What? How can you know that?"

"I have led the Academy for ten years. In all that time, I have never failed to see it long before it surfaced." The headmaster slowly shook his head. "If a student has the potential to ascend, the potential to manifest the Bond, I always see a glimmer. I examined you when you arrived today. There is nothing there, nothing at all. There never has been."

Eldred frowned. "It could come late. I have—an unusual bloodline."

The headmaster raised his palms. "An odd mixture of Deiran, Mercian and Maldavian blood. They granted you a Deiran stone—as they should have. But why also a Mercian and Maldavian stone? What was the sense in that? Rather a muddle, Eldred."

"There's no muddle. My mother is of royal blood. She's your queen."

"Queen Ghyslaine has many fine qualities, but she is not Deiran. Is she?"

Eldred crinkled up his face in a pained expression. "No."

"And the Bond—the Night Mother bequeathed it to the Deirans and only the Deiran, did she not?"

Eldred looked back at the fire.

The headmaster reached out and patted Eldred's arm. "I don't fault you, Eldred. You have trained as hard as any squire ever has. I warned Alfred. Now you bear the cost. The first royal heir completely bereft of the Bond."

Eldred licked his lips. "You're certain?"

"I am. We are at the end. We need to consider other courses of action."

"Such as?"

"Not everyone leaves as a warrior. Squires go on to many professions. They become tradesmen, farmers, scribes, coopers. Some even become stewards and run the estates of lords."

Eldred grunted.

"You are friends with Tenny," said the headmaster. "I believe he will leave the Academy soon, no doubt to apprentice with his father."

"How do you know this?"

"I see—indications—and then there is his age. He is quite old as well. Will you think less of him when he takes up a blacksmith's hammer?"

"Of course not."

"Nor will I think less of you," said the headmaster. "We will find you some other—important role. I expect you will be a steward. If you marry well, your sons will have some chance to manifest the Bond. I would be honored to start their training myself, if I am still here."

Eldred shook his head. "No. It cannot be. I'm not meant to be a steward. I'm a fighter. I trained all my life for battle."

"I know. I directed your training. But now, it is time for something new. You will find another role—steward, farmer, blacksmith, scribe or whatever you decide."

Eldred's eyes glimmered with unnatural brightness as he stared into the fire.

"What about here, then?" Eldred met the headmaster's eyes. "I could instruct students at the Academy. I know the sword and staff as well as anyone, better than some current instructors."

"Oh, no, Eldred. All preceptors must have the Bond."

"Why? Why is that? You don't need the Bond to swing a wooden sword."

The headmaster smiled. "No, I suppose not. But we have rules we live by. As I said, I expect you will be a steward. But you are thinking, considering. You are taking the step. I knew you would."

Eldred folded his arms over his chest. "I see. Is that all?"

"No, there is another matter, one you will view more favorably. Your father has arranged a blood match with the Mercians, the most enormous tourney in years. A substantial grant of land hangs in the balance."

"Hmm. A blood match is for warriors."

"Warriors do the fighting, but your father has asked me to send a small band of worthy squires to witness, in the hope that some may experience transference."

"Transference?" asked Eldred.

"The acceleration of the Bond by being exposed to its use," explained the headmaster. "He asked me to make a list of candidates, but his meaning was clear. While he doubtlessly intends to take more territory from the Mercians, I believe this is primarily an exercise for your benefit."

"Does it work?"

The headmaster nodded. "I have witnessed cases where it did have some effect. We don't usually bother, since it only speeds the process a short interval. However, transference only surfaces the Bond in squires who possess potential. That is not your circumstance. Still, you will leave for the blood match in ten days, right after the fall trial."

Eldred's eyes glowed red again as he stared into the fire.

"When you return, we can discuss your future," said the headmaster. "You have forty-five days until the winter trial."

"And sixty-three until my day of ascension."

The headmaster smiled. "So quick with your sums."

DINING HALL

That evening, Eldred and Tenny sat at one end of the table for old-timers while Mance, Yeowars and Dreven huddled together at the other, talking quietly. The rest of the hall was bustling with activity as the younger boys crowded in at packed tables.

The two ate in silence, shutting out the laughter and clatter of the others. Eldred piled up the bones from his extra helpings of chicken in front of him. He usually enjoyed Cook's meals, but today he found it tasteless.

Eldred glanced toward Mance and Yeowars. "Preceptor Garaint said they signed up. Do you think they will pass?"

"Can't say."

"I haven't noticed any change. They're not devilishly fast like Traden and Noll."

Tenny shrugged and picked up a chicken leg.

Eldred glanced back at the boys. "What're they thinking?"

"Perhaps they just want to try before they give up. I'll leave without ever having attempted the trial."

"Then stay."

Tenny gave a short laugh. "I told you, I'm done wasting my family's gold."

"And I told you, I can speak to my father. He needs warriors. He can provide funds."

Tenny shook his head. "Why would I waste the king's coin?"

"It's not a waste. You're more than a year younger than I am. You're not close to approaching the age of ascension," said Eldred.

"I'm a year older than either Mance or Yeowars, and they're the next oldest after me."

"They're fifteen. They're still young," protested Eldred.

Tenny made a sweeping gesture across the hall. "Not for this. We're sitting at the old squire's table in a room full of children."

Eldred frowned. "I'll have to leave soon. You don't have to. Not yet."

"Don't fuss, Eldred. Like the headmaster told you, you're going to be a steward. You'll run one of your father's holdings and order a mess of vassals around. It won't be worse than being here at this wretched academy. Not in any way."

"If I'm not a warrior, then I can never be king."

"Why do you want to be king?"

Eldred pursed his lips. "I'm Alfred's son. I'm supposed to be king."

"Well, I wish you luck. For my part, I'm leaving as soon as my father arrives, the very moment."

"You so want to be a blacksmith you can't wait one more year?" asked Eldred.

Tenny gave Eldred a sharp look. "One year that costs more coin."

"The headmaster is picking candidates to attend the blood match. I can get you on the list. There could be transference."

Tenny sighed. "Yes. You told me and I'm sure someone will manifest, but not me. I'm done making excuses. Stop by and see me on your way back. Hog's End is close to the site of the match. I'll start on a piece for you, my first for a customer—maybe an oversized helmet to cover your thick Mercian skull."

Eldred gave a half-hearted grin. "I'm certain you will make an accomplished blacksmith."

"And I'm certain you will make a terrible steward. That is why it's fortunate you are the king's son."

Eldred snorted a laugh. "You're not wrong, Tenny."

PREPARATION

Preceptor Grimes, the master of the sword, ran the morning training the next day. He was middle-aged, a bit pudgy in the middle, but his eyes had the lively twinkle of a younger man.

"Today we're helping some of our squires prepare for the trial. Does anyone know why we conduct trials?" asked Preceptor Grimes, standing before the assembly, a wooden sword in each hand.

"We do it to ascend, to become bonded warriors," answered Mance from the front line.

"Correct," said Preceptor Grimes. "Now let's get into the specifics of how we conduct a trial. In the trial, there are five distinct actions. Someone list them off."

"Thrust, swing left, swing right, step forward, step back," said Yeowars, who was standing—as usual—at Mance's side.

"Correct. A pair of squires performs ten acts. They must match each other. What could be simpler? Traden, can you come up for a demonstration?"

Traden brushed past Eldred on his way to take the wooden sword Preceptor Grimes offered him.

Preceptor Grimes held up his sword. "Now we have a pair. We need a caller. Eldred, as the senior squire, will you do us the honor?"

Eldred nodded and walked over to stand in front of Traden.

"Show us the hand signals, if you would, Eldred," said the preceptor.

"For thrust, you point forward." Eldred pointed.

"And when Traden sees the signal, he will lunge forward. Now please, Traden."

Traden thrust the wooden sword forward.

"With flourish, with panache, Traden!" scolded Preceptor Grimes. "If things go well, you will only attempt the trial once. You must be crisp. You may have the Bond, but if you are lackadaisical, you may still not pass. Again, Traden!"

Traden lunged forward again, fully extending this time.

Preceptor Grimes smiled. "Better, I like it. Take us through the other acts, Eldred."

Eldred demonstrated. "Point left, and they swing to their right. Right, and they swing to their left. Push your palm out to make them step back. Pull your hand back to bring them forward."

Preceptor Grimes moved over to stand behind Traden while facing Eldred. "Now give us a full set of ten acts, if you would, Eldred."

Eldred pulled Traden forward as Preceptor Grimes looked over Traden's shoulder and stepped forward. The boys in the assembly laughed. Eldred smiled and shook his head.

Next, Eldred gave Traden the signal to swing left. Behind Traden, but out of sync, Preceptor Grimes swung left.

"You can't look!" shouted some boys.

"You have to face the other way!" bellowed Dreven.

Next Eldred pushed Traden back, and Preceptor Grimes mirrored the act.

"You're still looking!" came the shout from the squad.

Preceptor Grimes grinned. As Eldred went through the set, the boys grew louder and more hysterical.

When they were done, Preceptor Grimes turned to the assembly. "Ten matches, a perfect ten. Any problems?"

"You can't look! Turn your back!" yelled the boys.

"Oh, my. You may be right. You have to turn your back. So how can you match anyone?"

"The Bond! The Bond! The Bond!" shouted the squires.

"The Bond. I hope you all manifest it, the greatest blessing the Night Mother ever granted any of her people. It makes you come alive, imbued with strength and speed beyond the reach of ordinary people, even other Deirans. Working with your brothers, in your pod, you will feel a connection that goes deeper than anything other people experience. Normally, we use the Bond to kill our foes, but the trial is not a fight. Instead, we work together. Noll, will you come up front?"

Eldred frowned as Noll made his way to the front from the second row.

He seemed pleased with himself. Preceptor Grimes handed him the wooden sword.

"First, we line you up, eight paces apart, facing away from each other." said Preceptor Grimes. "Good. We need auditors. Tenny, Mance, Yeowars and Dreven, please come up."

The four squires, the balance of the old timer's row, stepped forward.

"Your job is to watch the signals and determine whether Noll matches the acts Eldred shows Traden," said Preceptor Grimes. "The act must match and be in sync. Now that we're situated everyone, let's run a test set. When you're ready, Eldred."

Eldred took a second to make up the order, then started the set. Traden and Noll performed their exaggerated steps and theatrically swung their swords. They did not match on every act, but they matched on seven. Seven times they performed the same act perfectly in sync.

"How many matches was that?" asked Preceptor Grimes.

The auditors each held up seven fingers. Preceptor Grimes grinned. "Well done. Quite well done. A hand for them, if you please."

Eldred rubbed his chin while the assembly clapped. Traden and Noll were not particularly strong or brave or smart, but they had something better than any of those qualities. They had the Bond. He felt sure they would prove as much in the upcoming trial. Eldred would have to watch another pair ascend while he stayed behind.

Preceptor Grimes retrieved another pair of wooden swords from his bag. "Mance and Yeowars also committed to standing for the trial. Eldred, Tenny and Dreven, please work with them on the other side of the square."

Mance and Yeowars took the wooden swords, and the five older squires trudged to the far side of the exercise yard. Behind them were calls of encouragement as Traden and Noll started another set.

The crew kept glancing back at the other group as Eldred tried to start the exercise. Eldred furrowed his brows. "Keep your eyes here. Focus on our practice!"

Eldred started the pair on their first set, going through ten actions. At the end of the set, Tenny and Dreven held up their fingers to show that only one matched.

Preceptor Grimes called over to check their results. "How many was it, Eldred?"

"One, Preceptor."

Preceptor Grimes pursed his lips. "Well, it's a start. Give them a break and then run through again with Yeowars taking the signals."

"Yes, Preceptor," said Eldred.

Mance and Yeowars huddled off by themselves while Preceptor Grimes started another set for Traden and Noll.

Dreven laughed. "I guess getting none right is a start too."

"That's enough from you," said Eldred.

"Do either of you think they can pass the trial?" asked Dreven, turning to Eldred and Tenny.

Eldred shrugged. "They need not match every step. They can ascend with only five matched acts so long as the auditors say they felt the Bond."

"True enough. But what do you think? Will they pass?" said Dreven.

Eldred considered. "They might."

"Will you make a wager?" asked Dreven.

"What?" said Eldred.

"You think they will pass the trial. Will you make a wager?" persisted Dreven.

Eldred frowned. "We're not allowed to bet on trials."

Tenny stepped forward. "What do you even have to wager, Dreven? Eldred's the king's son. His family has more gold than your family ever will."

Dreven grinned. "Eldred has loads more gold than my family does. I'm not betting gold. I wager my attendance here at the Academy. If these two fools pass the trial, I leave. If they don't, Eldred leaves."

"It is nothing we should bet on," protested Eldred. "And even if Mance and Yeowars don't ascend this time, they will just be more prepared for their next attempt."

"Exactly," agreed Tenny.

"So says the blacksmith," said Dreven.

"Shut up," said Eldred.

Dreven pointed at Tenny. "You mean me or the quitter?"

"You're a fool," said Eldred.

"I may be a fool, but I'll manifest the Bond someday, unlike you or this feeble pair." Dreven waved his hand toward Mance and Yeowars. "It is only a little while longer you get to pretend at being a squire, Eldred. You should take my wager. Better to leave on your own than to get kicked out."

Eldred scoffed. "How amazingly instructive, Dreven. Can we return to our testing session? You can count, can't you, Dreven?"

"I can count to one, though I doubt their performance will warrant it."

Tenny walked over and grabbed Dreven by his tunic.

"What is going on here?" asked Preceptor Garaint, who appeared from around the side of a nearby barracks.

Tenny released Dreven and stepped back next to Eldred.

"Are you running this session, Eldred?" continued Preceptor Garaint, turning to Eldred.

"I am, Preceptor," said Eldred.

Preceptor Garaint glared up at Eldred. "Is it a trial or a brawl?"

"A trial, Preceptor."

"Then clean it up. I will be watching from across the yard." Preceptor Garaint glowered at Tenny before heading over to join the assembly.

Eldred sighed. "Let's get on with it. Yeowars, let's have you up for signals."

TRIAL DAY

The morning of the trial, fifty-five days before Eldred's day of ascension, Eldred and the other squires gathered all the chairs they could find and placed them in a semi-circle on the northern side of the arches. The arches were an odd architectural feature of the Academy, five freestanding black stone arches off by themselves, a hundred yards north of the other buildings. Built for some unknown purpose, they had become a centerpiece of the advancement trial for squires. Each arch was twenty feet high, twenty feet across and ten feet wide, separated by stone walls two feet thick.

In the late morning, visitors started arriving. Some were relatives of the four squires taking the trial; others included bonded warriors interested in learning who would be joining their ranks. As noon approached, everything had been made ready. The only thing left to do was wait for the warriors conducting the trial, and King Alfred, who was accompanying them.

The visitors waited on their seats. Squires formed up in lines on the south side of the arches. Mance. Yeowars, Traden and Noll stood in the first row, the participants. Then came a row with the oldest boys, comprising Eldred, Tenny and Dreven, followed by longer rows of the younger boys. Headmaster Tibbot hovered halfway between the arches and the squires, accompanied by a few of the senior preceptors. Other preceptors walked the lines, keeping the squires at attention.

"Your father is late," said Tenny.

Eldred nodded. "He is. It's odd he's coming. He has not come to any trials for the last few years."

"Perhaps he wants to see your cousin conduct the trial. The preceptors say Harold's pod is highly accomplished," said Dreven, who was standing off the side.

Eldred frowned. "So they do."

"I would be more impressed if they showed up on time," said Tenny.

"What about our wager, Eldred?" said Dreven.

Eldred crossed his arms. "Make your bets with someone else."

Dreven smirked. "Suit yourself, Eldred."

Finally, a contingent of riders appeared in the distance, approaching down the lane behind the seated visitors. Eldred noted his father among them. King Alfred had changed little from when Eldred had last seen him two years ago. His face remained stern and humorless. The small patch of hair remaining on top of his head was smaller and grayer, but he didn't look any weaker. He was still the same hard man, despite his age. Harold rode by Alfred's side, a dandy in black leather armor with a red sash.

Tenny squinted. "Is that them?"

"Yes, my father and Harold, arriving at last."

"Too bad you can't trade Maldavian eyes for something more useful," said Dreven.

"Far sight is helpful, which is more than I can say for you," said Eldred.

"Quiet, boys!" said a preceptor who had walked up behind them.

"Sorry, Preceptor," said Eldred.

The squires stood in silent attention as the warriors arrived at the arches. Alfred dismounted and took his seat at the front of the visitors.

Eldred studied Harold as he marched through the center arch, leading the four men in his pod. Eldred could beat Harold with the sword, spear or staff. Eldred could outrun Harold. Eldred could pick up Harold and throw him through the air. But today, Eldred would stand with the squires while his younger cousin judged who was fit to be a warrior.

Harold approached the headmaster. "Present your first pair!"

"Traden and Noll, to the arch!" called Headmaster Tibbot.

Traden and Noll strode forward, wooden swords in hand.

"We begin in the center arch," said Harold.

The squires walked to the arch and took their position eight paces apart, facing away from each other. Harold approached Traden and waited for his men to situate themselves for auditing.

"First attempt!" shouted Harold.

Harold started the set and put Traden in motion. Noll matched Traden's act as often as not. Both squires moved with clearly delineated actions, as they either stepped forward or back, slashed left or right or thrust their swords. After ten acts, they were done and Harold huddled with the auditors.

Dreven nodded. "Not bad."

"They only made five matches, the minimum to pass," said Eldred.

"They passed," said Tenny.

Harold broke the huddle with his men and approached Traden and Noll, who were standing under the center arch. Harold spoke animatedly with the squires, then turned to the headmaster.

"My men count five matched acts, and we attest to the Bond, but Traden and Noll do not accept!" shouted Harold.

Murmuring erupted among the rows of squires and the crowd of visitors.

Dreven frowned. "They don't?"

"You can choose to test again," said Eldred.

"Why would anyone do that?" asked Dreven.

"Pride," said Eldred. "They don't want to advance with the minimum."

Dreven laughed. "They might fail."

Eldred looked at the ground. "They might." He felt sure they wouldn't.

Harold stood in front of Noll, who was taking the signals for this run. "Second attempt!"

This time the set went better for the pair. After a quick huddle, Harold stepped towards the headmaster and called, "We count eight matched acts! They passed the trial!"

"Well done!" shouted Headmaster Tibbot.

The squires, leaving out Eldred and Tenny, roared their approval.

Harold returned to speak with Noll and Traden. Then Harold turned again to the headmaster and called out, "They will try one arch removed!"

Eldred raised his eyebrow. "How bold. They only scored eight. You should score a perfect ten if you want to try across an arch."

Tenny scratched his arm. "They passed. It's all for show now."

"Why even attempt an arch removed if you only matched eight acts? That's never been allowed before," said Eldred.

"When I advance, I want to pass at three arches removed," said Dreven.

Eldred scoffed. "Not going to happen. The last pair to succeed at three arches removed was Norris and Piers six years ago. They only had the minimum in the final arch."

"I'll reach three arches. I just need a solid partner," said Dreven.

"You won't get near three," said Eldred.

"Perhaps not, but I can pass the trial. Wouldn't you like to do that, Eldred?" asked Dreven.

Tenny sighed while Eldred glowered at Dreven.

"First attempt at one arch removed!" shouted Harold.

For this set, Noll stayed in the center arch with Harold and two auditors while Traden and the other two auditors moved to the next arch over. The auditors walked out to the side of the arches, so they could keep both squires and Harold in constant view. It was not a smooth set. After Harold huddled with his men, he came out holding two fingers in the air as he walked over to talk with the boys.

Eldred gazed quizzically at the arches. Walls blocked the Bond. Why was that?

After a quick exchange, Harold called to the headmaster, "We count two matched acts at one arch removed. The squires will switch roles, and we will test again."

Traden joined Harold in the center arch while Noll went to the next arch over.

"Second attempt!" shouted Harold.

This attempt went no better than the first. Harold came out of the huddle holding up two fingers.

"I think that was more like one," observed Eldred.

"One, two—it makes no difference," said Tenny.

"Still, I don't know where they saw two matched acts in the set. On the third act, they both stepped forward. So there is your one. I didn't see a second match."

Tenny shrugged.

Harold turned to Headmaster Tibbot. "We count two matched acts with one arch removed. The squires will switch roles for a last attempt."

"They seem to do better with Noll," commented Dreven.

"They should have stopped after eight in the center arch," said Eldred.

"Third and final attempt!" shouted Harold.

The set was ragged but improved on their earlier efforts. When Harold came out of the huddle with the auditors, he held up five fingers as he walked to confer with the squires.

Dreven grinned. "They did it."

"Only if Harold and his men attest they felt the Bond," said Eldred.

"They got five, Eldred," said Tenny.

Harold stepped out of the arch towards the headmaster. "We count five matched acts, and we attest to the Bond. Traden and Noll pass the trial at one arch removed!"

A cheer went up on both sides of the arches.

"I haven't seen anyone pass at one arch removed in my time here," said Dreven.

"At least the first pair is done," said Tenny.

Traden and Noll exchanged hugs with Headmaster Tibbot, then they passed through the center arch and approached the king. Eldred glared as his father embraced the former squires and handed them each a dagger.

"What did he give them?" asked Dreven.

"Daggers," said Eldred.

"What sort of dagger?" said Dreven.

"Just normal daggers. Not named daggers. They barely passed at one arch removed."

"It was impressive," said Dreven.

"Perhaps it is becoming so. It seems like every year, fewer squires advance even in the center arch," said Tenny.

Harold signaled the headmaster. "Headmaster, present your second pair!"

"Mance and Yeowars, to the arch!"

Mance and Yeowars trudged over to Harold with their heads down.

Mance lined up facing Harold with Yeowars facing away behind him.

"First attempt!" shouted Harold.

The squires looked nervous as they went through their paces, flustered and out of sync. After the set, Harold shook his head as he went to huddle with the auditors.

"Oooh, that was none," said Dreven.

"None," agreed Eldred. The poor showing both delighted him and horrified him.

"We saw it the other day. What was the most we counted? Two?" asked Tenny.

"With two more tries, they might have some luck," said Dreven.

Harold stepped out from the huddle and called to the headmaster, "We count no matched acts in the first attempt! We will conduct a second attempt."

Yeowars cringed under Harold's glare as he lined up.

"That's not right. Harold is intimidating them," grumbled Eldred.

"I don't think it's making a difference," said Tenny.

"Second attempt!" called Harold.

The second attempt was more ragged than the first. Yeowars couldn't even execute the steps Harold signaled. At the end, Harold said something that upset Yeowars, who appeared to be on the verge of tears.

It was a quick huddle, barely formed before Harold stepped away. "We count no matched acts in the second attempt."

"No matched acts in twenty tries. You should get a few by accident," said Dreven.

"Unnecessary foolishness. The headmaster could have just told them they lacked the Bond," said Eldred.

"They stood for the trial of their own accord, Eldred," said Tenny.

For the third set, it was Mance facing Harold for signals as the visibly unsettled Yeowars faced away.

Eldred glared at Harold. "They can't possibly pass while Yeowars is upset."

"They were not going to pass in any case," said Tenny.

"Third and final attempt!" called Harold.

Mance moved well to Harold's signals, but once again Yeowars delivered a stuttering performance, stuttering and out of sync.

Harold appeared vexed as the test concluded. He did not pause as he walked past the huddle of auditors. "We count only one matched act. The squires failed the trial!"

Headmaster Tibbot nodded solemnly.

"Did they match one? I didn't see it," said Dreven.

"No, they didn't. Charity in some form, though not any that I would want," said Eldred.

"Perhaps they will be wiser farmers or woodcutters for their lesson today," said Dreven with a laugh.

"That's enough," said Eldred.

Mance and Yeowars left the arch and walked hurriedly through the crowd towards their quarters with their heads bowed. The other squires were being directed to the dining hall where a celebration feast was being laid out. Traden and Noll remained on the other side of the arches. Their time at the Academy and its dining hall had ended.

Eldred started to walk towards the arches.

"Aren't you coming to the feast, Eldred?" asked Tenny.

"I need a word with my father."

"Our table will be nearly empty. I doubt Mance and Yeowars will be present," said Tenny.

Eldred nodded. "I'll be there presently."

As Eldred passed by Headmaster Tibbot, the headmaster gave him a quizzical look but did not obstruct him.

Harold paused when he saw Eldred coming and waited in the center arch with an imperious smile. "How truly excellent to see you, cousin."

Eldred set his jaw. "And you, cousin."

"When I volunteered to run the trial for today, I expected you would be standing for the trial. You do plan to take the trial, don't you?"

"I'll take the winter trial."

"At least this was interesting, a mixture of success and colossal failure," said Harold. "I don't recall ever seeing such a comical attempt when I was here at the Academy with you all those many years ago. No acts out of thirty tries."

"I believe you scored them with one act," corrected Eldred.

"Oh, you're right, Eldred. I forgot. One act. Well, I won't keep you. I expect you want to greet your father before you go to the feast with the other boys."

"Yes, I'll see my father."

"Don't miss the feast, Eldred. You'll miss them when you finally leave the Academy. I certainly remember them fondly."

Eldred brushed past his younger cousin and walked over to his father, who was regaling Traden and Noll with some tale.

Alfred paused as Eldred approached, looking Eldred up and down. "Ah, here's Eldred."

Eldred frowned down at Alfred. He had not seen him in two years. "Mother's blessings, Father."

"You must be proud of your fellow squires. It's been some time since a pair passed at one arch removed."

Eldred favored the boys with a dour look. "Four years."

"Well, you would know, son."

Eldred flinched. "Yes, I suppose I would."

Alfred took a quick glance toward Harold and motioned Eldred to join him. "Excuse us for a moment, young warriors. I need to discuss something with my son."

As Alfred led Eldred up the lane, away from the celebration, the noise of the crowd dropped to a low murmur. "I'm glad you possess the wisdom to wait until you're ready. The second pair was a disgrace. The headmaster made a mistake. That shameful display should never have happened."

"I don't know that it was shameful," said Eldred.

Alfred pulled down his eyebrows and wrinkled his nose. "It was to me. Disgusting. The Academy takes a pretty chunk of taxes. If the staff can't do better, I'll replace them all."

"Well, it's not easy. Everyone's under pressure, and there's the cost. Not every family can afford the Academy."

"What's that to do with it? The Academy has always cost gold," said Alfred.

"Fewer squires are ascending, fewer have the Bond in each class. That makes the cost more daunting. My friend, Tenny, feels—this pressure. If you could support his training, he could stay on."

Alfred waved dismissively. "What? Why are we discussing this? That's for his family to manage."

"Tenny's strong and has excellent skill with the sword. He's the only one who can challenge me. You'll add a talented warrior to your army if you help him."

"The Academy's not a place for playing favorites. If I pay for your friend's fees, other families will want the same."

"Well, can you at least consider it?"

Alfred snorted. "There's nothing to consider, Eldred. Now let's speak on another matter. Did the headmaster mention a blood match coming up in the next few days?"

"He did."

Alfred reached up and placed his hand on Eldred's shoulder. "Good. I created this opportunity for you. I arranged the most prodigious blood match with the Mercians I could stomach. I had to give them favorable terms, damned favorable terms. The Mother must be laughing at me. I allowed them four times the men and put up four times the land, a considerable tract of land. I still need to find a captain to lead my forces. Most difficult, as the position comes with considerable personal risk."

"Why not have Harold do it?" suggested Eldred.

Alfred stepped back and chuckled. "Your cousin is too important. He'll fight, many are interested in fighting, but few wish to serve as captain against a force possessing such an advantage."

"I thought Mercians were easy to kill."

"They are giant and unpredictable, like yourself."

Eldred scowled. He was Deiran, not Mercian.

"That is how things stand. I arranged a monumental blood match. That's the limit of what I can do for you."

"Thank you, Father," said Eldred coldly. Such limits. It was not a long way to Boar's Tusk, but he had heard nothing from his father for two years.

His mother, Ghyslaine, sent monthly letters, but Alfred couldn't even bother to do that.

"Now, you must deliver your side of it. You must never attempt the trial unless you're certain to pass. Those squires today, the second pair, their failure was inexcusable. It'll be years before anyone forgets their disgraceful display. Do you understand?"

Eldred's face grew hot. "I understand, Father."

"See that you do. Now you best return south of the arches with the other squires. We can only bend the rules so far."

"Of course, Father."

Eldred proceeded back through the crowd, weaving around the tiny Deirans, with their tiresome celebration.

Harold smirked as Eldred reached the arches. "Did things go well with your father, cousin?"

Eldred strode by with a sour expression. "Splendidly, cousin."

"Enjoy the feast."

BLACKSMITH

The next day, fifty-four days before Eldred's day of ascension, Preceptor Grimes led a sword training exercise in the yard. He had the squires paired up in full gear, leather armor and wooden swords. As was usually the case, Eldred sparred with Tenny, who was throwing everything he had into his attack.

"Die, you scoundrel!" shouted Tenny as he drove Eldred back under a flurry of blows.

Eldred smiled as he retreated across the yard, parrying Tenny's attacks. As Eldred approached a wall, he turned the onslaught back on Tenny. Tenny was quick, but Eldred was stronger. Eldred closed on Tenny, locking up their wooden swords. After a brief struggle, Eldred knocked Tenny to the ground. Eldred advanced, his sword ready.

"Hold up, Eldred!" called Preceptor Grimes.

Eldred stopped. "I wasn't going to hurt him."

"Tenny's father is meeting with the headmaster. It's time for Tenny to go."

Tenny jumped to his feet. "About time he got here."

Preceptor Grimes offered his hand. "May the Mother smile upon you, Tenny. I enjoyed instructing you."

Tenny clasped Preceptor Grimes's hand. "Thank you. Sorry to be a disappointment."

"Never to me," said Preceptor Grimes.

Mance approached. He had been sparring nearby with Yeowars. "You're leaving?"

Tenny nodded. "I've been ready to leave for some time."

"Best of luck to you," said Mance.

"And to you," said Tenny. He warmly embraced Mance and Yeowars.

Dreven walked over. "So you're out."

"Come to crow, Dreven?" asked Tenny.

"No, come to wish you well. I'll miss you," said Dreven, extending his hand.

Tenny eyes widened as he shook Dreven's hand. "You'll miss me?"

"Once you leave, they'll pair me up with Eldred. That's months of beatings till they kick him out."

Eldred flashed an angry look, but when Tenny laughed, Eldred turned his frown into a weak smile. "A few months of beatings sounds right."

"I'd best fetch my things," said Tenny.

"I'll help you. That is, if I may, Preceptor Grimes?" said Eldred.

"You're dismissed, both of you."

They dropped off their equipment and made their way through the grounds to their quarters, where they shared a room.

Eldred watched as Tenny slid some bags out from under his bed. "You are already packed?"

"Just a few more things. I don't have much."

"What about staying for dinner?"

"I'm ready to leave, Eldred. I'm sick of this place. Not of you, of course. Not even of the preceptors. Well, at least not all of them. When I consider it all, I want to run out the door."

"I understand."

"Don't avoid the outside world, Eldred. Other people never give the Academy a second thought. They just live their lives. I'm happy to join them."

"I'll miss you, Tenny."

"Not for long. Stop by and visit me in Hog's End."

"It's a waste of your sword arm. You'd be a challenging opponent for any warrior."

Tenny stuffed a shirt from the floor into his bag. "You know that was never the issue. There, that's everything." Tenny paused. "I hope you find your own escape from here soon."

Eldred shrugged. "Something has to happen."

As they walked back towards the yard, they met Headmaster Tibbot and a man who was leading two horses.

"Good to see you, son," said the man.

Tenny stepped forward to hug him. "Father, this is Eldred, the king's son. Eldred, this is my father, Pate, the finest blacksmith in south Guaraci."

"It's an honor to meet you, Eldred," said Pate.

"Tenny became a very accomplished swordsman in his time here," said Eldred.

"Ah, yes," said Pate.

Tenny shook his head as he tied a sack to his horse's saddle. "Thank you, Eldred."

Pate turned to the headmaster. "I'll be in touch about the balance."

The headmaster smiled. "I am sure we can work something out. I wish you and Tenny a pleasant journey home."

Pate mounted his horse. "Very kind of you. We have fair weather and excellent roads from here to Hog's End, thanks to the king." Pate nodded to Eldred.

The pair turned their horses and rode out between the academy buildings while Eldred and the headmaster walked slowly after them. Pate only had smiles for Tenny, who seemed to be in high spirits. Eldred and the headmaster stopped at the southern edge of the Academy. The road south soon took Tenny and his father down into a line of trees and out of sight.

"So they owe you a balance," said Eldred.

"That is none of your concern," said the headmaster.

Eldred frowned and turned to look at the woods.

"You leave for the blood match tomorrow," continued Headmaster Tibbot. "Dreven and Mance will accompany you. I am sending Wybert and Daw from the younger squires."

"You see no glimmer in me. What about them? Do they all have the Bond?"

"They each possess gifts. Just as you do. Just as Tenny does."

"My father made you send me, but you picked them. You must think they have the Bond."

"You will be there to learn what happens. Good day, Eldred."

Headmaster Tibbot turned and walked back into the academy grounds. Eldred remained, gazing into the distance. This had to work.

DEPARTURE

The next morning, fifty-three days before Eldred's day of ascension, before the dining hall even finished serving breakfast, Eldred and the other chosen squires formed up in the yard. Each of them had a bag or two of clothes. Dreven and the younger squires, Daw and Wybert, kept pacing about excitedly. Mance slumped and stared off into the distance.

"Why is Yeowars not coming, Mance?" asked Dreven with a smirk.

"Headmaster Tibbot did not ask him," replied Mance.

"Why not?" said Dreven.

"I don't know," said Mance.

"Did Yeowars want to go?" persisted Dreven.

Mance shrugged.

Eldred sighed. It had to be Yeowars terrible performance at the trial.

"It's the biggest blood match in years. And against the Mercians, too. It'll be a very bloody affair," said Dreven.

"We won't kill all the Mercians," said Eldred.

"There'll be carnage, Eldred," said Dreven.

"Yes, but the match comes down to the captains. Once they enter the field of battle, they stay until one captain is dead. Others will die, of course, but we won't slaughter them at the end. We'll both collect our wounded."

"I know the rules. I'm telling you that we'll butcher the Mercians. There'll be hundreds of Mercians gathered around their captain. We'll carve our way through them."

"It's hard to kill a Mercian," said Eldred.

"Yes, I know. You all have thick skulls," said Dreven.

"I'm not Mercian."

"You're part Mercian. Your skull appears to be one of those Mercian parts."

Daw and Wybert laughed until Eldred silenced them with a glare.

Preceptor Grimes approached the squires on horseback, followed by stable hands leading more horses. "Mount up. We have three days to reach Finches Field. We need to make reasonable time."

"Are you issuing any equipment?" asked Eldred.

"Such as what, Eldred?"

"We need swords in case we come under attack."

"My sword will suffice for the territory we are traveling through."

"And if it doesn't?"

Preceptor Grimes smiled. "Then you had best hope one of your enemies brings you one."

The squires mounted their horses and accompanied Preceptor Grimes out of the Academy to the south road. A few well-wishers came out and shouted encouragement. Dreven and the younger boys crowded Preceptor Grimes in their enthusiasm to keep up with him. Eldred and Mance followed at a more restrained distance, with Eldred bringing up the rear.

They rode for eight hours with few breaks. They stopped to camp near the wide dirt road in the basin of a valley set with a smattering of trees. Preceptor Grimes had the squires search for wood and started a small fire.

As evening came on, Preceptor Grimes softened up a mess of hardtack and fried it in a small skillet.

Eldred blew on his portion to cool it. "This is the furthest south I've been."

"We will reach the Mercian border in two days. The lands we ride through the rest of the way will be at stake in the match," said Preceptor Grimes.

"Including Hog's End?" asked Eldred.

"Yes, Hog's End and several other villages."

"What if we lose? Will the Mercian's kick the villagers out?"

"I'm sure not. We trade these borderlands back and forth—though this match is offering up a bigger chunk than usual. Your father had to tempt them into battle."

"King Alfred arranged the match to benefit Eldred," said Dreven.

"Who knows why he wants it. The king has had luck with big matches in the past. He won a huge patch of territory as well as Eldred's mother from King Julian nineteen years ago," said Preceptor Grimes.

"Who's our captain?" said Mance.

"A warrior by the name of Dederick," said Preceptor Grimes.

"Can he really command a golden pod?" asked Mance.

"That's the question. You squires have never attempted anything of the sort, but you will learn even filling a regular bronze pod of five men with the Bond can be a strain. It takes great spirit to put everyone to full use. Now, take five times the men for a silver pod, only a select few can run one properly. A golden pod is another five times more men. Only a true champion can hope to master one. The king can."

"What if Dederick can't? Will we lose?" asked Dreven.

Preceptor Grimes tilted his head as he made his assessment. "Not necessarily. It means we won't fight as one. Multiple voices take hold. You fall to smaller groups taking their own lead. We could still prevail."

"Do you think we will win?" pressed Dreven.

Preceptor Grimes gave a small smile and nodded. "Mercians are rugged. The individual Mercian is as hard as they come. The Night Mother made them so. But though they were granted a thick skull, they don't come with the smartest brain."

"Careful, you'll upset Eldred," said Dreven.

"No, no, Dreven. Eldred appears Mercian, but he's Deiran," said Preceptor Grimes.

"That's right," said Eldred.

"But he has the thick skull you mentioned, Preceptor Grimes," said Dreven to the delight of the younger squires.

"Careful there, Dreven. Don't get Eldred stirred up. Now, on the blood match, the matter we were discussing, I was saying the Mercians are stout warriors. If they all clumped around their captain, that would be a tough nut to crack."

"Like Eldred's skull," blurted Dreven.

Preceptor Grimes shook his head while Eldred glared at Dreven. "Don't be rude, Dreven. The Mercians, the Mercians—though—are always too eager to stick their spear into someone. I expect Dederick will draw some Mercians off and then send in a few warriors in to kill their captain. Now, we—by which I mean you squires—don't want him to succeed too quickly. The longer the fight, the better the chance for transference."

"What if you don't have the Bond in you, say if you are a Mercian? What happens then?" asked Dreven, smiling mischievously.

"Nothing. The Mercians aren't walking away from the match with the

Bond. The Night Mother only shared her best gift with Deirans. I'll cross my fingers for each of you squires. With luck, we bring all five of you back, with each of you ready to take the winter trial."

"If we don't gain the Bond now, can we manifest it later?" asked Mance.

Preceptor Grimes pursed his lips and paused for a moment in reflection. "Of course, you could. Sometimes, rarely, the transference comes after a day or two, or so they say. Well, enough talking for tonight. Finish your hardtack and into your blankets. We will ride at dawn tomorrow."

The other squires and Preceptor Grimes soon drifted off to sleep, but Eldred lay awake throughout the moonless night, staring at the hills of the valley and the stars slowly turning in the clear sky. This would be his last chance. He shifted this way and then that, but never got comfortable. The blankets kept twisting off as he turned, leaving him cold and miserable.

THE VALLEY

As they started the second day of their journey, fifty-two days before Eldred's day of ascension, Dreven and the two younger squires rode in front, followed by Preceptor Grimes. Eldred and Mance trailed behind. Eldred's mouth tasted terrible after his sleepless night.

After riding a few hours, Mance spoke up. "Do you think this will work?"

"You mean the transference?"

"Yes."

Eldred held up his hand to shield his reddened eyes from the sun. "It might for some of us. Probably not for me."

"Why do you say that?"

"The headmaster can sense who will manifest the Bond. He saw no glimmer in me."

"Then why did he pick you?"

"My father insisted."

"So your father thinks you possess the Bond?"

Eldred frowned. "No. I doubt he does."

"Huh."

Eldred rubbed his neck. "I'm nearly eighteen. If I were meant to manifest the Bond, it would have happened by now."

"Yeowars and I had similar thoughts when we put our names up for the trial. Of course, we're not as old."

Eldred rode closer to Mance. "You were brave to try it."

"I wish we hadn't. We only had one matched act in thirty tries. Your cousin was so furious. We thought he was going to strike us, or expel us from the Academy."

"You just need the right partner."

"You mean not Yeowars?"

Eldred shrugged. "Well, no, maybe Yeowars. You need someone you are in tune with."

"Who will you pair with?"

"I'm not supposed to make an attempt unless I'm sure I can pass."

"That's what I would recommend. Those were the worst moments of my life."

Eldred gave a small smile. "Well, the headmaster sent you down for this match. Your luck might change. You might return and succeed."

"With Yeowars? Or do you think I should switch to another partner?"

"The trial did not go well with Yeowars. Changing partners might benefit both of you."

"No, it didn't go well." Mance fixed his gaze on the squires riding up ahead. "Do you suppose the headmaster thinks these three are the best? Is that why he sent them?"

Eldred nodded. "Could be."

"I'm half a year senior to Dreven, but I don't like Dreven. I'm two years older than those other two. With Tenny gone, I'm the next oldest after you." Mance frowned. "Once you go, I'll be the oldest."

"True, but you're only fifteen. You have years left."

Mance frowned. "This has to work. I don't like Dreven. I think disliking him will block the Bond. You saw how poorly it went with Yeowars."

"Do you dislike Yeowars?"

"No, but I find Dreven quite common."

Eldred raised his palms. "Squires seek to move on however they can. If you can pass the trial with Dreven, I suggest you do so. You're older than Wybert and Daw, but I don't think it matters much. If they can advance with you, they'll be keen to pair up."

"I won't pair with Dreven."

That night, the other squires descended into sleep before the sun was fully set, leaving Preceptor Grimes to tend the fire and hum to himself. As the darkness settled and the temperature dropped, Eldred was the only one still awake. The stars shone clear and bright in Eldred's eyes as his mind raced. Was the blood match a heroic opportunity or simply the last and most epic humiliation? The stars turned through a full quarter of the sky before Eldred finally drifted off to sleep.

A BIRD

They spent the morning of the third day, fifty-one days before Eldred's day of ascension, riding up steep switchbacks as the trail climbed west out of the valley. By noon, they reached a ridge with a vast panorama. Eldred fell behind as he slowed to take in the view.

He was looking down the hill when he saw a furious gray bird streak down from the sky and seize a groundhog with its talons. The bird tore at its squirming prey, ripping it to pieces before settling down to eat it.

Eldred called the others back and pointed down at the bird, which was around a hundred feet away. Preceptor Grimes and Mance came over while the other squires continued on.

Preceptor Grimes squinted at the bird. "Oh, that could be a Gray Mori. Does it have a small black circle of feathers around the base of its neck? I can't make it out."

"It does," said Eldred.

"Then that's it for certain. A favorite of the Night Mother, but very rare. I last saw one more than five years ago."

"It caught that groundhog easily. It could eat them all day up here on the hill and in the valley."

"It could. It definitely could."

"So why is it uncommon? Why doesn't it empty out the valley of vermin and feed an army of Mori chicks?"

Preceptor Grimes chuckled. "You're smart enough to revere the Night Mother, but nobody's smart enough to understand her ways. When she made the Gray Mori, I expect she knew what a dangerous bird she made for small prey—the groundhogs and rabbits hereabouts. But she admires all of her creatures, even the weak, so she created a balance."

"How?"

"I don't know. There could be many ways she slows them down. Perhaps they have to perform some elaborate dance to win a mate. Maybe they die in the cold of winter or make shoddy nests that drop their eggs. She finds a way. She can do anything."

"Praise the Night Mother," said Mance.

"Praise the Night Mother," repeated Eldred.

Preceptor Grimes looked up from the feasting bird and gazed into the distance. "You can see Hog's End. It sticks out beyond that hill."

Eldred studied the distant settlement, mostly shacks with a few farms. "Seems small."

"Yes, not much compared to Boar's Tusk."

Eldred examined the landscape, noting a few farms scattered in the distance. "Tenny told me my father owns an estate down here somewhere."

"Well, of course, your father's castle is in Boar's Tusk. He might own estates down here, but I don't know of any. Perhaps Tenny was talking about one of the ranches down in the valley. Your father might own one or two of those."

"Those lack the size of an estate."

"They may be what passes for one out here."

Eldred studied the terrain with an unhappy expression as Mance and Preceptor Grimes rode on.

FINCHES FIELD

A s evening came, the trail led down the ridge to a flat grass-covered plain divided by a meandering river. Several camps were pitched, including a substantial camp to the north and an enormous camp to the south.

Preceptor Grimes pointed to the northern base. "That's our men. Those smaller campsites in the middle belong to the Maldavians and the Torvid. They're here to officiate the blood match. The Mercians are set up in the massive camp."

"Are we in time for the feast?" said Dreven.

Preceptor Grimes wagged his finger. "No banquet for us. You're still squires. We'll make our own dinner tonight."

"Why is that?" asked Dreven.

"You'll understand soon enough if things go according to plan. Bonded warriors avoid the company of unbonded folk before a battle. Mixing with normal people puts us out of sorts."

"Whatever happens for me, I won't ever forget that squires enjoy roasted meat," said Dreven.

"Perhaps tomorrow night, if our men win the day and if you are lifted by their spirit," said Preceptor Grimes.

"A certainty," said Dreven.

Eldred and Mance rolled their eyes.

After the squires found firewood, Preceptor Grimes got a fire going to warm the hardtack, and the lads laid their blankets out on the soft grass. Preceptor Grimes was passing out bowls when visitors descended on their camp.

"Good evening, Preceptor!" called Harold as he sauntered up a bit unsteadily with two members of his pod in tow.

"Lord Harold, gentlemen, you do us quite an honor coming to visit our camp. I brought these squires down for the match."

Harold smiled oddly at Eldred. "Ah, and there he is, my cousin."

Eldred got up from his blanket and looked over Harold and his men. "Hello, Harold."

Harold pointed at Mance. "The boy from the trial. What's he doing here?"

"We are trying for transference for these squires," said Preceptor Grimes.

"Transference for this boy and Eldred?" asked Harold, slightly slurring Eldred's name.

"So we hope, Lord Harold."

"That's a lot of hope, Preceptor Grimes. I fear you may be disappointed. If you want transference, you need a lengthy battle. But I tell you, my pod is in the fight and I don't expect the Mercians will last long."

"They won't," declared one of Harold's podmen.

"You were one of my sharpest pupils, Lord Harold. If you're rested, I expect you'll exert considerable influence on the outcome," said Preceptor Grimes.

Harold frowned. "Who was your sharpest pupil?"

"What?" said the preceptor.

"You said I was one of your sharpest pupils. Who was your sharpest pupil?"

"I don't know if there was one specific pupil. I've taught at the Academy for over nine years. Many students came and went."

"One came and didn't ever leave. I mean my cousin, of course. Is he the best?"

Preceptor Grimes gave Harold an appraising look. "Eldred is a proficient swordsman."

Harold smiled broadly. "He's much more than that. Eldred's a truly excellent squire. He outshines everyone. How unfortunate the job is only suitable for children."

"You're drunk," said Eldred.

"You're calling me a drunk? You insult me, cousin. Are you forgetting your place?"

Preceptor Grimes strode quickly to Eldred's side. "I'm sure he meant nothing by it, Lord Harold."

"I said you are drunk, not that you are a drunk. Is the distinction lost on you, cousin?" said Eldred.

"And I'm a bonded warrior, and you are but a lowly squire. Is the difference lost on you, cousin?"

"I'm not confused about what you are, Harold."

Harold put his hand on the grip of his sword. "I think you may be."

"Now hold up, Lord Harold," interjected Preceptor Grimes, speaking quickly. "Best you think clearly on your course of action. These two young squires come from some formidable families. Mance is the son of Lord Farhan. Young Wybert is the heir of Lord Trenth. Those are important houses in court."

Harold glowered at the boys, his sword half out of the scabbard. As he hesitated, an old man in a baggy gray tunic came bustling into the camp on horseback.

"Uncle Benedict!" shouted Eldred.

"Mother's blessings, Eldred." Benedict gave Harold a reproachful look. "Ah, there you are, son. Dederick is going over the plan for tomorrow's match. He's asking for you."

Harold slammed his blade back in its scabbard.

"Alfred wagered a vast tract of land on the outcome," continued Benedict.

"So we all know, Father," said Harold in an exasperated tone.

"You should return."

Harold's face turned red as he cast a quick glance back at Eldred. "Yes. I'm not staying here. I just came to greet Eldred."

"Very good," said Benedict.

"Good luck to you in the match tomorrow, Lord Harold," said Preceptor Grimes.

Harold muttered something about luck as he stalked back towards the Deiran camp with his men. Once they left, Benedict dismounted and pulled out a baking tin from one of his saddlebags.

"Besides searching for my son, I thought the squires might appreciate some cake."

"Thank you, sir," said Dreven.

Dreven and the other squires clustered around Benedict, getting their portions, while Eldred and Preceptor Grimes watched Harold trudge away.

Eldred spoke softly. "I could have used a sword."

Preceptor Grimes shook his head. "Foolish talk."

"He was drunk."

"Then, unlike you, he had an excuse for his foolishness."

"Do you want some cake, Eldred?" called Benedict.

"Cake would be appreciated, Uncle."

BENEDICT

Eldred and Benedict walked down to the river bank, below the campsite. The burbling of the meandering river filled the air. On the far side, out in the middle of Finches Field, fires lit up the Mercian camp.

Benedict moved slowly in the dark. Though Benedict was Alfred's older brother, he appeared younger and had a full head of black hair. He bore a strong resemblance to Harold, though he was heavier and had more rounded features. Instead of Harold's piercing stare, Benedict's eyes had more of a haunted, quiet sense about them.

Benedict paused by the shore. "I am sorry about that, Eldred."

"Harold acted like a mad dog," snapped Eldred.

"He was not behaving as he should. I am sure he will apologize to you tomorrow."

"He was drawing his sword."

"Nothing happened."

"Preceptor Grimes seemed to think something might happen," said Eldred.

"But nothing did. The young squires are settling to sleep, and you are quite unharmed."

"What's gotten into him?"

Benedict gazed off towards the Mercian camp. "Your situation is troubling to others beyond yourself, Eldred. You are—and have been—the presumptive heir. These next weeks will finalize the matter. Harold also faces a difficult time. What he had once perhaps distantly hoped for has come nearly in reach. Now it is perhaps what he has come to expect."

"It seems he is not alone in his expectations," said Eldred.

"Me? No, Eldred. I would be glad enough if you succeeded your father. If it were for me to choose, then we would not be waiting until this late date to learn the outcome. I would be happy if you ascended years ago, the same as Harold."

"Would you?"

"Of course. Did you forget, Eldred? I am the older brother, not Alfred. I was in line for the throne, just as you are now. Like you, I faced challenges."

"I heard you surrendered the throne to my father."

Benedict smiled. "Surrendered? Makes it sound like I had a choice. I had none." He shook his head. "Your father passed in the fifth arch, four arches removed. I passed in the center arch. That decided everything. It took me a while to understand, but the outcome was set, just as it might be now."

"You seem quite certain Harold will be the heir."

"That may be, Eldred. I don't know if the Bond will thunder in you tomorrow or if it will ever come. Whatever happens, I support you. You don't have to be king to enjoy a worthwhile life. The best things in life have nothing to do with rank."

Eldred looked out over the river and frowned. "If I fail, I won't live your life, Uncle. You're not king, but you're a warrior. You've fought in battles. People respect you. If I don't manifest the Bond, I won't experience any of that."

"Perhaps not. Those are things in my life, things people value, but they are not the dearest things to me."

Eldred's eyes blazed. "They would be to me, Uncle. I was born to fight. I have trained for battle all my life. Every day."

"I wish you well, Eldred. I always have. We will discover the outcome shortly. If you are to manifest the Bond before your ascension day, I expect it will come tomorrow."

"Tomorrow. It will—must be tomorrow."

"You should rest, Nephew. Your answers will come in the morning."

BLOOD MATCH

Benedict woke the squires and passed out warm bread and sausage he had brought over from the main camp. While the other squires gleefully devoured the food, Eldred sat stiffly on his blanket, watching the activity down on the field and the pockets of spectators setting up on the surrounding hills.

Preceptor Grimes was on his feet, gesturing down at the field. ""They're laying out white stones to mark the boundary for the southern and eastern sides of the field. On this side, the boundary is the river itself."

"The nearside of the river or the far side?" asked Mance.

"The far side. If anyone goes in the river, they're out for the rest of the match," said Preceptor Grimes.

"So we can watch from within the river. We can get closer," said Mance.

"I suppose we can. What do you think, Lord Benedict?" said Preceptor Grimes.

"If the far side is the boundary, then being in the river should be permissible," replied Benedict.

"Is the Bond flowing yet?" asked Mance.

"No, not till the actual match," said Preceptor Grimes.

"Harold said the match would be quick," complained Dreven.

"With five hundred Mercian warriors milling about, our men will require time to reach their captain," said Benedict.

"What about Dederick? Will he hang back? If hundreds of Mercians run at him, what can he do to stay on the field?" asked Eldred.

"Good question, Eldred. Your father had to work hard to find the right captain for this battle. Many accomplished warriors declined the honor.

Perhaps they entertained the same concern. Dederick took up the challenge. I expect he has plans to deal with a full out charge," said Benedict.

"It'll help that the Mercians are on foot," said Preceptor Grimes.

After the boundary was marked, representatives of the four peoples met in the center of the field, the Deirans under the red blade banner, the Maldavians under the blue crescent moon, the Mercians under the red fist, the Torvid under the crossed daggers.

Benedict pointed down at the field. "Their captain is marked by a red plume in his helmet. Dederick wears our plume. That's his honor guard."

"Should I feel anything yet?" asked Mance.

"No. I'll let you know when the Bond stirs. You need not keep asking," said Preceptor Grimes.

"Eldred, I believe you have cousins both in the Maldavian contingent and among the Mercians," said Benedict.

Eldred frowned as the other squires smirked. "I recognized Oudin— Uncle Julian's younger son—with the Maldavians, but none of the Mercians."

"Alfred mentioned some relatives among the Mercians, but it is of no matter," said Benedict.

Eldred nodded. Mercians certainly did not matter.

"There they go!" said Preceptor Grimes.

The rest of the Deiran warriors rode through the river and lined up behind Dederick's honor guard. The Mercians were taking their position on the southside of the field.

"They will need time to count with so many Mercians," said Benedict.

The Maldavian and Torvid contingents split in half, circling around the Deiran horsemen and the Mercian footmen.

"That's quite a few Mercians," said Eldred.

"Five hundred of them," said Preceptor Grimes.

"Do we have enough men?" asked Eldred.

"It depends on Dederick," said Preceptor Grimes.

"I predict a competitive match," said Benedict. "Mercians possess advantages beyond their numbers. They are very strong and enjoy a simple kind of courage. But I wouldn't doubt our warriors."

After the counting, the Maldavians and Torvid exited the field to patrol the boundary. Dederick and his honor guard wheeled around and positioned themselves behind the main body of Deirans. The Mercian captain and his bodyguards jogged back through a gap in their lines to stand at the rear of their formation, near the southern boundary.

"We should get closer," said Mance.

"Yes, we should," agreed Preceptor Grimes.

They hurriedly mounted their horses and rode down the slight hill, splashing into the shallow river. Two Maldavians approached rapidly on horseback. Eldred could tell they had the gift by the glint of their eyes.

"The match is closed," shouted one of the Maldavians.

"Of course, these are squires. We're just here to observe," answered Preceptor Grimes.

"We will accompany you," said one of the Maldavians as he stared back into Eldred's eyes.

Eldred nodded. They recognized him.

"You are most welcome to," said Benedict.

They reached the center of the river, the water nearly to the horses' knees, when horns sounded and the men on the field set in motion.

"You might sense something now, boys!" called Preceptor Grimes.

They all paused to stare at the action. The Mercian lines were advancing and the Deirans spread out in their pods.

"Follow me!" called Preceptor Grimes as he splashed east, up the middle of the river.

The squires filed after Preceptor Grimes. Benedict and the Maldavians trailed behind. On the field, the Mercians continued to push forward, but their lines stretched thinner. Whenever a pod of Deirans circled close to the Mercian line, the Mercians would hurl their spears and chase the pod as it disengaged. The Deirans kept narrowly out of reach. Meanwhile, other Deirans opportunistically rode down any Mercians who had fallen out of formation.

Preceptor Grimes stopped at a slight curve where the river pushed out into the field. "This is as near as we can get."

The squires lined their horses up next to Preceptor Grimes. Eldred surveyed the action. Dozens of Mercians lay on the ground but only a few Deirans.

Eldred pointed across the field. "Two more Deirans down."

"Stop looking. Shut your eyes, Eldred. Reach inside. Feel the Bond," said Preceptor Grimes.

Eldred glanced at Preceptor Grimes, then—along with the other squires—closed his eyes. The sounds of the battle filled his ears, shouting Mercians and screaming of all sorts. The river also made noise, soothing burbles and splashes. After a few minutes, Eldred peeked at the others. Mance,

Daw and Wybert appeared to be in a trance. Their hands underwent sporadic twitches, their faces blank. In contrast, Dreven's face wrinkled in concentration.

"Concentrate, Eldred," said Preceptor Grimes.

Eldred gave the battle another glance and closed his eyes. This time, he kept them shut longer. When he opened his eyes, only Dreven had his eyes shut. The other squires had their eyes open and relaxed. They were studying their hands, which still showed slight spasms.

Preceptor Grimes frowned. "Focus, if you can, Eldred."

"Try with your eyes shut again, Eldred," said Benedict.

Eldred made a quick check of the battle. Fewer Mercians remained on their feet. Those left standing were split into smaller groups beset by harrying packs of Deiran riders. Eldred snapped his eyes closed and drew a deep breath.

Eldred had his eyes shut for only a few minutes before he heard horns echoing around the field.

"The match has ended," said Preceptor Grimes, with a dour tone, as he studied Eldred. But he smiled as he turned towards the three squires who had been twitching.

"What happened? Did I manifest the Bond?" asked Dreven.

"Not as yet, Dreven," said Preceptor Grimes softly.

"Oh, what about the others?"

"Mance, Daw and Wybert show promise," said Preceptor Grimes.

"What about you, Eldred?" said Dreven.

Eldred crinkled up his face. "I'm the same as I was before, like you."

Preceptor Grimes sighed.

"What happened? In the battle?" asked Eldred.

"Proof once again the Mercians cannot hold a line. They lack discipline when any opportunity to engage presents itself. Dederick used their weakness against them time and again," said Preceptor Grimes.

Eldred gazed out at the field. Both sides carried away their dead and wounded, while the Maldavians and Torvid took the tally. "How did Harold fare?"

"Two of his pod were slightly injured," said Benedict.

"Did any Deirans die?" said Eldred.

"I felt some two dozen die," said Preceptor Grimes.

"You could sense them die?" asked Eldred.

Preceptor Grimes nodded. "Yes."

"I felt it too, Eldred," said Mance.

Eldred turned away and stared at the field. "How many Mercians do you think died?"

"The total doesn't matter. Their captain died. That was enough," said Benedict.

"But how many do you think? It must have some importance. They're out there counting it."

"Perhaps one hundred fifty Mercians killed and more injured. Takes a lot to kill a Mercian. Some of those on the ground will end up back on their feet," said Benedict.

Eldred nodded his head slowly. "Quite a victory."

"I predict a feast in the making. I am sure all the squires will be welcome to join now the match is over," said Benedict.

Mance laughed. "How perfect."

Dreven glared at Mance.

"I need to visit Tenny at Hog's End," said Eldred.

"We can stop on the way back. We must not miss the feast. This'll be a proper feast," said Mance.

"I won't keep you, Mance. I can ride there on my own," said Eldred.

"Now, hold on. We are out in the middle of nowhere. I don't believe I can split you lads up," said Preceptor Grimes.

"I'll be fine," said Eldred.

"I can go with him," said Dreven.

"Or I can go alone," snapped Eldred.

Preceptor Grimes rubbed the back of his neck.

Benedict gestured at Eldred. "Preceptor Grimes, I am sure Headmaster Tibbot would not want a squire to ride off without supervision, not even one as accomplished as Eldred. Why don't you accompany Eldred and Dreven—if that is Dreven's wish—to Hog's End. I will take charge of these other squires and return them to the Academy."

"Thank you, Lord Benedict," said Preceptor Grimes.

"I'm off. Just headed to the camp to grab my gear," said Eldred.

"We will follow behind," said Preceptor Grimes. "Keep to the road. The turn to Hog's End is marked about eight miles up the track."

"I'll find it." Eldred urged his horse across the river.

As Dreven started to follow him, Preceptor Grimes held him up.

"I will pass your regards to your father!" called Benedict.

Eldred glanced back at Benedict and continued on.

HOG'S END

Eldred started the ride at a quick pace, but soon slowed to an unhurried walk as he started up the green grassy hills. He felt stuck; he wanted to leap down from the saddle and run away.

Fifty days would pass quickly. He should do something. But what? Alfred's grand gesture, the blood match, had worked for Mance and the others, but had done nothing for him. He was running out of time.

Idly, he reached up and rubbed his Deiran stone, his fatum lapis. He could feel it attached inside the skin. He could imagine its tendrils descending through his body. His body had accepted it well enough. Why didn't it work? Eldred scowled. He had always thought it would start working one day. They always did for everyone else. A muddle, the headmaster had called it. Muddle or not, a crystal blessed by the Night Mother herself ought to work!

Eldred stopped when he reached the turn, staring at the signs. The road north to Boar's Tusk climbed a steep ridge covered in waves of grass, rippling in the breeze. That way lay pointless drills he had done a thousand times and the headmaster's nagging insights on prospective professions. The trail west to Hog's End dropped down into a plain and carried off into the distance, disappearing into a small woods. That way led to a friend, though not one who could help.

Eldred hunched over on his horse and looked at the two paths, not caring to take either one. He had been sitting for a few minutes when he caught sight of a large yellow and black butterfly a few hundred yards away, crossing the road to Hog's End. The beautiful insect flitting across the grass, carried on the wind. It had accomplished amazing feats, passing from egg, to caterpillar, to chrysalis and now to this, a master of haphazard flight. Truly amazing.

Eldred straightened his back and turned his horse towards Hog's End. He might not have the Bond but he had a friend.

After a few hours, he passed through an outer stretch of farms and ranches to reach the town center of Hog's End, three short streets encompassing a few businesses and several residences. Eldred found Tenny sitting on the porch of the foundry debating some matter with a young Deiran man, with typical wiry build and black hair. He appeared to be about the same age as Tenny.

"Mother's blessings, Tenny."

Tenny leapt to his feet. "Eldred! Come down off your horse and meet Jenkin, my fellow apprentice." He turned to Jenkin. "This is Eldred, the king's son."

Eldred dismounted and shook Jenkin's hand, which gripped him like a vice.

Jenkin grinned. "I'm honored, Eldred. Tenny is full of tales about you."

Tenny looked down the road. "Where are the others? Did you abandon them?"

"I did, though Dreven and Preceptor Grimes should be along shortly."

"And the match?"

Eldred shook his head. "Bloody. Many Mercians died and—nothing changed for me."

Tenny nodded. "I'm the same too. That is to say, I am free, free of that dreadful academy."

Eldred frowned. "As I'll be soon."

"What about an ale," said Jenkin after a pause.

"Oh, that sounds good," said Tenny.

"I'll join you, but I can't drink," said Eldred.

"Why not?" asked Jenkin.

Tenny laughed. "Academy vows. Foolish stuff. They sell lemonade at the inn, Eldred."

After a short walk to the Hog's Breath, they were seated with their drinks in a nook of a cozy common room. A few patrons glanced at Eldred with interest, but none of them imposed on the trio as they fell into conversation.

"Everything here seems to be named after pigs," said Eldred.

"No, that's not true," said Jenkin.

"Hog's End, the Hog's Breath?" said Eldred.

"Those are, to be sure, but not much else," said Jenkin.

"The main store is called 'Hog's Supplies'," volunteered Tenny.

"Fair enough," said Jenkin.

"Was there some famous pig in these parts? I did not pass any hog farms as I rode into town," said Eldred.

"Well, Jenkin?" said Tenny.

"No famous swines come to mind. The town, the inn—each could boast another name."

"But they don't," said Eldred.

Jenkin took a sip of his ale. "Nope, but it's all good this way."

After a pause, Eldred noted Tenny's wide smile. "You seem happy, Tenny, happier than I have seen you in a long time."

Tenny nodded. "I'm back home, Eldred."

"Have you started smithing yet?"

"I only arrived here two days ago."

"So you have not made me a piece?" asked Eldred

Jenkin laughed. "No, he won't make quality pieces for anyone for a year or two."

"That long?" asked Eldred.

"Jenkin would know," said Tenny. "He's your age, Eldred, but he's already apprenticed with my father for years. He can craft gauntlets so masterfully, they pass as my father's own work."

"No, no," protested Jenkin. "I never said that."

"But I did," said Tenny.

Jenkin smiled and raised his mug towards Tenny, and they both took a hearty swig. As they drank, a towering thickset man with black hair walked in the door. Eldred stared with wide eyes.

"That's a Mercian," Eldred whispered.

Tenny and Jenkin looked at each other and laughed.

"Why are you laughing?" asked Eldred.

"What do you think people say when they see you?" said Tenny.

Eldred rolled his eyes. "What's he doing here?"

"He lives here. Felix, come and join us! Come meet my friend, Eldred," called Tenny.

Felix came over and stuck out his hand to Eldred while he inspected Eldred's clothes. "Well met. Are you from Tyrus?"

"No. I'm not a Mercian. I'm from the Academy, near Boar's Tusk."

"Are you fooling me? You sure do have the look of a Mercian."

"But I'm not a Mercian. I come from Deiran blood, mostly Deiran blood, anyway."

"Are you one of them bonded warrior fellers?" asked Felix.

Eldred frowned. "No."

Felix pulled up a seat. "Good. I hate them bastards."

Tenny grinned. "So do I."

Eldred pointedly did not drink while the others toasted to their mutual dislike of bonded warriors.

They had been chatting for an hour when someone called Eldred's name. Eldred turned to find an angry Preceptor Grimes with Dreven lurking behind him.

Preceptor Grimes marched up to their table. "Were you drinking, Eldred?"

Tenny waved Preceptor Grimes off. "No, no. He's quite innocent. Look, he had lemonade."

Preceptor Grimes examined the contents of Eldred's glass, picking up the glass to sniff it. "Thank the Mother for that."

Tenny pointed at the bar. "Can I offer you a drink, Preceptor Grimes? You're surely past the age of ascension."

"I most certainly am. I would be glad for it, and a lemonade for Dreven, if you would."

"My pleasure."

Preceptor Grimes and Dreven pulled two more chairs up to the table.

"We had some blood match today. Quite a few—people died," said Preceptor Grimes, finishing weakly under Felix's withering glare.

"Mercians, for the most part," said Dreven in a cheerful voice. "Before we left, they counted one hundred sixty-seven slaughtered Mercians. They said the number might come down though if some Mercians recovered."

"But they were dead?" said Eldred.

"They were probably dead. They were laying them out. They were in no rush to bury them," said Dreven.

"How many fancy warriors killed?" asked Felix.

"Twenty-three," said Preceptor Grimes.

Felix smirked and took a drink.

Preceptor Grimes gave Felix a puzzled look. "Only twenty-three. And since we won the match, we continue to hold these lands, including Hog's End."

Jenkin chuckled. "Nobody truly holds the borderlands."

"There's the yearly tribute," said Preceptor Grimes.

Jenkin smiled. "Some years we pay Tyrus, other years we pay Boar's Tusk. The best years are when we don't pay anyone."

"That's the one I like. I hate giving my pigs away," said Felix.

Eldred pointed at Felix. "So you're the one who raises hogs."

Felix glowered at Eldred. "I keep some pigs. I also grow potatoes. I am not the 'one' who raises hogs."

"I meant no offense. I was just joking."

"I want to fight," declared Felix.

"What?" said Eldred.

"You insulted my honor."

"He did no such thing, you muddle-brained Mercian," said Preceptor Grimes.

"Don't be alarmed, Eldred, Preceptor Grimes. This is a Mercian custom. He's offering to fight for some sport," said Tenny.

"Is that right, Felix?" asked Eldred.

Felix slapped the table. "I want to fight."

"To the death?" said Eldred, with a glance at Tenny.

"No, it's simply a fistfight. Mercians have them all the time. They hardly damage each other. Come on, Eldred. You'll be great," said Tenny, with a loud burp that set Jenkin laughing.

"So long as nobody gets too badly hurt," said Eldred.

"Outside everyone!" shouted Jenkin.

"Now, hold up," said Preceptor Grimes.

"Don't fret, Preceptor Grimes. They're simply enjoying some fisticuffs," said Tenny.

Preceptor Grimes followed them out the door with a displeased expression. Eldred and Felix stood across from each other in the dusty street. The inn patrons watched from the porch, holding their drinks. Now they were outside and standing, Eldred realized Felix was three inches taller and had longer reach. He had not fought someone bigger than himself in years.

Felix took a fighting stance. "Put up your fists, schoolboy."

At first, they circled each other while the crowd cheered on both combatants. The cheers were mixed; a few Mercians shouted for Eldred while several Deirans clapped for Felix.

The circling ended abruptly with Felix chasing after Eldred, throwing punch after punch. Eldred retreated, ducking away from the punches until one caught him right in the eye and dropped him to the ground. The crowd whooped, and Felix danced back to take a bow before them. Eldred lay there stunned for a moment before wiping the dirt from his lips and heaving himself to his feet.

"So we're not done, then," said Felix brightly.

Eldred shook his head and advanced on Felix with his fists up.

"Careful, Eldred!" called Preceptor Grimes.

As Eldred approached, Felix started throwing punches. Eldred blocked the first few, but then a glancing swing caught Eldred on the side of the head. Eldred stepped into Felix and hammered his ribs with five quick, powerful blows before Felix backpedaled out of reach.

"Ouch! The schoolboy has some sting," said Felix, laughing along with the crowd.

Eldred charged Felix, swinging wildly, but Felix hit Eldred hard on the chin, staggering him. Felix landed two more blows on Eldred's face before Eldred tumbled on the street.

"Felix, Felix!" chanted the crowd.

Eldred was seething with rage as he rolled onto his side. Tenny and Jenkin dashed over to help him up.

"It's over, Eldred," said Tenny.

Eldred spat blood on the ground. "Not yet!"

Jenkin grabbed Eldred lightly on the arm "No. You're done, Eldred. This was only for fun. You're too angry."

Tenny nodded. "He's right, Eldred."

Eldred glared at Tenny and Jenkin before taking a deep breath. "So what now?"

Tenny smiled. "Well, you could buy Felix an ale to show you are a good sport. If you were not so stuck on staying at the Academy, you could enjoy one too."

"I don't have any coins," huffed Eldred.

"Of course you do," said Tenny, pressing a few copper coins into Eldred's hand.

Eldred gave a half smile to Tenny.

"Are you up for more, schoolboy?" called Felix.

"Time to drink, Felix."

Felix clapped his hands together. "I like this lad. He has some punishing fists."

The crowd filed back into the inn and Eldred bought Felix a large ale.

As they sat back at the table, Dreven examined Eldred. "You look terrible. Doesn't your face hurt?"

"Oh, I barely touched him," said Felix. "He has two black eyes is all."

Eldred felt his face gingerly. "It doesn't feel bad."

"But you lost to a Mercian," said Dreven.

"There are lots as can do that, son," said Felix.

Tenny wagged his finger. "Few can win a fistfight with Felix. Preceptor Grimes, you should have taught us brawling instead of sword work."

"Don't underestimate the value of a sword, Tenny," said the preceptor.

"Wooden swords?" said Tenny.

"Even wooden swords. That's how warriors get their start."

MORNING

The next morning, Eldred sat with Dreven at the kitchen table in Tenny's house while Tenny finished up preparing a beef steak compress for Eldred's blackened eyes. Tenny's parents were out in front of the house showing pieces of armor to Preceptor Grimes.

Tenny placed the treated steak on a plate. "Try this."

Eldred placed the steak over his right eye.

"That color won't go away quickly. Those will still show when we return," said Dreven.

Eldred shrugged. "I doubt this adds much to my shame."

Dreven chuckled. "I'm not so sure. Preceptor Grimes is pretty unhappy with the whole business."

Eldred glared out the window. "Perhaps collecting payment from Pate will cheer him up."

"We're paying what we owe. We're not complaining, Eldred," said Tenny.

Eldred frowned.

"If injustice bothers you so, you can pay my fees," said Dreven.

"Your case is not the same. If you manifest the Bond, then, of course, the cost makes sense."

"I have not manifested anything as yet," said Dreven.

"You will," said Eldred.

Dreven grinned. "I hope you're right."

"When you're done with the Academy, come to Hog's End, Eldred. You'll fit in better down here," said Tenny.

"There are actual Mercians here, I suppose."

"Exactly."

Eldred rubbed his chin. "Where's my father's estate? I didn't see it on the way into town."

"Your father owns a ranch ten miles west of here."

"A sizable one?"

"I gather some ten or twenty men run it. You could be the steward."

"Does a ranch that size need a steward?" asked Dreven.

"I don't know," said Eldred.

Tenny gestured grandly. "Of course, it does. And down here, you can fight. Mercians love to fight. They don't merely brawl; they conduct real duels with armor and swords."

"I suppose you'll sell me equipment for these battles?" asked Eldred.

"Yes, at a fair price too."

Eldred smiled and switched the steak to the other eye. "I'll hold you to your word."

After a spell, Preceptor Grimes summoned the squires outside, where he stood in front of a pile of armored gauntlets and helmets. "We need to carry some goods back with us. Each of us must take a share. Your horse will take the largest portion, Dreven. Eldred's already bears a large enough load."

Dreven scowled at the heap. "This'll slow us down."

Preceptor Grimes folded his arms. "We'll save Pate a trip and set the books right for young Tenny. I'll not debate the matter."

Dreven gave an exaggerated sigh.

As they loaded their gear and the armor, Tenny's mother, Cisly, brought out a basket filled with bread, fruit and some smoked meat. "For your travels, Preceptor."

"Oh, there is no need, dear lady. Your hospitality last night was more than enough. Besides, I packed plenty of hardtack for the journey."

"I'll take the basket, then. I'm done with hardtack unless I'm starving," said Dreven.

Cisly smiled at Dreven and held up the offering to Preceptor Grimes. "For the young squires, then. We were honored to host a preceptor and two well-mannered guests in our house."

"And you're saving me a long ride," threw in Pate as he walked up behind Cisly and put his arm around her.

Preceptor Grimes took the basket. "Thanks again for your gracious hospitality."

"You're quite welcome," said Cisly.

Dreven gave a slight bow from his saddle.

Tenny stepped next to his parents and waved. "Mother's blessings, Eldred. Enjoy your last days at the Academy."

Eldred nodded. "Thank you, Tenny."

Preceptor Grimes led the squires out the north side of Hog's End. The day was fine, perfect for riding, except for the rattling pieces of armor.

Eldred felt a headache coming on. "What's the headmaster going to do with all this?"

"I expect we'll barter this lot in the market at Boar's Tusk."

"It makes quite a racket."

Preceptor Grimes shrugged. "We're not carrying it for our convenience, Eldred."

Eldred scowled at Preceptor Grimes. Thereafter, he trailed a fair way behind Preceptor Grimes and Dreven, which is how they clattered through the first day.

The night was quiet. Preceptor Grimes warmed up hardtack for himself. Eldred and Dreven ate the victuals from the basket Cisly had given them.

TRAIL

The next morning, they set off through wooded valleys with the expectation of reaching the Academy in the late afternoon.

"Your eyes are green and yellow now. They don't look good. You probably shouldn't have fought Felix," said Dreven brightly as they started down the trail.

"There's some sense to your thinking," agreed Eldred.

"Mance was a surprise," said Dreven, hanging back with Eldred as Preceptor Grimes trotted ahead.

"What do you mean?"

"You saw how he did with Yeowars. He had about the worst trial anyone has ever seen and here he is only a few days later with transference at the match."

Eldred shrugged. "Good for Mance."

"He went from being appalling to being enviable in a brief span. His story inspires me."

Eldred nodded without much interest.

"When the winter trials come, Mance is certainly going to pair with either Daw or Wybert. He will not be trying with Yeowars again," said Dreven.

"He suggested as much to me."

"So who will you try with? You won't partner with Yeowars. He was a disaster. He was not even making clean acts for his part. And Mance and one of the two others will be out. Tenny is gone. Perhaps we should pair up?"

"Us?" said Eldred, in surprise.

"Who else is there? You need to pass the trial too. This is your last chance before your ascension day," said Dreven.

Eldred sighed. "Seems as if everyone knows that."

"Well?" said Dreven.

"Thanks for your offer, but you just mentioned Mance's failed attempt. I would not survive something of that sort."

"They had bad luck, and you've an advantage. If you match the minimum, nobody will face your father and declare they didn't feel the Bond. Your father would kill them on the spot."

Eldred tapped his chest. "My father will disown me on the spot if I fail."

"We get three tries. And the steps; we can focus on those."

"What do you mean?"

"Stepping forward and back," said Dreven with emphasis. "That usually makes up three to four of the acts. In the last trial, more than once, the first act in the set was a step forward."

"Mance and Yeowars did not match once in thirty acts," observed Eldred.

"Yeowars was rattled. Besides, what if we knew when someone stepped? We could lightly scrape our feet. If we had a signal, we might get all the steps."

Eldred raised his eyebrows. "You want to cheat?"

"Nobody would dare say that if you passed. They would not want to face your father."

Eldred shook his head. "My father is all set to make Harold his heir. He's not concerned about me."

Dreven scoffed. "The histories don't have many tales of kings giving away their lands to a nephew when they had fathered a son."

"The auditors would know. You can't fool them."

"Not for long, that's for sure, but perhaps we can trick them for one trial. Then you don't need to serve as someone's steward, and I don't need to till someone's land. Besides, we might eventually develop the Bond. Nobody can be certain we wouldn't. You are set with a Deiran stone, aren't you?"

"I am."

"Think on it, Eldred. We can find time. If we practice, if we match five with confidence, we can change everything."

They rode in silence for a spell as Eldred considered, chasing the idea around in his mind. What if you could trick the auditors? They mostly just counted. How smart was Harold anyway?

Eldred looked over at Dreven. "These winter trials are my last. Why are you so rushed?"

"This will be my last attempt as well, Eldred. I won't age out, but my family, we're farmers. They've paid about all they can."

"That's the same situation as Tenny found himself in."

"So you will consider it?"

"I'm not sure. Perhaps."

Dreven grinned. "Think on it!"

Dreven gave his horse a kick and rode ahead with Preceptor Grimes.

RETURN

They arrived back at the Academy in the late afternoon. Squires swarmed out of the barracks to surround Preceptor Grimes and Dreven as they rode into the compound. Eldred detoured around the crowd and made his way to the stables without attracting attention. After leaving his horse, he made his way back to his quarters, emptier now that Tenny had left. Eldred plopped down on his bead with a history book he had on loan.

He had been reading for an hour when Preceptor Grimes knocked. "The headmaster wants to see you."

Eldred huffed as he set the book down. "May as well get it over with."

"He only wants a word, Eldred."

"Fine."

As they crossed the grounds some squires caught sight of Eldred and burst out laughing as they mimicked boxing.

"Dreven's been talking," muttered Eldred as they continued on.

"Dreven returned from an adventure," said Preceptor Grimes. "You can't be surprised that he would relate his exploits. Besides, your black eyes are plainly visible. He saved you from having to provide the explanation."

Eldred grunted.

When they reached the hall, Preceptor Grimes knocked on the door of the headmaster's study.

After a moment, the headmaster appeared. "Ah, thank you for bringing Eldred," said Headmaster Tibbot, then he noticed Eldred's face. "Oh, what happened?"

"Just a bit of brawling, Headmaster," said Preceptor Grimes.

The headmaster raised his eyebrows and beckoned Eldred into the study. Once inside, the headmaster took a seat at his desk and waved Eldred into a chair.

"One moment, Eldred," said the headmaster. He leaned forward and studied Eldred. After a pause, the headmaster sat back, apparently satisfied with his examination. "I hope you found the trip interesting, Eldred."

"I suppose I did."

"What did you make of the blood match?"

Eldred smiled wryly. "Quite a spectacle, though I might have appreciated the battle more if I had kept my eyes open."

Headmaster Tibbot pursed his lips somberly. "How was your experience relating to the transference?"

"As I'm sure Preceptor Grimes informed you, there was no transference for me. Mance and the two younger squires had some awakening, or so everyone said."

"You felt nothing?"

"Yes, as I'm sure Preceptor Grimes informed you," said Eldred, with an edge in his voice.

"Preceptor Grimes spoke with me, but these matters shape the kingdom. I need the information from you directly."

"Do you? Events transpired exactly as you predicted they would. You needn't have bothered sending me."

"I do not agree. Given the circumstances, sending you was most prudent."

"If you say so, Headmaster."

The headmaster nodded. "I do. So what is your plan? What do you wish to do now?"

"My plan? What is there to do but to prepare for the winter trial as best I can?"

"Really? The winter trial? Do you have a partner in mind?"

"Dreven and I discussed it. I think we make a reasonable pairing."

The headmaster jerked back in his chair. "You would pair with Dreven? I thought you two did not get along."

Eldred clasped his hands in his lap. "Well, this is a serious business. Any option must be considered." Eldred cleared his throat. "I need you to excuse us from training and allow us to practice for the trial each day. I certainly don't require any more instruction with the sword or spear."

The headmaster narrowed his brows. "Hmm, which preceptor do you want to work with?"

"No preceptors; just ourselves. To succeed, we must remove all distractions."

Headmaster Tibbot rubbed his chin. "You seem to have given this some thought."

"Yes, we both did."

"This is quite ambitious, Eldred."

Eldred set his face. "No other plan gives me a chance. Forty-eight days—that's all I have left. The Academy, my Deiran fatum lapis—nothing's worked so far. I need to do things my way for this last stretch. Don't disturb me. Don't block me. When the time is done, I'll ascend or I'll—as you repeatedly insist—choose from my other opportunities."

Headmaster Tibbot tilted his head and considered. "I see you helped yourself to some extra time. The winter trials are in thirty days."

"My father can send a pod to audit me at any time. The snow is not going to block the arches. I can shovel them clear myself, if needed."

"Very well. I will support your effort, Eldred. I will excuse you both from training, though, frankly, Dreven could benefit from more time with the staff. But please note, I examined you when you came in. Nothing has changed. When the time comes for the trial, be it the winter trial or your own special trial, don't forget the king's explicit instructions. You must not make the attempt unless you are certain to pass."

"I recall my father's demands. He made them clear enough. Still, as a squire, I have the right to the trial. But don't fret—only a fool would seek to disappoint my father."

"Very wise. I will move Dreven to your quarters. As the trial draws nearer, I expect you will come to understand the situation better. Come and speak to me then. I will help you."

"Thank you, Headmaster. But, perhaps it is you who will enjoy the realization."

The headmaster sighed. "Just come to me when it is time."

TRAINING

The next day, forty-seven days before Eldred's day of ascension, Eldred and Dreven stood examining the center arch while the other squires were training with spears in the main yard.

Dreven laughed as he watched the distant figures go through their paces. "You did this right, Eldred."

Eldred grunted and continued staring at the arch.

"Just one mention from you and we get to skip training."

"A last favor; I don't expect the headmaster holds much hope of us taking the trail, let alone passing it."

Dreven frowned. "Why would he think that?"

"He can sense the Bond in squires. He examined me yesterday. He knows I don't have it."

Dreven pointed at the arches. "His word is not the trial. The trial takes place right here. Three sets of ten acts settle the matter."

"True."

"We are working with a stone floor, not dirt. This will help us listen for steps. We can brush a heel when stepping forward, like this." Dreven took an exaggerated step which scraped the ground.

"Don't! People can see us," snapped Eldred.

"Right, well, stone benefits us. When we move back, we can drag our toes."

"And that will sound different?"

Dreven nodded. "Yes."

"We must step at the same time or the auditors will take note."

"Practice," said Dreven.

Eldred rubbed his ear. "That still leaves us a few acts short. We will still need some sword acts to match. I can't count on chance."

"What about your hearing? You possess Maldavian sight; do you have Maldavian hearing as well?"

Eldred shrugged. "The Night Mother did not grant better hearing to the Maldavians, just the sight."

"Hmm. Unfortunate. In any case, we'll figure something out. For now, we need a private place with a stone floor where we can practice."

"I'll ask the headmaster," said Eldred.

DINNER

That night at dinner, Mance invited Daw and Wybert to the senior squires table. The three had arrived back in the morning before the first training session. They sat near the middle of the table while Eldred, Dreven and Yeowars edged down to the end.

"You and Dreven missed an amazing feast; so much better than this slop," said Mance.

Eldred ignored Mance and worked at cutting his boiled beef.

"I wager we had a much more interesting time in Hog's End. Eldred fought a Mercian and bears the black eyes to prove it," said Dreven.

"I heard he didn't win," said Mance.

"No, but he landed some hard punches in the Mercian's gut," said Dreven.

Mance gave Dreven a dismissive glance, and the squires went back to eating their food.

After a pause, Mance waved a small piece of beef on his fork. "Your uncle was a great host at the feast and for the return, Eldred. Please give him my regards."

"Mine too," added Wybert with his mouth full.

"He was extremely kind," said Daw.

"I'll pass on your good wishes," said Eldred in a solemn tone, though he had no intention of following through.

"So, you and Dreven are training together? You'll put your names forward for the trial?" asked Mance.

Eldred kept his eyes on his plate. "We're working together."

Mance cocked his head. "Is that wise? Neither one of you experienced transference."

"We are both prepared to train hard for the trial," said Eldred.

"It's not as if we could do worse than you and Yeowars did," said Dreven.

Mance frowned. "Oh, you could so do worse."

Dreven smirked. "No, we couldn't. You had no matched actions out of thirty."

"We had one act," said Mance.

"That's right," said Yeowars.

Eldred put down his knife and waved off the dispute. "Dreven and I will face our own trial if we go forward. You and Yeowars had a rough time of it, Mance, but you're both doing well now."

Mance nodded emphatically. "Quite well."

"With you excused from training, Mance and I are the senior squires present," said Yeowars.

"How nice for you," said Eldred.

"I found your absence today odd, Eldred," said Mance. "You've been around for as long as I've attended the Academy."

"I'm still here," said Eldred.

"I heard you were seeking a role as a steward at a ranch down by Hog's End," said Mance.

"What?" Eldred narrowed his eyes at Dreven.

"My father owns several estates. If you do end up in need of a position, I'm sure we can find a suitable opportunity for you," continued Mance.

"My family also holds estates," said Wybert.

"As does mine," said Daw.

Eldred's face flushed. "How thoughtful of you all, but I'm not seeking a position as anyone's steward."

"You don't want to move down by Hog's End. You would be hard-pressed to find a less important place," said Mance.

"I'm not moving anywhere. I'm preparing for the trial. That's all I'm doing," said Eldred.

"I'm just trying to help," said Mance.

Eldred straightened his back. "I don't need your help. I don't need anyone's help."

Later, in their dormitory, Eldred sat on the edge of his bed facing Dreven, who leaned against the wall with his arms crossed. "Why did you tell them about the ranch? I didn't intend to share my plans with everyone."

Dreven shrugged. "I'm sorry. That part slipped out as I was telling the squires about the fight with the Mercian."

"In the future, consider everything I say in your company private. Now these stupid boys are offering me positions as their father's steward."

"That doesn't sound so bad to me," said Dreven.

Eldred stared at the floor in front of him and took a breath. "Neither one of us wants to be a farmer or a steward."

Dreven nodded. "Not if we can be warriors."

"We need to trust each other completely, if we're even going to have a possibility of passing the trial."

"I know," said Dreven, sounding serious for once.

"Don't speak of me or my life again to anyone."

Dreven frowned. "I won't."

"Good."

Dreven pointed at Eldred. "But stop speaking down to me."

"What?" said Eldred.

"You're all high and mighty. You're the king's son and your worst nightmare is being some rich steward. In this—our plan, I'm taking equal risk. Don't forget it."

Eldred shifted uncomfortably. "We're in this together."

RUSE

The next morning, forty-six days before Eldred's day of ascension, while the other squires reported for training, Eldred and Dreven took their wooden swords and went to a storage hut on the outskirts of the Academy. As they stood at the entrance, Eldred cast a lingering glance towards the yard where the boys were lined up.

"You honestly like those stupid exercises, don't you?" said Dreven.

Eldred nodded slowly. "Yes, I do."

Dreven pushed the door open and went into the windowless hut, examining the dusty room full of scattered odds and ends. "Delightful."

Eldred set his sword down on a barrel. "It offers us privacy and a stone floor. We just need to clear things up."

Dreven walked to the opposite wall, scraping his sword along the ground as he went. Eldred started clearing debris. After a pause, Dreven joined in. Once they had enough space cleared, they inspected the room in silence.

Eldred laughed mirthlessly. "We can't do this. We can't get away with this."

Dreven picked up a loose stone and hurled it across the floor where it made a sharp crack. "Are you such a quitter? Do you want to spend the rest of your life as Mance's steward?"

"No! I'm no steward, and I would sooner kill Mance. But it doesn't work."

Dreven's face was intense. "We'll use a sound, something subtle." Dreven got up and started pacing around the hut, taking exaggerated steps.

Eldred gestured dismissively. "You won't be able to do any of that."

"No, I suppose not." Dreven stared at his shoes.

"Well?"

"My shoes aren't as fine as yours."

Eldred looked. Dreven's shoes were shoddy. "They look serviceable."

"I'm not complaining. In this case, my station helps us."

"How so?" asked Eldred.

"Nobody is likely to think much about what I wear. Everyone knows my family are farmers who can barely pay the academy fees."

"Not everyone does. I didn't," said Eldred.

"My point is that I can show up with noisy shoes and an ancient leather cuirass—two sizes too small—and nobody would comment," said Dreven, with a touch of pride.

"Not on your clothes, but they will notice you scraping your feet. They're not blind."

"I won't drag them much. You need to listen carefully and step quickly."

Eldred sighed. "You would already be moving before I react. We won't fool anyone."

"You saw Yeowars's form. He was terrible and nobody complained. I expect I could straighten my foot before stepping. Then we can go together, as we must."

Eldred leaned against the wall and shook his head. "They'll catch us."

Dreven took off his shoe and started inspecting the sole. Then he rummaged through the shelves until he found a small claw hammer, which he used to dig into the leather.

"There," said Dreven, replacing the shoe on his foot and dragging it over the stone, making a scratching noise from an exposed tack. "You will know I am about to step forward when you hear that."

"And for stepping back?"

"I'll soak the other one to make it squeak. For the sword acts, my cuirass will make sounds like no garment you have ever heard. You are the son of the king and can't wear such things, but I can."

"So it squeaks?" said Eldeed.

"No. You'll see. Every movement generates an infernal noise, which normally makes me embarrassed—or even angry. But now, while the auditors cringe, you'll spring into action. And I thought my grandfather's old armor was worthless, I was wrong. You'll see tomorrow."

"I hope this garment lives up to its reputation."

"You won't be disappointed, but you need to be lightning quick. We had best start practicing with the footwork. Line up."

Eldred grudging picked up his sword. They practiced for hours.

NEWS

Three weeks later, twenty-five days before Eldred's day of ascension and a week to the winter trial, Eldred and Dreven were at practice when someone started pounding on the door.

"Open up!" It sounded like Mance. "Open up. We hear you in there."

Dreven lowered his sword and unlatched the door, opening it a crack. "What do you want?"

Mance pushed the door open and crowded past Dreven, followed closely by Wybert and Daw. Yeowars hung back in the doorway looking in.

"Hey," said Eldred, a look of irritation across his face..

Mance looked around the room, taking in the furnishings that Eldred and Dreven had added. "So this is where you've been keeping yourselves."

Wybert pointed at the carpet. "It's nicer than the dorms."

Daw frowned at the beds against the walls. "Are you sleeping here?"

Eldred crossed his arms. "We're here a lot. Now what do you want?"

Mance rolled his eyes. "We have some questions. We won't take long."

"What do you know about it, Eldred?" asked Wybert.

"Will your father allow it?" asked Daw.

Eldred gave them a quizzical look. "Allow what?"

"Allow the Wretched his request?" said Mance.

"Who?" said Eldred.

Wybert stepped forward. "A Wretched presented himself to your father's court. He requested your father's aid in killing a dragon."

"A real dragon," said Mance excitedly.

"One of the Wretcheds from Turicum?" said Eldred.

"I don't know where. Someplace up north," said Wybert.

Eldred rubbed his chin. "That's odd. My Uncle Julian usually manages dealings with the Wretcheds. The Maldavians killed the last dragon that attacked the Wretcheds, back, well, back before any of us were born."

"Right. Well, this time the Wretcheds want the dragon killed properly, so they came to us," said Mance.

"I heard from my father that the Wretched arrived yesterday. What'll your father do?" asked Wybert.

Eldred looked back and forth between the boys. "This is the first I've heard of it. I've been training with Dreven all day."

"That's all you do every day," complained Mance.

"As we should," said Dreven.

"You don't understand, Dreven. When a squire is ready, the Bond comes naturally and without effort," said Mance.

Dreven scoffed. "Now you are the expert."

Mance straightened his posture. "I'm taking the trial this winter. Wybert is working with me. We hardly train at all."

"I wish you luck, Mance," said Eldred.

"I don't," said Dreven.

"I don't need your luck, Dreven. And we don't need much training. What are you even doing all day? You're missing out on drills. Your fighting will get sloppy."

"Once we pass the trial we can make up for any missed training," said Eldred.

Mance shook his head. "Only if you pass the trial, Eldred. You won't need great fighting skills to be a steward."

"He'd be a fierce steward. He's already bigger than everyone," said Wybert.

"I'm not aiming to be a steward," said Eldred hotly.

"And I'm not aiming to be a farmer," added Dreven.

Mance and Wybert laughed.

"It's not funny," said Dreven, raising his training sword.

Mance choked on his laughter, fighting to regain control of himself as tears rolled down his cheeks. "What if—what if—Dreven was the steward and Eldred was the farmer?"

"He would be a regal farmer, bigger than his donkey," sputtered Wybert.

Dreven turned red in the face, and Eldred glared furiously at the chortling squires.

"I'm sorry. I'm sorry. I was only joking," said Mance, finally calming down.

"We were jesting," said Wybert.

Eldred gave a thin smile. "Very humorous. Perhaps you should seek positions as jesters."

"So what do you think about the dragon?" said Mance.

"I just learned about it," said Eldred.

"Do you think your father will wait until after the winter trial to send an expedition?" asked Daw.

Eldred took a breath. "Ah, now I understand. You hope to go. Well, I last spoke with my father before the blood match. I don't know when he'll send an expedition, or whether he'll send one at all."

Mance raised his fist. "He has to. He can't miss a chance to kill a dragon."

Eldred scoffed. "More like a chance to be killed by a dragon. The Maldavians sent forty men against the last one. Only a handful returned."

"Why even fight the creature if all it's doing is tormenting the Wretcheds?" asked Yeowars quietly.

Wybert nodded at Yeowars. "That's a point."

"We can't let it eat them all," said Eldred. "There's only a limited number of Wretcheds."

"What do you mean?" asked Mance.

"We only allow the Wretcheds a certain number. They have to keep to it. Every year the Maldavians send an expedition to count them. If they're over their allotment, the expedition corrects the situation."

"With a battle?" said Mance.

"No, with executions," said Eldred.

"That doesn't make much sense," said Daw.

Eldred shrugged. "Perhaps not, but the Night Mother made the covenant before she left. We can't question her law. The count might explain why the Wretched came here. My uncle had some problem on a recent one, too, some issue that enraged the Wretcheds. I guess they don't want Maldavians in Turicum, not even to kill their dragon."

"If the king sends an expedition after the winter trial, perhaps we can all go," said Daw.

"They say the dragon is the strongest creation of the Night Mother, outside of us," said Mance.

Eldred glanced out the door. "Quite an adventure." An adventure for warriors.

INTERROGATION

The next morning, twenty-four days before Eldred's day of ascension, Eldred and Dreven were training in the storage hut when someone knocked at the door. Eldred opened the door to find Headmaster Tibbot.

The headmaster offered a courteous smile. "Good morning, Eldred. Good morning, Dreven."

"Good morning, Headmaster," said Eldred.

"May I come in?"

"It's better if we come out. It stinks in here," said Dreven.

The headmaster stepped back as the squires exited the hut.

"What do you need, Headmaster?" asked Eldred.

"The winter trial is in six days. It is time to declare your intentions."

Dreven glanced at Eldred. "I'm game for it."

Eldred crossed his arms. "We're ready."

The headmaster studied each squire intently before shaking his head. "Eldred, your father was most explicit. He does not want you to take the trial unless you are certain to succeed."

"I believe we will," said Eldred.

"On what do you base this confidence? None of the preceptors worked with you. You haven't even completed a practice run with your fellow squires."

Eldred shrugged. "Not yet. We've been focused on working with each other. We find it's the best approach."

The headmaster's expression darkened. "I wish I shared your optimism. But counting on luck will lead to disaster. I can't conceive of how you convinced yourselves to make this attempt, but it is time both of you checked your understanding of the situation."

"We train every day," said Dreven in a cheerful tone.

The headmaster shook his head. "That does not matter. The trial tests ability, not effort."

Eldred bristled. "You can't prevent us from taking the trial."

The headmaster fixed Eldred with a stern gaze. "I can't bar a squire from making an attempt, but I can determine who remains a squire."

"What're you suggesting?" asked Eldred.

"I wish you to go through a test session tomorrow, under the supervision of Preceptor Grimes. I will be in attendance."

Eldred gestured at the hut. "You can't all fit in there."

"Then we will conduct the session at the arches," said Headmaster Tibbot.

Eldred clenched his fist. "You're rushing us."

"I will humor you for three sets. Afterwards, we will discuss whether you should proceed."

"So we have no choice?" complained Eldred.

"No," said the headmaster.

"I'll be there," said Dreven.

"Eldred?" said the headmaster.

Eldred shrugged. "Fine. If I must."

The headmaster nodded. "Very well. I will leave you to your—activities."

Eldred and Dreven watched the headmaster walk back to the training yard, where the students were performing sword drills with Preceptor Grimes.

Dreven stuck his chest out. "We trained well. I expect we can tally seven acts or more."

Eldred sat down on a barrel by the door. "We don't know how it looks. Are we even in sync? Besides, the headmaster is aware I don't possess the Bond. It's probably the same for you. If we have a run of matches, he'll give our performance a hard look."

"Then we mix it up."

"What do you mean?" asked Eldred.

Dreven wagged his index finger. "I lead on the first set, but you ignore the sounds, so it looks bad with me leading. Then you take your turn, which also goes badly in any case. On the third set, I lead and give you the signals. We try to match five, maybe four or five, perhaps not enough to pass but close."

"It comes down to the third set."

"Right."

Eldred nodded. "That might work."

TRAINING DINNER

The cook prepared beef stew for dinner, one of her most popular meals with the students. Eldred took an additional helping as well as his usual extra helping, carefully balancing three full plates on his way to the table.

Mance looked over as Eldred sat down. "So we finally see you at work tomorrow."

"Did the headmaster invite you to be an auditor?" asked Eldred.

"Preceptor Grimes did," said Mance.

Eldred took a bite of stew.

"Are you ready?" asked Wybert.

"I suppose. Did they make you do a trial run as well?" asked Eldred.

"Yes, this afternoon," said Mance.

"How did it go?" asked Dreven.

Mance beamed. "Quite well. We had a few low sets, but we mostly scored between five and eight acts."

Eldred nodded. "How perfectly satisfactory."

"Did the headmaster attend?" said Dreven.

"No, just Preceptor Grimes and Preceptor Garaint," said Mance.

"Daw and Veril also ran through a few," said Wybert.

"How many did you tally, Daw?" asked Dreven.

Daw smiled and shook his head. "Not good. I won't be standing for the trial, but I'll serve as your auditor tomorrow."

"Thanks," said Eldred.

"If we pass, we might be in time for the expedition against the dragon," said Mance.

"Was there an announcement?" said Eldred.

"No, but the Wretched's still there. Why keep one around if there's no expedition?" said Mance.

Eldred dug around the vegetables, looking for meat. "I suppose if forty Maldavians defeated the last dragon, we should be able to kill this one with enough warriors."

"The Wretched told everyone that this one is bigger," said Wybert.

"As if he can remember the last," said Eldred. "They killed it more than forty years ago. I doubt that anyone who saw it then is still alive."

"I hope it's bigger," said Wybert.

Eldred shrugged.

"So, will you and Dreven manage eight matched acts?" asked Mance.

"Anything is possible," said Eldred.

"Tomorrow is for practice. The count is of no great concern," said Dreven.

"True, but the trial is in less than a week," said Mance.

"You'll want to be ready. The trial can be—really difficult," said Yeowars with a downcast expression.

"Right," said Eldred after an uncomfortable silence.

"We're ready," said Dreven.

PRACTICE

Just before noon the following day, twenty-three days before Eldred's day of ascension, Eldred and Dreven made their way to the center arch with their wooden swords. The weather was cool with overcast skies. Eldred donned a fine cotton tunic, black pants and leather dueling shoes. Dreven wore his creaky leather cuirass and his mangled shoes.

Dreven watched as Eldred kept tapping his sword on the ground. "Are you nervous?"

Eldred paused. "No."

"Don't score too high a count."

Eldred raised his eyebrows. "I'm sure we can't."

Preceptor Grimes arrived with the auditors: Mance, Yeowars, Daw and Wybert. "It's about time we had this rehearsal. Seems like ages since either of you had any proper instruction."

"We practice hard every day," said Eldred.

"Tenaciously," said Dreven.

Preceptor Grimes smiled. "I hope to good effect. We'll start once the headmaster arrives. He should be along shortly."

"Must we wait?" asked Eldred.

"Yes, he requested as much."

"But it is only a trial run," protested Eldred.

"True, but he has taken an interest," said the preceptor.

Eldred resumed tapping the ground with his sword. "If he were really interested, he would be on time."

Mance frowned. "You should be honored, Eldred. I wish the headmaster would come by and observe my practice."

Eldred stared at the mud streaks on the tip of his sword. "I suppose."

"Here he comes," said Yeowars.

Eldred glanced over to see Headmaster Tibbot bearing down on the assembly bearing a stern expression.

Preceptor Grimes clapped his hands. "Auditors, take your positions. Eldred, you begin on the right with me, Dreven to the left."

"You mean to have Dreven on the right. He will start us off," said Eldred.

"But you are the older squire," spluttered Mance.

Preceptor Grimes looked Eldred in the eye. "You're having Dreven take signals on the first set?"

Eldred nodded. "Yes."

Wybert chuckled. "The senior squire won't even lead his own trial."

Eldred bristled. "It's not a rule."

Preceptor Grimes patted Eldred on the shoulder. "No, I don't suppose it is. All right. We'll start with Dreven."

The squires moved into position. Eldred and Dreven stood in the middle of the center arch, facing away from each other. Mance and Yeowars faced Eldred for scoring. Wybert and Daw lined up to audit Dreven.

The headmaster arrived as the last auditor situated himself. "I hope I did not hold up the proceedings."

"Not at all, headmaster. I was enjoying a pleasant visit with the boys," said Preceptor Grimes.

The headmaster paused and examined the layout. "So Dreven begins as the lead?"

Preceptor Grimes nodded. "Yes, that's how they wish to proceed."

"Interesting."

Preceptor Grimes walked over to face Dreven. "Are you ready for the first practice set, squires?"

"We stand ready!" said Eldred and Dreven together.

"We begin!" said Preceptor Grimes.

Preceptor Grimes silently signaled Dreven, running Dreven through a series of acts. Eldred and Dreven made crisp movements for each part of the sequence, but outside of a step back on the fourth act their actions did not match.

When the set was complete, Preceptor Grimes did a quick check with his auditors. "One match."

The headmaster shook his head. "Not nearly good enough. Particularly for you, Eldred."

"It's just the first set, Headmaster," said Eldred.

"Is there a reason why we should not make this the last?"

"A trial is three sets, Headmaster," said Eldred.

"Very well. Commence with the second."

Eldred and Dreven switched places, with Eldred facing Preceptor Grimes.

"Are you ready for the second sequence, squires?" asked Preceptor Grimes.

"We stand ready!"

"We begin!" said Preceptor Grimes.

Again, Eldred and Dreven had crisp movements, but their acts rarely matched. When the set was complete, Preceptor Grimes consulted the auditors. "We count two matches."

"Two matches to follow one match," said Headmaster Tibbot.

"An improvement, Headmaster," said Eldred.

Headmaster Tibbot distractedly rubbed his chin. "Do you understand the consequences, Eldred?"

"Yes. We didn't give our best effort, Headmaster. We'll do better on the next set."

Eldred and Dreven switched places again.

"Are you ready for the third and final sequence, squires?"

"We stand ready!"

"We begin!"

Though not anything of beauty, Eldred mirrored Dreven more often on this run and both kept their movements crisp.

After checking with the auditors, Preceptor Grimes nodded. "We count five matches."

As Eldred and Dreven exchanged grins, Headmaster Tibbot cast a cold glance at Mance and Yeowars, who had been facing the blind partner in each set. The headmaster approached Eldred and examined him carefully for a moment before repeating the same with Dreven. Everyone kept silent as he made his inspection.

Once the headmaster completed his examination of Dreven, Eldred approached him. "We matched five, Headmaster, enough to pass."

"I heard the tally, Eldred," said Headmaster Tibbot dryly.

"We just needed time to warm up," said Dreven.

"A charitable assessment," said the headmaster.

"And we still have more time to practice. Almost a week," said Eldred.

Preceptor Grimes walked over and grabbed the boys by their shoulders.

"You need more training, lads. That was a narrow thing, too narrow."

Eldred nodded. "You're right, Preceptor Grimes. Best we start practicing right away. May we be excused, Headmaster?"

"Yes, you may go about your activities."

"Thank you, Headmaster."

Dreven took off in a sprint, pounding his feet as he ran. Eldred took off after him and soon caught up.

"You had better practice!" called Mance.

CELEBRATION

At dinner, Mance wasted little time before he shared his thoughts. "Those were weak sets today."

Wybert smirked. "You were both terrible."

"We had eight matched acts in total, seven more than you had in your last trial, Mance," said Eldred.

"Eight more. You and Yeowars didn't match a single act," said Dreven.

"They gave us one," said Yeowars quietly.

Dreven made a dismissive gesture. "Based on today, we would have passed. Nothing else matters."

"Only if the auditors agree they felt the Bond," said Mance.

Dreven pointed at Eldred. "He's the king's son. They'll certainly say they did."

Eldred flashed a sharp look at Dreven.

"I'm not so sure," said Mance.

"We'll see, Mance," said Eldred. "I would be more comfortable with a higher tally. We did not do our best today."

"Have you done better?" asked Mance.

Eldred picked up a chicken leg. "I'm sure we have. No auditors are present when we practice, but we've had some excellent sets, and our movements are crisp."

"They're not bad," conceded Yeowars.

"That's right," said Dreven.

"Wybert and I don't intend to pass with any charity. We'll score seven acts for certain," said Mance.

"I hope you do, Mance. We're merely looking to get by as well," said Eldred.

Mance frowned. "I suppose I expected more after all your secret training."

Eldred shrugged. "I never asked you to expect anything."

A DELIVERY

A few days later, when Eldred and Dreven returned to their quarters in the evening, Dreven found a package at the foot of his bed along with a note.

"What's that?" asked Eldred.

Dreven tore the wrapping open and laid out the contents. "A cotton shirt like yours, wool pants, leather dueling shoes."

"What does it say?"

Dreven read through the note. "It's from Tibbot. He says I need finer garments for the trial."

"Your clothes—how could he tell?"

Dreven smoothed the wrinkles out of the shirt with his hand. "The way he was staring at Mance and Yeowars, I was sure he suspected them of passing the signals to us."

Eldred gave a deep sigh. "He knows everything."

"Perhaps not. Perhaps he merely noticed I was dressed like a beggar."

Eldred shook his head. "No, no. This isn't some chance occurrence."

"It might be. In any case, we can make this work."

"You mean you won't wear these clothes? How would that look?"

Dreven picked up a shoe. "The clothes won't make any noise, but I can adjust these. We can match the steps. If we rack up all the steps and catch some luck with the sword, we can squeeze by."

Eldred felt his chest tighten. "I have to be certain. My father warned me. I must pass. Anything less is a disaster."

Dreven tossed the shoe on the bed. "Nobody is certain to do anything.

We have time. I'll wreck these shoes. I might hurt the headmaster's feelings, but no one else will give it any notice."

A pained expression crossed Eldred's face. "Three steps in the first set today, four in the second and third. It won't be enough."

"So what?" said Dreven. "Warriors face risks all the time. This is our chance. Or, if you don't have the heart for it, you can just become someone's servant."

Eldred stared dejectedly at the shoes on Dreven's bed.

"We'll practice tomorrow with these. I'll adjust them when we get to the hut. I might be able to sneak in one grunt. I can grunt on swing left, just for the first time."

Eldred walked to his bed and sat down, cradling his head in his hands.

Dreven rolled his eyes. "Don't look like you died. Steward is better than farmer."

LAST PRACTICE

The next morning, twenty days before Eldred's day of ascension and two days before the winter trial, Eldred and Dreven rushed over to the hut right after breakfast. Eldred sat on a barrel as Dreven adjusted his dueling shoes, cutting into the sole of one shoe and soaking the other.

Dreven eyed his handiwork. "They don't look too bad, but they'll sound terrible. Even I wouldn't wear them out of embarrassment, except the headmaster himself gifted me these fine shoes."

Eldred gave a noncommittal grunt.

Dreven put on the ruined shoes and paced around the hut. "I'm hearing these now. Listen, Eldred." He stepped forward and back, grating on a tack and squeaking the shoe, respectively. "It's not so different. Do you have it, Eldred?"

"I do; it just won't be enough."

"Perhaps not, but we won't be the disaster that Mance and Yeowars were. Their failure will make us seem like a near miss at worst. In the best case, we pass."

Eldred slowly got up. "I understand."

They set to practicing.

Around noon, someone knocked on the door. They cast a quick glance at each other before Eldred opened it. Framed in the door was Eldred's Uncle Benedict.

"Mother's blessings, nephew."

Eldred stepped back. "What are you doing here?"

"Your father sent me to fetch you. He wants to see you."

"In Boar's Tusk?"

"Yes."

Eldred eyed Benedict warily. "What's this about?"

"I will fill you in as we ride."

"I can't go. We're training for the trial."

Benedict shook his head. "Oh, but you can. It only takes two hours if we trot. Pack some clothes. You will be spending the night."

"But my training. The trial is in two days."

"Your training can wait."

Eldred crossed his arms. "You said you would support me."

Benedict gave him a firm look. "It can wait."

Eldred stepped forward to loom over his uncle, his face growing red.

Dreven grabbed Eldred on the arm. "You just need to be back for the trial."

Eldred took a breath and nodded.

Benedict trailed after the boys as they walked across the compound. Dreven's shoes squeaked with each step. Headmaster Tibbot and several preceptors were waiting by Eldred's door.

"I will pack your things, nephew." Benedict sidled past Eldred as Eldred stood staring at the gathering. Dreven ducked off to the side.

Headmaster Tibbot gave a stiff short bow. "I wish you a pleasant trip to Boar's Tusk."

Eldred licked his lips nervously. Preceptor Garaint had a ghost of a smile. Preceptor Grimes wouldn't meet his eye. "It's just a two-hour ride, if we trot."

"Pass my regards to your father," said Headmaster Tibbot.

Eldred nodded. "I will."

Benedict came out the door carrying two bags stuffed with clothing.

"Hey, that's all my clothes," said Eldred.

"I didn't know what you needed. Anyway, we must be off."

Two men from Benedict's pod came up leading horses. Benedict walked past the preceptors and stuck the bags on his saddle. Eldred hesitantly followed after him.

As Eldred mounted an offered horse, Preceptor Grimes called out, "May the Son walk beside you, Eldred!"

"Thank you, Preceptor Grimes. I'll be back tomorrow."

Preceptor Grimes turned away.

"Look after Eldred, Lord Benedict," said Headmaster Tibbot.

Benedict glanced over, but did not reply.

They rode through the Academy grounds towards the north road to

Boar's Tusk. As they passed the training yard, the boys stopped their exercises to watch them pass. At first, Eldred thought they were all staring at Benedict, brother to the king, but then he realized they were all staring at him.

Heading out to the north side of the Academy, they came to the arches and passed through the center arch to meet up with the road.

Eldred glanced back. "We had a trial run yesterday. We matched five."

"Did you? That's acceptable. Or I should say, it could be acceptable," said Benedict.

"What do you mean?"

Benedict signaled his men, then fixed Eldred with a stare as his men rode up ahead of them. "If you and your partner—excuse me, but his name escapes me—could match five acts, we would all be pleased. But the thinking of the people involved is that you cannot."

"We could use more practice."

"What you could use, and what apparently neither of you possess, is the Bond."

Eldred stared at Benedict in stunned silence for a moment as they rode. "We matched five acts!"

Benedict shook his head. "This is why I insisted on fetching you. You're taking the wrong tack. I much prefer you attempt it with me than with my brother."

"You want Harold to be king," growled Eldred.

"He will be, regardless of my desires. Even if you could squeak out five matched acts, he would still be king. I told you—I passed with seven in the center arch. When Alfred triumphed at four arches removed, I lost the crown before I ever wore it."

"Your son did not make it to the fifth arch."

"No, but he made it to the second."

Eldred narrowed his eyes at the two men riding in front and gripped his reins tighter.

Benedict shook his head. "No, Eldred. No tricks. You are as safe with me as you would be with the Mother herself. I convinced Alfred to let me collect you. You will make it safely to Boar's Tusk. If you want to be safe beyond that, you had best listen to me."

Eldred glowered down at his uncle. "I can ensure my own safety."

"Perhaps, if you act wisely. When you meet Alfred, you must start by admitting your guilt."

"What's the sense in that?" asked Eldred.

"While you can't bring Alfred honor, you can bring him shame. He will do terrible things to protect his name."

"So you would have me tell him I planned to cheat?"

"A bold and honorable admission might redeem you in his eyes. You can say it was the other boy's plan."

Eldred scoffed. "You've a twisted sense of honor."

"I understand necessity."

"And then?"

"And then you tell him you accept my offer to be a steward in my household."

Eldred shook his head. "Your steward? You want me to be your steward? Why? So I can fetch things for you and Harold?"

"Yes, my steward. Sometimes a steward might run an errand, but that is not why I am suggesting it."

"Then why are you?"

"My steward, so people forget about you," said Benedict softly. "Like they largely forgot about me. My steward, so you can live to a ripe old age."

"Oh, how exciting!" said Eldred. "I always dreamed of being someone's old, forgotten steward."

"Perhaps not your first choice, but as a steward in my household, you could do as you pleased, for the most part."

Eldred gave him a hard look. "You're old, Benedict. Even older than my father. Once you die, you would leave me as a servant in Harold's house. Whatever I may have dreamt of, it's not that. I'll return and take the trial. I'll pass. You'll see."

"No, the Academy will block you," said Benedict, almost apologetic.

"As long as I'm a squire, I can demand to take the trial."

Benedict shook his head. "You are not listening. Do you hear anything I say? You will not take the trial. You will likely never set foot in the Academy again."

"Whatever happens, I'll never serve you."

"Use your brain, Eldred. You have little time left to figure this out. Alfred is waiting for us."

"You are not my father, Benedict. You're a useless uncle. Save your tiresome lectures for Harold."

Benedict extended his hand. "I beg you, Eldred. Pay heed. You are in danger, but not from me."

After a last glare at Benedict, Eldred kicked his horse and rode up past Benedict's men. Eldred led for the rest of the journey to Boar's Tusk.

BOAR S TUSK

Eldred pushed his horse harder as they approached Boar's Tusk, leaving Benedict and his men behind. The castle was set by itself near the south wall of town. It had been two years since Eldred last visited, but the castle was unchanged. It was a fortified castle, with a twenty-foot-high curtain wall marking its perimeter. Within the walls, the keep was visible, along with the roof of the Great Hall and the topmost peak of the stables. As usual, the gate stood open.

When Eldred reached the gate, he leapt down and handed the reins of his horse to a young groom who gazed at Eldred in confusion.

"Just take it," said Eldred irritably.

"Who you are, sir?" asked the groom, who appeared no older than fifteen years of age.

A guard who was standing by piped up. "That's the king's son, Eldred."

The groom cringed at Eldred. "I'm so sorry, sir."

Eldred brushed by without comment and marched through the inner courtyard. As he walked, people stopped and stared, but he pressed on, greeting no one, not even the few he knew. Eldred reached the Great Hall and pushed through the doors to find the long tables and many chairs empty, except for the last table before his father's throne. King Alfred sat, drinking an afternoon beer with Pounder and Mack, men from his pod.

Alfred looked up with a sour expression. "Where's your uncle?"

"Back there somewhere," said Eldred.

Eldred crossed the room to the table where the men were sitting.

"We need to talk," said Alfred.

"Do we?" said Eldred.

"We do if I say we do," answered Aldred, an edge in his voice.

Eldred sat down across from his father, who remained flanked by Pounder and Mack. Eldred gestured at the men. "Do you need them?"

The men rose and left the hall without comment. Once they had gone, Alfred leaned forward. "Why all of this? What are you doing?"

"What are you accusing me of?" asked Eldred.

"I spoke to you at the last trial. I was clear with you. You were not to make an attempt unless you were certain you could pass. Don't tell me you don't recall."

"I recall," said Eldred.

"I asked you not to disgrace me, not to dishonor our family." Alfred paused. "I did not imagine you would devise an even worse humiliation."

Eldred glared at Alfred.

Alfred tapped the table. "My son would never cheat. Perhaps that did not occur to you, due to your thick Mercian skull, but it should have been clear."

Eldred's face turned red.

"Well? Don't you have anything to say for yourself?"

Eldred rose to his feet.

"I am glad to see you two talking," said Benedict as he walked into the hall.

After a pause, Alfred answered. "This isn't a matter of your concern, brother."

"That depends, dear brother. Eldred and I discussed many possibilities on our ride here. One option we considered was having him join my household as a steward. I recommend he does."

"Do you really, brother?"

"Yes."

Alfred locked eyes with Eldred. "Is this what you want, son? Do you want to be Benedict's servant?"

Eldred continued to glare at Alfred. "No."

Alfred smirked. "I didn't think so."

"I believe it deserves careful consideration," said Benedict.

"But we don't," said Alfred. "Take your leave, brother. This is a matter for Eldred and myself."

Benedict gave Eldred a worried look. "Very well Eldred, remember what we discussed." Benedict turned and left the hall.

"So what now?" asked Eldred.

"I'm going to make you a hero of sorts."

Eldred narrowed his eyes. "A hero? What're you talking about?"

"You'll find out soon enough."

"I demand to take the trial."

Alfred stared at his drink. "You don't want to ponder what I can demand. In any case, your partner—the farmhand—left the Academy."

"Dreven? You made them expel Dreven?"

Alfred waved his hand dismissively. "They had an obligation. I merely reminded them."

Eldred slammed his fist on the table. "Why did you do that?"

Alfred took a long drink, then stared at Eldred with cold eyes. "Duty. I know mine, and I was clear with you about yours. But you knew better. Now your friend has paid some of the price. You owe the balance."

"What are you planning?"

"You'll learn of it after dinner."

GHYSLAINE

Eldred sat on a sofa in his mother's brightly colored parlor while one of her maids brought him a cup of tea and a biscuit.

"Thank you," said Eldred.

"Excuse me, ladies. I need to speak to my son in private," said Ghyslaine.

As the maids swept out of the room, Eldred studied his mother. She was a proud, handsome woman with piercing Maldavian eyes. Her age only showed slightly in the white strands in her hair and a few lines on her face. A distinctive feature, one which deeply embarrassed Eldred, was her height. Her Mercian and Maldavian blood had combined to make her taller than most Deiran men, including Alfred.

"You've not changed," said Eldred.

"Oh, no. If only that were true, son. Your father and I are growing old."

Eldred crinkled up his face. "And he's angry."

"He has proper cause for once. You were planning to cheat at the trial. The letter from the headmaster was clear on that front."

"He sent the message to you?"

"He addressed it to your father, but Alfred had me read it to him. The headmaster thought he had handled the matter in some subtle way, but your father was not satisfied. He took over the situation, as he is always inclined to do."

"Why did the headmaster have to say anything?" said Eldred bitterly.

Ghyslaine narrowed her eyes. "Why did you cheat?"

Eldred shook his head and sighed. "I don't remember. It just happened."

"It was that boy—" started Gyslaine.

"No—it was me," said Eldred.

"Why?"

"I had to pass. It was finally my turn. It had to be."

Ghyslaine shook her head. "If you want to be a warrior, be one with our people. My brother Julian will welcome you with open arms. You don't appear Maldavian, but you passed our trials. You proved true your sight."

Eldred folded his arms. "This is my home. These are my people."

"Can you truly believe that? Deirans are cruel. They don't often pass up a chance for a rude word. I hear their comments, remarks about my height, about my eyes. Is it different for you, Son? Do you honestly find these people welcoming?"

Eldred grimaced.

"Headmaster Tibbot was not clear in his letter. How were you planning to cheat?" asked Ghyslaine.

Eldred pursed his lips.

"How did you and that poor boy hope to trick Harold?" she continued.

"Sound, noises. We were going to use the sounds of his creaking shoes to signal the acts to me. He had a creaky leather cuirass. We trained on it for weeks."

"Such effort. What a waste. And now you tell me Alfred had him sent away."

Eldred nodded slowly. "He was a worthy squire."

"Not for a Deiran. Only one thing matters to them."

Eldred wiped his right eye. "Father says he has a plan for me."

"Whatever it is, refuse it. We must press on to my brother's court."

"I don't like Emon."

Ghyslaine raised her eyebrow. "It's a fine city. You will learn to appreciate it."

Eldred drank some of his tea and took an absent-minded bite of his biscuit. "Uncle Julian cares for you. He doesn't care for me."

"Nonsense—you are too sensitive. You confuse your uncle's feelings for you with his concern about your situation. The uncertainty has made it difficult for everyone. Nobody knew what to do with you. Now that the matter of the Bond is settled, we can finally move forward."

"What would my position be? Julian fathered two sons and a daughter."

"You won't end up with the crown, but you will be a lord in my brother's court. You won't find such honors offered here."

"Being a Maldavian lord would be a fine thing, but it does not sound like something that would happen to me."

Ghyslaine frowned. "Why not? We descended from the oldest Maldavian bloodlines."

"It makes no sense, no more sense than if I were to go to Tyrus to challenge the king to a duel. That's all the legitimacy a Mercian ruler requires. He simply needs an audience to witness him kill the previous monarch."

"The Mercians? What has gotten into you? You are tall, but you are no more a Mercian by nature than I am."

"Perhaps not, but if I killed the Mercian ruler in a duel that would make me the legitimate Mercian king. I wouldn't be asking anyone for a favor or a handout."

"How foolish. What makes you think you could win? You are barely more than a boy."

"I fought a Mercian," said Eldred.

"And you lost. I heard the tale. You fought a common ruffian."

"I can hold my own."

"You're overconfident, but you should not be so certain. Not yet."

"I'll see what Father says."

Ghyslaine shook her head. "Whatever your father says, it will work to his benefit, not yours or mine."

LAST DINNER

Dinner was a much larger affair than Eldred expected. A full half of the Great Hall was called into use. Several unfamiliar nobles with their pods had arrived in the afternoon. Harold came as well. The head table comprised Alfred with Ghyslaine—in her fine blue and gold Maldavian robes—to his left, followed by Eldred. To Alfred's right sat Benedict and Harold. The visiting lords were intermixed throughout the hall, scattered among Alfred's men at arms and some local lords Eldred knew by sight.

The food was better than the fare served at the Academy. Eldred especially enjoyed the boiled beef with cabbage. Eldred bothered himself with eating and ignored the guests as best he could, but he still noticed their stares, both for himself and for Ghyslaine.

After some time, Ghyslaine nudged him. "Are you acquainted with these men?"

Eldred looked up from his plate and glanced blankly around the room. "They're merely some of Father's pledged lords."

"They are that, but odd choices for a dinner party in your father's hall. These are men for whom your father expresses little affection. Lord Vance, you must have heard of him. He is of some renown." Ghyslaine nodded towards an older man with thick bushy eyebrows.

"I have," said Eldred in surprise. The famous warrior was short even for a Deiran.

"Your father does not care for the love the people show him."

Eldred reached for a bread roll. "I see."

Ghyslaine indicated a middle-aged man with a wrinkled forehead and an earnest expression. "Your father holds Lord Kenelm in a similar state of contempt. And Lord Thom, he was a favorite of your grandfather, Berdic, but not of Alfred."

Eldred studied Lord Thom, an old man, who had thin gray hair and a gray wedge shaped mustache.

Ghyslaine gestured towards a younger, thickset man with shoulder-length hair and a thick beard. "Lord Osbert does not fit the pattern. Your father likes him."

Eldred chewed the bread roll as he surveyed Lord Osbert. "Even Father can't hate everyone."

Ghyslaine sipped her wine as she cast a darting look at a middle-aged man with narrow-set eyes and a weak chin covered with a patchy goatee. "In Lord Ferris's case, I agree with your father. Lord Ferris is a snake."

Eldred chuckled. "Father welcomed me home with a feast of disappointments."

"Something is afoot. Be on your guard."

Eldred sat up and paid more attention to the proceedings, but the boastful conversations bored him. He slouched with relief as the meal ended and the staff cleared away the plates and refilled the guests' wine glasses.

Alfred took a heavy draught of the wine, and fixed Eldred with a measured gaze that Eldred met with disdain. Alfred wiped his mouth and turned away. After another sip, he addressed the hall.

"My lords and ladies, valued subjects, you must be wondering why I invited all of you here."

Lord Kenelm stood up. "I was not asked; I was summoned. I had to come at quite a pace too, I should say."

Alfred waved Lord Kenelm back to his seat. "Yes, then, summoned. I brought you here so you can witness an important event, one people will speak of for many years to come. Bring in the Wretched!"

The guests turned expectantly towards the doors of the hall, which opened as the Wretched entered under guard. Eldred had never seen a Wretched before, and stared at his blond hair and gray eyes. All the children of the Night Mother had black hair and brown eyes. The Wretched was an older man with receding hair and wrinkles around his oddly colored eyes. He was as tall as a Mercian, but lanky whereas Mercians were generally thickset. He wore a finely woven red and gold tunic tied at the waist with a purple sash that showed his knees and left his arms bare. His long, narrow feet were clad in leather sandals.

The guards marched the Wretched through the hall. Finally, he stopped, some ten feet from Alfred, shifting as he gazed at the hard-faced Deirans in their plain woolen tunics who were sitting at the tables with their drinks.

"You have traveled far to my court to visit me and to beg for a favor, isn't that so?" proclaimed Alfred.

"I have come to request aid," said the Wretched.

"If you want my help, state your case."

The Wretched bowed. "Thank you for your courtesy and kindness in granting me your attention, Alfred, king of the Deirans. I, Sammanus, have traveled here from the far north, from the ancient city of Turicum, where I live in the company of my people who you and the other tribes so graciously allow to exist. It is not without some trepidation I seek to disturb you, but we face a matter of utmost urgency."

"And the nature of your emergency?"

"We are beset by an enemy far beyond our measure, perhaps the most deadly creature to ever live—a terrible dragon of unprecedented size, a nightmare woven out of terror and blood by your revered Night Mother. It killed several of our citizens before I left to seek your aid. The count, the count of the unfortunate dead, stands at three already. I hope—as a small gesture of your majesty—you will send forth some of your vaunted warriors to free my people of this evil scourge."

Alfred glanced slyly at Ghyslaine. "Why me? Why not pester Julian? Didn't Maldavians kill the last monster that beset your people?"

"This is a dragon of immense size. With all due respect to the Maldavians, we felt this was an adversary only matched in ferocity and cunning by you brave Deirans. I beseech you. Grant us freedom from this fearsome peril. The ages will remember your valor and courage for a considerable period of time."

"More sense than I might have expected." Alfred surveyed the assembled nobles. "The last one was killed by a band of forty Maldavians. I allow that Maldavians are fierce fighters. I fought them early in my reign. I did well. I won huge tracts of lands as well as my fair wife. Dangerous as a Maldavian may be, the Mother made the Deirans a damned sight more deadly. Compared to us, this dragon is a lesser construct. I'll send an expedition of our finest to slay this beast, not out of any affection for the Wretcheds, but to prove our greatness."

Eldred nodded as the guests cheered. Ghyslaine appeared unmoved. Alfred stood up and drew his sword, Capito, blessed by the Night Mother herself, and pointed at Lord Osbert. "Lord Osbert, you're strong. Are you up to the task?"

Lord Osbert stood and raised his fist. "I am, sire!"

The guests banged their cups and Alfred smiled. "There's a brave man for you."

Alfred pointed Capito at Lord Kenelm. "Lord Kenelm, valiant warrior of the north, will you join this mission?"

Lord Kenelm rose and bowed stiffly. "Yes, sire."

"You do not disappoint." Alfred turned to Lord Thom. "Lord Thom, do you still possess the wiles to battle a dragon?"

"I hope so, sire."

"Old, but still plucky." Alfred gave Lord Ferris an imperious look. "Lord Ferris, you're considered manful. Will you prove the truth of it?"

Lord Ferris glanced at the other lords. "Yes, sire."

Alfred offered Lord Vance a thin smile. "Lord Vance, some say you are our greatest warrior. If true, who better to lead this expedition? Will you show everyone the meaning of courage?"

"If I must," answered Lord Vance in his deep baritone voice.

"Then, let it be noted, whereas the Maldavians sent forty men to battle a dragon, we will defeat this larger and more monstrous creature with only five bonded warriors. It can be done! It will be done!" proclaimed Alfred.

Eldred looked on questioningly as the guests shouted their approval.

As the din quieted a bit, Lord Kenelm spoke up. "Excuse me, sire. Did I hear correctly? Do you mean to send only us? Not our pods?"

"Your hearing is true. We could dispatch five hundred warriors to defeat this dragon, but there would be no glory for anyone. This is a single beast we face, not an army."

Lord Kenelm stood frozen, staring at Alfred.

The Wretched raised his hand. "Oh great king, might they not require some assistance in this endeavor to slay this mightiest of dragons? All understand the extraordinary prowess of bonded warriors, but can even five peerless soldiers such as these accomplish the task?"

Alfred smiled. "You raise a worthy point. They'll have help. That future generations might better recall what happened and to assist these brave men, I'll arrange a squad of five squires. To show my personal commitment, I offer to send none other than my only son, Eldred, as one of the same." Alfred raised his goblet to Eldred. "Eldred, quite a dangerous undertaking. None would question you if you were to decline. Do you accept?"

All eyes in the hall focused on Eldred. Ghyslaine pinched Eldred under the table and shook her head.

Eldred stared at his father's face, which bore a mocking grin. "I accept, Father."

"I knew you would, son. It's settled then. We have our gallant lords and the first of our five brave squires. I'll send a rider to the Academy tonight, so we can receive the remainder of the lads first thing in the morning. We have the men. I've gathered the provisions. The expedition can depart for Turicum tomorrow."

Lord Ferris cleared his throat. "Excuse me, sire. While I would very much like to join this enterprise, I do not see how I can leave as soon as tomorrow. There are matters in my fiefdom that require my attention. Several Corporians were sighted near the Vindius Mountains, close to my borders. I expect I can deal with them and be ready to leave within the month."

"How unfortunate, Lord Ferris, though I wonder why the appearance of a few Corporians should worry you so. In any case, the snow will cover the northern passes by then, making Turicum unreachable." Alfred tapped his fingers on the table. "I selected each of you with care. My only son is going on this expedition. I chose leaders I trusted to succeed, to keep him safe. Nonetheless, I understand the challenges in running a fiefdom. I'll allow you to step aside as long as you name a replacement to go in your stead. As this is a matter of my son's safety, I insist the man be a braver and more accomplished warrior than yourself. Can you name this man? Can you offer me a candidate more worthy than yourself?"

Lord Ferris's face twisted in discomfort. "No such warrior comes to mind, sire."

"Does this expedition frighten you, Lord Ferris? Is this a matter of courage?"

"No, sire. I have no fear of the dragon."

"Then I would bid you to honor the commitment you just made in front of these lords and ladies."

"I—will, sire."

"Do any other lords have concerns? I need not ask Eldred. I know he possesses courage."

"He goes as a squire," said Lord Vance.

Alfred gave Lord Vance a steely look. "What did you say?"

"I said Eldred is going as a squire."

"What did you mean by it?"

"I made an observation. In your wisdom, you are sending along squires," but I don't expect they'll engage the dragon. They'll be busying themselves with cooking and cleaning and polishing armor."

"Correct, Lord Vance. We are of like mind. The squires are not shields for you to hide behind. The warriors, such as yourself, must do the killing."

Lord Vance glared disdainfully at Eldred. "Indeed."

"Let there be wine and laughter and merriment of all sorts. Tomorrow a great expedition leaves for the north. More wine! Bring out the best vintages for my guests!" shouted Alfred.

The guests beat their cups on the table in anticipation as servants started carrying in bottles of wine from Alfred's cellar. Ghyslaine rose from the table and tapped Eldred's shoulder. As Eldred rose to follow his mother, he glanced across the table, beyond his father, to see Harold's amused countenance and Benedict's somber expression.

LAST NIGHT

Ghyslaine walked hurriedly to her sitting room while Eldred trailed after her. She shooed out a maidservant and shut the doors after her.

"We must leave here tonight," said Ghyslaine.

"What are you talking about, Mother?"

"We must ride for Emon. If we start now, we can build a sizable lead before any of those drunken oafs notice we are missing."

"Why would I desert them? I agreed to go. Everyone witnessed it."

"He trapped you. He set you to it. This expedition, this glorious dragon hunt for the ages—it's all for you, Son. Your father has turned against you, Eldred. He wants you dead."

Eldred shook his head. "He's only acting to prevent me from attempting the trial. He doesn't need to kill me. Why would he care if Uncle Benedict enlists one more steward?"

"Perhaps you do have a Mercian brain," muttered Ghyslaine. "Your father's intentions are obvious. He is ridding himself of you and those five lords."

"Why do you think Father is getting rid of anyone? You said yourself he's friends with Lord Osbert. Besides, we can succeed. Lord Vance is a truly accomplished warrior. If forty Maldavians can kill a dragon, why would the deed be beyond a pod of Deiran lords? We're the Night Mother's champions."

Ghyslaine frowned. "You are full of tales from the Academy. Bonded warriors are strong, but five Deirans are not equal to forty Maldavian men at arms."

"I attended the Blood Match. We routed a force of Mercians that outnumbered us four to one. And Mercians, even they are stronger than

Maldavians. Superior eyesight won't kill your enemy."

Ghyslaine narrowed her eyes. "The power of our people lies not in our vision. That merely serves as our test of the Night Mother's design. The strength of Maldavians is our wisdom."

"The Maldavians are not my people. They're your people, Mother. And, though I enjoy having sharp vision, we must all agree that bonded warriors are the Night Mother's greatest creation."

"That is a matter for some debate, a discussion we have no time for at the moment. We must go. We must go now. Those five lords will not kill the dragon. Lord Ferris realized it. You are not using your Maldavian brain if you do not realize it."

"Father's not tricking me, Mother. Everyone at the Academy has been talking about the chance to battle this dragon. Everyone in the hall heard me commit to the expedition. They can all say I don't have the Bond. That might be true. But if I leave with you now, they can say I'm a coward, which would be needless, since I'm not afraid."

"You could be a lord in my brother's court."

"I'm not going to Emon. I'm fond of you, Mother, but I am not Maldavian."

"You are such a fool, Eldred. Your time at the Academy has clouded your thinking."

"Don't be angry, Mother. I'll return from Turicum after they kill the dragon. Perhaps I'll play some minor role. When I'm back, we can discuss Uncle Julian's court. Now I am off for some rest. Tomorrow an adventure begins."

Ghyslaine eye's watered. "I can't stop you, can I?"

"No."

DEPARTURE

Eldred woke up early to the sound of the kitchen servants clattering about as they started the day. He had argued with Morris, Alfred's head steward, but Morris had insisted on putting Eldred in a storage room of the Great Hall on a tiny bunk. Eldred rubbed his eyes. When he had last stayed over, two years ago, he had been up in the tower, in proper apartments, not an oversized cupboard. As he viewed the piled sacks of nuts and flour, it reminded him that Harold was the heir. The official announcement would probably come the moment Eldred rode out the gate.

Eldred got up and rummaged through the bags Benedict had packed. He found warm clothes and boots for the ride to Turicum. Benedict had been right—Eldred had needed everything from his room, but he would need a few more items for the trip.

Eldred yawned as he entered the kitchen with his baggage in hand. Old Wilky, the head kitchen steward, caught sight of Eldred and walked over to him. The half-dozen cooks he supervised continued their work behind him.

Wilky smiled. "What can I get for you, Eldred? The first loaves are still baking, but I have gruel, and I can have someone fry you up some pork and eggs."

"Thank you, Wilky. I'll take all of that. It sounds delicious."

Wilky beckoned Eldred out towards the Great Hall. "I have oat muffins coming up too, but not for an hour."

The hall was empty save for Lord Kenelm and his men, who were speaking softly to each other at a table on the far side of the hall. Lord Kenelm turned to watch Eldred enter, as if sizing him up.

Wilky waved to them. "I'll have your food out shortly, gentlemen. Just after I take care of young Eldred."

Eldred sat down at the head table, taking his seat from the previous evening and setting his bags on the chair Ghyslaine had used.

Wilky leaned on the table. "Lord Kenelm is a strong one. He's seen his share of fighting and come out of it well enough."

"Right. Still, I'll need my own steel. Who should I see for that?"

"Oh, I can send someone to the armory for you. You need a saber?"

"Thanks, Wilky. A saber and a greatsword; I would like both, if you please."

"Both? You're going as a squire."

"I need to be prepared."

Wilky raised his eyebrows. "Two swords might be a bit much. I'll see what I can track down while you eat."

"That would be wonderful."

Wilky was about to duck away when Eldred tapped him lightly on the arm. "One last thing, Wilky. How do you like it here? Do you like being a steward?"

Wilky looked blankly at Eldred. "Do I like being a steward? I suppose." After a momentary pause, he straightened up. "I mean—yes, of course. I mean, your father's a fair man."

"Thank you, Wilky."

Wilky hurried away.

True to his word, Wilky presented Eldred with two swords—a saber and a greatsword—before Eldred finished his breakfast.

Eldred set the swords on the table before lifting the saber to check its balance. "These are excellent. The chops are tasty too."

Wilky smiled and bobbed his head. "I'm glad. You'll have to return them both, though, once you are back. They are just a loan from the garrison—only a loan."

Eldred grinned. "Count on it."

The hall was filling up with men when Eldred made his way over to the stables. The stablehands were busy outside the stables, preparing a line of pack horses with supplies. Eldred approached Harkin, the steward in charge, who was tying a bundle of provisions to one of the horses.

"I need a mount for the journey to Turicum."

Harkin looked up briefly before returning to his work. "You can have the horse you came in on yesterday."

"No, that was barely more than a pony."

"Very well. I'll find another one for you once I'm done here."

"I'll save you the trouble. I will pick one myself."

Harkin groaned. "Not all the horses are available. Your father—"

"Can hardly begrudge his only son a choice of mount for an expedition such as this."

Harkin followed Eldred through the stables with a clenched jaw as Eldred inspected the horses. Eldred checked each stall, inspecting each horse in turn before returning to the stall housing the largest horse.

"What about this one?"

Harkin pressed his lips together. "That's Thunder."

"Does he have good feet?"

Harkin idly grabbed the stall door. "Uh-huh. Is he the one you want?"

Eldred nodded. "Yes. I need him fitted with a saddle. And groomed, I suppose. It'll be a while before he gets groomed again."

"Well, everyone is packing supplies. I can have someone fetch a saddle. I don't know about any grooming."

"Thank you, Harkin."

Outside, the pace of activity increased steadily. Stewards kept bringing more supplies over to load on the pack horses. They brought rope, blankets, shovels, axes as well as various parcels that Eldred took to be food.

A number of visitors showed up, apparently with an interest in seeing off the expedition, including Lord Trenth, Wybert's father, whose holdings were only a few miles away.

Eldred was standing off to the side of the stables, enjoying the busy scene, when Pounder—one of Alfred's podmen—entered the courtyard, leading a crew of squires: Mance, Yeowars, Wybert and Daw.

"Eldred!" shouted Mance.

"Mance! I wondered if you would be coming. I thought you would stay for the trial."

"That can wait for later. We have a dragon to kill."

"Yes, we do."

Eldred examined their mounts. "Are these your horses for the expedition?"

Mance hopped down. "Yes, from the Academy stable."

"Very good, and you have some steel."

Yeowars dismounted and handed his sword to Eldred. "Yes. Not wooden swords. For once, we each got a saber."

Eldred inspected their swords before holding forth his own freshly issued arms.

Yeowars hefted Eldred's greatsword. "This is castle steel."

"We don't have greatswords, just sabers," said Mance.

Eldred shrugged. "A loan from the garrison, to be returned after the expedition."

Mance glanced at his saber. "Once we pass the trial, we can claim finer blades."

"Perhaps a named blade if you help kill the dragon."

Mance chuckled and reached up to punch Eldred in the shoulder.

At that moment, Eldred spotted Lord Vance striding towards them. His forehead had a sweaty sheen and his eyes were bloodshot.

"Lord Vance, these are the other squires going on the trip. May I present to you Mance, and—"

Lord Vance waved Eldred out of the way as he entered the stables. "Not now!"

After Lord Vance rushed past, Eldred turned to the squires. "That was Lord Vance."

"I've heard of him," said Daw.

"Now you've met him," said Eldred.

Shortly after, the other lords on the expedition started appearing. None of them showed any interest in the squires. They checked the provisions on the pack horses or saw to their own horses inside the stable. Wybert and Mance left to find Lord Trenth.

Near the tenth hour, Eldred saw the Wretched making his way through the inner courtyard, trailed by his guards. He wore a thick leather coat, half blue and half gray, worked through with elaborate designs in red and gold thread. Green wool trousers stretched from his waist to the smooth skinned leather boots that rose over his ankles.

Eldred pointed at the clownish figure. "That's the Wretched."

"Yellow hair. How odd," said Daw.

"He's as tall as you are, Eldred," said Yeowars.

"So he is," said Eldred.

Not far behind the Wretched came Alfred in the company of his pod.

As the Wretched strode past into the stable, Alfred approached Eldred and extended his hand. "I wish you luck, son."

"Thank you, Father. These are a few of the other squires, Yeowars and Daw."

Alfred shook each of their hands in turn. "Mother's blessings."

"An honor, sire," said Daw.

"You're headed on a real adventure," said Alfred. "Once the lords have done their work and you return bearing the dragon's head, everyone will know your names."

The squires smiled. Alfred nodded and entered the stables, calling after Lord Vance. The Wretched came out of the stable leading his horse.

"If the Wretched's ready, it must be time to leave," said Eldred.

Eldred hurried into the stable, passing Lord Kenelm and Lord Osbert as they exited. When Eldred reached Thunder's stall, the young groom who had taken Eldred's horse the previous day presented Thunder, saddled and packed. "He's all ready, Master Eldred."

"Thank you," said Eldred.

Eldred reached into a saddle bag and pulled out his bright green Maldavian riding cap bedecked with purple cloud sparrow feathers. He noticed a look from the groom as he quickly set it on his head. It was gaudy by Deiran standards, maybe even by Maldavian standards. But Ghyslaine would appreciate him wearing it. She had gifted it to him when he had passed his vision trial. She had been happy that day.

Eldred came out of the stables to find the expedition lined up, five lords, four squires and one Wretched. Alfred stood across from them at the front of a crowd, with Benedict and Harold off to his side. Eldred searched the courtyard. Ghyslaine had not come.

"A special day!" proclaimed Alfred to scattered applause. "These brave warriors and squires are riding into history, riding towards a danger most men would seek to avoid. When they return, after the successful execution of their mission, they'll prove the supremacy of Deiran warriors. Our honor rides with them! Our honor's in their hands!"

"Hear, hear!" called Harold.

"I give you the leader of the expedition, Lord Vance, some say our greatest warrior. From the north, I give you Lord Kenelm, an accomplished fighter. Lord Osbert, a great warrior and a true friend. Lord Thom has seen a few more days than these other lords, still formidable. Lord Ferris, are you actually going? You were speaking of a replacement last night."

Lord Ferris glared. "I'm going, sire."

Alfred grinned. "I'm heartened by the news. As for squires, we have my son, Eldred, as well as a number of accomplished lads from the Academy. I'm sure they'll prove the bravery of their generation."

Alfred paused for another round of scattered applause and gave a final wave. "There you have it."

Lord Vance gave Alfred a sour look before mounting up and heading towards the gate. The other lords followed after him. As Eldred climbed up into his saddle, Benedict approached, followed by Harold. "Be careful, Eldred."

"To be sure, I will, Uncle."

"Return safely. We can discuss plans then."

Behind Benedict, Harold fixed Eldred with a cold stare.

"Of course, we can, Uncle." There would be plenty of time for talking then.

Mance squeezed his horse between Thunder and the wall of the stables. "Move forward or move aside, Eldred."

Eldred maneuvered Thunder out of the way as Mance and the other squires pressed past.

"May the Son walk beside you, Eldred," said Benedict.

"Mother's blessings, Uncle."

As the last squire disappeared out of the gate, Eldred gave Thunder a light heel and followed after him.

FIRST DAY

They rode at a measured pace the first day through the wide green fields north of Boar's Tusk. Lord Vance took the lead. His face was gray, and his brow was sweaty. He argued intermittently with Lord Kenelm. Eldred could not clearly hear their exchanges, but it seemed Lord Kenelm wanted something.

The lords rode behind Lord Vance in single file. First came Kenelm, then Osbert, then Thom and then Ferris. They were trailed by the Wretched, who in turn was followed by Eldred and the other squires. Mance and Wybert proceeded side by side, as did Yeowars and Daw. The pack horses were in two lines, split evenly between Yeowars and Daw.

After an hour of riding, Eldred dropped back, even with Mance and Wybert. "Do you have any news about Dreven?"

Mance showed a tight smile. "I do."

"Well, what happened?"

Wybert gave a short laugh. "Why don't you guess?"

"I don't want to guess."

"He left the Academy," said Mance.

"Did they say why?" asked Eldred.

"No," said Mance.

Wybert raised his left eyebrow. "What about you, Eldred? Do you have some insight on the matter?"

"I didn't know he was leaving," said Eldred.

Wybert laughed. "You trained with the farm boy every day for weeks. Don't you know why he left?"

"No."

"Not for a happy reason, judging by his face," said Wybert.

Eldred glared at Wybert. "How unfortunate."

Eldred kicked his horse on and moved away from the boys, up past the Wretched and drew even with Lord Ferris.

"What's our route?" asked Eldred.

"It is not your concern," said Lord Ferris.

"Perhaps not, but I would like to know."

"We are taking the old road, which is not to Kenelm's taste."

"Why does it matter to him?"

Lord Ferris gave a slight shrug. "He would prefer to ride through his own lands, which are directly north of Boar's Tusk. Lord Vance has chosen another course."

"Will this route save time?"

"Some days, perhaps, though I doubt enough to keep us out of the snow through the final passes into Turicum."

"It'll be a hard journey," said Eldred.

"A hard journey? Is that your idea of a deep insight?" scoffed Lord Ferris.

"Won't it be?"

"We are riding through the Eryx Mountains as winter is setting in. When we arrive, the five of us will battle a creature whose match might have never been seen. We don't have our pods; instead, we are in a mixed state due to your father's trickery. Five men against an enormous dragon. It is not a hard journey. It is a final journey."

"Then why did you come?" asked Eldred.

"I was willing to go on a sensible mission. With five full pods, we could have killed the dragon as well as anything else that dared trouble us. That was the expedition I believed I was agreeing to, not this harebrained plan to feed an old man's vanity. You didn't help things by being so eager."

Eldred made a face. "The dragon could kill me too."

"For all your crowing about your bravery, you will be at the camp when we face any true risk."

"I'm not afraid of battle," protested Eldred.

"Stop meddling and keep to your place. You and your father are a right pair, both of you meddlers—making things worse for warriors who actually fight battles."

"I doubt he would like to be called a meddler or to have his personal bravery questioned."

Lord Ferris glared at Eldred. "Very well. Get back with the other squires."

Eldred slowed Thunder's pace. As Lord Ferris rode ahead, the Wretched came even with him. "He did not seem happy with what you had to say."

"I just asked him the route."

"This is the old trading road to Regillium. I expect we will skirt Regillium, but we will see the city."

"Does much of it still stand?"

"Yes, all of Regillium stands. That is where Regula's power was strongest. The buildings are in fine condition, though, of course, the city is deserted."

Eldred gave a slight shake of his head. "We call her the Night Mother."

"Naturally, but when Regillium was her capital, she was called by the name 'Regula', which is why I referred to her in that way."

"I suggest you not call her by that name again. We find it offensive."

"Thank you for your kind advice. We have not been properly introduced. I am Sammanus of Turicum."

Eldred frowned. "Well, you're the Wretched."

"So you call us. Nonetheless, there are more of my people than just me, which is why I have my own name, 'Sammanus'."

"I'll call you 'the Wretched'. It would be odd if I started calling you by your name."

"I see. You are worried about maintaining the high opinion the other members of the expedition hold you in."

"No, it's not that. It just isn't proper to speak to you at all, I suppose."

The Wretched smiled thinly. "Your people have your own rules of etiquette. By what name or title should I refer to you? I can't call you 'the Deiran', since you are all Deirans."

"No, it's probably best if you don't call me anything. We shouldn't have to speak."

"I see. Let me know if you change your mind. I should be very interested to hear your point of view on various matters."

Eldred blinked. "Really?"

"Yes," affirmed the Wretched.

Eldred shrugged. "Well, I should rejoin the others."

The Wretched nodded and rode on. As Eldred dropped back closer to the squires, Wybert edged forward. "What were you talking to him about?"

"The Wretched?"

"Yes."

"Nothing much. He let me know where this road goes. It passes by Regillium."

Wybert frowned. "That's a horrible place."

"We will skirt around the city," said Eldred.

"Of course, we'll avoid those ruins. We won't be entering Regillium, especially not in the company of a Wretched," said Mance.

"Why does his presence make a difference?" asked Eldred.

"Regillium is their old capital. He likely knows some tricks by which he could maim or kill us."

Eldred smiled. "Why would he do that? The lords are going north to help his people. He has no reason to harm us."

"They don't think like we do, Eldred. They are wicked, treacherous beasts."

Eldred glanced at the spindly man with neatly cropped blond hair. "He's just one man. I don't expect he will get up to much treachery."

"He could cut our throats while we slept," said Wybert.

"How would that serve him or his cause?" asked Eldred.

"You are as dumb as a rock, Eldred," said Wybert.

Mance laughed.

Eldred turned red. "Shut up!"

"He was thrown out for cheating," said Wybert.

"What?" said Eldred.

Wybert smirked. "Dreven. I heard a rumor that he was expelled for planning to cheat at the trial."

Eldred glared at Wybert.

Wybert raised his eyebrows. "Don't you have anything to say?"

"You had best watch what you say," snapped Eldred.

Wybert straightened up. "Have you forgotten what happened when you and Dreven teamed up against Traden and Noll? They whipped you."

"That's right," added Mance.

"That was Traden and Noll, not you two."

Mance pointed at his chest. "We are the same as them now. We would have passed if we had stayed behind."

Eldred narrowed his brows. "You don't know for certain."

Mance pushed his shoulders back. "Not in the center arch either—one arch removed at least."

"Mercians can't pass the trial without cheating," said Wybert.

"I'm not a Mercian," snapped Eldred.

"You are not one of us either," said Wybert.

Eldred rode to the side and stopped. Eldred glared at the laughing squires as they passed and waited until they were fifty feet ahead before he trailed after them.

DINNER

As they settled that night, the band split into three groups. The lords gathered together and started building a fire at a flat spot adjacent to the road. With the exception of Eldred, the squires were at work, excitedly setting up their own camp a hundred feet down the road. The Wretched tied his horse to a tree halfway between the two groups.

Eldred weighed his options and decided to tether Thunder next to the lords. Eldred started gathering branches and stray bits of tinder which he took over and added to the lords' fire.

"What's this?" said Lord Vance.

Eldred ignored him and perched on a log near the fledgling blaze, holding out his hands to warm himself.

Lord Kenelm pointed to the other camp. "This is not the spot for you, Eldred. You should be with the other squires."

"I don't get along with them. I find them childish."

Lord Vance scowled. "Nobody disputes you are too old to be a squire, but you are—nonetheless—a squire. Get over there."

"You should go, Eldred," said Lord Kenelm.

"I'm the king's son. I'm not going to associate with those idiots."

Lord Thom chuckled. "I should think you would be quite at home, as you describe it."

Eldred frowned at the old man.

"Are you stupid, boy? Go over with your betters, or I will teach you a lesson," barked Lord Vance.

Eldred fixed Lord Vance with a glare. "They're not my betters."

Lord Ferris shook his head. "Stubborn and half-witted; true Mercian charm."

"Your father's not here. You had best start listening to me, boy," said Lord Vance.

As Lord Vance started to step towards Eldred, Lord Kenelm stepped forward and nudged Eldred to his feet. "I'll take care of this, Lord Vance. Let's go for a walk, Eldred."

Eldred grudgingly went with Lord Kenelm. They walked down the deserted road together as dusk began to settle on the open fields to either side. Twisted oak trees lining the road at regular intervals marked the way ahead, disappearing into the distance.

"What's this about? Why won't you camp with the other squires?" asked Lord Kenelm.

"I hate them," said Eldred.

"Do you get along so much better with the lords?"

Eldred pondered. "No. I don't suppose I do."

Lord Kenelm spread his hands. "We're not at the Academy. We're not even at your father's castle. We're on an expedition, and each of us must make allowances. We're not the closest of friends, not as yet, anyway. When you volunteered to come on this mission, you made a commitment. Honor your commitment."

Eldred glanced away from Lord Kenelm into the growing darkness. "I agreed to battle a dragon. This is camping with the worst people I ever met."

"In the end, if we reach Turicum, we might face the dragon. That will be a part of the expedition. This journey is days and days of riding and camping, days of time with people, some lords and some squires, with whom neither of us might particularly wish to spend our time. In some ways, this poses a greater challenge. The creature—we'll kill it, or we won't—but it will be a relatively quick matter either way."

"I can't stay with Mance and Wybert."

"Perhaps not, but you definitely cannot associate with Vance and Ferris. The other lords don't like being near someone lacking the Bond either, for that matter."

Eldred huffed. "You really find it that vexing?"

Lord Kenelm clasped his hands in front of him. "We're a mixed pod, which makes everyone unhappy to begin with. As we strive to form a balance, the disturbance from people without the Bond poses a serious distraction."

"So I should camp with the Wretched?"

"Definitely not. Don't even speak to him. When we return, set your blankets near the other squires and ignore them. Tomorrow, ride with them and do your best to be agreeable. If you want to be an asset for this expedition, your duty is clear." Lord Kenelm stopped. It was now quite dark. "Are you ready to head back?"

"Yes."

As they started back toward the camp, Lord Kenelm gestured out at their surroundings. "So this all appears the same to you as if it were day? I heard you possess the Maldavian gift through your mother."

"I can see everything clearly enough, but it does not look the same as in daylight. Colors shift. Something black in sunlight might appear to be the brightest object to my dark vision."

Lord Kenelm pointed. "But if someone were lurking by that tree, you could see them?"

Eldred nodded. "I could."

Lord Kenelm looked up at the sky. "What about the stars? How do they appear to you?"

"I have far sight, so I see many more stars than you do. And they are all different colors, thanks to my dark vision. Most Maldavians only have either far sight or dark vision. I have both."

"I envy you those gifts from the Night Mother. The night sky is a thing of beauty even to my simple eyes."

"I'm not Maldavian. I'm not a Mercian either, despite Ferris's opinion on the matter."

"No, you're not. But you have some of their blood."

"I'm a Deiran, the same as you."

"I wish you well, Eldred, but we are not the same. It won't serve you to pretend that is the case."

They walked the rest of the way back to the camp in silence.

SPLIT

The next morning after breakfast, the expedition lined up, ready to depart. Eldred looked up the formation at Lord Vance, who no longer appeared hungover, though he didn't seem any happier for it. As he took his position at the front, he glowered down the line of horses at Eldred and called Lord Kenelm up for a discussion which quickly turned into an argument. Everyone waited while they whispered angrily back and forth. Finally, Lord Kenelm shook his head and broke off, riding down to where Eldred and the Wretched were sitting astride their mounts.

Lord Kenelm motioned to Eldred and the Wretched. "You'll have to go to the back."

"Behind the other squires?" asked Eldred.

Lord Kenelm's forehead wrinkled even more than usual. "Behind the pack horses. Lord Vance requests you stay a hundred paces behind them."

Eldred raised his eyebrows. "A request?"

"No, Eldred. I'm sorry, you must comply. Lord Vance feels the two of you interfere with the balance of our pod."

"What about the other squires?"

"They don't bother Lord Vance. I don't like the two of you trailing behind like this, but Lord Vance makes a valid point. We're not coming together as readily as we might like."

"I think the problem is you should lead, not Lord Vance," said Eldred.

Lord Kenelm's eyes narrowed. "That's not a matter of your concern, Eldred. If and when you gain the Bond, you might have some insight into how warriors coalesce into pods. For now, though, you would do better to avoid discussing such matters as you will likely give offense. What you must do is to ride at the back as Lord Vance commands."

The Wretched bowed his head and stepped his horse off the side of the road. Eldred sat where he was for a moment, lips pressed tight together, before following the Wretched's example. Lord Kenelm rode up the line and the column of riders set off. Wybert smirked as he passed by.

The party was well ahead and the dust from the pack horses was mostly dispersed when the Wretched turned to Eldred. "I think that is far enough."

The Wretched gave his horse a nudge and started down the road. Eldred followed after the Wretched.

After half an hour, the Wretched turned back to Eldred. "Why are your people so rude to you?"

"Not everyone treats me poorly. Some on this expedition don't care for me, such as Lord Vance and that idiot, Wybert. I get along with most people well enough."

The Wretched slowed his horse, so he only rode a few feet ahead of Eldred. "Some people dislike each other. There are always differences. But you are the son of the king, the son of their ruler. Usually those circumstances would require them to treat you with respect."

"I suppose so."

"Why is that not the case?" said the Wretched.

"I can't pass the trial. If I had the Bond, everything would be different."

"When is this trial you speak of?"

"I'll miss it. There'll be no trial for me."

"So you will remain a squire?"

Eldred scowled. "No, I'll reach the age of ascension soon enough. After that, I'll no longer be a squire. I'll become a steward—or take some trade."

"Warrior or not, squire or not, won't you have the ear of your father, the king?"

Eldred shook his head. "My father has no great love for me, and he's very old in any case, nearly forty. The kingdom will soon pass to my cousin, Harold, who holds even less affection for me."

"Yours is an odd situation on an odd expedition."

"Odd situation? Odd expedition? The only odd part of this expedition is that we're going at all. I don't know why we're going to help your people."

The Wretched raised his hands in an appeasing gesture. "I meant no offense. Your predicament is unfamiliar to me, that is all I intended to convey."

"We might die. We could all of us die, trying to save a few Wretcheds," complained Eldred.

"That could happen. I must confess, I expected your father to send more warriors."

"He's a proud man—too proud."

REGILLIUM

Over the next few days, they wound higher up into the mountains. During the day, Eldred and the Wretched rode behind the others, well behind the pack horses. At night, the lords sat around their fire in silence until they slept. Eldred camped a bit to the side of the other squires who roundly ignored him. The Wretched camped by himself, each day moving off a bit further from the others though always in sight. Eldred was hardly more sociable and said nothing to anyone outside of a few words with the Wretched during the day's ride.

Around noon on the fourth day, they reached the Hobart Gap. The day was cold and snow topped the nearby peaks, but the sun peeked out of the clouds from time to time, lending a bit of warmth. The road was wide and in good repair as they crossed the pass, heading north, cutting neatly through a green alpine meadow.

As usual, Eldred and the Wretched were riding well behind the rest of the expedition.

"You will see them soon," said the Wretched.

"See who?"

The Wretched sat higher in the saddle. "The towers of Regillium. If the clouds would only break a bit more, I think we could see them."

"Last night I heard them say we were still a day from the cursed city," said Eldred.

"The towers are tall, taller than any you have ever seen, and Regillium is not cursed. Why would you think such a thing?"

"That's where you opposed us. That was your capital before we drove what was left of you to Turicum."

"Regillium was her capital, the center of Regula's power."

Eldred's eyes flashed with anger. "You mean the Night Mother. I've already warned you. You should refer to her properly. And the city was never the center of anything. Regillium is evil. That's why nobody lives there to this day."

The Wretched smiled sadly. "The city sits empty, but your people would be most welcome there. They would find it in better repair than other cities your people live in, such as Botrus."

"Where?"

"Your father's capital; your people renamed it Boar's Tusk. Before your people settled the area, it was the fair city of Botrus. Many of its buildings are from those distant days, even your father's castle. The structures have held up well, though not as well as those in Regillium. The residue of her power here keeps the buildings from wear."

"You say your people built Boar's Tusk?" said Eldred in an incredulous tone.

"Not all of the structures, just the more elegant ones. I noticed some shacks that appeared to be newer construction. Unfortunately, not everything has held up as well. I found the remnants of the gardens a disappointment. My people wrote poems about the roses of Botrus in olden times. They used to say on a warm summer's day the perfume would place everyone in a delightful slumber, giving them the sweetest and most memorable of dreams."

"That sounds terrible."

The Wretched shook his head. "On the contrary, it was most pleasant, I assure you. In the summer months we organized evening lawn parties with dancing and singing. Poets held competitions. They were among the most celebrated people of the day."

"You make me wonder why the Night Mother needed us to defeat you. The Mercians and the Maldavians may not match us in war, but they should have been able to kill a motley collection of poets and gardeners."

The Wretched nodded. "You should not doubt that they did. Many died at their cruel hands, though the savagery was more on the part of the Maldavians. The Mercians were strong, but at least they did not appear to kill us for pleasure."

"My people say your people were difficult to defeat, that the weakness of the Maldavians and the Mercians moved the Night Mother to create us to finish you," said Eldred.

"When the Night Mother created the Deirans, she did indeed preordain our doom. Please note I call her by your name for her, the 'Night Mother'. While the bonded warriors were a terror to behold in battle, some among my people maintain that fierce as they were, you Deirans did not tip the balance of the war through your arms. They say that until that time the Night Mother still had some aspect of Regula in her—some part of her supported my people—but when she created the Deirans that part was no more."

"Yet she left a few of you in Turicum—the very reason for this expedition."

"Yes, we were spared, as per the covenant."

Eldred pointed off into the distance. "The towers; they're showing now."

The clouds had lifted, leaving the top of a white stone wall and the lower portion of some towers visible, but the peaks of the spires were still shrouded. Before them, the road descended sharply into a valley of bright green meadows where it skirted a jewel blue lake. The city stood on a hill beyond the far ridge, which hid the lower extent of the walls.

"Our city is beautiful, is it not? Hardly the look of a place which is cursed," said the Wretched softly.

Eldred shrugged. "It looks fine. Would you really want my people to live there? We're your enemies."

"Why not? It is a wondrous place. Better it is enjoyed and celebrated than left to eventually fall into ruin. I would entreat you and your fellow colonists to develop your skills at gardening. And, of course, I would expect you to revere the hallowed creations Regula produced in Regillium before she became the Night Mother."

"What creations?"

"There are so many. We built fountains fed by springs that run playfully through the city for miles. The towers themselves are miraculous. If the clouds continue to lift, you will witness their full glory. Sky bridges connect the tallest structures. In former days, poets, artists and historians would take their tea on high as the sun descended behind these mountains we just crossed. Our masons fashioned statues that moved to follow the sun as it passed through the sky. The cobblestones in the streets exhibit geometric patterns so vast that you could walk for a mile before you notice any sequence of stones repeat. We had nothing but wonders."

"Weren't all of those things destroyed when we sacked the place?" asked Eldred.

"No, the city was not pillaged. Regillium was Regula's own heart and she ensured it came to no harm. When the time came, we opened the gate and the majority of my people walked out to meet their fate. Some others stayed behind and took their own lives. Perhaps their suicides are why your people think Regillium is cursed, but it is not. It is just a place where many people lived and died in the past."

"That's not what I learned at the Academy. We demolished your city and killed your people by the thousands."

The Wretched held forth his arm. "Does Regillium appear destroyed?"

Eldred looked, but he saw no trace of damage. "Well, we slaughtered those who came out, aside from the few sent for confinement in Turicum."

"That is not true. None of the Sun People who came out were killed, certainly not in the moment."

"What became of them, then?"

The Wretched tilted his head. "They weren't dispatched—in any case. It truly is the most wondrous place in the world. How unfortunate we are rushing to Turicum. I wish I could show you the city myself."

"That would never happen. If we did venture inside, it would never be in your company or the company of another Wretched."

"Why?" asked the Wretched.

"Tricks and traps. You would use your wiles to spring some long hidden trap to ensnare us."

The Wretched stared at Eldred. "It was our home. We raised our children, we held our weddings, we studied arts and science and built wonders. It is not a den of traps. Have you discovered traps in Botrus? That was also our city. Why would Regillium be any different than Botrus regarding the placement of traps?"

"Because Regillium is cursed," snapped Eldred.

Eldred gave Thunder a kick and rode ahead while the Wretched followed after him shaking his head.

QUESTIONS

That evening they camped on a broad grass-covered ridge across from Regillium, which enveloped the hill rising across the valley. The clouds had cleared, leaving the white walls and towers of the city gleaming in the red light of the setting sun. Eldred studied the buildings as he sat on a log near the road, eating some mush and stale bread for his dinner. As usual, the lords camped apart from the squires and the Wretched was off on his own.

The other lads huddled nearby around a small fire arguing about how the lords would vanquish the dragon. Their conversation faded from Eldred's hearing as he lost himself in the vision of the vast and beautiful city that sat across from him. Dozens of spires rose taller than any Eldred had ever seen. As the Wretched had mentioned, the towers were connected by bridges that hung majestically in the air. Lines of statues wound up the hill, but they stood immobile. Eldred looked for fountains, but spotted none. Had the water sources dried up?

Eldred was lost in thought when he realized the other squires were talking to him for the first time in days.

Mance stepped close and waved his hand in Eldred's face. "What was it?"

"What was what?" replied Eldred.

Mance stared at Eldred with a determined expression. "What was the Wretched saying? You talked for hours."

"He spoke to me about Regillium. He told me of the city's treasures and how it fell."

"Most likely he was lying to you," said Mance.

Wybert scowled. "We know what happened. We sacked it and killed the cowering Wretcheds."

"That's not what he said," offered Eldred.

"Lord Vance told us yesterday that the Wretcheds are born liars," said Mance.

Yeowars broke his gaze off from the towers. "What did the Wretched say?"

"The Wretched said Regillium did not fall. At least to say, it was not sacked. He said when the time came, the Wretcheds opened the gates and came out to meet their fate."

Wybert laughed. "That's stupid."

Mance straightened his shoulders. "We sacked Regillium."

"Did we?" said Eldred. "The walls are unbroken. The buildings are all standing. No damage from fire. Even the gates appear intact."

"It's too far to see from here. And besides, we can't examine the other side of the city," said Wybert.

"I see quite clearly," said Eldred.

"Oh, right," said Mance.

Yeowars looked at Daw, who was stirring the pot of mush on the fire. "Maybe we starved them out."

Eldred shrugged. "I'm not arguing with you. I'm letting you know what the Wretched told me. You can observe for yourselves that Regillium appears undamaged."

Yeowars looked Eldred in the eye. "You shouldn't speak to the Wretched so much."

"I'm bored riding back there all day. I'm almost ready to talk to the flies buzzing around my head."

"Do that instead," said Yeowars.

"At least you don't have to lead the pack horses," said Mance. "That is an irritating chore if there ever was one."

"He said Boar's Tusk was a Wretched city in the past, that they made all the nice houses," said Eldred.

"That's a damned lie," snarled Wybert.

"Right. Lord Vance said they lie," said Mance.

"That could be," said Eldred nonchalantly. "He said the Wretcheds built my father's castle."

"That can't be true," said Daw.

"I thought the same at first, but then I considered—my father never repairs anything," said Eldred. "If a wall or outer building falls down, he just leaves it. Maybe it's not laziness. Maybe we don't know how."

"They're not better builders than we are," said Wybert.
Eldred raised his hand, directing Wybert's gaze to Regillium.
Yeowars shook his head. "Just don't talk to him anymore."

TO THE NORTH

The next morning was cold and overcast. Clouds obscured much of Regillium, but enough remained visible to capture Eldred's attention as he ate breakfast. After they packed up, they headed north along the ridge, passing roads which wound down into the valley and up to the gates.

The Wretched kept his eyes on the city as he rode, watching it with a tense passion. When the road entered a pine forest, he pulled up his horse and sat, fixing his gaze on Regillium as Eldred followed the others into the darkness of the trees.

Twenty minutes later, Eldred heard the Wretched trotting up from behind.

Eldred glanced back. "I almost thought you weren't coming."

The Wretched's eyes were moist. "It's difficult for me to ride so close without stopping. The memories, they all come back—the good and the bad."

"Have you visited the city?"

The Wretched sighed. "Long ago."

"How can that be? Uncle Julian doesn't give the Wretcheds the right to ride freely around Guaraci. Aren't you constrained to stay within a few miles of Turicum?"

The Wretched straightened up in his saddle. "You are correct regarding the current state of affairs, but enforcement of our imprisonment in Turicum was more tempered under previous kings."

"You find my Uncle Julian a restrictive ruler?"

"He serves the role of our jailor, not our sovereign. He sends his men to count us every year. Other than that, we have no dealings with him."

"If you don't like being ruled by Uncle Julian, why don't you just flee, escape from Guaraci?" asked Eldred.

The Wretched shook his head. "Have you ever left the blessed realm and traveled to barbarian lands? Or even worse, the lands controlled by a foreign stone bearer? You would not like it. You would feel sick. Your mind would be clouded."

"I would never go to such a place. I live in the heart of the Night Mother."

The Wretched nodded.

After they rode a few minutes, Eldred turned to the Wretched. "I heard it was a harsh count two years ago."

"Yes."

"What happened?"

The Wretched sighed. "Your uncle's men acted in the way they thought was correct. We lost a citizen at sea from one of our fishing boats. Your uncle's men thought it was a trick, that she had escaped the city. They murdered another woman to settle the balance."

Eldred raised his eyebrows. "I see."

The Wretched held his face tight. "While I was saddened by what transpired, I understand the motivations and reasoning your people exhibited during the incident."

"Not my people. I'm Deiran," protested Eldred.

"Of course, of course."

"And this unfortunate incident, is that why you came to my father about the dragon? Not to my Uncle Julian?"

"My thinking, which is aligned with the views of other elders in Turicum, followed along the lines I presented to your father and his lords the last night in Botrus. We considered that a smaller—and presumably weaker—dragon had quite nearly obliterated a force of forty Maldavians leaving but a few survivors. Given the tensions with your uncle, I was not sure he would volunteer his men for such a dangerous quest."

"But you thought my father would," said Eldred.

"As he did." Sammanus gave a slight smile. "It seemed poetic to us that a vicious creation of the Night Mother be dealt with by an even more menacing construct. We thought he would send more warriors."

"He sent five squires as well."

"Of course. Of course. That he truly did."

THE FOREST

Three days of steady downpour followed them into the forest. Eldred and the Wretched rode in single file behind the party along the road which was covered by a thin layer of soupy light-brown mud. Eldred's riding hat was soaked through by the rain; its wet feathers drooped and water kept running down his forehead into his eyes.

As they came to the edge of a long meadow, Eldred was startled to find himself staring into the eyes of a humongous wolf—twice the size of a southern wolf—hidden in the shadows of the trees across the field.

"Wolf!" shouted Eldred.

The Wretched jerked up in his saddle. "Where?"

Eldred pointed towards the trees. "It's gone now. It was just there. I have to tell the lords."

Eldred pushed Thunder up the road, but the horse struggled to move quickly on the slippery footing. The squires observed with interest as Eldred scootched past them.

When Eldred caught up to Lord Ferris, he was favored with a sharp look. "Get back with the Wretched. You will make Vance angry."

Eldred gestured toward the field. "I saw a wolf in those trees, Lord Ferris."

"We are in a forest, Eldred. Many creatures live here."

"This was a large wolf," said Eldred emphatically.

Lord Ferris smirked. "Did it frighten you?"

"No, but it could be a threat."

Lord Ferris groaned. "Very well, go back with the Wretched. I will pass on your report."

Eldred maneuvered Thunder to the side of the road.

As Mance came up, he stopped. "What were you saying to Lord Ferris?"

"I saw a wolf."

Wybert laughed. "A wolf—that's the least of our worries. You should have warned him about the rain."

Mance joined in the laughter. "I'm very wet."

Eldred raised his palms. "An enormous wolf."

Mance glanced across the meadow. "Where is it?"

Eldred pointed. "It was under those trees."

Wybert squinted. "I don't see anything."

"It left. It may have observed me as I spotted it."

"You think it observed you while you observed it?" said Wybert.

"From over there?" said Mance.

"It might have. I let Lord Ferris know."

Wybert grinned. "Well, I wouldn't want to be you and the Wretched, hanging off the back of the column, but if the wolf comes around the lords will kill it."

The squires pushed ahead after the lords, pulling the pack horses along. Eldred waited for the Wretched, then continued the slog through the mud.

"I am surprised your lords don't make more of an effort to guard your pack animals," shouted the Wretched through a cloudburst.

Eldred afforded the Wretched a quick glance before continuing his survey of the surrounding woods. "I protect them."

The Wretched's lips twitched. "The wolves of the Hercynian Forest are not easily dealt with. They are a creation of your Night Mother, not Regula. As my friend—who studies such things—would tell you, they have many advantages over an ordinary wolf. They have a larger cranial capacity that shows in their enhanced intelligence. They also enjoy more complex social interactions, in particular, an unwavering loyalty to the members of their pack. If they came upon us now the horses would scatter, diminishing the effectiveness of your warriors. I expect some of us would be killed, perhaps all of us."

"What do you suggest?"

"We should tighten our formation and a few of the lords should join us here, at the rear of the column."

Eldred shook his head. "I don't imagine having Lord Ferris closer would make either us or the pack horses any safer."

"We might have to disagree on that point."

"How did you pass through here on your own if you're so frightened of everything?" asked Eldred.

"I skirted the forest."

They rode without incident until they halted to make camp in the late afternoon. Lord Vance picked a section of the road where the surrounding woods were less dense.

It was raining as Lord Vance addressed the expedition. "You, squires! I want the horses tethered right here—along the road. I need them tied tightly. If wolves come and a horse pulls loose, it might be killed. Collect the supplies and put them in two piles, one on either side of the road under these trees. For each watch, I want one squire positioned on either end of the horse line. I need one lord on constant patrol. If you are off duty, you can bunk near the supplies, but be ready for action."

"I'll keep my sword at hand, Lord Vance," said Eldred.

"No, Eldred. I want you, the Wretched and Yeowars to keep your swords sheathed no matter what happens. Your job is to grab for any horse that gets loose. If we encounter wolves, we'll engage them with the support of the advanced squires, that's Mance, Wybert and Daw."

"I carry a sword, Lord Vance," said Eldred. "If a wolf comes near, I plan to use it."

"No! You're not listening. Lord Kenelm, relieve Eldred and the Wretched of their weapons. Yeowars, can you follow a simple direction?"

Yeowars nodded as Lord Kenelm approached Eldred and the Wretched, who were standing at the edge of the group.

"Your weapons, please," said Lord Kenelm.

"This is outrageous," sputtered Eldred as Lord Kenelm collected the Wretched's blade.

"Don't carry on. This is not the time for it," said Lord Kenelm.

"So I'm to be unarmed when the wolves attack us?"

"We'll keep you from harm. Hand over your weapons, Eldred."

Eldred's face turned red as he passed his great sword and saber to Lord Kenelm.

"I'll return them to you tomorrow," said Lord Kenelm.

As the camp preparation moved forward, Eldred found himself securing horses in the company of Mance and Yeowars. Eldred was pushing the animals into position while Mance secured their ties.

"It makes sense, Eldred," volunteered Mance, after they tethered a few.

Eldred frowned. "What does?"

"Taking your swords. If the wolves attack, keeping you and the others without the Bond out of the way is best. Otherwise, we might trip over you."

Eldred glowered at Mance. "How many times have I sparred with you, Mance? Have you ever won? Even once? No! Don't be surprised that I would rather depend on the sword in my hand than the sword in yours."

"What about you?" offered Mance. "You're not even really a squire anymore. Dreven was thrown out of the Academy for cheating. You should have been thrown out too."

"The wolves are not going to care about any of that," said Eldred.

Lord Osbert trod up through the mud. "More focus on the task at hand. Save your chatter for another day."

Eldred glared at Lord Osbert, but joined the other squires in securing the animals.

After the camp had been laid out as Lord Vance instructed, Eldred sat against a tree trying to nap, but he could not sleep. Instead, he tiredly tracked Lord Ferris as he navigated through the mud in a slow circuit around the horses. The first squires on duty, Yeowars and Daw, stared dejectedly up and down the road as the rain soaked them through.

Lord Kenelm worked with Wybert to start a fire, but it kept sputtering out. After an hour of sitting in wet clothes, Eldred ate damp bread and turnips for his supper.

As dusk faded into night, Lord Thom came to fetch Eldred and Mance for their watch. They took their place at opposite ends of the horse columns while Lord Thom trudged ponderously between them, taking lingering breaks under the shelter of the trees.

Near the fire that Lord Kenelm had started, the squires and lords were starting to drift off to sleep. Eldred shivered and hoped the rain would stop.

Soon it was fully dark. Eldred had a faint smile as he watched Lord Thom creep forward, tapping the edge of the road with a stick to find his way.

"Is that you?" asked Lord Thom as he grew closer.

"Yes, just a few more steps this way."

"You are the one who should be making the circuit with your damned sight."

"I suppose so."

Lord Thom reached out to Eldred, who stepped forward and took his hand.

"Ah, there," said Lord Thom, walking to the middle of the road in Eldred's grip.

Lord Thom stood next to Eldred, peering around in all directions. "What can you see?"

"Some ways up the road. The area around the men and the supplies is clear."

"We should put you on watch all night. You're the one who says he spotted the wolf in any case."

"I'm the one who can see in the dark, which means I'm the one who should be holding a sword," said Eldred.

"Right, well, Lord Vance expressed himself on that matter. He wants you and the other two out of the way if it comes to a fight."

"I could beat any of those squires with sword and staff."

Lord Thom chuckled. "If the wolves propose a duel, I suppose Lord Vance might reconsider."

"I'm suggesting that we don't know what this night will bring. Perhaps no wolves come, perhaps one hundred. We don't know. That's why I want my arms."

"If that many wolves come, you won't need anything but your legs," said Lord Thom. "But don't worry, I doubt the forest boasts enough game hereabouts to support such a large pack. And whatever does come, we have Lord Vance and Lord Kenelm to kill it."

Eldred's sour expression was lost on Lord Thom in the darkness.

"Carry on," said Lord Thom. He headed to the side of the road, tapping his way.

The watch ended without incident. Eldred was settling in near a supply pile when Mance approached and sat by the fire.

"Was there really a wolf?" asked Mance.

"Yes."

"Next time, keep it to yourself."

"I will," snapped Eldred. He twisted around, trying to find a comfortable position against the knobby tree trunk.

Eldred kept jerking awake as he tried to keep his eyes on Yeowars and Wybert during Lord Osbert's patrol. Finally, when the rain stopped and a sliver of moon cast its light on the road, Eldred slept.

When Eldred woke later in the night, the drizzle had resumed. Lord Osbert hunched near the fire warming his hands. The others slept, scattered among the supplies. Eldred watched drowsily as Lord Osbert fed wood to the blaze. Eldred could feel a trace of the warmth. Eldred glanced along the horse line. Wybert stood forlornly at one end but Yeowars was nowhere to be seen.

Eldred shook himself awake and took another look for Yeowars but did not spot him. Eldred struggled to his feet and walked over and sat down on the ground next to Lord Osbert. "Where's Yeowars?"

"He's relieving himself."

"Where did he go?"

Lord Osbert waved his hand aimlessly. "Out, away from the camp."

"When?"

A look of concern passed over Lord Osbert's face as he rose to his feet. "He should be back." Lord Osbert walked towards the horses. "Is he here?"

"No."

Lord Osbert pointed off into the trees. "He must have gone over there. Go find him. Perhaps he's unwell."

"I need my sword."

"No, just take a quick look."

Eldred stood with his arms crossed.

Lord Osbert shoved Eldred. "Go look."

Eldred recovered his balance and glared down at Lord Osbert, who scowled back. Eldred cursed and walked to the side of the road. Tracks led off into the woods.

"Stupid Yeowars," muttered Eldred.

Eldred followed the footprints out into the trees. After forty feet, Eldred discovered the spot where Yeowars had squatted down. The trail continued on in the wrong direction.

"Idiot."

After another thirty feet, Eldred heard a noise behind a bush. "Yeowars, is that you?"

The sound stopped. Eldred paused for a moment, then he walked off to the side of the trail, angling to look through the undergrowth.

There they were, looking at Eldred with blood soaked muzzles as they crowded next to Yeowars's body. Eldred froze in amazement, spellbound. Twenty pairs of yellow eyes considered him, weighed him, hungered for him. The moment stretched, then one of the wolves shifted, breaking the spell. Eldred turned and ran towards the camp with all the speed he could muster, hollering as he went.

As Eldred cleared the last trees, the horses were snorting and tugging against their tethers. The lords charged forward with their swords free, Lord Vance and Lord Kenelm out in front. Eldred dashed past them, then turned as the lords engaged the wolves.

One of the wolves knocked Lord Thom to the ground, but before it could tear into him, Lord Kenelm ran it through the neck. The lords moved with amazing speed and dispatched the wolves as quickly as they came. As the lords commenced their butchery, Eldred glanced down the horse line to see four wolves making for Wybert and the horses at the far end.

Just as the lead two were almost upon Wybert, who stood with his sword drawn, Mance and Daw dashed forward to support him. Wybert stabbed the chest of the first wolf as Mance slashed at the head of the second and drew blood. The second knocked Daw to the ground, but kept running and disappeared into the woods.

The other two wolves ripped into the horses. Eldred watched in amazement as Mance got Daw to his feet and the squires drove the snarling animals back.

Near at hand, the lords killed a number of wolves, and the survivors retreated back into the woods, howling in defeat. The skirmish had only lasted a few minutes. Lord Vance stared off into the darkness after his vanquished foes. Lord Kenelm went to the trio of squires to check on their welfare. The Wretched hunched down by the fire.

Lord Osbert approached Eldred. "Where's Yeowars?"

"He's in the woods. They killed him."

Lord Ferris favored Lord Osbert with a haughty smile. Lord Osbert glowered back.

"Take me to him," commanded Lord Osbert.

The first glimmerings of predawn showed as Eldred led Lord Vance, Lord Osbert and Lord Ferris to the body. Yeowars's corpse remained behind the bush where Eldred had last seen it. As they approached, they could see the damage.

"He didn't suffer. They took his throat right away," said Lord Osbert.

Lord Ferris smirked. "He might have suffered some."

"That's enough! Don't make this about status. This one should not have been here any more than that one should be," said Lord Vance, gesturing at Eldred.

Eldred bristled. "I didn't get him killed. I told you about the wolves."

"He did not say you did. He said Yeowars should not have been here," said Lord Ferris.

Lord Vance took off his cloak and laid it down next to Yeowars's body. Then he and Lord Osbert gently moved the corpse onto it. Lord Vance wrapped the body and lifted the remains. The others followed him back towards camp.

"I want it deep, Osbert. I don't want them digging him up once we're gone," said Lord Vance.

Lord Osbert looked away unhappily.

Back at camp, Lord Osbert started to work on Yeowars's grave. Lord Kenelm approached Lord Vance with the other squires in tow.

"What's the damage?" asked Lord Vance.

"We lost two horses for certain. I already put those down. There are two more that were badly injured. We might take them, but they can't bear a rider," said Lord Kenelm.

"So we are three horses short," said Lord Ferris.

"Yes," said Lord Kenelm.

Lord Vance studied the horse line. "Whose mounts?"

"Osbert's and Ferris's are dead. Mance's and Daw's are injured."

Lord Vance nodded. "Fine. Osbert takes Yeowars's as a reminder. Ferris can have Eldred's. Mance can take the Wretched's mount."

"What am I going to ride?" protested Eldred.

"We'll have you on a pack horse, same as the Wretched and Daw," said Lord Vance.

"Thunder is mine!"

"Fine, he's your horse. Ferris is just going to ride him," said Lord Vance.

Eldred was about to protest again when Lord Kenelm interjected. "That's enough, Eldred. This is what you signed up for."

Lord Vance gazed reproachfully at Lord Kenelm and Lord Ferris raised his eyebrows.

"Glad you have this in hand, Kenelm. Mance and Wybert, go find some stones for Yeowars's grave. Eldred and Daw, start packing up the supplies. We break camp as soon as he's in the ground. I'm not going to waste good weather sitting here," said Lord Vance.

Lord Osbert dug with manic effort, working hard long after Mance and Wybert collected their rocks, but nobody helped him dig. Lord Vance paced impatiently. Lord Thom passed the time harvesting teeth from the dead wolves.

After six hours, Lord Vance walked over to the pit to check on Lord Osbert's progress. "That's deep enough."

"I can make it deeper," said Lord Osbert, covered in mud and breathing heavily.

"This is all that's needed. Put him in."

Lord Osbert placed his shovel beside the hole and held up his arms to take Yeowars's body, still wrapped in Lord Vance's cloak. After carefully placing the corpse, Lord Osbert climbed out and the lords, along with Wybert, Mance and Daw, started to fill in the grave. Eldred started forward to help, but Lord Kenelm waved him back.

The pit filled quickly with everyone pitching in. Mance and Wybert laid out the stones, which Lord Osbert stamped into the muddy soil. As the last stone was stomped into place, the company turned their gaze to Lord Vance who studied the grave dispassionately.

"He should never have come. All that he accomplished is that he died a long way from home."

Lord Vance dusted the mud off his hands, walked to his horse and mounted up. The others followed after him and soon they were riding out from the camp with a slight change in order—Lord Osbert now rode behind Lord Thom.

As Eldred and the Wretched took their position at the back of the column, they had to fight with their mounts, which wanted to walk with the other pack horses.

Eldred fumed. "They stole Thunder."

"For my part, I am not happy my horse was given to a child, though I cannot say I am surprised."

"You're a Wretched and I'm son to a king."

"A great injustice, indeed."

TO TURICUM

The weather improved from that point onward. The nights were chilly, but there was no rain, which sped their progress. After nine more days of riding, they passed through a thicket and came out on the crown of a hill covered with low-lying bushes and grass, which rippled in the breeze. Below, nestled against the sea, stood a city, surrounded by tall walls of white stone, filled by a maze of buildings, towers and green spaces. Tilled fields and cow pastures made a patchwork around the city.

The Wretched gestured grandly, as if presenting the city to Eldred. "Turicum, our long journey has at last come to an end."

Eldred studied the scene and grunted. "Not as impressive as Regillium. Where's the damage? You said a dragon attacked."

"A dragon most certainly did kill three of our citizens. The damaged buildings are by the shore. It attacks from the sea."

Eldred gestured towards two small wooded islands near the horizon. "From those islands?"

"No. Those are the islands of Imbros and Sarnia. We are not sure where exactly the creature comes from, but it appears to be up the coast, to the northeast. As regards Regillium, nothing can match its majesty, but—unlike Regillium—Turicum does not stand empty."

Eldred grinned. "That's an advantage?"

"Huh. My people, the Sun People, possess culture and knowledge that has disappeared elsewhere in Regula's realm. It seems quite possible, even probable, that we represent the pinnacle of civilization that remains in the world, though we are but a small fragment of the empire Regula abandoned."

Eldred rubbed his chin. "What sort of knowledge?"

The Wretched held his hand out. "Knowledge of all things. We have copious stores of books along with exhibits and laboratories. The greatest scientists living today are down below. And culture, the finest works of art, the most elaborate plays, creative work developed over more than a thousand years."

"Knowledgeable maybe, but still Wretched."

The Wretched pointed at the company ahead. "You call us the Wretcheds, but look at your stunted and nasty companions. Strong and dangerous, they may be, but any person with more than a thimbleful of grace would find more pleasant associations with the Sun People. Our gifts were honed by Regula over a millennium. She created the most graceful, intelligent and beautiful people the world has ever seen."

Eldred raised his eyebrow. "Was that her gift to you, then? Intelligence and beauty? Are you certain it wasn't modesty?"

The Wretched reddened. "You inquired. In any case, I am glad to be home."

Up ahead, Lord Vance veered to the left, and trekked to a grass covered mound a hundred yards off the side of the road. The rest of the troop followed after him. Reaching the top of the grassy knoll, Lord Vance dismounted and looked over the city, squinting against the bright winter sun. Lord Ferris rode around the other lords and hopped down to stand by Lord Vance's side. The two studied Turicum with hard eyes.

Lord Vance beckoned the Wretched. "Come over here!"

Eldred followed the Wretched over.

Lord Vance gestured down the hill. "Where's this dragon we need to kill so urgently?"

The Wretched nodded solemnly. "The creature was attacking Turicum sporadically when I departed. I will inquire about recent sightings. This might be a task best accomplished working on my own."

"We have no wish to mix with you Wretcheds. Go fetch the news. When you return, bring three horses to replace the ones we lost."

The Wretched bowed his head. "Yes, lord, but I will supply you with four horses, for I would like my own horse returned to me, if that is permissible."

"Any objection, Mance?" called Lord Vance.

"As long as it's better than this nag, I have no concern."

Eldred stepped forward. "Perhaps I should accompany him, Lord Vance."

"What? Why do you want to enter that cursed city?"

"I have a good eye for horses. I can make sure we get suitable replacements."

Lord Vance's eyes widened. "Eldred raises a good point. Thom, you have the most equestrian knowledge. Why don't you go with the Wretched?"

"Let the boy go. He picked a fine mount for Ferris."

Lord Vance shrugged. "Very well. Eldred will accompany the Wretched."

"Can I take my horse now, squire?" asked the Wretched.

"No. I'll examine the replacement before I surrender this wreck," said Mance.

Lord Vance waved dismissively at the Wretched and Eldred. "Be on your way. We'll be setting up camp here."

Eldred and the Wretched mounted their pack horses and headed back to the road as the expedition went to work.

TURICUM

The Wretched fidgeted as he and Eldred rode down the hill to Turicum, tapping his fingers together absently as he gazed at Eldred.

"What?" said Eldred.

The Wretched shrugged. "Nothing."

"You seem bothered."

"No, not at all. I am glad to be home."

"And?"

"Well, I find it curious."

"What?"

The Wretched put his hands out, palms up. "I find it curious that you are choosing to enter our city, when you needn't. I can find suitable replacements. You can wait here."

"Picking horses is the best job I've had on the expedition, the only proper job, really."

"One I am certain you can perform well, but the stablemen can bring out a dozen prospects. No need to enter Turicum. The city is full of us 'Wretcheds', as you and your comrades would say."

Eldred pursed his lips. "I see some sense in your words. I think before all this, I would have been glad to avoid the company of the other Wretcheds. But, after our time together, I find you and your people less—bothersome."

The Wretched gave a slow nod. "How very kind of you. Still, I would not want my people to be an annoyance. We Wretcheds can be difficult and unpleasant. I will bring the horses out. It's for the best."

"No, no. I'm the one who is curious," said Eldred. "Why should I not want to meet the Sun People? As you described them, they are the most beautiful, graceful and intelligent people who ever lived. To travel this far and not visit, that would be a shame."

"I might have exaggerated."

"Well, after spending time with Lord Ferris and Wybert, your Wretcheds are bound to show in a good light. Enough debate. I'll check the horses myself," said Eldred.

"Hmm, well, if you insist on entering the city, allow me to make a suggestion. Perhaps you might consider refraining from referring to my people as 'Wretcheds'. You can start by calling me by my name—'Sammanus'."

Eldred cast a quick glance up towards the mound, some two miles behind them. "I know your name."

"What a pleasant surprise. How should I introduce you to the citizens of Turicum?"

"Just 'Eldred' will do."

"Very well, Eldred."

Eldred frowned. It was disconcerting to hear the Wretched use his name, but there was nobody around.

As Eldred approached the city, its size came into focus. The wall had looked small from the hill, but now it towered up some thirty feet high and appeared surprisingly clean too. Did they wash it?

Sammanus rode to a tall black gate with two sturdy doors that appeared to be made of iron. He dismounted. "Calvus, open the gate!"

A small window set up above the gate opened, and an old man looked down, narrowing his eyes as he studied Eldred. "Who is that with you?"

"This is Eldred; he is one of the Deirans who has come to battle the dragon."

Calvus scanned the surroundings. "Where are the others?"

"They are camped up on Galla's Mound. Everything is quite safe."

Calvus muttered something and disappeared from the window. The left door opened, and Eldred steered his pack horse inside onto an empty cobblestone street. The only people in view were Sammanus and Calvus.

"Have there been more attacks, Calvus?" asked Sammanus loudly as he watched Calvus bar the gate.

"It claimed three more victims: Fulvius, Loukia and Drusus. Last week, it stalked the streets for an hour before it found one of Domitia's pigs. Ate it in one bite."

Sammanus sighed. "That is terrible. The count is now six, Eldred. Take note."

Eldred shrugged. "We're not here for the count. Did you know them?"

"There are just under a thousand of us. I know everyone." Sammanus turned to Calvus. "Have I missed the festivals?"

"Drusus's festival is set to happen in three days, weather permitting. You still have time to enter the lottery," said Calvus.

"Poor Drusus. Was he at home when it happened?"

"He was. He left you a note. Opimia has it for you." Calvus eyed Eldred. "Why did you bring this Deiran inside the city?"

"He is here regarding some horses. Don't worry. I will keep my eye on him."

Calvus glared at Eldred. "Make sure you do. Can't have Deirans wandering around."

They tethered their pack horses and set off through the deserted streets with Sammanus leading the way. "Sorry about that. As I mentioned, some Sun People are not all that friendly."

Eldred smiled. "I don't mind being called a Deiran."

"Well, prepare for more of the same. You can't expect the citizens to be overly pleased by your visit."

"Speaking of them, where are they?"

"At this hour, they would mostly be home for tea. As you know, we have but a small population."

The stables were a few minutes' walk from the gate, set against the outer wall, adjacent to a grass field surrounded by a low wooden fence. Several horses were out. Two men sitting outside the stable stood up when they saw Eldred. They wore finely woven gray and white tunics and black trousers.

"Gallus, Hortensius, this is Eldred, one of the Deirans who has come to battle the dragon."

The men looked past Eldred, not meeting his eye.

Eldred smiled his most pleasant smile. "Pleased to meet you."

"Welcome home, Sammanus. Welcome, Deiran. I am Gallus," said the older of the two.

Hortensius appeared slightly older than Eldred. He stood behind Gallus, looking Eldred over with cold eyes. He stood three inches taller than Eldred but was spindly, like Sammanus.

"Eldred is here on a matter of some horses. The Deirans lost a few on the journey. They require four replacements."

"From us?" asked Hortensius.

"That is correct," said Sammanus.

Gallus exchanged a worried look with Hortensius. "Some elders on the council are most particular about their mounts."

Sammanus nodded. "I am well aware, Gallus, but this is where we find ourselves."

"This is a matter for the council to decide," interjected Hortensius.

"Unfortunately, there is nothing to debate. The Deirans must have their due."

Gallus sighed. "Very well, but this is on your authority, Sammanus."

"Agreed."

As Eldred followed Gallus inside, he was struck by the familiarity of the place. "Your stables are laid out like ours in Boar's Tusk. It's exactly the same, down to the carvings of a horse on the wooden doors on each stall."

"Yes, of course. We have made such stables for centuries." Sammanus walked over to a stall with several chestnut mares. "What about these? They appear suitable."

Eldred shrugged. "They might do, but I'm tasked to find the best horses."

Sammanus continued. "Whose horses are these, Gallus?"

"Those belong to Gaius and Longinus. They won't be happy to find them seized by this Deiran."

"No, I do not suppose they would be," said Sammanus. "Still, they are both easier to reason with than some. Are they decent trail horses?"

"They are middling, but they would be taxed carrying someone of his girth," said Gallus.

"Oh, the other Deirans are much smaller. Eldred here is part Mercian, as well as part Maldavian. We will take these."

"Wait a moment! I'm choosing the horses," snapped Eldred.

Sammanus's eyes widened. "Why do you care what horse Lord Ferris or Mance sits on?"

"It's my task to find the best. Besides, one is for me, and I have ridden that cursed pack horse for far too many miles."

Sammanus sighed. "These horses are fair enough, and we can acquire them without stirring up much trouble."

Eldred set off walking through the stables. "I'll look at the others."

The others reluctantly fell in line behind him. A handsome black stallion caught Eldred's eye.

Gallus cleared his throat as Eldred stopped to inspect the steed. "That is Avitus's horse. I do not think we can do that. I do not believe this mount is available."

Eldred stared at Gallus. "You said it will take a strong mount to manage a rider of my girth."

"Choose another horse, please, Eldred. This would be an extremely difficult matter to settle," said Sammanus.

"And he bites," said Hortensius.

"How fearsome. Fine, I will check the others," said Eldred, but the stallion suited him. He was a beautiful horse.

As they came to the back of the stables, there was a group of tall white horses, taller than any horse Eldred had ever seen. "What sort are these?"

Gallus turned red. "No! Not these. You cannot have them."

"Eldred, these are not an option," said Sammanus.

Eldred fixated on the tallest of them. "What sort are they?"

"These are Nonus horses. They—they are prized horses, highly prized," said Gallus.

"Are they swift? Do they have endurance?" asked Eldred.

Gallus shook his head. "They are ill-suited to the trail."

"They are not pack horses," said Hortensius.

Eldred leaned on the gate, admiring the stallion gazing back at him. "He looks quite strong."

Sammanus stepped next to him. "These are stud horses, Eldred. Not a fair exchange for the meager animals your people lost."

"I value Thunder. Besides, didn't I just ride for weeks through the rain to come here and fight a dragon for your people?"

Sammanus grimaced and turned away.

"I'll take him and three of those suitable ones."

"Unbelievable," said Hortensius.

"Already in trouble and I only stepped through the gate," muttered Sammanus.

"What's his name?" said Eldred.

"His name is Jupiter. Can you not take any other horse? Any other horse at all? What about Avitus's horse?" asked Gallus.

Eldred weighed the name on his tongue. "Jupiter? That sounds so formal. I will call him 'Hobbie'."

"Hobbie? You are renaming him 'Hobbie'?" said Hortensius.

"I just did. I need a saddle for him."

While Gallus went in search of equipment, Eldred opened the stall and approached Hobbie.

"He might kick you," warned Hortensius, but Hobbie stood still as Eldred scratched him on the neck.

Eldred smiled at Hortensius as he patted Hobbie's neck. "Friendly and well-mannered, a model for others."

Once outside, Eldred climbed up Hobbie. Sammanus mounted one of the chestnuts with the other two in tow.

"So you are off again just like that?" said Gallus.

"I will be back in an hour," said Sammanus.

"I want to visit the site where your friend died before we leave," said Eldred.

"What?" said Sammanus.

"Drusus," said Eldred. "He has the festival coming up. Your gatekeeper said the dragon killed him at his home."

"What for? We ought to be on our way. Not everyone will be so accommodating regarding your choice of mounts," protested Sammanus.

"Nonetheless, I want to see it. I want to see some sign of the dragon after all this Mother-cursed riding."

Sammanus sighed. "Very well. It was his house by the harbor, was it, Gallus?"

"It was."

"Follow me," said Sammanus.

A DEAD MAN'S HOUSE

E ldred found the ride through Turicum odd. The buildings were similar to those in Boar's Tusk, only with greater scale and better kept. Almost every building had a well tended garden, which you wouldn't find back home. But while the city felt familiar, it was also deserted. What few people they did encounter went from excitement at seeing Sammanus to surprise and distress as soon as they noticed Eldred riding along behind. The gaudily dressed citizens took one look at Eldred and made pains to leave the area without taking a second.

The air took on a salty taste as they reached the waterfront. Eldred looked out on a large harbor, with row after row of empty stone quays. Three small boats were docked, but there was room for a hundred more of the same. A line of stately buildings and squares stretched along the water, down to the start of a sea wall, which branched off into the water a mile or more down the road. The wall looped back, protecting the calm waters of the harbor. Beyond the wall, the waves kicked up and the water stretched unbroken to the horizon. Eldred squinted, but there was no trace of the islands he had seen from atop the hill.

Eldred was still searching for some sign of the islands when Sammanus came to a sudden halt and gestured at a lot strewn with piles of stones. "This is it, the remains of Drusus's house."

"A house?" Eldred leapt down from Hobbie and walked onto the lot. Some flagstones on the ground marked the sign of a foundation, but there was not a trace of a wall standing. Sifting the rubble with his foot, Eldred found bits of cloth and broken wood mixed in with the loose rocks.

"Drusus's home. The dragon may have caught a pig in the streets, but it catches my people in their homes."

Eldred studied the nearby buildings. "It did not damage the other houses."

"No, the creature chooses a house, always with at least one person inside. It demolishes the dwelling and devours the occupants. This time Drusus made the sacrifice. We will honor him at the festival. Everyone will be there. We cannot kill the dragon, but we can throw wondrous festivals."

"Why didn't he run? Why didn't someone come to help?"

"Oh, you will understand once you see it, Eldred. Then you will know. Once it sets its mind to something, it cannot be stopped."

"We will stop it."

"Of course you will. Now, we had best be going. You will not be welcome while you are riding Jupiter."

"You mean Hobbie?"

Sammanus sighed. "Yes."

They were a third of the way back through the city when they encountered a band of five elderly Wretcheds on Nonus horses, four men and a woman. The woman led the pack. She had long white hair and stern gray eyes and wore a silver gown, embroidered with gold. The men wore blue and gray tunics, with swords on their belts. They blocked the street.

The woman looked over Hobbie with cold eyes before sparing a quick look at Sammanus. "Brother, you have spoiled the pleasure of your return by giving away that which was not yours to give."

"Lady Agrippa, as I explained to Gallus and Hortensius, we owe the Deirans a debt. Unfortunately, the Deiran picked Jupiter. You know we will—"

"Who knows what you have contrived to owe them, brother. For my part, I invited no Deirans and harbor no wish that any should trouble themselves to stay." She glared at Eldred. "Climb down from that steed, young man. Climb down and return south, where you most assuredly will be safer."

Eldred smiled at Lady Agrippa. "I won't be returning Hobbie, or any of the others, but I'm not greedy. I'm only taking the four we are due. As for threats, it will take more than an old woman and her ancient minions to frighten me."

Her eyes flashed with anger. "How dare you speak to me so!"

"I traveled for weeks to reach your city. Along the way, we lost one of our companions, a squire younger than me. He was ripped apart by wolves in the Hercynian Forest. Now we're here to battle a dragon for you. It might behoove you to show some gratitude," said Eldred.

Lady Agrippa's thin face grew taut as she frowned. "I am quite certain I do not require instructions on manners from an ill-dressed horse thief. I am done asking for your cooperation. My companions can ease you down from Jupiter if you are too stubborn to climb down on your own." The four riders set their hands on their swords.

"Hold up, sister!" said Sammanus raising his hand. "He means well. He is here to help us. You would find he is one of the better ones. Now, his companions are setting up camp on Galla's mound. They aren't nearly as pleasant as he is. Please, sister, have care. Remember the time and place we are in at this moment, the time and place."

The cords tightened in Lady Agrippa's neck. "This is your doing, brother. I warned you, but you went on your way. It took forever to breed him. An eternity. I will not forget this transgression."

"I will make it up to you, sister. I am not sure how, but I will seek to make it up to you."

"Yet another sorry entry to my ledger." Lady Agrippa took one last look at Hobbie, then turned and left, followed by her escort.

Eldred watched them ride away as their hoof beats echoed through the deserted streets. "Is she really your sister?"

"A manner of speech. We consider everyone in the town to be part of our family."

"That's neighborly of you."

"Let us get you back to your comrades, where you belong."

GALLAS MOUND

A fter they left the city, Eldred kept racing ahead on Hobbie and then doubling back. Sammanus plodded along, towing the two other chestnuts as well as the two pack horses.

"What speed he has!" cried Eldred, as he raced back to Sammanus.

Sammanus gave Eldred a blank look. "Yes, quite swift."

"I'll see you at the camp. You're too slow."

Eldred sped ahead. When Eldred reached the field that led to the mound, he urged Hobbie into a gallop and shot towards the camp. The lords and squires heard the pounding hooves and hustled to that side of the mound. Eldred kept the gallop until the last twenty feet before the top of the mound, when he slowed Hobbie to a walk.

Eldred dismounted. "This is my horse, Hobbie. Sammanus is bringing the other replacement horses."

Lord Vance narrowed his eyes. "What sort of horse is that?"

"He's a Nonus horse. He's the finest in Turicum," said Eldred.

"He has a distinctive appearance, distinctively Wretched," said Lord Thom.

"Yes. The mount Mance took from the Wretched was more acceptable," said Lord Vance.

"Did you call him a nonsense horse?" asked Lord Ferris.

"Nonus, the word is Nonus," said Eldred.

"The others are not nonsense, are they?" asked Lord Vance.

"It's Nonus!" said Eldred. "No, they are plain ordinary mounts of the sort you prefer. Hobbie is mine."

Lord Vance shrugged. "Fine. Once he breaks his leg, you can go back to riding your pack horse."

Lord Ferris smiled. "A pack horse is more fitting for Eldred. One stubborn creature serving another."

Lord Thom noted Sammanus approaching. "You did better with those. You should have gotten one more of them."

Eldred sputtered. "Do you care to race, Thom? I'll race any of you across the field and back."

Lord Thom scowled. "You should not be so familiar."

"That's enough, Eldred. You picked a good mount for yourself. Let's leave it at that," said Lord Kenelm.

Eldred felt hot. Looking past the men, he saw their blankets laid out in lines on a flat patch. "Is that the camp? Just there, exposed on the hill?"

"For tonight. Tomorrow we set to building our lodge," said Lord Vance.

"We should stay in the city. It's mostly deserted," said Eldred.

"The city is infested by Wretcheds. This is as near as I care to get."

"How will you protect the citizens from here?"

"We're not here to protect anyone. We're here to kill a dragon."

BUILDING CAMP

The next morning, after breakfast, Lord Vance addressed the group. "We will be staying here for some time. Even if we kill the dragon today, the mountains are too treacherous to cross in winter. With this in mind, I have asked Thom to plan the layout for a lodge and direct you in building it."

Eldred glanced down the hill towards the city. "You would find Turicum is much the same as Boar's Tusk. The stables are laid out exactly the same."

"What does that matter?" asked Lord Ferris.

"We are not staying in that Motherless town," said Lord Vance.

"You needn't worry about the Wretcheds," said Eldred. "It's empty enough that we could have our own district. I'm certain they would avoid us."

"Are you lured by the comforts of Turicum, Eldred? Can you not bear any hardship at all?" asked Lord Ferris.

Eldred rolled his eyes. "If we were on the outskirts of Boar's Tusk, entering the depths of winter, we wouldn't be building a shelter on an exposed hill. We would go into town."

"That's enough, Eldred," snapped Lord Vance. "All right, everyone, this will take some work. Thom thinks it'll take three days. Thom, take them through your plan."

Lord Thom beckoned them over to the side of the mound. "This will be the site of our lodge, here on the leeward side, where this sharp slope levels out along this wedge. To begin with, we need to haul up a number of tree trunks. Our first task."

"I want Kenelm, Osbert and Thom on the logging. Squires haul. Time for work!" said Lord Vance.

They had a slow start while Lord Thom sought out the proper trees, but once he found a few, the lords set to it, chopping them down. The lads skidded the trunks back up the mound using pairs of pack horses. Eldred harnessed Hobbie and showed off his power, easily out pulling the others.

The lords were busy limbing a tree when Lord Thom paused to take a break, leaning on his ax and breathing hard. Lord Kenelm and Lord Osbert continued to work. Eldred, Mance and Wybert were lined up, waiting for something to haul.

"Can I take your ax, Lord Thom?" asked Eldred.

Lord Thom mopped the sweat from his brow. "I am just taking a moment to consider how many more trunks we need."

"We only have the three axes. Perhaps I can use yours while you ponder."

"I will be back to it shortly."

"I can borrow it while you rest, then," said Eldred.

Lord Thom glared. "You seem quite insistent, Eldred."

Lord Kenelm walked up next to Lord Thom. "Lord Thom, why don't you go back to the camp and check the suitability of what we collected. If we need longer trunks, best we know now. Besides, cutting trees is better left to the young."

Lord Thom considered for a moment, then leaned his ax against a tree. "Very well."

Lord Kenelm and Lord Osbert went back to work on the trunk. Lord Thom took a pack horse and departed.

As Eldred picked up the ax, Mance interjected, "I'll take that."

"What?" said Eldred.

Mance walked up to Eldred with his chin jutting out. "I'm the most advanced squire. Lord Vance said as much."

"Give Mance the ax," said Wybert.

"Don't tempt me," said Eldred. "But if we're discussing chopping wood, I'm stronger than either of you. Stronger than both of you together, I expect."

"You're not an advanced squire," said Mance.

Lord Kenelm paused his ax. "That's enough. In the matter of cutting down trees, I expect Eldred is better suited than any of us, including Osbert and myself. We cannot match him in strength or stamina."

The two young squires stared at Kenelm with their mouths open. Eldred took the ax and set at the tree. Lord Kenelm and Lord Osbert stepped aside as Eldred finished the job.

"Fast work," said Lord Kenelm.

"Decent," allowed Lord Osbert.

From then on, Eldred worked on one tree while Lord Kenelm and Lord Osbert labored together on another. Eldred always finished his first. Soon, they had felled eight more trees.

While the other squires hauled the trunks and collected branches, Lord Kenelm led Eldred and Lord Osbert to a white birch tree.

"So we chop these down next?" asked Eldred.

"No need; we just want the bark. We only need knives, not axes. Watch." Lord Kenelm dug his knife into the tree as high up as he could comfortably reach, then smoothly made a long incision down to the height of his boots.

"There. You don't want to go too deep and damage the tree. Now we peel. At the right time of year, it pops off, but it's chilly now, so we have to work it free." Lord Kenelm pried the bark off into a thin sheet, seven feet high and three feet wide.

Eldred examined the piece with interest. "How do we use this?"

"This will serve as a panel for our roof. We need dozens."

Birch trees were common in the woods, and the harvesting went quickly. After the panels started to pile up, Lord Kenelm had Wybert and Daw haul loads of them. They worked into the late afternoon, spreading out into the woods in search of the birch trees.

In the early evening, everyone reassembled at the camp. Lord Vance, Lord Ferris and Lord Thom had already bound nine of the tree trunks into three framed sets. Other trunks were piled on the bark panels to flatten them out.

Lord Vance surveyed the progress with satisfaction. "Well done! We might finish tomorrow at this rate. We'll resume in the morning."

The next morning, Lord Thom demonstrated how to cut turf for the squires. He used the edge of a shovel to cut parallel lines through the grass one foot apart and ten feet long. He then pried up the sod, cutting through the grass roots and shaking out the rocks and dirt as he rolled it up. "Work in pairs. Keep bringing rolls over until I tell you otherwise."

Eldred reached down and picked up the roll. "Are you certain you don't need me for raising the frames?"

"I am," answered Lord Thom.

"I'm the strongest one here. I should help with the heavy lifting," said Eldred.

"Just do as you're told," said Lord Thom. "Didn't they teach you anything at the Academy?"

Mance shook his head. "They never taught Eldred to mind. He always did just what he felt like."

Eldred frowned. "That's not true."

"At the end it was," said Mance. "You were off pretending to train."

"We were training," said Eldred.

Lord Thom waved them to silence. "That's enough. None of that matters. I need you cutting sod. You are here to help, not chatter. Get to work!" Lord Thom grabbed the roll back from Eldred and walked back to the lodge.

Mance frowned. "You're making us look bad."

Eldred picked up a shovel. "I make you look weak."

"We're the advanced squires," said Wybert.

"One of you advanced squires can follow after me and roll up the sod," said Eldred.

"You can work alone," said Mance.

"Fine. Perhaps you can use the Bond to intimidate the grass."

The work turned into a competition. The other squires kept even for the first two hours, but they started to tire. By noon, when Lord Thom had all the rolls of sod he wanted, Eldred had delivered the most.

The outlines of the lodge were clear once the lords leaned the framed sets of trunks against the hill. Lord Thom sent the small squires up the trunks, laying out the bark panels and covering them with sod. Eldred was put to work weaving grass panels to serve as doors. Once Eldred finished the doors, he sat off to the side and watched the other squires work.

When night came, the lower third of the roof remained incomplete, but the expedition members crowded into the shelter. The lords settled in the spots with more headroom, leaving the squires to squeeze into the lower, unfinished areas.

Eldred banged his head on the low frame as he laid out his gear and muttered under his breath.

Lord Ferris looked up from where he was sprawled on his blankets. "What's wrong, Eldred? Does the lodge not meet your standards?"

"It's fine."

"But what?"

Eldred sighed and waved his hand in a slow circle. "We're sleeping, crammed together on cold damp ground, when we could just as easily be enjoying fine, spacious, warm rooms in Turicum."

"That's enough, Eldred. We agreed this is the proper base for our expedition," said Lord Kenelm.

"We can't even see the town. The dragon could be ripping through Turicum, killing people by the dozens. We wouldn't know until morning."

"Killing Wretcheds, you mean," said Lord Ferris.

"Killing people by whatever name you want to give them," insisted Eldred.

"The Night Mother named them the Wretcheds," said Lord Ferris.

"I don't intend to ever set foot in Turicum," said Lord Vance.

"So you would avert your eyes while the dragon razed Turicum?" asked Eldred.

"No. I would watch with interest. Who knows, perhaps the Wretcheds have an ounce of courage between the lot of them. But only a fool would engage one enemy while surrounded by another. That's enough discussion. Everyone, get your rest. I'll give orders in the morning."

THE HUNT BEGINS

The camp had a somber air as the expedition stirred to life the next morning. The lords rose and dressed for battle. After breakfast, they grabbed provisions and mounted their horses.

Lord Vance surveyed the squires from his mount. "Finish the roof, then go hunting for food. We'll return tonight."

The lords set forth, riding back to the road and heading down the hill in the direction of Turicum. Eldred stood at the top of the mound, watching them go.

"Eldred, get over here and help! You can reach the lower parts without climbing," called Mance.

Eldred tracked the lords in the distance. "You're doing a fine job without me."

"What are you doing then?"

"Hunting for food, as Lord Vance ordered."

Ignoring the protests of the squires, Eldred mounted Hobbie and rode over the mound and down the hill towards Turicum. The lords had disappeared to the north by the time he reached the city. "Open the gate, Calvus. It's Eldred."

After a pause, Calvus peered out the window. "What do you want?"

"What I already asked—open the gate."

Calvus scanned the surroundings. "Why are you here?"

"I came to gather provisions for our camp. Open the gate."

Calvus shut the window. A moment later, Calvus opened the gate. "Sammanus did not say anything about giving you supplies."

Eldred brushed by. "Why should he have? It's our decision."

Calvus frowned. "This is a matter for the council."

"No, it's not."

Eldred walked Hobbie down the street to the stables. He groaned inwardly to find Hortensius manning the stables by himself. He found the tall, gangly Wretched a nuisance. "I need to leave Hobbie for a short time while I conduct some business."

Hortensius crossed his arms. "He is filthy. What indignities have you inflicted on him?"

"I used him to haul some timber. He's quite strong as you promised."

"Timber? He is not meant to drag stumps." Hortensius shook his head. "He may not be here when you return."

Eldred handed over the reins. "He had better be."

"Or what? You will steal someone else's horse?"

"That's enough. Make sure he is here. Now, on the matter of my visit, where is the festival?"

"The festival?"

"Drusus's festival. Sammanus invited me."

"I do not believe you. This is not an occasion for outsiders."

"Where is it? I'm here on expedition business, the expedition your people begged for," said Eldred.

Hortensius glared at Eldred but pointed to a ring of towers visible over the rooftops. "They are gathering on the green next to the Hall of Ages. You have no place there."

"Thank you, Hortensius."

Eldred walked through the city, navigating towards the towers. As he passed through the streets, the few citizens he encountered scattered before him. They either changed direction and fled away from him at a measured pace, or they ducked inside buildings to avoid him.

Eldred stepped out into a vast square with the Hall of Ages to his left. The hall consisted of a circular building topped with a huge dome surrounded by eight evenly spaced towers that stretched eighty feet into the air. It was constructed of polished white stone that gleamed in the winter sun.

The festival green was across the square. Hundreds of small tables heaped with knickknacks, flowers and candies spread across the lawn, and at each table sat a blond haired Wretched woman clad in an ornate dress. Wretched men in resplendent togas circulated among the women, many carrying bouquets of flowers. Eldred had never beheld such finery.

As Eldred took in the festival, an awareness of his presence passed through the crowd. The warmth of the occasion disappeared, and soon everyone was staring at Eldred in silence.

Eldred stiffly returned their gaze. A pack of twenty men coalesced and strode across the square towards Eldred. They paused fifteen feet from Eldred, and a tall blond man with a serious expression stepped forward. He appeared to be the youngest in the group.

"What are you doing here?" asked the man.

"I heard there was a festival. I came for provisions."

The man studied Eldred's face. "You are Eldred, are you not? Sammanus made some mention of you."

"I am. Who am I addressing?"

"I am Valens. If your company needs food, come with me."

"Of course, but first, can you explain your festival?" asked Eldred.

"Explain the festival?" said Valens.

"Yes. Why are your women sitting at these tables? What're you doing?"

"How did you learn of our event?"

"Calvus mentioned it to Sammanus."

Valens gave Eldred a quizzical look. "Do you really need supplies or have you come to sneak into our celebration?"

"I require provisions, and I'm interested in your festival, but I'm not sneaking anywhere. It's easy enough to pick me out of the crowd."

Valens looked Eldred up and down. "Enough food to fill a basket or to load down ten mules?"

"I only brought Hobbie to carry it back."

A small smile stole across Valens face. "You rode 'Hobbie' back here?"

"Yes."

Valens turned to one of the older men next to him. "Very well. Tullus, find Eldred some meat, cheese, bread and wine."

Tullus bowed stiffly to Valens and departed.

"And the festival?" asked Eldred.

"Why not?" said Valens, which spawned a murmur of displeasure in the men arrayed behind him.

Valens smiled. "I will mind him, gentlemen. I will ensure he causes no disruption. Excuse us. Some of you still have your own business to conduct."

Valens took Eldred's upper arm. Eldred fidgeted uncomfortably in Valens's grip, but walked forward with him past the angry men.

"The first note for you is to control your gaze. Do not stare at the women. They may have come to be admired, but not by you."

"What's wrong with me?" asked Eldred.

"Your people have gained a reputation with us, something to do with all your violence and killing. Some here might think of you as a rabid dog, which is why I keep hold of you."

"Hmph."

Valens guided Eldred to a stone path that wandered through the green. "Why are you so interested in our festival? Are you some sort of Deiran scholar, or is there even such a thing?"

Eldred shrugged. "It's a special day."

As they wound through the green, Eldred stole quick glances at the Wretched men and women, but mostly stared at the path in front of him. After a few minutes, the Wretcheds grew more comfortable with his presence and resumed their activities.

Rounding a turn, Eldred paused to observe a Wretched man setting a bouquet of red flowers on a woman's table and engaging her in conversation. Their discussion faltered as they noticed Eldred's attention, which prompted Valens to jerk Eldred onward.

"Don't let your gaze linger or you will have to leave," said Valens, keeping his tone surprisingly pleasant.

"Sorry. Are these flowers in honor of your fallen citizen?"

"In a manner of speaking. This is a courting ceremony."

"These men are picking a wife?"

Valens held up his index finger. "There is one man who has departed, Drusus, leaving room for a single replacement. Any more than that would spark a disagreement with your uncle."

"Then what's happening?"

Valens appeared thoughtful as they walked. Finally, he looked at Eldred. "Since a man was lost, the men pick today, hence their bouquets."

"So one man will get a wife?"

"It could lead to that."

"All of this is for one man?"

"In the end. Later we will choose the man by lottery. For now, we all take part in a fanciful celebration. We leave our flowers with the partner we would have chosen if we had the honor and the fortune."

Eldred paused to stare at the middle-aged woman sitting at the table nearest to them. Her blond hair was streaked with white strands, and her gray eyes seemed lost, matching her forlorn expression. Her table was decorated with well-crafted ceramic plates and piled high with dozens of bouquets.

"Mind your eyes, Eldred. You are staring again," warned Valens gently.

Eldred looked away, and they continued on. "She has quite a sizable pile of flowers. The largest I have seen so far."

"Cassia is not short for suitors."

"Does that make sense?"

"What do you mean?"

"The young woman ahead has no flowers," said Eldred, under his breath.

"Which woman? Oh, I see—Opimia," said Valens, looking at the woman sitting at the table in front of them.

Eldred stole a glance at Opimia, a beauty in a white dress, with gray eyes. Her face hinted of amused grace, but her table, though decorated with elaborate glass work and beads, had not a single bouquet.

"How could she not have flowers?" asked Eldred quietly.

"You think she should have the bouquets?" said Valens.

"Your people are comely enough, but she, well, she's the fairest, isn't she?"

Valens raised his eyebrows.

"Isn't she?" said Eldred.

Valens pursed his lips and seemed to weigh the matter. "Perhaps her glass work is lacking. Let us visit her and cheer her up."

As they approached Opimia's table, the expressions of the nearby Wretcheds turned hard.

"Is she a princess?" whispered Eldred.

"No," said Valens.

Opimia smiled at Eldred, the only person to do so that day. "Who is this young man you have brought to my table, Sir Valens?"

"I present you with Eldred. A young man blessed with royal blood both from the Deirans and from the Maldavians. Perhaps the Mercians as well. He is part of the expedition Sammanus requested of the Deiran king."

Opimia nodded graciously.

"And to you, Eldred, I present Opimia, a virtuous woman of Turicum."

"You do me too much honor, Sir Valens."

Eldred gave a low bow. "The honor is all mine."

"That is sweet. So tell me, Eldred, why did your father send only five warriors to battle the largest dragon ever seen, even considering the old times."

Eldred smiled. "My father was moved to create a moment of glory for our expedition, if we have the will and strength to succeed."

"So you believe you can kill this dragon? No less than brave Sir Valens hung back from the quest. I recall his circumspect answer that it was too dangerous."

"It is foolish for anyone who wants to live a long life to engage even a weak dragon," said Valens.

Eldred looked at Valens in surprise. "You're a warrior?"

"Sometimes a warrior; on other occasions a poet. Usually I am the opposite of what the moment necessitates."

"I really hadn't thought about any of you being warriors," said Eldred.

"Why not? Does Sir Valens appear weak to you?" asked Opimia.

Eldred examined Valens. "No."

Valens nodded. "That is kind of you, Eldred. I know we possess a reputation for cowardice among your people."

"Some people say things, but what do they know?" said Eldred. "My compatriots won't enter your city. They say they will not, even if that entails missing their opportunity to battle the dragon."

"Where do they hope to make their stand?" asked Opimia.

"They plan to find its lair and kill it there," said Eldred.

"Deirans are efficient warriors," said Valens. "I expect they will find the right time and place to engage the creature."

"The Deirans are deadly, but so is the dragon. Both rank high among the most dangerous creations Regula ever made," mused Opimia.

"You should call her the Night Mother," corrected Eldred.

Opimia smiled. "Before she was the Night Mother, Regula made many things. She made us, the Sun People. She created every plant and animal that grows in Guaraci. The dragons, when she first crafted them, were marvels, beasts of wonder and intellect. She made the first to impress Korinna, the stone bearer of the Moon People. It was mesmerizing to watch, beauty and power inextricably intertwined. What we should have seen was the malice of it, not even hidden. The first one ate its trainer and laughed as they beat it with sticks in a poor effort to free the bloody corpse. Evil, but fashioned by Regula. At the time, a rarity."

"Excuse me, Eldred. She is starting to tell her tales. Perhaps we should go find Tullus and your supplies."

"Nonsense, Sir Valens," said Opimia. "You brought me the only man present who could set a bouquet on my table. I will not let you take him away so easily. Why don't you run along and find Tullus while I take Eldred back to my house for lunch? Are you hungry, Eldred?"

"I'm never not hungry," said Eldred.

"Now, this might not be entirely proper," said Valens.

"You started it, dear," said Opimia, rising from her seat. "Will you take my arm, Eldred?"

"Of course," said Eldred, disengaging himself from Valens's grip.

They left Valens in their wake as they walked away together, arm in arm. The Wretcheds in the area stopped and glared at Eldred, watching him go.

Eldred swallowed. "Are you a princess?"

Opimia laughed. "No."

"Why aren't you afraid of me? Except for Valens, everyone I met today scurried away."

"Many of them were raised in fear. They are locked in a pattern of thought that limits their ability to perceive your nature. As for me, I see you for what you are, an interesting visitor who has traveled an enormous distance to offer us his aid at great personal risk."

Eldred blushed. "I'm just a squire."

LUNCH

When they reached Opimia's home, which was only a short distance from the Hall of Ages, Eldred gazed over the huge mansion, made of polished white stone, four stories high, set among gardens thick with fruit trees and densely planted flowers of every color. "This is your house?"

"Yes."

"Is it just your house, or do others live here as well?"

Opimia smiled. "Others do."

As they entered the front door, Opimia called out, "Marcia, are you home?"

"Yes, mistress," answered Marcia from another room.

"I have a guest for lunch. Can you bring us sandwiches in the solarium?"

"Yes, mistress."

Twin marble stairways draped with thick red rugs led up from the entry room on both the left and right walls. Eldred followed Opimia to the right. As they started up the stairs, Eldred glanced at a large gilt-framed picture along the stairs and jerked to a stop.

"Is that of you?" asked Eldred.

"Hmm, oh, yes," said Opimia.

In the painting, Opimia sat resplendent in plate armor atop a Nonus horse, raising a sword over her head. Behind her rode a dozen other Wretcheds in similar gear.

"What is it? What does it mean?" asked Eldred.

"It is merely a work of art, Eldred. I had a friend who enjoyed painting."

Eldred looked over the pictures hung on the other staircase. "I guess he did. You are in most of the paintings across the way."

Opimia started back up the stairs. "I make a compelling subject."

They journeyed up three more flights of stairs and through carpeted halls with marble display stands set with decorated terracotta vases. Everywhere Eldred looked, the walls and carpets were clean—no scuffs, no mud or stains.

After a maze of corridors on the fourth floor, Opimia opened the door to the solarium and entered. Eldred felt a blast of heat as he followed after her. The circular room, thirty feet in radius, was covered by a glass dome that showed the sun and sky. As Opimia crossed to sit in a reclining chair, Eldred gazed up, tracking the flight of a distant blackbird. Potted plants were set around the perimeter; an earthy smell filled the air.

"I hope you find the heat agreeable."

Eldred sat in a white wicker chair next to Opimia, wiping the damp from his brow. "Yes, I like warmth."

"I must say, in appearance, you seem rather more Mercian than you do Deiran. Mercians prefer it warmer, do they not? They did settle the furthest south."

Eldred nodded. "You're not the first to notice. I'm almost a foot taller than the average Deiran, but then so are many of your people."

"As a people, we are tall, as fit Regula's fancy before she assumed her new identity, your Night Mother. But coming back to you, why is it you so resemble a Mercian when Valens introduced you as being from the royal families of Deira and Maldavia?"

"I have an eighth share of Mercian blood through my mother, Ghyslaine. She is the half-sister of Julian, the Maldavian king."

"I thought your people did not mix, that you kept to your separate lands and avoided each other."

"Mostly we do. My lineage is rare, perhaps unique, not that it has done me much good."

Opimia tilted her head. "Can the son of a king rightly complain of his circumstances?"

Eldred wiped off more sweat. "Sometimes."

Suddenly, a woman screamed and Eldred turned to see a middle-aged woman drop a tray as she lurched backwards. Delicate plates and cups shattered on the ground, mixed with scattered sandwiches.

Opimia rushed to the woman's side. "There is nothing to fear, Marcia. This is Eldred, my guest."

Marcia stooped to gather the mess, taking a quick peek at Eldred as she did. "I am sorry, mistress. So sorry. I will clean this up immediately."

"It is quite alright, Marcia. I should have informed you regarding the nature of my visitor. It is my fault entirely, dear."

Marcia took a few deep breaths. "I will tidy this up and fetch another platter."

Opimia gently patted Marcia on the shoulder. "There is no rush, dear."

Marcia deftly gathered up the debris and left, as Eldred—coated in sweat—watched in dismay. "Perhaps I should leave. I upset your servant."

"Oh, Marcia is not a servant. It is no bother. Stay and tell me more about yourself."

Eldred felt a trickle of moisture run down his back. "Very well."

Opimia returned to the recliner and shut her eyes. "I am just resting my eyes. You were just explaining your lineage. Please continue."

"I'm Deiran. My father, Alfred, is the Deiran king. But, as you noted, I have the general appearance of a Mercian, which comes through my mother. She was part Mercian, though rather more Maldavian, except for being too tall. Not that there's anything wrong with being tall. You're tall, and that seems good in a—well, one of you. But she is married to my father, a Deiran, and she is actually taller than he is." Eldred watched as a drop of sweat splashed loudly to the floor beneath the wicker chair.

Opimia lay back on her chair, eyes closed and face relaxed. "Can you see in the dark?"

Eldred gave a short nod. "Yes, I have both dark vision and far sight."

"Good tricks. What of the Bond? Do you possess what Deirans call the Bond?"

"No."

"Oh, how unfortunate. I gather you Deirans have run out of your fatum lapides. Ours were exhausted long ago."

"Actually, I'm set with a Deiran fatum lapis. I also bear a Maldavian fatum lapis and a Mercian fatum lapis." Eldred brushed back his hair to show the stones to the side of his left temple.

Opimia sat up in surprise. "Three fate stones! Are they not rare?"

"Yes. At the Academy, only my cousin, Harold, had one aside from me. I don't believe many remain. Unfortunately, mine does not work."

"How could you know whether it works, if you bear two other fatum lapides?"

"I lack the Bond."

Opimia settled back. "Nobody can own every blessing. Whoever gave you three fatum lapides appears to not have understood that basic principle."

They sat in silence for a spell until Marcia returned. She set a tray down gingerly on a table between Eldred and Opimia and scurried away.

Opimia remained reclined. "Help yourself. I am not hungry."

Eldred examined the platter, stacked high with sandwiches packed with meat. Eldred took the thickest one. "These look tasty."

"Marcia is a good cook. How nice to have a young man with an appetite to enjoy her handiwork. If you don't mind, I might take a short nap."

Elder shifted in his seat. "Of course."

Eldred ate two sandwiches and sat, bathing in his own sweat, waiting for Opimia to stir. After ten minutes, he was roused by Valens beckoning him from the doorway.

"What?" said Eldred.

"Come on, it is time for you to go," hissed Valens.

"Oh." Eldred quietly rose to his feet and left a dripping trail of sweat as he walked over to join Valens.

Valens curled his lip as he examined the wet splotches on the tile. Eldred paused.

Valens motioned Eldred onward. "It is fine! Marcia can clean it up once you have gone."

Outside, Eldred took a deep breath. His clothes clung to him, but the breeze was refreshing.

"Tullus packed you two baskets of food. If you are done harassing our citizens, perhaps you can be on your way," said Valens.

Valens started in the direction of the stable and Eldred hurried after him. "I did nothing improper, Valens. I merely had a sandwich or two. Opimia invited me to lunch."

Valens's expression softened. "I suppose that is true. Nonetheless, it was not proper. If you aim to visit again, you must follow our rules of etiquette."

"What are they?"

"To start with, given your situation, you need a minder. You should always be under the guidance of either Sammanus or myself. It is for your own safety. If you anger the citizens, they could harm you."

Eldred laughed. "Harm me? How could the Wretcheds—I mean, your people—hurt me?"

A cold glint showed in Valens's eye. "A punch in the gut seems a viable option."

Eldred held his tongue the rest of the way to the stable.

THE RETURN

When Eldred arrived back at the lodge, the squires were putting the finishing touches on the roof.

Eldred dismounted and examined their handiwork. "Not bad."

"No thanks to you," said Wybert.

"Where were you?" asked Mance.

"Hunting," said Eldred.

"What did you catch?" said Mance.

"I'm not sure." Eldred lifted down the baskets Tullus had provided, and sat down to rummage through them. "Let's see, freshly baked bread, some fruit, some cheese and some wine. There should be some meat. Hmm—I don't see the meat. Nonetheless, gifts from the people of Turicum."

Daw shook his head. "I wouldn't eat any."

"The Wretcheds poisoned it," said Wybert.

Eldred ripped off a hunk from a soft white loaf and wrapped it around some gooey orange cheese. "We went through this before. Why would they bring us all the way up here to harm us? We're here to kill their dragon. Who wants some?"

Wybert glowered at Eldred. "I'm waiting to watch you choke and die."

Eldred took a bite, then uncorked a bottle of wine. He sniffed it before taking a sip.

"What in Mother's name are you doing! Have you forgotten your vows?" shouted Mance.

Eldred made a face. "No, I didn't. This is too sour. The food is good, though."

Mance strode over to Eldred and loomed over him. "You've done it this time, Eldred. First, you cheat at the Academy. Now, you are disobeying orders and breaking vows."

Eldred smiled. "Lord Vance ordered us to hunt. You can search, but you will find no better food in the area."

"Nobody but yourself is so degenerate as to eat that Wretched garbage," said Mance.

"Calm yourself, Mance. It's food, just regular food. Actually, it's very tasty."

Mance kicked one of the baskets over, spilling a round of cheese and two loaves of bread into the dirt.

Eldred snatched up one of the loaves and dusted it off. "Hey! What are you doing? Have you lost your senses?"

"You'll catch it when they return," said Mance. Then he stalked back to the others, and they entered the lodge, shutting the door behind them.

A few minutes later, the squires exited the lodge, wearing their swords and carrying their veruta, small throwing javelins. They mounted up and went down the mound towards the woods on the southern edge, away from Turicum.

Eldred watched them go, then took his baskets to the top of the mound and sat in the sunlight, taking in the view. The outlines of the two islands, Imbros and Sarnia, were visible across the choppy sea and below, Turicum presented a magnificent, though still, cityscape. But it was the birds and their songs that caught Eldred's attention.

Species he had never seen or heard of ranged up and down the hill. A large beaked bird with blue plumage sat in a tree a hundred yards off, marking its territory with shrill squawks. A bird with green plumage, a white face and red markings on its head, worked at pecking through the bark of a fallen tree. Eldred kept hearing a shriek that sounded like an owl, but he could not find the source. No southern owl would be so active during the heat of the day.

The end of his time alone was forewarned a few hours later when he spotted the lords returning across the fields northeast of Turicum. Nearer at hand, he saw the squires riding along the edge of the woods on their way back to the lodge. Eldred sighed and stood up, pausing to dust off his pants. The first pleasant break since before he left the Academy was over.

Eldred was waiting at the lodge when the squires arrived. The carcass of a small rabbit swung from Mance's saddle. Daw cradled two massive tubers in his arm.

Eldred raised his left eyebrow. "That looks—edible."

Mance glared at Eldred.

The squires set in motion putting a meal together. Mance skinned the rabbit while Wybert started the fire. Soon, the rabbit was roasting on a spit and the tubers were heating between rocks on the edge of the firepit.

The sounds of the lord's horses announced their return. Lord Vance had barely dismounted when Mance and Wybert raced over to him.

Mance pointed at Eldred. "Eldred went into Turicum today instead of helping on the roof. He came back with that Wretched trash in those baskets, which he gorged on. He even guzzled some wine."

Lord Vance walked over to Eldred, his expression severe. "Is this the truth, Eldred?"

"Essentially."

"Then you disobeyed my orders and broke your vows."

"I did neither. You gave the order to hunt. I gathered the best food we've had on this expedition, with plenty for each of you. And while I had a taste of wine, no vows were broken."

Lord Ferris came up behind Lord Vance. "You don't think your oath applies to Wretched swill?"

"Mine doesn't."

"And why is that?" asked Lord Vance.

"Because my vows expired this morning. Today is my eighteenth birthday."

Lord Vance turned to Lord Kenelm. "Is that right?"

"I don't know," said Lord Kenelm.

"So he is not a squire anymore," said Lord Osbert.

"Not if he is eighteen," said Lord Thom.

"He is definitely not a warrior. None of us see him. There is nothing there," said Lord Ferris.

"He was going to become a steward," said Mance.

"That's true. I heard Benedict offered him a position," said Lord Kenelm.

"I declined," said Eldred.

Lord Vance crossed his arms. "So whose steward are you?"

"I am nobody's steward. I'm free."

"What do you mean?" said Lord Vance.

"Just what I said. I am a free man. I can drink wine if I wish to, though this is somewhat sour. I can eat food from Turicum as well, if I prefer it to half-cooked roots."

Lord Thom frowned. "I wouldn't touch anything the Wretcheds gave you, not unless you watched them make it."

Lord Osbert surveyed the delicacies in the baskets. "Not even then."

Eldred helped himself to a hunk of bread and cheese. "Quite tasty, as delicious as that last banquet at my father's table. You're all welcome to share. The people of Turicum will provide more if we ask."

Lord Vance clapped his hand with his fist. "No! Touched by a Wretched. Made for a Wretched. None of that's fit to eat." He glanced over at the fire. "Now where are the other rabbits?"

Mance looked down. "There is only the one."

"Oh," said Lord Vance.

Wybert pointed at one of the tubers. "Daw found these."

"I see," said Lord Vance. "Well, tonight it's simple fare. Tomorrow, we join the hunt."

Lord Vance ate the rabbit. The other lords and the squires shared slices of roasted tubers. Lord Osbert and Lord Thom eyed the pile of food around Eldred's baskets several times.

Eldred threw up his hands. "I invited you to eat what you please."

The lords glared at Eldred as they gnawed on their wooden roots.

MORNING OF DECISION

Eldred sat at the peak of the mound, listening to the morning chatter of the birds while he ate Wretched apples for breakfast. They had provided a variety of apples: green, red and pink. The pink apples were sweetest, and Eldred nibbled his to the core before tossing its remains out into the field for one of the birds to find.

He was about to start on a green apple, which he knew to be much more sour from the previous day, when he spied Lord Ferris trudging up from the lodge. Eldred slipped the apple back into his pocket and waited for his visitor.

Lord Ferris stopped ten feet away, directly behind Eldred. "Get up! I need a latrine dug below the lodge, down by the woods."

Eldred shifted his seat, but remained facing away. "Hmph. Get Mance and the others to start. I'll be down to help after a bit."

"They are training with Lord Osbert. This task is for you alone."

Eldred twisted around. "What?"

Lord Ferris smiled. "You have done so well with your other chores. I am sure you can dig it faster than anyone."

Eldred gazed back down the hill. "I decline. You dig it!"

"I'm not asking for a volunteer."

"It's your turn. I haven't noticed you do anything useful in ages."

Lord Ferris sighed. "Once more, you have achieved new heights of insolence. I'm impressed, though not favorably so."

"Good!"

"Is that it, then? Shall I go and report to Lord Vance that you decided to spend the day up here sulking? Does that constitute your royal contribution to the expedition for the day?"

"Why don't you?"

Lord Ferris chuckled. "You just keep digging yourself deeper. If the Mother gave you any sense at all, you will fetch a shovel and run down the hill before I return."

Eldred was still admiring the birds when Lord Ferris returned to the mound with Lord Vance. Lord Vance strode up and stood right in front of Eldred, blocking his view. "I believe Lord Ferris gave you an order."

"He did."

"Then why're you sitting? Get up and do as you were told."

Eldred glared and slowly rose to his feet to loom over Lord Vance.

Lord Vance smiled. "You boast the bulk and strength of a Mercian, so much to the good, but you are as stubborn as a Mercian as well. If you want to remain on this expedition, you need to cease this behavior."

"In what way am I on this expedition? You took away my swords when we faced the wolves. You'll do the same with the dragon. Won't you?"

Lord Vance gave a sharp nod. "You're not fighting the dragon. That's a job for warriors, true warriors—bonded warriors. The other squires, young as they are, might prove useful, but not you. In a dangerous situation, I can't predict what you will do. You lack the Bond. You knew this before you came."

"So I dig latrines and sod strips."

"You can cut down trees, too. I heard you were a real wonder at that. We have plenty of chores to keep you occupied, but you're not joining us in battle. We don't fight alongside Mercians or Maldavians or Torvid or First Born or whatever you are. We're Deirans, the bonded warriors. You know this. You went to the Academy all of your life."

"I withdraw from the expedition."

Lord Vance grunted. "Fine. It's no matter to me. I welcome it. Once you die on your own, we'll bury you here. You're too big to drag all the way back to Boar's Tusk."

Eldred poked Lord Vance's chest. "If you die, though you are a small man, even for a Deiran, I'll also leave you here. If circumstances permit, I'll cover you with dirt."

They stood staring at each other until Lord Vance broke the silence. "My camp, my lodge. Get your Wretched horse and go."

Eldred turned away and went down the hill. Lord Ferris trailed after him with a broad smile.

Eldred stalked past the squires, who were lined up outside the lodge, facing Lord Osbert. After saddling Hobbie, Eldred went inside to grab his gear.

Lord Kenelm hailed Lord Ferris. "What's happening? Where's Eldred going?"

"He is leaving the expedition."

"What do you mean?"

"Lord Vance asked him to leave."

Mance and Wybert looked at each other and grinned.

Lord Kenelm jogged over to Eldred, who had come out to pack his horse. "Now hold on a minute, Eldred. Let's discuss this."

"What is there to discuss?" said Eldred.

"We're in enemy territory. We've insufficient numbers. Nobody should be splitting off."

"Lord Vance asked me to leave."

Lord Kenelm turned towards Lord Osbert and Lord Thom, who were standing back from the commotion. "This is not well thought out. I don't pretend to understand King Alfred's feelings for Eldred, but I don't envision him being pleased to learn we abandoned his only son. As every lord on this mission is aware, Alfred finds ways to punish behavior he does not appreciate. Every lord on this mission ought to think carefully."

Lord Thom stared off into the distance. Lord Osbert adjusted his collar and looked at the ground.

Eldred climbed up into his saddle. "My father may not be as angry as you think, Lord Kenelm. In any case, I quit the expedition. Let everyone be witnesses. Lord Vance asked me to leave after I withdrew. Good luck to you. I hope you succeed."

"This is rash," said Lord Kenelm.

Eldred nudged Hobbie forward. "Mother's blessings, Lord Kenelm."

A NEW HOME

As Eldred approached Turicum, he heard a bell pealing. Glancing up, he saw a few Wretcheds on the wall. When he reached the iron gate, Calvus was peering out of the window overhead.

"You must wait," said Calvus.

"Why?" asked Eldred.

"You need a minder to enter the city. Sammanus should be along shortly."

"What if I were being chased by the dragon?"

"You aren't."

"But what if I were? Would you keep me outside the gate then?"

Calvus sighed. "I am following orders."

"I'm sure," said Eldred.

It was ten minutes before the door swung open to reveal Sammanus. "Good morning, Eldred."

Eldred walked past Sammanus, leading Hobbie. "Good morning, Sammanus."

Sammanus fell in step with him. "Why are you back? Do you need more provisions already?"

"Yes. I also need a house."

"What?"

"I need a place to stay," said Eldred.

Sammanus stuck his hand in his pocket. "I do not know, Eldred. This is not something I can grant. This requires the full council. Why not stay on Galla's Mound with your comrades?"

Eldred shrugged. "I'm the liaison with the city. I'll be finding out what you know about dragons, looking over the places where it attacked."

"This was never discussed."

"I remember you pleading with my father to save your people. I don't recall you mentioning our plans would need approval from your council. That might have been the time to raise your concerns. You would have saved us all quite a bit of trouble. Yeowars would not be dead."

Sammanus frowned. "A tragic event."

"Good. Now convene your council. I want this sorted out."

After a lunch that included two roast chickens, Eldred accompanied Sammanus to the Hall of Order, which was rather plain and small by the standards of Turicum. The entrance was up a short flight of stairs into a single room which comprised the entire building.

Opposite the doors was a dais with seven throne-like chairs. Only the two rightmost chairs and the leftmost chair were occupied. Lady Agrippa sat in the chair second from the right. She eyed Eldred coldly as he entered the chamber. Two old men occupied the other seats. Dark wooden benches ran the length of the room, split down the middle by a carpeted aisle. Twenty or so Wretcheds were scattered among the benches. Eldred recognized Opimia, Valens, Tullus and Hortensius. Opimia and Valens smiled pleasantly.

Sammanus led Eldred up the aisle to a single chair at the front, set below the dais. "Sit here, please."

"I prefer to stand."

Sammanus went to the left side of the dais, walked up the stairs and sat next to the man at the end. "I call this session of the council to order. The purpose of this meeting is to consider the request of Eldred of Deira, that he be granted a temporary residence in Turicum for the duration of the Deiran expedition. He further requests the freedom to roam the city in pursuit of knowledge regarding dragons, including the examination of sites where the dragon has attacked."

Lady Agrippa raised her hand. "A point of information."

"The chair recognizes Lady Agrippa."

"I question the motives of this Eldred of Deira. I first came to know of him when he entered the city and seized my most prized possession, my horse, Jupiter. Are you all familiar with Jupiter?"

"We are all well-informed regarding said horse, Jupiter," replied Sammanus.

"I will make this short and to the point. Jupiter is a horse bred to a level of excellence on par with horses two centuries or even four centuries ago, in the age before Regula betrayed us. While other horses fell into gradual decline,

I trained Jupiter to match the documented speed and agility of famous horses from history. I will not go through an exhaustive list, but I submit the only horses on Jupiter's level would be Saturnina or perhaps Maximus. The record will prove that Tiberius was not Jupiter's equal."

"Your point, dear sister?"

"My point, dear brother, is that Eldred entered our city and took from me that which was mine. He reportedly used Jupiter for dragging lumber. All of us here possess things we value, be they family heirlooms or horses raised and trained from birth. Will any of us find any pleasure in the day while this grasping young man wanders the town deciding what he needs or—more accurately—desires?"

Sammanus nodded. "Thank you sister; a point of concern. Eldred, how do you respond?"

Eldred snorted. "You were there, Sammanus. At the start, Lord Vance was sending you to get the horse replacements, but I said I could make sure we got the best. That's why I came to the city and picked Hobbie. Now, I'm not informed on all the history your sister mentioned. I don't know the names and achievements of the ancient horses, but I agree Hobbie is a good horse, exactly what I was sent by my comrades to obtain. On the point of family heirlooms, I'm not here to rob anyone. If any of you own a weapon that can help us, I might borrow it. It's no certain thing with this dragon. There are five lords and four squires now with Yeowars's death. Even if we succeed, I expect more of us to die."

Eldred turned towards the audience. Only Opimia wore an agreeable expression. Eldred paused, and noticed the man sitting next to Valens appeared exactly like Valens, except for having shorter hair.

Eldred was still staring at the man when Sammanus continued. "Are you satisfied with Eldred's explanation, Lady Agrippa?"

"No."

"Duly noted. Do others on the council have points of concern?"

The old and wizened man sitting next to Lady Agrippa motioned with his hand. "A request."

"The chair recognizes Sir Aemilanus."

"I discussed the Deiran with Lady Opimia and was surprised to learn he is marked by three fatum lapides. If he is staying here in the city, I would like to examine him to understand how his fatum lapides are working together."

"Interesting point, Sir Aemilanus. Eldred, do you consent to participate in Sir Aemilanus's research?"

"What? No!" Eldred turned to Opimia with a concerned expression.

"Young man, you will not suffer any pain from my investigation. I heard perhaps one of your fatum lapides was not working as you expected. I would merely be checking your stones in a manner that should not discomfort a robust young Deiran such as yourself."

Opimia nodded. "I assure you, you will come to no harm, Eldred. It might help you."

"The chair belatedly recognizes Opimia."

"Well, if that is your intention, I might participate," said Eldred. "No bloodletting though."

Sir Aemilanus smiled. "No blood. Not at this time."

"Sir Crispinus, have you any concern regarding Eldred's visit?" asked Sammanus.

Sir Crispinus, sat in silence for a moment. "My concern is whether this is a temporary situation. We are under the control of the Maldavians, who police us from afar. I understand Eldred is of the Maldavian royal line, which I find troubling. Can we get a clear statement that this is a matter of providing provisional lodging to Eldred expressly for the campaign against the dragon? This must not be taken as a precedent regarding lodging for Maldavians in the future."

"What say you, Eldred?" said Sammanus.

"This is just lodging during the expedition. Besides, everyone only desires to avoid your city."

"Are you satisfied, Sir Crispinus?"

Sir Crispinus pursed his lips. "Perhaps."

Sammanus rubbed his chin. "I also must enter a point of concern. To avoid problems with the citizens, I propose you always be accompanied by men of our choosing."

"Even when I sleep or wash?" protested Eldred.

"Perhaps not at those times. I do not wish to cause you irritation, Eldred. We traveled some time together and I respect you, but while you are in our city, you must always have a minder."

"Valens suggested you and he would be the minders."

"That might have worked for the occasional visit, not if you live here. Will you consent to work with the men we appoint?"

Eldred glanced at Hortensius. "If they're not irritating."

"Noted. We can try to change minders if you request, but if you don't accept our candidates, you must leave."

Eldred nodded.

"Any questions or concerns?" asked Sammanus, examining the audience. "The chair recognizes Opimia."

Opimia rose from her seat. "I should just like to say this creates a wonderful opportunity for us to get to know Eldred and for him to know us. I am certain Eldred will respect the concerns the council has raised. For us, perhaps, we can let go of our fear. Perhaps it is time we start considering a Deiran, or a Maldavian, a neighbor, instead of an enemy."

Eldred bowed to her.

"A wonderful sentiment, Lady Opimia. Does anyone have any other questions or concerns? No? Very well. Now we shall proceed with a vote on the matter of granting Eldred temporary residence, with the conditions previously noted. A vote of 'yea' signifies agreement Eldred can stay. A vote of 'nay', the opposite. Your vote, Lady Agrippa."

Lady Agrippa stared at Opimia blankly. "Yea."

Eldred raised his eyebrows.

"Sir Crispinus?"

Sir Crispinus sighed. "Yea."

"Sir Aemilanus?" said Sammanus.

Sir Aemilanus smiled weakly at Opimia. "Yea."

"I also vote 'yea'. The council unanimously votes in favor of your request, Eldred. On the matter of where he will stay, has anyone a proposal?"

Valens stood up. "I have a suitable residence for Eldred."

"Thank you," said Eldred.

Sammanus nodded. "The matter is decided. I hereby close this session of the council."

As the audience rose and quietly started leaving the Hall of Order, Eldred approached Opimia, who was standing next to Valens and his lookalike. "Thank you for your vote of confidence, Opimia. I think you made a difference."

"Perhaps in some small way. In any case, the council made the right decision."

"Eldred, may I introduce you to my brother, Avitus," said Valens.

"Glad to meet you, Avitus. Are you and Valens twins?"

Avitus shook his head. "I cannot claim such an honor. We are merely brothers."

"Would you care to see where you will be staying?" asked Valens.

"Thank you. I would."

CITY LIFE

Eldred's house was set in a narrow alley rising up an incline, not far from the stables. It had a smallish footprint but rose three stories, matching the other houses along the street. The first floor was a kitchen and dining room, the second floor was a lounge and the third was Eldred's bedroom. Judging by the other houses they passed, it may have been small by the standards of Turicum, but it suited Eldred. The shelves of the larder were lined with food, including fruit packed in glass jars. The furnishings were comfortable for someone of his height. Large windows let in light and fresh air. Each floor had its own fireplace for keeping warm.

Eldred was sitting on a couch near the fire on the second floor eating a bowl of peaches when he heard a knock at the door below. He rose and made his way down the stairs to open the door. He found a tall, thin man with neatly trimmed blonde hair and a bland expression. The man seemed perhaps five years older than Eldred.

"Good day, sir. I am Gaius."

Eldred looked Gaius over. "Hmph. They said I should wait for you. So you'll be here watching me?"

"No, I will not intrude, sir. I have lodgings across the street. Whenever you go out, please come and fetch me. If I am not available, my brother, Longinus, in the house to the left of mine, will escort you around the town."

"That sounds reasonable." Much better than being spied on all day.

"Now, if it is not impertinent, may I ask you a few questions?"

Eldred shrugged. "I suppose."

"Perhaps we might better converse inside rather than in your doorway."

"Oh, of course."

Eldred trudged back up the stairs and returned to the couch. Gaius stood in the middle of the floor with his hands clasped behind his back.

"Please sit," said Eldred.

"No, sir. I prefer to stand."

"What do you want to know?"

"I have a number of questions for you, sir. Firstly, I would like to ask what you desire for dinner. I wish to provide proper notice to the cook."

"What cook?" asked Eldred.

"Lady Opimia's cook, Marcia, has volunteered to prepare meals for you, sir. That includes breakfast, lunch and dinner. She will still be at Lady Opimia's house for the most part, but I can send Longinus to fetch the meals when Marcia is not available to cook here."

"She would cook here?"

"We prepared the house to the left of yours to serve as a kitchen. Again, that is for when she is here. For simple meals, either Longinus or I can prepare you something. The question for the moment is what you would like to eat."

"Her sandwiches from the other day were tasty."

"You desire a sandwich for your dinner, sir?"

"Is that not available?" said Eldred.

"I am sure it could be, sir. A sandwich is no bother, but if you were of the mood, sir, a number of other dishes might be more adventurous."

"What dishes?"

"Shall I list the entrees Marcia cooks most capably, sir?"

"Yes, please."

"I find her steaks are well-prepared. She seals in the flavor by searing the exterior. Served with a baked potato drizzled with lark's sauce, it is quite a delight."

Eldred grimaced. "Lark's sauce?"

"Lark is not an actual ingredient. That is just the name."

"What else is there?"

"If you prefer fish, you will find your stay in Turicum most rewarding. I expect the fishmonger has a variety of mussels and eels in stock, if you care for the same. Otherwise, he may have cod or whitefish, depending on the fortune of our small fishing fleet. Marcia could turn any of these into a delicious meal, sir."

"I don't eat fish. What else is there?"

"For some tastes, nothing will match a simple pork chop or roasted chicken. Does that interest you, sir?"

"It does. Boiled chicken is my favorite."

Gaius wrinkled his brow. "Boiled chicken, sir? Not roasted?"

"Yes, perfect. I'll go for a walk first and then return for dinner."

"Of course, I will escort you, sir, if that is what you wish, but I would advise against it in the present circumstances."

Eldred sat up. "The agreement specifically mentions my freedom to roam the city."

"And you shall, sir, but, as a word of caution, you might consider the effect of your appearance on the citizens of Turicum."

"What do you mean?"

"Sir, I heard of the hardships you and Sammanus endured on your journey here. They sounded terrible, if you do not mind me saying. What I mean to say is, you have a rough look, as anyone might, if they had experienced such a journey. If we were to adjust your appearance appropriately, you might find the citizens of Turicum have a much more favorable impression of you. Perhaps they should not care, but these are the things that matter to them."

"What do you suggest?"

"Well, sir, your clothes are a trifle worn. Lady Opimia volunteered her tailor to prepare a new wardrobe for you."

Eldred looked Gaius up and down. His clothes did not look that odd, a suit similar to what a wealthy merchant might wear. "I suppose I could wear something like what you have."

"Excellent, sir. Additionally, your hair is quite long and tangled. If it were combed and cut, perhaps in a style more common to Turicum, you might be seen in a less ominous light."

"I'm not against grooming, but not too short."

"And bathing, sir. This might be the most important consideration, if you will excuse me for emphasizing it. The house to the right of yours has a bath on the first floor. I can start a hot bath for you now. The barber can attend to you after. I can make an appointment for the tailor to come by after dinner."

"You have it all planned."

"Thank you, sir."

Eldred caught the ends of his hair in his fingers "Tell Lady Opimia's barber my hair can't look too strange."

"It is my barber, sir."

NEW MAN

The next morning, after a breakfast of honeyed ham and fresh bread rolls, Eldred headed to the Hall of Ages accompanied by Gaius. Eldred wore the brown tunic and black pants the tailor had stitched together the previous night. The fabric felt soft and smooth against Eldred's skin. While the citizens he encountered paid close attention to Eldred as they passed him, they no longer scurried off.

"You were right, Gaius. The change of clothes put the people at their ease."

"Yes, sir. If you study them, you will observe the residents of Turicum take pains with their appearance. We value grooming in ourselves as well as in others."

Eldred nodded. They had not passed many people, but they all—both men and women—appeared highly presentable, bedecked with richly appointed tunics, mostly white and gray, but some were an explosion of color. "Do you think I should visit Opimia? To thank her for the loan of her cook and her tailor?"

"Oh, no, sir. It's a fine thought, but I must recommend against that course of action, especially as Sir Aemilanus is waiting to start your examination."

"We could be quick. I could briefly stop in and thank her."

"You sound very well-intentioned, sir, but you would put her in a difficult position. Trust me regarding the customs here in Turicum."

"I see. So thanking someone is a problem in Turicum. Perhaps just a visit then?" suggested Eldred.

"In time, sir, that could make sense. I will let you know when that might be appropriate."

"Hmph. Well, do let me know."

When they reached the Hall of Ages, Eldred followed Gaius up the stone steps to a massive door, which Gaius pulled open. Eldred paused and stood stock still in the doorway. Stretching before him in all directions across the vast interior were skeletons of animals of all sizes and shapes. Some known to Eldred, some not. The skeletons faced the door, as if preparing for a stampede.

"What's wrong, sir?"

"There's a graveyard in there."

Gaius peered around Eldred. "An exhibit, sir."

"Of the dead!"

"Of some animals which are no longer alive. Yes, sir."

Gaius stepped around Eldred. "It's quite alright, sir. To examine things, scientists, such as Sir Aemilanus, take the remains of animals of all sorts and remove their residual flesh. They then attach the bones in the form the animal had while it lived."

Eldred gazed slowly around the hall. "Why do they do that?"

"To better understand them, sir. To acquire knowledge. To gain mastery."

Eldred snorted. "Mastery? Mastery does not come from playing with bones. It comes from strength. When the wolves attacked, Sammanus cowered by the fire while the lords slew the beasts. Who showed mastery?"

"Perhaps a rudimentary form of mastery, sir. But would not true mastery be demonstrated through the ability to direct the wolves, to have them do your bidding?"

Eldred shook his head. "No."

"I see, sir. Well, if I can trouble you to follow me to the back of the hall, there is an exhibit you must see. We have a dragon on display."

Gaius walked along a narrow path through the maze of animal skeletons. Eldred trailed after him, stopping to examine the small portraits set below each skeleton, comparing them with the skeletal remains. Eldred stopped in front of a towering skeleton whose neck stretched high up into the air.

"What's a giraffe?" asked Eldred.

Gaius spun around. "You can read, sir!"

"Yes. I was at the Academy for thirteen years. I can read."

"This is marvelous, sir. I never heard Maldavians or Deirans could read. This is sure to impress the citizens."

"What about Opimia?" said Eldred.

"She is a citizen, sir. She may well be impressed. The giraffe is interesting, but if you come back here, past the pachyderms and tigers, you can see the dragon."

Eldred walked unhurriedly past the massive tusked skeletons of the pachyderms and caught up to Gaius, who was standing in front of the five-foot-long skeleton of a low, squat creature that had its jaws fixed in an open position, exposing its metal capped teeth.

"This is your dragon?"

"Yes, sir. The only one on display anywhere, even before the collapse of the empire."

"It does not seem like much. We came all this way to fight this? Your people can't defeat such a meager creature as this?"

"A young dragon, sir. A full-grown one is much longer than any specimen in the hall. Not as tall as a giraffe, perhaps, but much more dangerous."

Eldred started to reach his fingers towards the dragon's teeth when Gaius grabbed his hand. "Don't, sir. No creature is more venomous."

"It's dead, Gaius. Long dead. And its teeth are wrapped in metal."

"The venom remains potent. It is not a being like any other, sir."

Eldred shrugged.

Sir Aemilanus came up behind them. "You found our famous Balbina."

Eldred turned to Sir Aemilanus. "Balbina?"

"Her name. She was introduced to the hall some five centuries ago. She is an early dragon. Later dragons had a number of improvements."

"They were improved?"

"Oh, yes. By Regula. She developed them. Some say she created them for a contest, but that is not accurate. There was a period when Regula was quite active in the creation of new animals of all sorts. Dragons were the most impressive, which led to her entering them into contests, but contests with her sisters were never the singular reason she created anything."

Eldred knelt down by Balbina and pointed at some fragments of scale next to the display. "She has black scales in the picture, but these are green."

"Oxidation, Eldred. Very astute. When Balbina came to the hall, those were lustrous black scales, but time extracted its due as it always does. These scales are brittle now, but I can assure you such was not the case while she lived."

"What is their weakness?"

Sir Aemilanus shook his head. "Physically, a dragon has no weaknesses. Its scales are proof against almost any attack. Even its eyes are resilient. If you struck a dragon in the eye with your sword, you might impair its vision, but you certainly wouldn't kill it. An adult dragon is the strongest animal to ever live, and they run faster than a horse on clear ground."

Eldred rose to his feet. "So no weaknesses?"

"None worth noting."

"How do you drive them off?"

"While dragons are extraordinary physical specimens, they are weak mentally."

"You mean they are stupid?"

"No, they are highly intelligent, likely smarter than—some people—but they are easily bored. We use that against them. When one attacks, we take no action. Each citizen goes to the deepest part of their house and stays put. Even if the dragon picks their house to demolish, the citizens stay calm, sitting as still as a statue. If the dragon breaks through the defenses of the building, which is no easy matter with our well-constructed homes, the dragon is forced to work, which is not its inclination. Our acceptance of fate denies the dragon its triumph, no chase, no cries of terror, no reward."

Eldred put his palms out. "So you let it kill your citizens? You don't raise a force to strike at it?"

"That would be the worst thing we could do. If we create an arousing experience for the dragon, it would dispatch all of us and likely level the city in the process."

"So if the dragon came now, we would just stand here in place?"

Sir Aemilanus nodded. "We would move to my library, but yes, we would have to wait and see if the dragon chose us. If it did, we would be required to let it take us without resistance."

Eldred scoffed. "I wouldn't do that. I'd put up a fight."

"It was discussed that you might feel this way. My assessment was you would only mildly interest the dragon while it killed you. So long as the rest of us adhere to sensible practices, it should wander off without doing too much damage."

"So I can confront it?"

"If you are so inclined. I would not recommend it. We showed you all you could wish to know about dragons through this display of Balbina, our own beloved specimen. You had an opportunity to examine her scales, which are still beautiful, even though they are aged. Now, if you please, I would like to begin my examination of your fatum lapides."

Eldred narrowed his eyes. "And you know enough about them to help me?"

"Anything is possible. Follow me."

EXAMINATION

S ir Aemilanus led Eldred halfway up one of the towers of the Hall of Ages, which required climbing many flights of stairs. By the time they reached their destination, Sir Aemilanus was winded and took a few minutes to recover while Eldred stalked around the room. The large windows with sweeping views of the city did not capture Eldred's interest. Instead, he examined the fatum lapides. There were more than a hundred of them on tiny stands encased in small glass displays.

Eldred stopped before a display of small blue stones. "Where did you get these? These look like they're Deiran."

Sir Aemilanus stood holding the back of a chair. "Yes, we have three Deiran stones. We also have a few Maldavian stones and even one Mercian stone."

"How did you get them? We are running short. I'll have to take these back with me."

"Of course, if you wish, though I doubt you will find them of much use. They are spent, taken from the dead, the same as the others."

"How did you get a dead Deiran's stone?"

"Before your people imprisoned us here, we were at war."

Eldred frowned. "What do you want with all of these useless stones?"

"I study them. I find them quite extraordinary. Each once contained the power to shape an individual. If you are ready, I will have a look at yours. Take a seat here by the window. I need the light." Sir Aemilanus lightly patted the back of the large leather chair he leaned on.

Eldred frowned and looked back at the Deiran stones.

Gaius cleared his throat. "It is an ancient display, sir. I would not read too much into the presence of some old stones. Do your people not have similar artifacts? The skulls and bones of Sun People your ancestors defeated in battle?"

"No, we don't."

Sir Aemilanus chuckled. "It is a tad barbaric, if you think about it. Still, if you want my help, I need you over here."

Eldred took the measure of the two Wretcheds and crossed the room to take a seat.

Sir Aemilanus moved to his side. "Now, if you can show them."

Eldred pulled his hair back from his left temple to reveal three stones. The topmost stone flashed bright red, the middle was blue and the bottommost was green.

"Interesting setting. The Deiran stone is set in the center, below the Mercian stone, and above the Maldavian stone."

"Does that matter?"

"It might. I have never seen a subject with three fatum lapides. In many ways, it is a questionable choice."

"Why?"

"Because they work against each other. Regula was the first stone bearer to fashion fatum lapides. She began crafting them for my people almost a thousand years ago. I have samples from that distant time over there." Sir Aemilanus pointed to a cabinet across the room.

"The early ones are the most visually striking with ornate symbols and designs, but they were weaker in effect than her later creations. She increasingly focused on their raw power and less on their appearance. The stones accentuated the properties that she wanted to develop in her subjects. In your context, if she wanted to make a Mercian taller and stronger, she would set them with a Mercian stone. If she wanted a Deiran with a more vibrant Bond, she used a Deiran stone."

Eldred gave a slight shake of his head. "My stone did not work."

"So I heard."

Sir Aemilanus took a small white cloth from a nearby table and dabbed it in a musty smelling liquid, which strung and felt cold as he rubbed the skin around Eldred's stones.

Sir Aemilanus picked up a lens and examined Eldred, gently stretching Eldred's skin with his fingers. "The Deiran stone appears well set." Sir Aemilanus lightly tapped it with a metal instrument he took from the table, making Eldred wince. "The Mercian stone and Maldavian stone also took root. They are so much more colorful and vibrant in a live specimen."

Eldred rubbed his temple. "The Deiran stone is definitely not working."

"Not as you expect. You want to be a normal Deiran."

"Yes."

"Knowing the handiwork of Regula—".

"For Mother's sake, call her by the proper name, the Night Mother!"

Gaius's eyes went wide. "Please be respectful, sir. Sir Aemilanus is one of our most revered elders."

Sir Aemilanus smiled tightly. "It is no bother, Gaius. Eldred is a young Deiran and follows their ways. I will humor his request. The Night Mother, if you will, Eldred. She did not make mistakes, but a fatum lapis can only augment what is already present. The only case where a fatum lapis did not function properly came in the person of Bonitus, whom you call the Dark Son, a famous narrative to be sure. One we consider a significant regression, but one I expect you celebrate as a triumph, given his role in destroying my people. That is not likely the situation here."

"Then what's happening?"

"I see two possible alternatives, one which is perhaps a bit shocking. Would you like to hear it?"

"Yes, what is it?"

"And you will listen calmly?" said Sir Aemilanus.

"Of course."

"Perhaps you are not at all Deiran. Given your appearance, it seems possible that some Mercian mated with your mother instead of your supposed father."

Eldred slammed his fists down on the arms of the chair. "How dare you!"

"Now, now, sir. Sir Aemilanus is just explaining the situation. We are not making any judgments," said Gaius.

"I've heard that drivel my whole life," snapped Eldred.

"It is just one possibility, Eldred," said Sir Aemilanus.

"And the other?"

"Your stones are in conflict. You have one stone telling your body to take the form of a Mercian. Judging by your appearance, it resonated with you. Lady Opimia informed me you possess the vision of a Maldavian, so that stone has shown its presence. Your Deiran stone may also be operating in some fashion, but its performance could be impacted by the constraints imposed by the other two. Perhaps the Bond is delicate, as might be in the case of an overbred line of cattle. It might require perfect alignment."

Eldred scowled. "I'm not a sickly cow. I have a problem. Can you fix it?"

Sir Aemilanus shook his head. "You do me too much honor, Eldred. None of us have the power of a stone bearer. If we did, you would find us in different circumstances. No, Eldred. I study fatum lapides, but I cannot fix them."

"What if we remove the other stones?" asked Eldred.

"Oh, an interesting thought, quite astute," said Sir Aemilanus. Your stones are in conflict, so uproot the others to resolve the problem. Sound thinking, Eldred, but there are problems with your proposal. For one, your fatum lapides did most of their work while you were young and growing. The child sets the stage for the man, if you will. Even if you detach the other stones, you are already fully grown. You would still be that which you are. For a second point, a fatum lapis is linked to its agent. Removing them would injure you over time, perhaps killing you. I am glad to make the attempt if you so wish."

Eldred frowned. "So the examination is complete?"

"On the contrary, we are just getting started. You are a unique specimen, Eldred. The only man to bear three fatum lapides. I had Gaius prepare a series of challenges to measure their effect."

"What challenges?"

"We will start with a race," said Gaius.

SPEED

Eldred looked over his Wretched competitors and shook his head. Gaius presented four men and four women to race him across the square adjacent to the Hall of Ages. They each appeared at least middle-aged, and one of the women looked old enough to be someone's grandmother. A crowd of a few hundred citizens had come to watch.

Eldred pulled Gaius aside. "Is there nobody younger who can race? I see Valens and Avitus in the audience. Surely they would be better competition."

"Sir Aemilanus is timing your performance so there is no need for other contestants. I merely added them to inspire you. But don't underestimate them, especially Drusa."

Eldred looked across the square to where Sir Aemilanus stood near a table covered with odd glassware. Opimia hovered behind him. "What is Sir Aemilanus doing? Is that Opimia's glass?"

Gaius raised his eyebrows. "She did make those hourglasses. How did you know? In any case, Sir Aemilanus will measure the time. In a sense, you will race against every champion in our history, not just these eight individuals."

Eldred grunted.

Gaius clapped his hands. "Let us get started. Everyone, take your mark!"

The racers crowded up to a chalk line drawn across the cobblestones. They turned to watch Eldred with hard faces as he took his stance.

Gaius picked up a stick with a white flag at the end and walked out twenty feet in front of the contestants. "When I wave this, the race starts."

The crowd started to call out encouragement.

"Run fast, Drusa!" called someone nearby.

"Show him your measure, Ahenobarbus!" yelled another.

Eldred scowled. He was Deiran. He had no intention of losing to any

Wretcheds. Gaius waved the flag, and several of the runners came out faster than Eldred. The fastest of them was the old woman—Drusa, by the sounds of the cheering. Eldred's eyes widened, but he did not slacken his pace; he pushed harder.

Drusa was still leading at the halfway mark, and the crowd shouted for her. She was the only one in front of Eldred, but he was still gaining speed. With a quarter of the square to go, he caught her and continued to accelerate. Eldred finished more than five paces ahead of Drusa, who led the others by three paces or more. The cries of the spectators trailed off, but some still yelled encouragement to their favorites as they crossed the finish line. Eldred sought out Drusa to shake her hand, which she placed limply in his grip.

Eldred walked up to Opimia. "How was that?"

Opimia lightly clapped her hands. "Impressive."

Sir Aemilanus harrumphed. "You lost."

"What, are you jesting? I was easily ahead of Drusa."

"Yes, of old Drusa, but not of young Drusa. You bested everyone who raced today, a reasonable effort, but I measured your time against every result we ever recorded. You ran the distance in just over twenty-two beats, but our fastest times are under twenty." Sir Aemilanus tapped an hourglass filled with red sand.

Eldred looked through the crowd to spot Drusa. "Drusa was your fastest?"

"No, Drusa's best time was just over twenty-one beats."

"How old is she?"

"Oh, don't ask that, Eldred. Manners," said Opimia.

Valens approached from across the square with Gaius and Avitus in tow. "Well run, Eldred."

"Thank you."

Avitus gazed at Eldred with an unblinking stare.

"Are you rested enough for your next challenge, sir?" asked Gaius.

"Of course."

Gaius gestured to a clump of Wretcheds, who were lining up, facing a street that led down to the harbor. "That was the test of speed, now we shall take the measure of your endurance. Three loops through the city for a total of ten miles."

"Ten miles?"

"Is that too far for you?" asked Avitus.

"No. I'll just be getting started."

ENDURANCE

Eldred studied his new competitors. They were an equal mix of four men and four women. And, as before, they were all at least middle-aged. Mindful of Drusa's surprise, Eldred picked out the most wrinkled woman, who appeared gaunt. She was short for a Wretched, barely taller than Ghyslaine. "What's your name? Are you the one to watch for?"

She frowned. "My name is Tatiana. I could be."

As they took the line, Eldred stood off to the right. He glanced over to find eight blank faces staring at him. He gave them a curt nod, to which they narrowed their eyes. The crowd started yelling encouragement to the runners. Gaius waved the flag, and they were off.

Two men—among the youngest of the contestants—went out fast, and Eldred followed. Before long, the three were well ahead. The men ran hard, with the one in second place nestled tightly behind the one in front. Eldred raced to the side. They took an equal stride to Eldred, but their feet landed lightly, while his feet pounded the ground.

For the first loop, Eldred just tried to hang on, fighting to keep up with the two runners, while they exchanged the lead back and forth between themselves. As they passed back through the square before the Hall of Ages, the crowd cheered the men, calling for Herius and Varro. Sir Aemilanus turned his hourglasses. Avitus wore a smirk on his face. As they left, the front runner—Varro, it had to be—grabbed his side and stopped, but Herius charged on with Eldred in pursuit.

At the halfway point of the second loop, Herius's steps grew unsteady, and he was breathing hard. Eldred was covered with sweat and panting too. He had never run so far at that speed.

As they came to the end of the second loop and passed back through the square, the spectators cheered, but they shouted for Rufina and Tatiana, not the flagging Herius. Eldred glanced back to find two women closing the distance. Eldred shuddered; the last lap would be painful. To the side, Sir Aemilanus glanced up from his hourglasses and jotted something in a book.

A short way past the square, the women passed them, running in tight formation. Herius exhaled and slowed to a jog. Eldred pressed on. He would not lose to a Wretched. The women settled in a hundred feet ahead, tracking him with steely looks and answering every effort he could summon. Eldred studied them as the spit burned in his throat. Tatiana plugged away admirably on her short legs, but Rufina bounded forward. Rufina was tall, even for one of the Sun People, standing taller than Eldred. Her long blond hair streamed behind her as she ran. When she looked back, her smile rang with confidence. If she had looked middle-aged before, she did not now.

At the halfway mark, Eldred slowed. Rufina noted the change and slackened her pace, preserving the hundred-foot lead. They were working hard too. They only wanted their gap. Eldred slacked off more, feigning increased fatigue, though it was barely an act. Rufina laughed and matched his speed.

And so they continued, until Eldred could see the square six blocks ahead. When Rufina next exchanged the lead with Tatiana, they lost their focus on Eldred, and he took back twenty-five feet before they noticed. Rufina broke formation, passing Tatiana, who turned to scowl at Eldred. It was Rufina. The race had always been with Rufina.

Eldred sprinted as fast as he could. He dashed past old Tatiana. How could that emaciated woman run with such speed? Rufina was stronger. Eldred gained, but he was running out of time. His breath tore through him as he pushed forward. They were on the last block and Rufina still held a twenty-foot lead.

As they entered the square, the crowd roared for Rufina. The Sun People jumped in the air, pumping their arms. Rufina grew faster. Eldred was barely gaining. A ribbon hung between two posts one hundred feet away. Rufina was ten feet ahead, two strides, one stride too many. Rufina took the race.

Eldred stood with his hands on his knees, breathing hard, watching Rufina wade through the crowd, exchanging hugs and clasping hands as the spectators chanted her name. Eldred had never lost a footrace before. Who knew a Wretched could be so fast?

Opimia and Sir Aemilanus made their way over to Eldred.

"Well run, Eldred," said Opimia.

"A reasonable time. Regula crafted strong legs and endurance for the Mercians," said Sir Aemilanus.

Eldred wheezed, sweat dripping off his face. "I'm a Deiran and it was— the Night Mother."

Sir Aemilanus nodded. "If you wish."

Eldred straightened up. "I should shake Rufina's hand."

Gaius came forward to stand next to Sir Aemilanus. "I am sure she would prefer you did not, sir. You are quite damp."

Eldred nodded slightly and grinned. "She's incredible! I never saw any Deiran women run like that."

"You are faster than the other Mercians—and Deirans?" asked Sir Aemilanus.

"Yes, any Deirans that ever were at the Academy, anyways, but it's not something they value much. They only care about the Bond."

"Of course, Regula's defining achievement as the Night Mother."

"So is that the last of the challenges?"

Gaius shook his head. "We have one more."

STRENGTH

The Wretcheds had placed a collection of five objects on a terrace, set in the steps leading up to the Hall of Ages. The smallest was the size and shape of a melon. The largest was a sculpture of a horse, standing with four legs set firmly on the ground. There was also a metal box, a coil of rope and a long rod, but Eldred ignored those and kept looking at the statue.

Eldred stood next to Sir Aemilanus, behind Gaius, looking out over the crowd, which spread out from the base of the stairs. The gathered Wretcheds occasionally burst into chants of 'Rufina' and wore ridiculous smiles. Eldred drew himself up to full-height and studied his lanky competition—four men and four women—who were standing off to the side. He would not allow them another victory.

He glared at Hortensius, who appeared to be on a break from his duties at the stables. While Eldred appreciated finally facing a younger opponent, he did not care for the gangly youth's previous disrespectful comments.

Gaius turned to Eldred. "Are you ready? Have you had enough rest?"

Eldred nodded.

Gaius addressed the crowd. "We now come to the lifting competition. Each contestant must lift and hold the article over their heads for thirty beats. They must set the item down without breaking it. We will start with the lightest object, the wooden melon, and move through the collection to the heaviest, the statue of the horse. Competitors will be allowed two attempts per object. Let us begin."

Hortensius strode forward and seized the melon with both hands, hoisting it over his head.

"Be strong, Hortensius!" came the cries from the crowd as Gaius counted down from thirty to one. When the count was complete, Hortensius set it down with a grunt.

Eldred chuckled softly. "It's just a little wood in the shape of a melon."

"That sculpture is carved out of Lignum Vitae, the heaviest variety of wood, sir," said Gaius.

Eldred waited through the round of contestants, who each successfully lifted the melon on their first try. When it was finally Eldred's turn, he picked it up with both hands and raised it to his waist. As he held it, he realized it was much heavier than it appeared and slippery, as well. But that did not deter him from transferring the melon into his right hand and hoisting it—single-handed—over his head with a flourish.

Eldred sought out Opimia in the crowd below as Gaius counted down. When he spotted her smiling at him from the audience, he lost his grip. The melon crashed down on his shoulder, before hitting the ground and rolling across the flagstones. The crowd broke into laughter. A few of the Wretcheds started chanting 'melon'.

Eldred darted after the rolling carving and grabbed at it twice before snatching it up. He was red-faced as he carried it back to where it had been set. "I have two tries!"

"Of course, sir."

"You can use two hands, Eldred. I recommend it!" called Hortensius.

"That makes it too easy!"

Nonetheless, Eldred held the melon aloft with both hands while Gaius counted down.

Gaius led the audience in a burst of applause. "Well done! Everyone came through that round, though the melon is quite heavy, almost half the weight of a typical citizen. The next challenge is an iron box with twice the mass. You are up, Hortensius."

Hortensius approached the box warily. After testing its handles, he grabbed them and pulled it up as far as his stomach. But that was as high as he could lift the box, though his face grew red with effort. Finally, he set it down with a loud thud.

"Well tried!" called a spectator. But that did not mollify Hortensius, who slunk off to stand in the audience, waving off his second attempt.

The next person up, a young woman with long blonde braids, named Sebine, also failed to lift the box.

The third contestant, an older man named Cnaeus, lifted the box for the full count, much to the delight of the crowd. He waved to the audience with shaking arms as he returned to stand with the remaining competitors. Two others matched his feat—a gray haired man named Albus and an old woman with short white hair named Decima.

"The older people in your city are amazing. They are stronger and faster than the young."

"We try to eat a healthy diet, sir."

On Eldred's turn, he tested the box briefly before trying to lift it. It was much heavier than the melon but easier to grip. Still, Eldred took no chances and lifted it over his head with both hands. It took more effort as the count went on, but Eldred held the box steady until the count was complete.

As Eldred shook out his hands, he studied the crowd. They looked sullen, especially Avitus, who was arguing with Valens. They were down to their last three champions. They had to realize they had no chance.

Gaius led another round of applause as the defeated contestants walked down the stairs. "We have four competitors left as we move to the third challenge, a rod of solid brass. Cnaeus, are you prepared?"

Cnaeus nodded and approached the bar, which was ten feet long. He tested its weight twice before locking his hands on it and pulling it up into his chest and throwing it up over his head. The crowd cheered as the countdown started, but Cnaeus grew shakier with each count. When Gaius reached ten, Cnaeus jumped backwards and dropped the rod with a clang.

"Will you make another attempt?" asked Gaius.

Cnaeus sighed. "No, thank you, Gaius. It is too heavy."

But notably, Cnaeus did not go into the audience. Eldred raised his eyebrows as Cnaeus returned to stand with the remaining competitors.

Albus was unable to lift the rod over his head. He declined his second try and went down to stand next to Hortensius. Decima lifted the rod and held it steady for five beats before she tossed it forward. It bounced down the steps, clanging loudly as the crowd scattered back.

"Disappointing," muttered Sir Aemilanus.

Hortensius and a few of the other defeated Wretcheds carried the rod back up to the terrace.

"You are the only one left, sir."

Eldred approached the brass rod and tested its weight. It barely moved. Eldred rapped the rod with his knuckles and stole a quick glance over the assembly. They looked expectant; they truly did not want him to succeed in the challenge. Eldred took a deep breath, grabbed the rod, snatched it up to his chest and threw it up over his head without hesitation. He swallowed and fought through a slight shudder in his legs as he held his position.

Gaius counted down slowly. Slower than for the others? As the count reached ten, the bar felt slippery in Eldred's hands. Finally, as the count completed, Eldred stepped back and dropped the rod on the cobblestones, with a resounding crash.

A feeling of warm relief passed through Eldred's shoulders and lower back; his legs stopped shaking.

Gaius came forward to stand next to Eldred. "We have our winner!"

A few Wretcheds in the crowd slouched. Others looked at the ground or stared blankly at Eldred.

Eldred raised his fist. "No! We're not done. I have to lift the horse."

"There is no need, sir. You have proven your strength."

"I would like to see the attempt. Recall, we are here to test him," said Sir Aemilanus.

Gaius nodded. "Very well. Should we go to the coil of rope first? That is the next challenge."

Eldred shook his head. "I'll just lift the horse. We could have done that and saved time. The tiny melon was never going to settle this contest."

Lady Agrippa stepped out of the crowd onto the bottommost step. "That is my horse sculpture. I do not want it damaged."

Eldred turned to her in surprise. "It's yours? It's one of the challenges."

Opimia appeared next to Lady Agrippa. "Eldred is correct. If you did not want it lifted, you should not have offered its use."

Lady Agrippa frowned. "Gaius told me Sir Aemilanus needed my statue for some important study. Watching this barbarian manhandle it hardly seems to qualify."

Avitus stepped forward on the other side of Lady Agrippa. "It is unlikely the barbarian can lift it in any case. He could barely manage the rod."

"I'm not a barbarian! I belong to the Night Mother," said Eldred indignantly.

Opimia raised her eyebrows at Avitus. "That's quite enough."

Avitus took a breath and looked at his feet.

Opimia smiled beautifully up at Eldred. "Please continue. I find this to be a fascinating demonstration."

Eldred smiled back and walked past the coil of rope to the statue, circling around it as he sought a means of hoisting it.

As Eldred completed his third pass, Avitus called up to him. "There is no shame in admitting your limitations!"

Eldred stopped and scowled. Then, he ducked under the horse and set his shoulders along its side while grabbing its two left legs. In a smooth movement, Eldred rose up from his squat, lifting the statue above him. As he reached a standing position, he released the left hind leg and sought a good place to set his freed hand. Then he released the left foreleg and placed his right hand on the chest. The statue rocked momentarily, but Eldred steadied it. With a final burst of strength, he raised the horse a few inches above his shoulders. Eldred could not hold it, so after an agonizingly slow count of seven beats from Gaius, Eldred ducked back to the ground, setting the statue down roughly but undamaged.

The crowd watched with silent detachment as Eldred came out from under the statue and raised his arms in triumph.

"Well done, sir," said Gaius.

"A surprising development," said Sir Aemilanus.

On the stairs, Avitus was arguing with Valens. Avitus pushed Valens aside and stormed up to where Eldred was standing. "You have won nothing, barbarian."

"I serve the Night Mother!"

Avitus ducked under the horse and grabbed it as Eldred had done. Eldred stepped back, out of the way, as Avitus hoisted the sculpture into the air. When Avitus was standing erect, he shifted his hands as Eldred had and raised it up off of his shoulders. He held it for only two beats before ducking out from under it and letting it drop. The two right legs of the horse shattered as they hit the ground, and the statue tumbled to its side.

"Avitus, Avitus!" chanted the crowd.

Lady Agrippa gave Avitus a cold look. "How clumsy of you, Avitus."

Eldred grew red and turned to Gaius. "What's this? Have you been making a fool of me, Gaius?"

"No, sir. What do you mean?"

"You had me racing old men and women. All the time you were laughing at me."

"No, sir!"

Eldred grabbed Gaius's shoulder. "I'll not be mocked!"

Opimia strode up the stairs. "Release him, Eldred. You have not been tricked. I forbade Avitus from participating."

Eldred dropped his hands. "Why?"

"Your people call us the 'Wretcheds'. You keep us here, penned, in the last of our cities. You control our numbers, killing our people if we grow too numerous."

"Yes, but how does any of that matter?"

"How could it not matter? We don't have much, but we have a few secrets. Avitus is one of our secrets. That is why I did not let him compete."

Eldred glanced down at Valens. "Is he also one of your secrets?"

Valens smiled back.

"Hmph. So this was not a pretend competition?" stated Eldred.

Sir Aemilanus cleared his throat. "This was not a competition at all. As I made clear to you, these are challenges that help me assess the efficacy of your three fatum lapides. There is no prize. The winner wears no laurels. As to the decrepitude of your competition, did not Rufina cross the line ahead of you?"

Eldred nodded grudgingly. "That's true."

"Are you satisfied? You will keep our secrets?" asked Opimia.

"No, I'm not! I demand a contest tomorrow with Avitus and Valens. We will spar with swords, wooden swords."

"You will be made sore by it, barbarian," said Avitus.

"Manners, Avitus," scolded Opimia.

Valens crossed his arms. "I must decline, Eldred, unless you mean to compete in poetry."

"Just Avitus, then. Avitus and whoever has the courage to hold a sword."

"But you are just sparring, is that correct? No one will be hurt?" said Valens.

"Yes, just sparring."

The crowd turned to Opimia as she mulled it over. "I will allow it, Eldred. But I must insist that you keep these contests secret from your Deiran comrades."

Eldred shrugged. "Even if I should tell them, they would never believe it."

BATTLE

G aius watched Eldred eat his third plate of flat cakes. "We should be going, sir. We are supposed to be there by now."

Eldred slathered jelly on another cake. "These are too good, like works of art. I can't waste them."

"I will ask Marcia to make you a fresh platter after the bout."

"I don't like to spar on an empty stomach. "

Gaius sighed. "You've already eaten enough for ten people. We are making them wait."

Eldred shrugged. "Avitus can wait."

"It's not just Avitus."

Eldred looked up. "Who else is there?"

"Everyone. Everyone in the entire city."

Eldred frowned. "A thousand people?"

"Just shy of that."

"The whole city is turning out to watch me fight Avitus? That seems odd. We had a few matches where everyone at the Academy turned out. But even those were well short of a thousand." Eldred set down his half-eaten cake and wiped his mouth with the back of his hand.

"There is considerable interest among the citizens, sir. Most of them have never seen one of us fight a Mercian, or a Deiran."

"A Deiran. I expect none of them have. You have been penned up here for more than a hundred years."

"I stand corrected, sir."

Eldred laughed. "Unless Sir Aemilanus is as old as he looks."

Gaius nodded as Eldred rose to his feet. "Good one, sir."

They encountered no one as they wound through the streets. Gaius darted ahead and Eldred hurried after him. Finally, they came to a four-story building with a vast cylindrical wall. Eldred paused to take the view.

"The Fabius Amphitheater, sir," said Gaius. "A highly appropriate venue. For the last millennium, it has been a setting for tamer gaming events, but in more distant and primitive times, it featured gladiator battles to the death. Not today, though."

"Not if Avitus has the wit to fall on his butt instead of his head."

"Best if nobody gets hurt."

Eldred waved his hand dismissively. "At most someone nurses a small cut."

"Come on. We are late."

Eldred followed Gaius as he rushed into an entrance on the ground floor and down a set of circular stone stairs into darkness. At the base of the stairs, a corridor led out to a pitch covered by a layer of white sand.

As Eldred stepped out into the arena, he marveled at the setting. The floor of the arena extended more than two hundred feet in length and was more than a hundred feet wide. A fifteen-foot high red stone wall marked the perimeter. More than twenty corridor entrances such as he had just exited were set at regular intervals around the walls, all shut, save for the one he had exited and one other. Four sets of gated stairs led up into the seats, which were sparsely populated by Sun People, who had switched their more common clothes for handsome togas and beautiful dresses with a variety of colors. Some sported gold and silver trim. Others had clasps made of elaborate sea shells.

It was likely all the Wretcheds, as Gaius had said, but the amphitheater was so massive it would take five times their number to fill it. The seats rose up four stories on each side of the arena. Most of the citizens chose the northern seats, which caught the warmth of the low winter sun. The floor of the arena and the south side remained cool—on the border of cold—in the shade.

Eldred waved to Rufina, who was sitting five rows up the north side next to Drusa, eating grapes. She looked away, apparently scandalized, and whispered something to Drusa, who laughed. Sammanus was seated next to Sir Aemilanus and Sir Crispinus a few rows behind the ladies. Further down, closer to the center of the arena, Opimia and Valens sat in the middle of a mass of citizens that included Lady Agrippa and Marcia among others.

Everyone wore their finery, but Eldred found Opimia's rose colored dress the most eye-catching. When she and Valens waved at him, Eldred smiled and waved back. Nobody else seemed pleased to see Eldred, not even Sammanus, who stared down blankly from above in his purple lined toga.

Gaius headed to the southern stairs. In the seats above stood Avitus, Hortensius, Cnaeus, Decima, Sebine, Ahenobarbus and two women Eldred had not met. They were passing around wooden shields and swords. Eldred grimaced as Decima picked up one of the swords. Four and four again?

"You are late, Gaius. You both are," said Avitus.

"You try getting him to hurry. In any case, he is here now."

Eldred walked over. "Am I fighting all of you?"

"You challenged everyone with courage enough to hold a sword. Did you forget, barbarian?" said Avitus.

Eldred stared at Decima and she scowled back. She was old, with short matted white hair and clouded gray eyes, but her sinewy arms had hoisted the rod, if only briefly. How many Deirans could do the same?

"Do not question my courage," said Decima.

"Nor mine," said Sebine, swinging her blond braids as she shook her head..

"Nor mine," said Hortensius.

Eldred rubbed his chin. They appeared honorable, not like cringing Wretcheds. "Very well, I'll fight each of you in turn."

"Bravely done, sir. Sir Aemilanus has provided the order," said Gaius.

"You have the privilege to fight me at the end, if you are still standing," said Avitus.

"As he will be," remarked Gaius. "Each round is to the first touch."

Eldred made a face. "No!"

"What?" said Gaius.

Eldred pointed at Avitus. "With first touch, I might lose a match. It increases the element of luck. I lost that way at the Academy. We fight to submission."

"To submission," agreed Avitus.

"That seems unwise, sir. That course of action could lead to serious injury," said Gaius.

"Not if people have any sense," said Eldred.

Gaius gestured towards the northern seats. "The reasonable people are seated over there."

"Do you possess the wit to submit before you are seriously hurt? If not, then we are going to encounter trouble with your comrades," said Avitus.

Eldred smiled. "I do. It's just sparring. What about you, Avitus? Will I have to knock you out before you submit?"

"Don't concern yourself on that point."

"We have the council members in the audience," said Gaius. "They will end the fighting in case anyone is seriously injured, or if they feel the event has taken too violent a turn. That was agreed this morning."

"How fortunate for you, Eldred," said Avitus.

Eldred laughed.

"Very well. Eldred and I will adjourn to the other side of the ring to prepare for the first contest," said Gaius.

Eldred followed Gaius across the arena to the other open door at the arena level, looking over the audience as he went. The view of the brightly dressed Sun People kept drawing his eyes.

Gaius pushed the door fully open to reveal a small dark room, still cool with the morning air. Inside, a helmet rested on a long table along with a set of padded armor and two wooden swords and two wooden shields. Water, fruit and other refreshments were set out on a side table.

"I can help you with the armor, sir."

Eldred picked up a wooden sword in each hand and tested their balance. The darker heavier one felt better in his hand. "No, thank you. I won't be using it."

"You should at least wear the helmet as a basic precaution."

"A Mercian skull is its own protection," muttered Eldred.

"You should take this seriously, sir. You face accomplished warriors."

Eldred looked through the doorway at his opponents across the ring. "Accomplished how? Who did they ever fight?"

"Well, that is hard to say, sir."

"Eight easy bouts."

"I would not be so certain, sir."

"No, you wouldn't."

On the opposite side of the arena, Hortensius came down the stairs, fully equipped with his arms, his helmet and his padded suit.

Eldred took the heavier of the two swords and grabbed a shield. "Time to get started, Gaius."

In the center of the arena, Hortensius approached Eldred slowly, holding his shield out well in front of him. Hortensius closed to eight feet and set himself. His eyes kept darting between Eldred's sword and Eldred's feet.

Through the mesh screen of Hortensius's helmet, Eldred could see drops of sweat on his face.

As Eldred waited in a relaxed stance, he noticed that Hortensius's neck was quite long. That is where he got his height. Some citizens shouted encouragement to Hortensius. Others shouted rude comments at Eldred. "Deiran dog!" "Mercian whelp!" "Maldavian traitor!" Eldred couldn't wait to swing his sword. This was far better than anything that had ever happened at the Academy.

Hortensius charged and whacked Eldred's shield with his sword. Eldred retreated with crisp, short steps, taking strikes on his shield as Hortensius spent himself at the urging of the crowd. Hortensius was panting when Eldred stopped retreating and leveled him with a thundering shield blow that sent him sprawling face down on the sandy ground.

Before Hortensius could rise, Eldred planted his foot in the square of Hortensius's back and gently tapped Hortensius's shoulder with his sword. "That's the kill."

Hortensius scowled and lay still. The crowd was silent as Eldred removed his foot and offered Hortensius a hand up, but Hortensius refused and got to his feet on his own. The Wretched hurriedly collected his gear and jogged back up the stairs to the other contestants.

When Eldred returned to the room, Gaius was setting out refreshments. "Ably done, sir. And—most importantly—nobody was injured."

Eldred took a seat and drank some water, which was refreshingly cold. "Not that round." Eldred looked over at the contestants and groaned. Sebine was descending the stairs. She appeared to be the youngest of the female competitors. Her reddish blonde hair was woven in long braids that bounced below her helmet as she walked. She hadn't lifted the iron box, but it had been heavy. Could Tenny have lifted the box?

"Have you not sparred with a woman before, sir?"

Eldred shook his head and sighed. "No."

"Just show her the same respect as you showed for Hortensius. That is all our etiquette requires."

"So I can knock her in the dirt and pin her with my foot?"

"If you can."

"You Sun People are very strange," muttered Eldred.

Eldred grabbed a handful of red grapes and ate them as he walked out to the center of the arena. She stopped twenty-feet away and started saluting the crowd, which roared its approval. Eldred turned to face them. They loved her. Was she their champion? Surely it was Avitus?

As the audience continued to issue a dull roar, she raised her shield and sword and closed in on Eldred, pausing just out of reach. Eldred set himself and waited for her onslaught.

She remained where she was, a wide smile across her face visible behind the helmet's mesh. "Is that all you can do, Deiran? Just stand there?"

Eldred charged, reaching out to tag her shield with his sword, but she ducked away to the left and cracked her shield into his, knocking him slightly off balance. Eldred recovered and pursued, only to have her duck away again and again.

She slid around the arena, twisting this way and then another as Eldred chased. She was quick and showed excellent ability at maintaining distance, which drove Eldred to charge faster. On the seventh exchange, instead of dodging away, she slid towards his feet under the cover of her shield and cracked Eldred hard on his left ankle bone.

Eldred yelped and crashed down on top of her shield with all of his weight, trapping her on her back underneath it. Her shield arm was stuck, but her sword arm was free, which allowed her a few ineffectual blows on the back of Eldred's legs. Eldred carefully kept her pinned and reached up with his sword to lightly tap one of her braids.

Sebine looked defiant but ceased her struggles. Eldred pushed off her shield and got to his feet. She popped up with a flourish and removed her helmet before taking a bow for the crowd, which cheered her even louder than before. Eldred grimaced as he tested his ankle.

Sebine smiled broadly. "Does that hurt?"

"A bit."

"Imagine the pain from a real sword. I would have taken your foot."

"If my sword had been real, you would have lost a braid."

Sebine snorted.

Eldred waited for her to head back to her comrades and started walking back to Gaius with as normal a gait as he could manage.

Gaius clicked his tongue as Eldred approached. "Can you continue?"

Eldred sat down and took a long drink of water and smiled. "I have already walked it off."

"Is that something you can do?"

"It is something Mercians can do. They are hard to damage. Still, I will take your advice. Let's get on that padding. The helmet also looks better crafted than it first appeared."

"Very sensible, sir."

The helmet covered Eldred's face with a tightly spaced wire mesh, tight enough to keep out a sword or an eye-gouging finger. It annoyed Eldred, but he preferred wearing it to being clubbed on the head.

As Eldred went out for his next fight with Naevia, some Wretcheds remarked on his garb, "Take it off, Coward!" But he pushed their comments from his mind. After the lesson from Sebine, he resolved to show more caution and not to over pursue. Naevia proved more formidable than Hortensius but less shifty and dangerous than Sebine. After a dozen clashes, Eldred knocked her down and brought the match to an end.

The next bout was with Ahenobarbus, a sprinter from the previous day's competition. His strategy was to run, which was sensible, given his speed. But Eldred had won the sprinting event and prevailed after chasing Ahenobarbus around the arena three times.

As Eldred returned to his table after the fourth match, the audience wore fewer smiles and more frowns. Even Opimia appeared deflated; her smile seemed forced. Valens looked unmoved, but he watched the proceedings carefully. Perhaps he was composing a poem?

Eldred beamed. Four matches, four wins. Sebine had been a surprise. The others, except for Hortensius, had been competent, but not serious threats. The children of Regula were no match for a child of the Night Mother.

Gaius poured Eldred a glass of water. The cool water was more welcome than ever. The sun had finally risen over the wall, heating the floor of the arena.

"Your ankle held up quite well, sir. I wondered whether it would when Ahenobarbus turned to flight."

Eldred sat down and unbuttoned his torso armor. "I told you it was fine."

"Do you find our warriors a challenge?"

Eldred took a drink and tilted his head. "They're decent, except for Hortensius."

"Then, excepting Hortensius, how would you say they compare to Deirans?"

"If we are speaking of the Academy, I don't like to say it, but Sebine would be a tough match for Tenny. He was the strongest fighter there, except for me."

"So she would win that fight?"

"Perhaps, but Tenny was just a squire. You should compare your fighters to bonded warriors."

"How does that comparison look?"

Eldred laughed and shook his head. "No! Deiran warriors with the Bond, they move too fast, too accurately. I watched them fight a blood match where they massacred the Mercians. I was there when the lords on the expedition slaughtered the Hercynian wolves. They wouldn't even take notice of Sebine as they killed her."

"But if they lacked the Bond, how would Sebine do? Without the Bond, would the Deiran warriors be as formidable as you?"

"No. Without the Bond, the Mercians are stronger. And—I'm like a Mercian, in that regard," said Eldred, trailing off.

"Interesting. They are signaling that Phabia is ready. Have you had enough rest?"

Eldred took a long drink of water and nodded. "Anything I should know about her?"

Gaius pursed his lips. "She is quite serious. I expect she will give her best effort."

"Everyone is making a strong effort, except for Hortensius. Why is that? Sun People pride? Or is it something more?"

"It could be something more."

"What is it?"

"Let us say Sir Aemilanus has put forth a proposition to motivate them."

"A reward?"

"In a manner of speaking. Something we all desire."

"I see. Unfortunately, honor dictates I deny Phabia."

"Quite proper, sir. You must strive your hardest in order for the competition to have meaning."

Eldred grunted and buttoned up his armor. He was first to the center and stood there as Phabia came down the stairs. She ignored the audience as they yelled for her. Eldred heard a note of worry in their cheers. They did want something. Just a victory, or something more? Her light gray eyes were lit with determination. She might give her best effort, as Gaius had suggested, but Eldred didn't allow that it would make a difference.

Eldred went on the offensive, but mindful of his foe, he did not overextend. She would tire first. That's how it would end. And so it went, Eldred chased after her, bashing her shield and swinging for her wrist whenever she showed her sword arm. So it went, for five, six, seven clashes.

On the eighth, she stumbled and went down. Eldred closed to finish her, when suddenly a cloud of sand was in his face, blinding him. Eldred stuck out his shield and tried to wipe his eyes with his sword arm, but the mesh helmet prevented him. Before Eldred could recover, Phabia grabbed his shield with two hands and swung him off his feet. The crowd erupted.

Eldred lost his sword in the fall, and was on the ground trying to detach his shield when Phabia walked up and kicked Eldred in the faceplate of his helmet. Momentarily stunned, Eldred grabbed for her leg as she kicked him in the shoulder, but she slipped away and disappeared.

Eldred got to his knees, still trying to blink his eyes clear. He was starting to stand up when she appeared, flying through the air, kicking him in the chest with both feet. Eldred was on his back as she rained blows down on him with her sword. No, it was his own dark hued sword! Eldred blocked with his arms. Despite the padded armor, it stung horribly. After four strikes, Eldred punched her in the hip and bought time to get to his feet.

The crowd was screaming for her, but she looked deadly calm as she assessed Eldred. She was armed, and he had nothing. She charged Eldred and took a powerful swing that cracked on his shoulder. Eldred roared with pain and grabbed her on the side of the neck with his right hand. She tried to slip away, but Eldred caught her on her waist with his left hand and lifted her from the ground. She rapped his hand with the sword, but before she could land a solid blow, Eldred raised her up over his head and flung her into the sand at his feet.

Phabia landed with a thud and lost her grip on the sword. As she tried to roll away, Eldred kicked her in the side and leaped on her back, pushing her helmet into the sand. Eldred pinned her, but she continued trying to break free. They struggled for several moments. Eldred was still trying to contain her when someone grabbed Eldred from behind and threw him to the side.

"It is over, barbarian," said Avitus as he dusted his hands.

Eldred scrambled up, soaked in sweat and covered in sand. "I don't think she quit."

Phabia shot up on her feet. "I did not."

Eldred retrieved his sword and stood facing the pair. Phabia stalked across the arena to retrieve her sword. Gaius jogged out to meet her. "It is a forfeit. Phabia, you must stop."

Phabia gave him a steely look. "I did not yield."

Gaius gently took her sword. "Avitus quit on your behalf."

"He had no right."

"Perhaps not, but the bout was getting out of hand. Be sensible. We cannot go beyond superficial damage."

Phabia pulled off her helmet and glared at Eldred. "He would have submitted before it came to that."

Eldred removed his chin strap and walked over to his shield. "I'm ready for the next match."

"I will have to confer with the council, sir," said Gaius. "We must moderate the level of violence. Please wait inside at your table while I consult with them."

Eldred walked back to the room and sat, checking his bruises, as Avitus followed Phabia up the stairs making feeble apologies.

Gaius was gone for some time. Eldred discovered a wrapped beef sandwich in a basket, which he devoured. As the day warmed, some audience members shifted to the south side of the arena, which was still shaded in places. Eldred was eating an apple when Gaius returned.

"How are you, sir?" inquired Gaius.

"I'm ready."

"There has been a change in plans."

Eldred frowned. "Are they quitting?"

"No. Not altogether. But the event has been abbreviated, out of concern for injury."

"If Avitus lacks the courage to—"

"He is the one who remains. The only one. In the manner of the lifting competition, we will skip to the final challenge. Will you be satisfied? Yesterday, you demanded that Avitus fight."

"To spar. Just to spar."

"You have your wish, sir."

"Decima will be disappointed."

"Most perceptive of you, sir."

The audience cheered as Avitus made his way down the stairs. Eldred buttoned his tunic and reached for his helmet.

"Be careful in this match, sir. You impressed everyone with your durability. It may tempt Avitus to forgo the usual courtesies."

"Phabia already dispensed with those."

Avitus stood, feet firmly set on the ground, waiting as Eldred donned his armor and walked out. His mouth curved into a smile as Eldred took his position. "You will learn your lesson now, barbarian."

They charged each other, shields crashing together. Eldred swung at

Avitus's helmet, but Avitus dodged. Eldred took the fight to Avitus, who retreated before Eldred's girth and strength. Then, on one charge, Avitus leaned into Eldred's attack and Eldred's shield shattered, leaving Eldred holding little more than a handle.

Avitus yelled in delight and landed a quick hard blow on Eldred's side. Eldred grunted and staggered back as the crowd surged to their feet. Eldred retreated before Avitus's onslaught, parrying most of the attacks, but taking hits on his arm and legs.

As they neared the wall, Avitus took a broad stance, seeking to close off Eldred's escape. Eldred took the opportunity to lock up swords, then stepped around to grab Avitus by the back of the neck. Avitus tried to twist away, but Eldred held firm and dropped his sword to throw Avitus into the wall with both hands.

Avitus dampened the blow with his shield arm, but was pinned by Eldred, who pressed him against the wall and slammed Avitus's helmet against the stone wall. After two batterings, the helmet came off in Eldred's hand. Eldred slugged Avitus in the face, and Avitus dropped his sword.

Avitus twisted loose and struck Eldred weakly with his shield. Eldred chased after him, grabbing his shield and striking him in the nose, which bled profusely. Avitus dropped his shield and tried to punch Eldred, but Eldred blocked the swing and hammered Avitus in the gut. Two more strikes to the face sent Avitus sprawling against the wall, where he slouched. Eldred stood panting, dripping with sweat and covered in dust, waiting to see what Avitus would do.

Avitus was breathing hard. "You are no swordsman. You, you—are a brawler. I would have bled you like a pig."

Eldred scoffed. "Stand up!"

Avitus wiped his mouth and smiled as he looked at his blood streaked hand. "You do not see it, do you? You think you are so grand." Avitus laughed.

Eldred frowned. "I'm ready for more if you are."

"You think she gave you the gifts. You are but a stout brute with good vision. What did she take away? The best thing—the thing everyone wants. That is your flaw, if you have the wit to reason it out."

"Reason what out?" asked Eldred.

Avitus heaved himself up and waved Eldred off as he walked back to the center of the ring. Eldred trailed after him.

Avitus pointed to Valens. "Valens!"

Valens looked down from his seat and raised his eyebrow.

Avitus spat out some blood and shouted again. "Valens!"

His fellow contestants lent their voices. "Valens!"

Then together, Avitus and the contestants shouted once more in unison. "Valens!"

Everyone in the amphitheater turned to Valens.

Eldred raised his fist. "Are you their champion, Valens? Come down and spar with me!"

Valens exchanged a whisper with Opimia and rose to his feet. "Thank you, Avitus, Eldred. What a magnificent demonstration. All in all, just a stupendous display. To those of you who took up the challenge and sparred with Eldred, well done. Each of you fought honorably against this most tenacious of competitors. For my own part, I have no interest in sparring with Eldred this morning, but I applaud you."

As Valens started to clap, other audience members stood up and joined in, though more than a few rolled their eyes. Avitus gave Valens a narrow-eyed look and stalked back up the south stairs. Eldred stood, smiling back at Opimia, when Gaius appeared at his side.

"Would you care for more flat cakes and a bath, sir?"

Eldred looked down at himself. He was caked with sand and sweat. "Why not?"

A VISITOR

After lunch and a bath, Eldred reclined on a couch in his living room and fidgeted with the bruises that marked his victory.

"Do your injuries bother you, sir?" asked Gaius.

Eldred patted his shoulder. "A bit. The bruise where Phabia struck me on the shoulder has an odd color. What did Avitus mean about a big flaw? Whatever my flaws, they didn't prevent me from winning."

"Quite true, sir. If your wounds irritate you, we could ask Sir Aemilanus to examine them."

"Is he some sort of healer as well?"

"His studies cover many disciplines."

"Perhaps we can look in on Lady Opimia on the way? I would like to thank her for her support at the contest."

"Visiting Lady Opimia would be inappropriate at this time. However, a visit to Sir Aemilanus appears in order."

Eldred rose to his feet. "Fine."

After a stroll, they arrived at the Hall of Ages.

"Is he always here?" asked Eldred.

Gaius opened the door. "His living quarters are up in one of the towers."

Eldred paused in the doorway and looked across the legion of animal skeletons that filled the hall. As Eldred glanced over the collection, he caught sight of a skull in the back. "What's that?"

"What, sir?"

Eldred strode purposefully through the hall with Gaius following behind. Eldred passed through the bones of a pack of wolves, around a long row of various dogs and past a clowder of cats to reach a display of three humanoid skeletons, nestled against the back wall.

"What's this, Gaius?"

"Some fossils, sir. Why do they concern you?"

"Did you forget I can read? The label for this one on the right describes the subject as a young Deiran. This is not a large skeleton. He's hardly more than a child. This middle one, the big one, the label names him as a full-grown Mercian. The one on the left is described as a Maldavian maiden, a woman! What reason, what right, have you to do this? We aren't animals to be placed on display!"

Gaius pressed his lips together. "Well, I am certain no disrespect is intended, Eldred. This is a hall of knowledge, filled with all manner of creatures. At some point, someone—some curator—must have added these specimens to commemorate Deirans, Maldavians and Mercians, Regula's later creations."

"The Night Mother! And we're people, not creatures. You don't have mastery over us. Did Sir Aemilanus add this exhibit?"

"No, not to the best of my knowledge, sir."

"We can ask him, then."

"We can meet with him once you are calm, sir."

Eldred made a fist at his side. "I am calm."

"Very well, but please recall we came here to seek his help, not to demand answers."

They walked in silence as Eldred followed Gaius up the north tower in search of Sir Aemilanus. First, Gaius checked a meeting room, with views over the square and green below, but Sir Aemilanus was not there. Up another flight of stairs, Gaius peeked in a strange room dominated by a massive stone table surrounded by smaller wooden tables with a variety of sharp instruments.

"What room is this?" asked Eldred.

"Sir Aemilanus's surgical room."

"More like a butcher's den."

"He does not hurt people; he heals them."

Up two more flights, getting near the top of the tower, they entered a library. Tall shelves full of finely bound books ran the length of both the inner and outer circumference of the room, disappearing out of sight with the curvature of the tower. Eldred stood in place, turning around to view the books. He had never seen so many.

Sir Aemilanus peered around the side of a high backed chair and set down a book on a side table. "Eldred. You gave quite a performance at the amphitheater."

Eldred stopped turning and glowered at Sir Aemilanus. "And you keep quite a display down in the hall."

"Yes. What? Do you mean Balbina?"

"No, I mean the Maldavian maiden and the others. I suppose the Mercian provided one of the fatum lapides you showed me."

"A maiden? Oh, I see. I am sorry if our exhibit upset you."

"You can't use my people as trophies. We're not beasts or barbarians."

"The latter is a debatable point, given the extended absence of the Night Mother. It would depend on how you defined 'barbarian'. But, regarding the exhibit, it is for knowledge, for our studies. Who knows, perhaps my own skeleton will be added upon my death. I have suggested as much. It is something of an honor really. Right, Gaius?"

Gaius nodded. "A great honor."

"Precisely, for knowledge."

Eldred crossed his arms. "And you will be on display yourself?"

"The ultimate decision will belong to those who remain, whatever recommendation I might make. They may choose to intern my remains in the crypts down by the harbor, but I wouldn't object to my bones resting here, where I have lived for so long. If they can convince the dermestid beetles that I am worth consuming, I think I would make a rather fine display. They could situate me near your friends."

Eldred narrowed his brows. "Who were they?"

"Hmm. They have been part of the collection for some time. Of the three, I most clearly recall the story of the Mercian. He somehow snuck into Regillium—the sewers were likely involved—and attacked citizens until the guards decapitated him. I do not know what he was thinking, attacking the city on his own." Sir Aemilanus smiled.

"He was killed in Regillium, yet his bones are displayed here?"

"You have the gist of it. He was quite an enormous specimen, even larger than you. Now, tell me, did you come here to discuss our friends in the hall below or for some other reason?"

Gaius stepped forward. "We came regarding Eldred's injuries. Eldred was dealt a number of punishing strikes."

"Yes, I saw. I would be glad to examine the injuries in question, if that is what Eldred desires."

"Well, that's what we came for, but then I spotted them," said Eldred.

Sir Aemilanus raised his palms. "With your sharp eyes. Of course, you would not miss them. Well, you are most welcome to take charge of their remains, if you so wish. I have made some study of what passes for your culture, but I must confess I have no knowledge of the ceremonial requirements for a burial so long delayed. But, if you are comfortable arranging and officiating their interment, by all means, please do. Have you conducted a ceremony of this sort previously?"

"Uhh, no."

Sir Aemilanus raised his eyebrow. "Well, you might want to give it some thought. It is not an action to undertake lightly. In the meantime, what are the symptoms that distress you so?"

Eldred hesitated, then slid aside his tunic to show a deep red bruise on his shoulder. "This mark from Phabia feels odd."

"A moderately worrisome sign. Let us move on to my study."

"The room with the stone table?" asked Eldred.

"No," said Sir Aemilanus with a slight shake of his head. "Not the surgical room; a room of wonders, one I am sure you will find more welcoming."

The study occupied the top floor of the tower. A maze of shelves, full of jars and metal boxes gave the room a disorganized feel. Tables, set in no discernible pattern, covered with plants and books added to the effect. Eldred spotted a small black and yellow snake in a terrarium.

"What are all these things?"

Sir Aemilanus gestured widely. "These are wonders, Eldred. Some were crafted by nature, others by Regula, a few by your revered Night Mother. If you look, you will find plants, worms, insects, minerals, crystals, reptiles and a few small mammals. I have a collection of eyes, which you might like to see. The answers to many mysteries are present here, for anyone who possesses the wit to ask the right questions."

"You answer questions?"

"I possess a store of knowledge collected over a long and studious lifetime."

"What happened to the Night Mother? Where has she been these last hundred years?"

Gaius frowned. "How could he know such a thing? Your people kill us if we wander too far from the city."

Sir Aemilanus chuckled. "Now, now, he is merely asking what we would all like to know, be it reasonable or not. We heard from the Maldavians that she disappeared on a visit to the council island of Mari while accompanied by a contingent of Deiran warriors. We were also informed that Bonitus—or as you call him, the Dark Son—led an expedition of vengeance against the Kingdom of Pergamon and was never seen again. A shame. But beyond this common knowledge, we—the Sun People—are not as informed on world events as we once were. As Gaius noted, our direct knowledge is limited to the immediate vicinity of Turicum, but we can make inferences."

Eldred smiled. "So you do know."

"Not precisely, but I have some thoughts. Come, sit here by the window."

Sir Aemilanus beckoned Eldred over to a seat next to a table on which stood by a plant no bigger than a pitcher of water, with a thick dark gray stem and shiny reddish-brown leaves, set in a pot filled with black sand. "Now, do not touch this. Do not even breathe on it."

Eldred sat down, keeping the plant at arm's length. "What does this have to do with the Night Mother?"

"I present to you the *Somnium ferrum*, the one and only specimen of its species and genus, created by Regula more than three hundred years ago."

"Very old, then."

"So are many things, but this is the only living thing made entirely of metal. A challenge—even for Regula—she needed all her will, her spirit, to make the plant come to life."

Eldred studied the leaves. "It seems small for having lived so long."

Sir Aemilanus pointed at Eldred. "A keen observation. The *Somnium ferrum* grows slowly. In the old days, we would only measure annual growth on the order of a fraction of an inch. But one hundred forty-two years ago, all growth stopped. Some thought the species had gone extinct."

"When the Night Mother disappeared?"

Sir Amilanus nodded. "Yes. The events appear correlated. The *Somnium ferrum* remained in stasis for some time. One day, thirty years later, it sprouted a leaf. It lived."

Eldred stared blankly at the plant. "So what happened to the Night Mother?"

"As Gaius mentioned, we are confined here, so the specifics elude us. But I find this evidence suggestive. I should note the plant grows much more slowly now than before, when Regula—was Regula."

"You think the Night Mother is injured?" asked Eldred.

"Perhaps. Or she could be far away, or any number of explanations suggest themselves. In any case, keep still and I will fetch a salve for your wounds." Sir Aemilanus wandered off through the shelves, tapping his lips. "I saw it just last month, Gel of the Elact, in a small stone capsule, a small gray stone capsule."

Gaius walked in the opposite direction from Sir Aemilanus. "I can help you search."

Eldred was watching them hunt through the shelves when he heard an odd sound. "What's that?"

"What is what?" said Gaius.

"That noise," said Eldred.

"From where?" asked Sir Aemilanus.

Eldred moved to the window. "From outside. Some sort of screeching."

"Oh, no," said Gaius, striding up behind Eldred.

Eldred pointed off towards the harbor. "It's coming from over there."

"It returned sooner than I expected," said Sir Aemilanus.

"The dragon?" said Eldred.

"Yes," said Sir Aemilanus.

Eldred leaned out the window. "I don't see it."

Sir Aemilanus shook his head. "It is not taller than a building."

"Where do you wait?" asked Gaius.

"The library. We should retire there," said Sir Aemilanus.

"Come away from the window, sir," said Gaius. "We do not want to tempt the dragon to destroy the Hall of Ages."

"What?" said Eldred.

"We must go to the library," said Sir Aemilanus.

"Come along, please, sir."

Eldred grimaced. "It can't—it couldn't destroy a building of this size."

Sir Aemilanus tilted his head. "It could destroy any building it wished."

Eldred sighed and left his observation point, following the men back down the stairs. At a table in the library, Sir Aemilanus laid out sheets of paper and handed Eldred a wooden pencil. Gaius fetched two quill pens and set a bottle of ink between Sir Aemilanus and himself.

Eldred held up the pencil. "What're we doing?"

"Very likely, we are simply waiting. The hall is enormous. I doubt the dragon possesses sufficient determination to take on such a challenging demolition project," said Sir Aemilanus.

"What are your men doing? What is Valens doing?" persisted Eldred.

Sir Aemilanus picked up a pen. "Wherever they are, they are doing the same as we are. I mentioned this to you before. This is how we drive the creature off. We stay inside until it grows bored and goes away."

"We are to stay here while the dragon hunts your citizens?"

Gaius selected a piece of paper. "The hunt does not always result in death, sir. It might wander off."

"Why do we need these sheets of paper?"

"In case we are chosen, we must write our farewells. Such is our practice," said Gaius.

Sir Aemilanus nodded. "This ritual places people in the right state of mind. Those who will live reflect on their loved ones, the people who give their lives meaning. Those who are to pass, who hear the dragon settle outside their door, reach out through their notes, and embrace their family one last time. A last embrace to distract them and strengthen their resolve, so they can wait in resignation and ignore the agent of death, even as it tears down the walls. We dare not excite it. That is the key aspect. Dragons feed on emotion, especially fear."

"So we just sit here?"

"And write," said Sir Aemilanus.

Eldred looked at the window as they set to writing. Outside the roars grew louder. Each cry started deep and powerful and then thinned to a whining note that lingered in the air.

Eldred strode to the window. "I can't stand this."

"You must not stand there, sir," warned Gaius. "You could instigate the destruction of the hall."

"I doubt we could rebuild now. We built this hall in the Golden Age. It's been my home for so long," murmured Sir Aemilanus.

Gaius motioned at Eldred. "At least crouch down, sir. Do not present yourself."

Eldred rolled his eyes, but knelt down. At the far end of the square, the dragon emerged from the street that Eldred had raced down the previous day. The massive lizard shuffled forward until its full length, bedecked in glistening black scales, came in view. Its head swung back and forth as its enormous dark blue eyes scanned the empty streets. It flicked out an enormous forked tongue, more than five feet long.

Eldred stared at it, frozen in place. "It's right there."

"Duck, man. Its senses are stronger than any we possess. Do not let it spot you. For the hall," said Sir Aemilanus.

"And for us, as well, sir," added Gaius.

Eldred accommodated them by peeking out from behind a curtain. Momentarily satisfied, the men went back to their writing. The dragon left the square, heading back for the harbor. Eldred heard it roaring in the distance.

After a few minutes, the dragon's roars subsided and were replaced with a new sound, a crackling din.

"What's that?" asked Eldred.

"It found its quarry. Something or someone caught its interest," said Sir Aemilanus.

Gaius set down his pen. "May they pass quickly and painlessly."

"It might take as long as an hour or be as short as a few minutes, depending on the size of the house," mused Sir Aemilanus.

"Do you think your comrades will intercede, sir?" said Gaius.

"No," said Eldred. "Lord Vance was quite clear that he intends to give battle outside Turicum."

"Thanks goodness. If your allies provoked it, the city might suffer significant damage," said Sir Aemilanus.

Eldred noticed the pens lying on the table. "You stopped writing."

"Yes, the sacrifice is chosen. This is not our day to bid farewell," said Sir Aemilanus.

Gaius sighed. "For some poor soul, the nightmare has just started."

Eldred grimaced. "We should not just be sitting here."

"Well, if you are entirely smitten with dragons, I can share a book with you," said Sir Aemilanus.

Sir Aemilanus stood up and went to the shelves of books that ran along the inner wall, adopting an exaggerated furtive manner as he moved.

Eldred stared at him with an incredulous expression. "There's no reason to sneak about."

"You do not know that for certain," whispered Sir Aemilanus.

Gaius glanced up at Sir Aemilanus and laughed. "I just realized one of my notes is to you. Not much point in that."

Sir Aemilanus shushed Gaius but smiled. After a brief search, Sir Aemilanus pulled down a massive tome and brought it to the table where Gaius was sitting. "I think you will want to examine this, Eldred. Come, sit and be still."

Eldred stole a last glance out the window, and went to sit down at the table. Sir Aemilanus slid the book over. The title was *A Study of Dragons*.

AFTERMATH

The small building was reduced to rubble. Its stones were scattered across the otherwise neatly kept yard. The wooden roof was crumpled up and pushed aside. Various furnishings were smashed. Eldred stood near what had been the kitchen, holding a book in one hand while the citizens searched through the debris. Eldred noted red splotches on a patch of white floor tile, and wrinkled his nose at a pungent odor.

After a few moments, an older man pulled a leather pouch out of the wreckage and raised it in triumph. "I found it!"

"Who did she write to?" asked a middle-aged woman.

The man inspected the pouch's contents as the crowd pressed in around him. "She wrote six notes."

"So many," said an elderly woman.

"She wrote to Camillus," said the man with the pouch.

"Of course she would," said the elderly woman.

"And she wrote to Gordianus, Vibius, Flavia, Agrippa and Opimia. Who will help me deliver these?" asked the man.

Several volunteers took letters. As they and the man with the pouch departed, a few citizens started to toss stones from the street up into the yard.

Gaius walked over to Eldred. "And such is the end of Aquila, a young woman of enormous potential. The count is now seven lives lost."

"How was she connected to Opimia?"

"Pardon, sir?"

"She left a farewell note for Opimia and Lady Agrippa. Was she related to them?"

"An interesting question, sir. But it would be rude to ruminate on whom she included and thus, by extension, on whom she did not."

Eldred started to place the book on a stone. "If you say so."

Gaius grabbed his arm. "What are you doing, sir? You cannot set that book down. You must attend to it carefully. Sir Aemilanus was quite emphatic that this volume is irreplaceable, a treasure, not something to balance on a pile of scrap."

Eldred gestured at the men clearing the street. "I was going to help them."

"I can assure you, they are content to continue in their labors without your assistance, sir. We should focus on getting the book back to your lodgings. You probably should have left it at the library."

"I'll be studying tonight. We need to learn how to defeat this creature—the dragon that just killed your friend," said Eldred with added emphasis.

"I am impressed by your enthusiasm for reading, sir. Nonetheless, there is no easy way to kill a dragon."

"It'll be bonded warriors that do the killing, not me."

"Let us just take the book somewhere safe."

THE RETURN

In the evening, Eldred studied in his bedroom. He scanned through hundreds of pages written in flowery cursive text and full of drawings, including several diagrams of dragon anatomy that detailed their glistening scales, their venomous teeth, their distinctive tongue and their thick necks. Intermixed with the images were accounts of how dragons had behaved and misbehaved. A key point discussed at length concerned whether they had a soul. It seems Regula thought they did. Unfortunately, during Eldred's investigation, he found no clear passage on how to dispatch one. Eventually, he put the volume aside and went to sleep.

Early the next morning, just as the sun was starting to rise, Eldred rose and dressed in his Deiran clothes and headed out the door with the book in hand.

As he stepped out into the alley, Eldred was approached by Longinus, Gaius's brother, who exited a door from across the street.

"You must always be accompanied in the city, good sir."

"It's so early. Surely you need your rest?"

"Such are the rules, sir. I am sure my brother, Gaius, made them clear."

"I suppose he did. Come along, then. I'm headed to the stables."

When Eldred reached the living quarters adjacent to the stables, he banged on the door. After a moment, Hortensius appeared in the doorway with his hair in disarray. "What are you doing here?"

Eldred gave Hortensius a disapproving look. "I need my horse."

Longinus tapped Eldred gently on the shoulder. "You are not taking the book, are you? It belongs to Sir Aemilanus's library."

"Yes. It contains useful information," said Eldred.

"Not again," grumbled Hortensius. "Why are you always seizing things from council members?"

"I didn't seize anything. I borrowed a book. A dragon swam to your city yesterday, crawled ashore and ate one of your citizens. But everyone's worried about books. Get my horse."

Hortensius unhurriedly stretched his back, neck and shoulders before ambling past Eldred to the stables.

"I also need my weapons, Longinus."

"Sorry, sir, the rules are quite clear, sir."

"Yes. No weapons in the city, but I'm headed up to Galla's Mound. You can hand over my swords at the gate if you fear me so much."

Longinus pursed his lips. "Very well, sir. I will meet you at the gate, sir. Have Hortensius escort you there, please."

Several minutes later Hortensius finally came out, leading Hobbie. "I washed him yesterday. Don't bring him back muddy, and don't make him drag lumber. He is too fine a horse for someone like you."

Eldred frowned. "Why can't you be more respectful, like Gaius or Longinus?"

"Oh, you think they respect you?" said Hortensius, with a smirk.

Eldred nodded. "Yes, it seems they do."

"You hear them say 'sir', but they mean 'barbarian'."

Eldred glared. "He wants you to follow me to the gate."

Hortensius handed Eldred the reins. "What an honor for me, sir."

Eldred mounted up and looked down at Hortensius. "Why did they let you fight? You were the worst."

Hortensius looked Eldred in the eye, a smile playing on his lips. "Time changes people. Perhaps we will fight again someday."

Eldred studied his face. "Who is your father?"

Hortensius shook his head. "That is none of your business."

Eldred grunted and they proceeded to the gate in silence.

Longinus was waiting with Eldred's weapons. "Are you leaving, sir? I mean, leaving permanently, sir?"

"No. I'll be back for dinner."

"I will let Gaius know, sir."

UNWELCOME VISITOR

As Eldred rode out of Turicum, a thick column of black smoke showed in the sky, rising over Galla's Mound. Eldred wrinkled his brow and urged Hobbie into a canter.

As he approached the lodge, he saw several smoldering fires burning halfway down the slope, towards the woods. Thunder was tied outside, along with Lord Vance's horse and a few pack horses. No other mounts were in evidence. Eldred dismounted and entered.

Eldred nodded to the occupants. "Lord Vance, Lord Ferris."

Neither man said anything, nor stirred from where they sat. They merely turned and stared at him.

"What's happening? Where's everyone?" asked Eldred.

Lord Vance frowned. "What's it to you? You left."

"So he did," said Lord Ferris.

Eldred pulled the tome out of a sack and handed it to Lord Vance. "I found something that might help."

"You brought me a book?" Lord Vance thumbed through the first few pages, pausing to examine a sketch of a dragon.

As Eldred took a seat, he noticed Lord Vance's grimy hands. "Be careful with it, please. It's extremely valuable to the people of Turicum, to Sir Aemilanus anyway."

Lord Vance shrugged and set the book on the dirt floor.

"Not there, please."

Lord Ferris languidly picked up the volume. "A Study of Dragons."

"It's highly detailed. It has drawings of dragons as well as accounts of their activity."

"Hmm," said Lord Ferris.

Lord Vance glanced at Eldred. "So that's why you came back, a book?"

"Yes. Where is everyone?"

Lord Vance studied Eldred's face. "The squires are dead."

"What?"

"They died," said Lord Vance, a note of resignation in his voice.

"How?"

"Tell him, Ferris."

Lord Ferris glanced up from his reading with a flash of annoyance. "Wolves, most likely the remnants of the pack we fought in the forest."

Lord Vance shook his head. "We don't know which wolves."

Lord Ferris resumed leafing through the pages. "Not with certainty."

"Wolves. Wybert killed one. Mance dispatched another. A respectable showing," said Lord Vance.

"I—I'm sorry. I should've been here," said Eldred.

Lord Vance frowned. "Better you weren't. Just would've added to the digging."

Eldred stiffened. "Hmph. What of Lord Kenelm?"

"He and the others are off in pursuit. A fool's errand. You can't bring an animal to justice," said Lord Ferris.

"I granted their request. They were quite upset regarding the squires," said Lord Vance.

Lord Ferris started skimming through the book faster. "We were tracking the dragon to the north when the attack happened."

"Did you find its lair?"

"We did," said Lord Ferris.

"When do you head back to confront it?"

Lord Ferris ignored the question and continued scanning the volume.

Lord Vance stared at the dirt floor. "Your father had a plan. Until I saw it yesterday, I thought we might surprise him. If forty Maldavians can kill one, perhaps the five of us could prevail, or so I thought." Lord Vance sighed. "Does the book speak of a weakness?"

"Not clearly," said Eldred. "There's quite a bit of discussion of dragons. They've deadly venom on their fangs, tough scales and are very fast. Regula thought they had souls."

"That's the Night Mother, not Regula," snapped Lord Ferris.

Eldred shook his finger at Lord Ferris. "This was before she changed."

"That's enough—it doesn't matter." Lord Vance drew a line in the dirt with a stick and stared at it for a moment before wiping it away with his palm. "Hmm. Shame as a weapon. We can't return while it lives. I didn't consider the squires. Yeowars disappointed me. He was weak. Now, I see they were doomed, right from the start. The squires were never going home."

"Eventually, everyone is doomed," said Lord Ferris.

Lord Vance looked up and locked eyes with Eldred. "They died because of you."

Eldred drew back. "What do you mean?"

"He couldn't just send you," said Lord Vance.

Eldred turned red. "He included them to—to bear witness to your great expedition. They died under your authority, not his. Your leadership—"

"That's enough," barked Lord Vance. "In any case, you're not going back with us. I'm done with you and your Motherless cur of a father."

Eldred frowned. "I didn't ask to go back with you."

"You won't survive the journey on your own, boy," said Lord Ferris.

"Sammanus made it," said Eldred.

Lord Ferris paused. "That's true."

"Goodbye, Eldred," said Lord Vance. "It's time you were gone and stayed gone."

Eldred got to his feet. "I'm leaving. I'm taking the book."

Lord Ferris tossed it over. "Take it. Some flowery pictures and pointless anecdotes. Like you—useless."

WANDERING

Eldred left the lodge and mounted Hobbie. As he turned to leave the camp, he saw three fresh mounds of dirt up towards the top of the mound. He paused, studying the graves, each marked by a sword driven in the dirt. On the left was Wybert's; his blade showed traces of dried blood. Mance's was set in the middle; his saber was the finest from among the squires. Last was Daw's.

Eldred sighed and turned away, riding back to the road. Lord Vance was right. It made no sense that any squires had come. They were not Eldred's friends, but neither were they his enemies. Now they were dead, ripped apart by wolves. Eldred shuddered. Nobody should die like that.

When Eldred reached the thoroughfare, he gazed to the south, where the road disappeared into the forest. Beyond the trees stood the mountains, shrouded in clouds and layers of snow. Beyond the peaks, somewhere was home. To the north, by the sea, lay Turicum. Eldred studied the city, marking the places that he had visited, the Hall of Ages, the Fabius Amphitheater and his own residence down a narrow alley. After a final examination of the mountains to the south, he rode towards Turicum.

After he descended the hill and was on the approach to the gate, Eldred pulled Hobbie to a halt and sat in silence. With a reproachful look at the Turicum, Eldred wheeled Hobbie to the northeast and urged him into a gallop. A smile played on Eldred's lips. He rode with abandon, faster than he had ever ridden a horse, crossing the fields in a blaze of speed.

The gallop faded in time into a trot as Eldred pressed on through the stands of trees and small hills which dotted the landscape. Eldred searched the land for signs of dragons and wolves.

After riding for an hour, Eldred reached a range of white cliffs which ran along the sea. Eldred kept as close as he could to the edge, scanning the rocky beaches below for some sign of the dragon's passage. Inlets made for lengthy detours.

At the end of one inlet, near a small woods, Eldred came across the ruins of a stone hut. He was riding by, paying little attention, when he caught the scent of the same pungent odor he had smelled at the destroyed house in Turicum. He dismounted.

Rocks were strewn about in all directions, but a bare patch of ground showed where the floor of the hut had stood. Near the doorway, Eldred found a hoof with a trace of hide and flesh still attached. Not fresh, but not ancient, either. A muddy path led down to a rocky beach below the bluff.

Eldred headed down and checked the beach for tracks but found nothing distinctive. He was walking back through the site when the scent grew stronger. Sniffing and hunting through the rocks, Eldred found a spot marked by shards of thin red glass mixed with a white sandy powder, the source of the odor. Up close, the stench was terrible, like all the rotten eggs and spoiled milk in Boar's Tusk mixed together and left out in the sun.

Eldred retreated feeling sick and mounted Hobbie, riding back towards Turicum. Riding only made him more nauseous, so he walked until he felt better. Eldred shook his head in dismay. He had set out to find a dragon, but had been defeated by an odor.

NEW DEMANDS

When Eldred reached Turicum in the late afternoon, Gaius was waiting just inside the gate. He motioned for Eldred's swords. "Where did you go, sir?"

Eldred slowly took off his blades and handed them over. "I visited the expedition."

Gaius passed the swords to Calvus and walked alongside Eldred towards the stables. "Calvus saw you ride north."

"I did. I searched for its lair."

"Interesting. What did you find, sir?"

"Nothing but rocky beaches."

"Likely for the best," said Gaius. "I would not want to count on Jupiter outrunning the dragon."

"Hobbie." Eldred rubbed the horse's ear. "His name is Hobbie."

They walked in silence for a stretch. Eldred gazed at the cobblestones. "There was an attack on the expedition. Wolves. They killed the squires, all three squires."

Gaius tapped his fingers together. "Up by Galla's Mound?"

"Yes."

"Hmm. How tragic, sir. It was just the squires? Nobody else?"

"Yes," said Eldred. "The wolves attacked yesterday, while the lords were away."

They walked the rest of the way to the stables in silence. Hortensius and Gallus were sitting outside. Gallus rose to his feet to take Hobbie's reins while Eldred removed a sack from the saddlebags. Hortensius stood back with his arms folded across his chest.

"Hobbie is looking well exercised and clean," said Gallus.

"He is an excellent horse," said Eldred.

"What about the book? Did you bring it back?" asked Hortensius.

Eldred lifted the sack. "I have the book."

"Sir Aemilanus will be wanting that," said Gaius.

Eldred paused as Gallus took Hobbie into the stables. "It was a trifle—soiled."

Gaius's face creased with worry. "You damaged it, sir?"

"Maybe a stain or two," said Eldred apologetically.

Gaius took the sack and pulled out the book. Lord Vance's fingerprints showed clearly on the front cover. Gaius turned the volume over to reveal light brown stains from the dirt floor of the lodge. "Oh, no."

Eldred waved dismissively. "Minor damage. The inside is fine."

Gaius flipped through the book, stopping on a page smeared with a thumbprint.

"That might have been there from before," suggested Eldred in a hopeful tone.

Gaius shook his head and stared off in the distance. "Doubtful, sir. I will need to see what I can do about this. In the meantime, I fear your library privileges are forfeit."

As Gaius stepped away, Eldred grabbed him lightly on the shoulder. Gaius squirmed loose and dashed towards Hortensius, who stepped forward with his fists up. Eldred put his hands out in front of him, palms out.

Eldred laughed. "Be calm, Gaius. I just wanted to let you know I need to meet with the council tonight."

"What? Are you jesting? Do you think you can just summon the council at will?" snapped Hortensius.

"I have news of the expedition," said Eldred.

Gaius raised the book. "A meeting at this time might be poorly received, sir."

"Tonight, Gaius. We must meet tonight."

UNHAPPY COUNCIL

Eldred stood in the Hall of Order before the four members of the council: Sammanus, Lady Agrippa, Sir Crispinus and Sir Aemilanus. For this meeting they occupied the center seats at the head of the room. A few citizens were in attendance. Gaius and Longinus had escorted Eldred. Lady Opimia was accompanied by Valens and Avitus. A dozen other citizens filled out the audience, notably Hortensius, Cnaeus and Drusa.

Sammanus looked over the hall. "Everyone who cares to be here is present. Eldred, please begin. Can you explain why this meeting of the council is necessary?"

Eldred searched the room for encouragement, but found little beyond a nod from Opimia. "My concern is the dragon. You all know it attacked yesterday, killing Aquila, destroying her house."

Sammanus nodded. "Yes. Tragic."

Eldred sighed. "The expedition suffered losses of its own. You knew them, Sammanus. The three squires were killed in an attack by wolves. That leaves only the five lords."

"In addition to yourself, of course."

"Yes, of course. I met with Lord Vance and Lord Ferris this morning."

"A friendly gathering. I am sure," said Sammanus.

"Well, they—mishandled Sir Aemilanus's book and painted a rather grim picture of the situation." Eldred noted Sir Aemilanus's deepening scowl. "The expedition's troubled. They—I am thinking they may not defeat the dragon."

Eldred studied the citizens, waiting for some reaction to his statement.

After a pause, Sammanus stirred in his seat. "Well, from the moment your father elected to send such a small detachment, there was always the possibility the dragon would prevail."

"With this meager force, it is a certainty," said Lady Agrippa.

"Do they at least have enough courage to fight?" asked Avitus.

Eldred turned towards Avitus. "They won't quit. But you can't expect them to protect you."

"Are you suggesting we seek the assistance of the Maldavians or the Mercians?" asked Sir Crispinus.

Eldred straightened his back. "No. You may be surprised to hear me say this, but I think the solution is to be found in you, the Sun People. That's correct. I dueled with your most accomplished warriors, and I won. But I learned your people possess grit and determination, far more than might be expected. Even Hortensius, a simple stable boy, was not intimidated after our contest of strength. He showed up the next day for a fight he must have known he couldn't win." Eldred looked over to see Hortensius glowering at him.

"That is all quite true, Eldred. We all respect Hortensius for his stalwart nature. What exactly do you propose?" said Sammanus.

"Rather than wait—helplessly—for the forces of the Night Mother to come to your aid, make your own army. I'll lend you my sword. I can lead you to victory. I trained at the Academy nearly all of my life. There'll be sacrifice, perhaps more than the forty lost by the Maldavians, but we can prevail."

The room was silent, save for a few citizens shifting on the benches.

"An interesting suggestion, Eldred," allowed Sammanus.

Sir Crispinus shook his head. "There are only a thousand of us left. We cannot afford to lose any more citizens from our reproductive pool."

"The Deirans should send a serious expedition," said Lady Agrippa.

"Deiran blood is cheaper," said Avitus.

Opimia shushed him.

"I apologize, Eldred. Having journeyed here with you, I am aware of the sacrifices the expedition suffered," said Sammanus.

Eldred surveyed the gathering with a bemused expression. "Thank you."

Sir Acmilanus pointed a crooked finger at Eldred. "I, for one, cannot sanction fighting the dragon. That is not what we are about. We build things; we do not destroy them. We fashion beautiful buildings, gardens, works of art and books, wonderful books."

Eldred crossed his arms. "The dragon will obliterate all of those things. It does not care about your books or the notes you write while you wait to die."

A shocked silence filled the room.

Sammanus grimaced. "You are correct on the specifics, Eldred. The dragon is a heartless beast, but you should know we do care. Please do not denigrate our dead citizens. We consider them heroes."

Eldred raised his palm. "Their writing is fine, Sammanus. Please don't mistake me. I'm offering to lead you. I would be putting my own life at risk."

Longinus stood up. "I am sure you make this offer with the best intent, sir. But we cannot be led by a Deiran, or by a Mercian for that matter."

Eldred faced him from across the room. "Why not?"

"Our history, sir. The history between our peoples. We are the last of the Sun People, the people Regula ruled for more than a thousand years. We perished at the hands of the Maldavians, the Mercians and the Deirans. That is you, sir. You personify our enemies, the very ones who destroyed us."

Eldred eyes grew wide.

"Longinus is right!" shouted Hortensius.

Cnaeus stood up. "Is he Mercian or Deiran?"

Opimia rose to her feet. "Take your seats, gentlemen. Whatever crimes were committed in distant times, Eldred is our guest. He never killed any of our people. I suspect he never killed anyone. He is only guilty of volunteering to help us."

"Interesting point, Lady Opimia. However, if Eldred summoned the council with the goal of becoming the leader of an army we do not possess, I see no support for his proposition," said Sammanus.

"And in your decision, you demonstrate wisdom, Sammanus," said Opimia. "As a citizen, I also do not advocate for us to wage a desperate battle against the dragon. Instead, we should seek help from the south. But put that consideration aside for a moment to celebrate the courage of this young man. He barely knows us, yet he would risk his life for our people."

Sammanus nodded. "So he promises."

"We have no army for him to lead, but he could represent us to the peoples of the south, our liaison to them, as he has been our liaison to the expedition."

"Would he count against our number?" asked Longinus.

Opimia waved her hand dismissively. "Of course not. We need to look out, beyond Turicum. There are opportunities in the world, even today. With a friend such as Eldred, we could make gains that would otherwise prove impossible. What does the council say?"

Sir Crispinus frowned. "He can make claims on their thrones based on his lineage. He might draw attention to us, attention that may lead to our annihilation."

Sir Aemilanus stared coldly at Eldred. "He is a careless man, careless with the property of others. I welcome him to battle the dragon, but we should not line up behind him."

"I echo the concerns of Sir Crispinus," said Sammanus.

"He is a horse thief," said Lady Agrippa.

Opimia smiled. "Now, now. I deeply respect the council, and like all citizens will adhere to whatever ruling you choose to make. But I must ask you to fully consider the benefit of having a diplomat with the advantages Eldred possesses. His entreaties would prove far more effective than our own. They call us the 'Wretcheds'. Isn't that what they called you, Sammanus?"

Sammanus glanced at Eldred. "Yes, they did."

"Did they not make you beg for assistance?" continued Opimia.

Sammanus took an exasperated breath. "I did not beg."

"No," said Opimia. "Of course not. Forgive me, Sammanus. In any case, the people of the south can be difficult and cruel. Why should one of us go forth and suffer such scorn when we can work through Eldred, a remarkable young man, so well-loved by his people that they granted him three fatum lapides? Three! It bears consideration, especially if the Deiran expedition has at last reached its breaking point. I respectfully suggest we appoint Eldred as our envoy to the southerners. Would you do me the favor of taking a vote on the matter, Sammanus?"

Sammanus stared at Lady Opimia for a moment, then turned to Eldred. "Very well. We can vote, but first, let us confirm his interest. Eldred, are you available for this position?"

Eldred paused for a moment before answering. "So you don't want me to lead you in battle, you want me to lead you in diplomacy?"

"You have the gist of it."

"I would keep my current residence. In return, you want me to raise allies against the dragon?"

Sammanus glanced briefly back at Lady Opimia. "Yes."

"Is that all? Would you also want me to represent you at the counting?"

Sammanus furrowed his brow. "At the counting?"

"Yes. If the Maldavians come for a count. I could represent your side of things."

"You mean you would count us?" asked Sammanus.

Eldred nodded. "I suppose I could, but my meaning was more to the point of representing you, smoothing over any issues that might come up during that difficult event."

Sammanus placed his hand on his chest. "Difficult. Yes, the counting is sometimes—difficult. Yes, perhaps you could represent us in this regard as well."

"I accept."

"I am glad to confirm your interest, but we must first conduct a vote before we offer you the position. What is your vote, Sir Aemilanus?"

Sir Aemilanus blinked. "He would be our envoy?"

"Yes."

Sir Aemilanus gazed up at the ceiling.

"Well?" said Sammanus.

"If it must be so," said Sir Aemilanus.

"Sir Crispinus, what is your vote?"

"I concur," said Sir Crispinus wearily.

"Lady Agrippa?"

"Never. We should drive this filth from our city."

Sammanus sighed. "Noted, sister. For my own part, I also concur, so— by a three to one margin—the council officially invites Eldred to be our envoy to the south for all matters relating to dragons and counts."

"I accept. But shouldn't we also fight the dragon?"

"No, we should not. If that is the last matter before the council tonight, I call for the meeting to adjourn."

TUNING DAY

The next morning at breakfast, as had become his custom, Eldred was eating enormous quantities of the thin cakes. Marcia was busy next door preparing larger and larger batches, but—however many cakes she made—Eldred consumed them all. Eldred was setting in on the last few cakes as Gaius came through the door.

"Good morning, sir," said Gaius.

"Good morning, Gaius," said Eldred between bites.

"I brought over the official document."

"What document?"

"The one which lays out the mutual obligations related to your new position as Turicum's envoy to the three principal kingdoms of the south: the Maldavians, the Mercians and the Deirans."

"I thought we settled that."

"This captures the details, issues not addressed in the meeting. I need your signature."

Eldred frowned. "What issues?"

"Well, for one, under absolutely no circumstances will you do the actual counting of the Sun People."

"I see."

"The document also specifies that in the matter of seeking assistance regarding the dragon, the council will determine which parties you contact and retains the power to amend any agreements you make."

Eldred slathered another cake with jam. "That seems foolish. Given those conditions, what can I promise anyone?"

"You can still fashion agreements. We might just need to add a few refinements. Also, a benefit for you is called out, a treatment, a tuning of your fatum lapides."

"What do you mean? You want me to submit to more testing from Sir Aemilanus?"

"No, no more testing or challenges. He will adjust your fatum lapides, the same sort of adjustment which he performs on the more elevated members of Turicum society."

Eldred looked up. "When would he do that?"

"Today, after lunch."

FIRST TUNING

Gaius was out of breath by the time he and Eldred reached the top of the east tower and stepped out into Sir Aemilanus's study. They found Sir Aemilanus gazing out a window with his hands clasped behind his back.

Sir Aemilanus turned and fixed Eldred with a stare. "Ah, you are finally here."

Gaius leaned against a shelf, catching his breath.

"The appointment was for after lunch. I just finished," said Eldred.

"Of course, of course. Why should I not stand here waiting for you to finish your meal. It makes perfect sense. I am a mere council member, and you are our grand ambassador, our illustrious envoy to the south."

Eldred paused for Gaius to say something before pressing on. "Well, I'm sorry we're late, if we are, but you arranged for this meeting."

"What gave you that idea?" said Sir Aemlianus.

"Your offer. I didn't add it to the agreement."

"Oh, the document? Yes, that is correct. We added the clause. I suppose I should thank you for coming by and granting me the privilege of tuning your fatum lapides, though—in reality—I believe it is quite impossible that we can effect the desired change on your Deiran stone, as I spent considerable time explaining last night."

"I don't recall you mentioning that."

Sir Aemilanus motioned Eldred to a chair by a table, across the room. "I raised my concerns at a subsequent gathering. Never mind. Sit here. This is not much more involved than the treatment I carried out for your bruises." Sir Aemilanus paused to examine the bruise on Eldred's shoulder. "That appears to be doing nicely."

"It feels better."

"Good. Then at least we can avoid the expenditure of more Gel of Elact, though I must now utilize materials which are considerably more valuable, virtually irreplaceable."

"Why are you doing this?" asked Eldred.

"Why indeed? A sound question, one I am struggling with myself. The optimistic view is that we are executing a treatment to wake up your fatum lapides, to stir them to action. If we activate your Deiran fatum lapis, that might trigger the Deirans' fabled ability in you. As I expressed, I rather doubt this process will accomplish anything of the sort, but that is the premise under which we are committing our scarce resources to this undertaking."

"So I will get the Bond?" said Eldred.

"That is possible," said Sir Aemilanus without enthusiasm. "I need to set a baseline for your current state by examining your fatum lapides. Move your hair, please."

Eldred pushed back his hair, revealing the three small colored stones leading from his left temple back towards his ear. Sir Aemilanus took a lens from a nearby table and leaned over Eldred to examine the stones. After a quick examination, Sir Aemilanus picked up a small metal instrument and firmly tapped the stones.

Eldred flinched at the sharp pain. "I don't like that."

Sir Aemilanus frowned. "And I do not appreciate people who damage my books. In any case, the settings appear sound. The skin around each stone is healthy and free of infection."

Eldred studied Sir Aemilanus warily. "What's next?"

Sir Aemilanus stepped to a table across from Eldred and started to place various powders and roots into a stone urn. "I will conduct a tuning. In any case, it is time I made a fresh batch."

"What is all that?" asked Eldred.

Sir Aemilanus gestured at the glass bowl of red powder he had just set down. "This is Carcinus powder, which comes from the ground up shell of a crab species that lives on the coast. The powder supplies the smooth texture and stickiness of the final product, essential for its proper application."

Sir Aemilanus picked up a small metal container and sprinkled the contents into the urn.

"What's that?" asked Eldred.

"Seeds of henbane to increase the circulation of the blood, which deepens the effect of the other ingredients. In particular, it amplifies the effect of the most important reagent, the powder of Balaur."

Sir Aemilanus held up a white woven cloth packet, an inch on each side. "This is the most rare and powerful ingredient. We synthesize it from the brains of dragons. We break down Regula's most powerful creation into its base components and so gain a small measure of her power. Today, we will use this precious substance, which can be used for innumerable useful pursuits, in an effort to transform you into a more normal Deiran."

Eldred gazed at the packet with interest. "From dragons? How did you get it?"

"We obtain it when the opportunity presents itself."

Sir Aemilanus solemnly cut the packet open and emptied the contents into the urn. He added water and stirred vigorously. When he was satisfied, he took a pair of tongs and placed the urn in a small fireplace above a small, but noisy, fire and stood, watching it.

"Who else will you treat?" asked Eldred, stirring in his chair.

Sir Aemilanus turned around. "What do you mean?"

"Well, who among your people are blessed with fatum lapides? Do any of you have them? Opimia said you had run out."

Sir Aemilanus wagged his finger. "Not surprisingly, that is a very rude question. One that you should never ask again."

"That is correct, Eldred," said Gaius.

Eldred shrugged. "Among my people, stones are rare. People even fasten fake stones to impress others. I don't see how it is rude to ask who has them. They're the touch of the Night Mother, or Regula, in your case. They should make people proud."

"We follow the old ways," said Sir Aemilanus. "We refrain from asking personal questions or boasting about our fatum lapides when we have the good fortune to possess them."

"Fine. What is the connection between Balaur powder and a fatum lapis, in any case?"

Sir Aemilanus nodded. "A more appropriate question. The powder of Balaur aids in this treatment by waking the body. It embodies the spirit of creation and can make flesh and bone young and malleable. It can open the body and the mind to the influence of a fatum lapis or serve as a powerful medicine in its own right. In your case, for your Deiran problem, I am quite sure that we are wasting it."

Eldred grunted. "So you said before, in a very rude fashion, questioning my lineage."

"Ah, yes," said Sir Aemilanus. "I apologize for that. If it makes you feel better, I reconsidered the matter. Though we can't rule out the possibility of cuckolding, or conflict between the stones, I believe your stone is actually working."

Eldred tilted his head. "It's working?"

"Yes, the handiwork of Regula, or as you call her, the Night Mother, could not have such a basic fault."

"So what's wrong?" asked Eldred.

"In my opinion, it comes down to a matter of resonance. You are functioning perfectly well for a Deiran, except that you don't resonate with the other Derians."

"That doesn't make sense."

"Very well; I will show you," said Sir Aemilanus. "We have a few minutes while the urn heats." He went off through the shelves and returned shortly with two small silver handbells and one larger one, which he set down on a table next to Eldred. "Take a small bell in your left hand. Hold it lightly and ring the other small bell next to it."

Eldred did as Sir Aemilanus asked.

Sir Aemilanus pointed at Eldred's left hand. "Do you feel it?"

Eldred nodded. The bell in his left hand vibrated slightly.

"Now the larger bell."

Eldred rang the larger bell. The bell was louder, but the small bell in his left hand remained still.

Sir Aemilanus smiled. "And now, nothing. Is that not so?"

Eldred frowned.

"Go on; ring it harder if you wish," said Sir Aemilanus.

Eldred shook the large handbell harder and harder, but the small handbell remained inert. Finally, on one last terrific shake, the clapper of the handbell came loose and flew over the head of Sir Aemilanus, as he ducked, smashing a terrarium. Two blue frogs leaped down from the shelf, and hopped away in separate directions.

Gaius ran to Sir Aemilanus's side, but Sir Aemilanus waved him away and straightened up. "Go! Go make yourself useful. You are his minder. Capture those frogs."

As Gaius hurried off, Sir Aemilanus turned and brought a shaky hand to his forehead. "You are a menace—a danger—even when doing something as simple as ringing a bell."

Eldred started to stand. "I'm sorry."

"No, stay still. You have done quite enough damage today."

Sir Aemilanus returned to the fireplace and picked up the urn with the tongs to check its contents. Apparently satisfied, he carried the urn to the table next to Eldred and poured the contents out on a small square metal plate. It looked like a thick paste, deep red in color. Sir Aemilanus smoothed the paste out with a small brush and shaped it into a red circle.

Gaius returned, carrying the two frogs in a glass bowl.

Sir Aemilanus nodded at the table. "Just set them there."

Eldred lifted his chin, looking down at the red paste. "What will happen to me when I take that?"

Sir Aemilanus shook his head. "The paste is not for consumption. I will apply a portion of it on your fatum lapides."

"Could this give me the Bond?"

"They seem to think so. I expect this will just make your large bell louder. You and others are welcome to harbor fanciful hopes; it is of no concern to me."

"But I could manifest the Bond?"

Sir Aemilianus rolled his eyes. "Oh, that is all you heard, was it not? Yes, yes, you could. Though how you would be able to tell without another Deiran present is unclear to me."

Sir Aemilanus fanned the paste with his hand while he lightly blew on it. Then he applied the hot paste to each of Eldred's fatum lapides. After he was done, he straightened up to examine his handiwork. "Do not remove this until tomorrow evening. You do not want to wash away your hopes."

EXPLORING

The next morning Eldred rose with a burst of energy. He quickly donned a red tunic and black pants that he had been gifted by the people of Turicum, grabbed some pastries Marcia had left out for him and headed out for a walk.

As Eldred bounded out of his front door, Longinus stepped out of his house.

"Hold up, good sir. I must escort you."

"Is that truly necessary? I'm your envoy. Besides, where's Gaius?"

Longinus hurried over to Eldred. "He has an obligation this morning. Where are you headed? Are you visiting the expedition?"

"No, not today. I plan to wander through the city. That is, if an enemy can be allowed such freedom."

Longinus smiled awkwardly. "Sorry, sir. I was caught up in the moment."

Eldred narrowed his eyes. "So you don't actually think I personify your enemies? You seemed pretty certain at the time."

"Well, our peoples share a history of conflict. We are still in conflict to this day. But regarding you, personally, perhaps I was rash. Besides, if you look back further, we are the same people."

Eldred frowned. "What do you mean?"

Longinus stepped back. "Well, I mean we are the people of Regula. You were fashioned by the Night Mother, the same stone bearer. We have much in common."

"Do we?" Eldred paused. "I suppose we might have a tiny fragment in common. We left Boar's Tusk in Sammanus's company, not as a friend perhaps, but we didn't harm him. However, the Corporians who turned up on Lord Ferris's lands, I guess we were going to kill them. Well, if they weren't just some excuse Lord Ferris made up."

"Very interesting, sir. Shall we go?"

Eldred headed through the streets of Turicum, looking over everything as he went. The buildings were similar to those of Boar's Tusk, but better kept, painted and tidy, despite being mostly empty. Almost every house had a well tended garden, even the empty ones. Watching the people come and go, Eldred discerned that the occupied houses were more likely to be planted with a vegetable garden, while the abandoned ones sported flower beds, a point of reason to the Sun People.

Down by the harbor, Longinus explained that a hall with two enormous towers and an extended nave was the Hall of the Dead, the resting place for the dead citizens. A group of four citizens by the doors gave Eldred a frosty gaze as he walked up, which successfully diverted him from an inspection.

Past the hall, Eldred reached his destination, the destroyed house of Aquila, the dragon's most recent victim. Some citizens had raked the yard and gathered up the scattered stones in piles of similar sizes. Whatever rubbish had been there before was cleared away; even the red splotches on the kitchen floor had been wiped clean. A lingering scent remained, though it was faint compared to the odor at the wrecked hut to the north that had made Eldred sick.

Longinus stayed in the street as Eldred picked through the piles, turning the stones over. "What are you doing, sir?"

"Checking."

"Checking for what?"

"I'm not sure."

"I am not sure this is entirely proper, sir," said Longinus with a hint of irritation. "That is Aquila's house, even if she is dead."

Eldred groaned as he strained to push aside a particularly large stone. "If I worried about being proper by your standards, I couldn't leave my house." Eldred studied the revealed patch of dirt as he caught his breath.

"True enough, sir. But can we move on from here?"

"Not yet."

Longinus was no less perturbed when Eldred made his way a few blocks down the waterfront to the ruins of Drusus's house, which he had first visited with Sammanus. The site had received less attention than Aquila's; some bits of wood were still mixed in with the rocks, which mostly lay where the dragon had scattered them.

Longinus stood with his arms crossed as Eldred picked through the remnants of the house. "If you told me what you were looking for, I could assist you."

Eldred grunted. "That's fine."

"Is a fallen house so interesting? Sammanus told us many of the dwellings in the south are in poor repair, barely standing hovels he called them."

Eldred spread out a pile of rocks with his foot. "Not from dragon attacks."

"Which is what this was."

As Eldred edged away from the house's foundations, towards the back of the lot, he started to sniff. The scent was present. Eldred bent close to the ground, prowling through the rubbish, sniffing like a hound.

"What are you doing now, sir?"

Eldred nudged rocks and debris aside. The scent was strongest near a low stone wall that marked the boundary of the garden. Eldred knelt down and sifted through the grass. He found small bits of red glass sprinkled in among the stems of grass, worked halfway into the soil. Carefully picking up one on his finger, he sniffed it. The shard bore the odor.

"What is that, sir?" said Longinus as he came up alongside Eldred.

Eldred stood up and dusted off his knees. "Nothing. Nothing of interest."

Eldred walked past Longinus out to the waterfront. The three fishing boats were out again. "So the dragon crawled out of the water here, and attacked this house, killing Drusus, before returning to the sea?"

"That is correct, as you can see, sir."

"That's awfully convenient."

"What do you mean, sir?" said Longinus in an aggrieved tone. "I knew Drusus. For those of us that knew the young man, we consider it a tragedy."

"Of course. I only mean that if your city were to be attacked by a dragon, you came off better than you might expect."

"I don't know, sir. He was a good fellow."

"I suppose. And, for Aquila, her house is just across a square from the waterfront."

"True, but the dragon wandered the town before returning there. You witnessed the event from the Hall. Gaius told me."

Eldred nodded. "Yes. But it returned to destroy her house and—again—slipped off into the sea."

"Because we did not trouble it," said Longinus, as if explaining the situation to a child. "If we had swarmed out and attacked, it would have killed us all."

"A long trip just to eat one person? It does not seem like much of a meal for a dragon. Why not devour more people?"

"The dragon has eaten seven people, sir. The count is seven. As for its thoughts, who can fully understand the thinking of this creature? Sir Aemilanus holds that dragons primarily eat large sea mammals. I would not try to reason this out too much. Dragons do as dragons do."

Eldred glanced over the sea wall to scan the horizon. "I don't see any boats. How far out do they go?"

"As far as is needed, sir. Wherever the fish require."

Boats

That night Eldred felt restless and could not sleep. He had washed off the paste at sunset, but he still coursed with energy. He sat by his bedroom window and looked up and down the dark alley, which was deserted, except for the two houses across the street occupied by Gaius and Longinus. Longinus was awake, sitting at a table near his front window, reading a book.

As the evening wore on, Eldred gazed at the stars, a passing owl, and two cats that roamed the alley. Longinus's head jerked as he tried to stay awake. After a particularly large twitch, Longinus moved his reading lamp and retreated to a cushioned chair, where he promptly fell asleep.

A smile crossed Eldred's lips as he rose to his feet and leaned out the window into the brisk night air. The eaves were just above him. With a last look at Longinus, Eldred stepped on the windowsill and reached up to grab the edge of the roof and pulled himself up. The slate tiles were slick, but Eldred kept his footing and walked up to the crown of the roof, where he looked out on his surroundings.

The alley wound up a small hill. Seeking a better view, Eldred made his way up along the rooftops, jumping over the gap between each empty house, till he reached the roof of the topmost house. Clouds blocked the waxing crescent moon, leaving him shrouded in darkness as he looked over the city.

Small birds flitted about. An owl strutted atop the dome of the Hall of Ages, looking for its dinner. A few cats and one dog prowled the streets, but the citizens took their sleep. So it seemed, until Eldred noticed some activity down by the harbor.

He had a narrow view down a street to the large square before the Hall of the Dead. Citizens were stacking crates and barrels in the square, while others moved the containers over to the fishing boats, which were back in port. They took half an hour to load one of the boats, which then cast off.

Eldred watched for an hour as the boat exited the harbor and sailed out to sea.

The next morning, after only a few hours' rest, Eldred jogged down to the Hall of Dead with Gaius in pursuit. A few people glared at Eldred from the steps of the hall as he stopped to examine the square. All three boats were out.

As Eldred waited for Gaius to catch up, he was pleased to see Cnaeus arrive in front of one of the buildings, one of the Sun People who had competed in the lifting challenge and had later been skipped for the sparring.

"Cnaeus! Hold up!" called Eldred.

Cnaeus paused as he went to open the door and looked over to Gaius, who had just arrived, out of breath, and stood with his hands on his knees.

"What do you want?" asked Cnaeus.

Eldred gestured at the building. "What do you do here? Is this your place of business?"

"Uhh, yes," answered Cneaus.

"Excellent. Will you show me around?"

Cnaeus looked to Gaius, but he was still panting. "I suppose."

Cnaeus briskly escorted Eldred and Gaius through the building, which was a storage facility for the city, containing room after room of supplies. Boxes, crates, bags and barrels filled each cavernous room. They ended up in the storage room closest to the water, near an assortment of barrels and coarsely woven brown sacks.

Cnaeus opened a large door facing the water. "When this was a functioning port, they would load and unload the ships right out here."

"What did you have to trade?"

"Mostly grain and beef," said Cnaeus.

"And what would you get?" asked Eldred.

Cnaeus tilted his head. "All manner of things. We might receive goat cheeses from the Corporians in Berisamo or Pergamon wine from Chalcis."

"You don't anymore?"

"No, no one trades with us now," said Cnaeus in a resigned tone. "Not since Regula became your Night Mother."

"But you still have your wares?" said Eldred.

"The portion of it we need. We don't need as much grain now, but we still harvest the fields. Likewise, with beef."

Eldred put his hand on a barrel. "What's in this?"

"That is wine, Chalcis wine."

"I thought you didn't trade anymore?"

"That wine is two hundred years old."

Eldred frowned. "Wine can't keep that long in barrels."

Cnaeus crossed his arms and fixed Eldred with an angry stare. "I am sure not in some shoddily fashioned Deiran barrel. It would rot within a year. But this wine was packed in barrels blessed by Korinna, stone bearer of the Moon People. This wine will be a delight long after you are dead."

"Perhaps it is time we left Cnaeus to his work?" suggested Gaius.

"Yes, please do," said Cnaeus.

REVIEW

That afternoon, Eldred and Gaius returned to the Hall of Ages and met with Sir Aemilanus in his study at the top of the tower.

Sir Aemilanus settled Eldred in a chair by the window and carried out his inspection. "The color of each of the fatum lapides appears deeper. Have you observed any difference in how you feel?"

Eldred took a deep breath and smiled. "Both yesterday and this morning I felt strong."

"Has anything changed with your vision?"

"No."

"Hmm, I should have measured that, created a baseline."

"Measured my vision?"

"Yes," said Sir Aemilanus. "Well, on the positive side, you suffered no deleterious effects from the treatment. We will have to wait and see whether you surface the Bond."

"I feel better. We should try another treatment right away."

Sir Aemilanus raised his eyebrow. "Perhaps next year."

Eldred glanced around the room. "What about the portion that was left?"

Sir Aemilanus walked over to stand next to Gaius, on the other side of a nearby table. "I shared the remainder with the appropriate citizens."

Eldred gestured at the corridors of shelves. "Don't you have the ingredients to make another batch?"

"I do, but we must make them last. I will brew another treatment next year. If we still enjoy the great honor of having you as our envoy, perhaps you will receive some small measure."

"You should give it to me now," insisted Eldred.

Sir Aemilanus looked over sharply. "I think not."

"Do not be demanding, Eldred," said Gaius.

Eldred rose to his feet and walked to the table, leaning on it with his hands. "I'm being sensible. If I had the Bond, I would be king. If I were king, I could change the covenant, or even end the covenant. You and your people could return to Regillium or stay here, whatever you liked. You could increase your numbers. It wouldn't matter to me."

Sir Aemilanus shook his head. "You report feeling stronger. That speaks to your Mercian nature, not your Deiran aspects. As with your eyesight, we have no indication that the Bond has grown any stronger. If you were to meet with your comrades and experienced the Bond, that would make a more compelling case for expending our precious resources."

Eldred rubbed his chin. "I'm supposed to be here. They're not expecting me up at the lodge."

"How unfortunate," said Sir Aemilanus without emotion. "Given our limited supply of Balaur powder, I am disinclined to invest more on this venture. We have already wasted more than enough on you."

"You can make more powder once the dragon is killed," said Eldred.

Sir Aemilanus gave a thin smile. "Only if the dragon is actually slain. Your own assessment suggests that is an unlikely outcome."

"Is there a smaller dragon somewhere?" asked Eldred.

Sir Aemilanus leaned on the table, mirroring Eldred. "Oh, now you are in the business of murdering dragons?"

"Yes. Isn't that why you requested we come?"

"We did, but only regarding a dragon that was attacking us."

"So you wouldn't want the powder from a young dragon?" asked Eldred.

Sir Aemilanus shook his head. "We respect the creations of Regula. We are not savage killers. Not like some people."

"You should use your powder on me. If I am your king, your problems disappear; no more counting."

Sir Aemilanus frowned. "You would never be our king. You would—at best—be the Deiran king."

Gaius glanced at Sir Aemilanus. "Still, an end to the counting, that would be a welcome change."

"I won't be king unless I manifest the Bond," said Eldred.

"If we knew that the treatment would work, I might agree," allowed Sir Aemilanus. "But the treatment will likely just make you a more robust failure as a Deiran. If we waste our resources to achieve such an outcome, we would pay a heavy price, an unthinkable price."

"What about the other dragon?" asked Gaius.

"What other dragon?" said Sir Aemilanus.

"The last one, the one the Maldavians dispatched," exclaimed Gaius.

Sir Aemilanus gave an exasperated sigh. "That was years ago, and we never reached the corpse."

Gaius gestured at Eldred. "Perhaps he could."

Sir Aemilanus made a face. "What would even be left now? All dead things rot."

"He might find something to harvest, perhaps enough to provide some treatments for himself or even enough to treat the city elders," said Gaius.

Sir Aemilanus looked Eldred up and down. "It would be dangerous. We would likely be putting our cherished diplomat at risk for a bag of slime."

"It's worth the risk," said Eldred.

YESTERDAY S DRAGON

Two days later, on a cool, cloudy day, Eldred ventured out from Turicum in the company of Gaius and Sammanus and headed along the coast in a north-westerly direction. Sammanus took the lead while Eldred followed on Hobbie, trailed by Gaius.

"This is a fool's outing," said Sammanus.

"We will not know till he checks the cave," said Gaius.

Sammanus glanced at Eldred. "Can you do it? Can you harvest whatever is left of its brain?"

Eldred nodded. "Sir Aemilanus showed me the steps."

Sammanus pursed his lips. "You should have informed your companions of your plans. Should an unfortunate event overtake you, I have serious concerns regarding how they may respond."

Eldred gave a small smile as he looked out over the ocean below the cliffs. "I doubt Lord Vance would even ask after me."

"Perhaps not," said Sammanus. "But this seems rash. And even if he does not care about you, your people are always looking for some excuse to torment us."

"For as much as the covenant limits you, it also protects you. They're not allowed to kill you without just cause." Eldred shrugged. "So the cave. You were there that day, forty-three years ago?"

"I was," said Sammanus quietly.

"You must have been a boy," said Eldred.

"I was younger, to be sure," allowed Sammanus.

"And that dragon attacked your city as well?"

"It did."

"Your people have bad luck with dragons."

Sammanus gave a curt nod. "A fair assessment."

"They say it was forty Maldavian warriors," said Eldred.

"Yes, far more than the five lords on the present expedition. I escorted forty-two warriors to the cave. Only four came out. One of those died within the hour."

"They would not go back in for your ingredients?"

"No, not even for their own dead," said Sammanus with a frown. "They broke camp and rode south the same day."

"And nobody has been back? Not you nor the Maldavians?"

"Not us," said Sammanus. "We discussed going. Sir Aemilanus wanted more than its brain. He wanted its bones. If you can navigate the passage, you can depend upon him trying to convince you to ferry out every last scale."

Eldred laughed. "That would make a more impressive display than Balbina. She is barely larger than a dog."

"Some respect, please, sir," said Gaius. "She has been in the hall for more than five hundred years."

"Perhaps the Maldavians returned later on one of the counts," mused Eldred.

"That is possible, though I doubt they would have had either the means or any interest in harvesting the dragon's brain," said Sammanus.

Eldred patted Hobbie's neck, a hopeful smile across his face. "We'll soon see."

CLIFFS

Two hours turned into three as they rode along cliffs overlooking the sea. Sammanus stopped several times thinking they had reached their destination, only to mount up again and press further down the coast. Finally, he spotted a narrow track that descended towards the water and called for the others to stop.

Eldred dismounted and surveyed the barren windswept hills leading off from the cliffs. "Someone should stay with the horses. I won't have my Hobbie falling victim to a wolf."

Gaius smiled. "I understand why you would dwell on the recent tragic occurrence, but I must emphasize that wolf attacks are extremely rare."

"Not that rare. The expedition was attacked twice."

Gauis shaded his eyes while he made a cursory study of the landscape. "Do you see any wolves?"

Eldred narrowed his eyes. "No. But someone should stay."

Gaius sighed and gave a slight shrug. "Very well. I will stay up top. I can chase off the fearsome pack if need be."

Eldred gave Gaius a blank look and started moving his supplies from the saddlebags into a backpack.

Sammanus stuck his sword in behind his saddle. "You should leave your blades here if you want to keep them out of the salt water."

"That's the final stretch, the passage," said Eldred.

"We will get soaked just getting through the mouth of the cave."

"Then I'll find a spot near there."

Sammanus led the way down the narrow path. The uphill side of the path was smooth chalky stone, with few grips. Downhill, the slope was covered with grass, but steep, and led to a sheer drop to the rocks and surf below.

"Why am I always with him?" asked Eldred.

Sammanus paused to look back. "What?"

Eldred wore a sour expression. "I'm always with Gaius—or his idiot brother."

"Oh, well, that is as it must be. You have to be accompanied by a minder. You agreed."

"But why them? I never see you, or Opimia, or even Valens."

"We each serve our role. This engagement suits Gaius's skills."

"When I go out in the town, nobody greets me."

Sammanus reached a point where the path had washed away. He carefully stepped over a three-foot gap, clutching a root that dangled down from the rock above.

Eldred waited for him to clear the spot and casually stepped over the drop. "It's rude."

Sammanus eased forward, taking small steps. "We have both sampled the hospitality of each other's people. You have a fine house, fine meals, fine clothes. Nobody calls you 'Wretched' or other names."

"But I'm helping you. If I get the Bond, I can end the count. Everyone acts as if I'm the enemy. You heard what Longinus said."

Sammanus raised an eyebrow. "Perhaps the citizens consider your interest in gaining the Bond primarily a matter of self-interest. In any case, this outing might aid your cause. If you scrounge up sufficient material and Sir Aemilanus extracts enough powder of Balaur to share, the citizens will appreciate your effort. They could grow more friendly."

"They should," said Eldred in a plaintive tone.

Sammanus pointed to the base of the cliff. A hundred yards ahead, the cave opening showed, halfway submerged.

The path petered out on a dusty ledge a hundred feet above the water. Sammanus stood at the edge, rubbing his hands and studying the rock face below.

"I do not remember it like this," said Sammanus.

"Is this the wrong cave?"

"No, it is the right place. The climb seems more difficult."

"You're an old man now."

"True."

Sammanus lowered himself over the edge and started down. Eldred removed his swords. He studied each blade a moment before leaning them against a rock.

Sammanus inched his way down the rocky face, considering each move with a wrinkled brow. At a sheer point, thirty feet above the water, he clung tightly to the rock face, searching desperately for his next move. Finally, he looked up and licked his lips. "It's eroded, impassable. We must go back."

Eldred gripped a hold with one hand and leaned out, looking down the cliff at the crashing waves below. "Oh, for Mother's sake. Just move to your left. There are plenty of holds just a few steps over. I'll show you." Eldred started to climb down.

"No, stay back! I will go, but do not crowd me."

Eldred laughed.

Sammanus glared up, with hard-set gray eyes. After a few deep breaths, he sidestepped along the narrow ledge, passing across a stretch of smooth rock with no solid holds. When he reached a spot where the ledge widened, he stuck his trembling hand in a groove and rested.

"You can just step down from there. I see plenty of foot holds."

Sammanus took a ragged breath. "Fine. Fine."

From there, the route grew easier. Sammanus descended until he was just above the crashing waves and scrambled along the spray-soaked rocks to the lip of the cave. He paused for a moment, glancing back at Eldred, before dropping eight feet down into the water, and paddling into the cave, carried by the waves.

Eldred blew out his breath. The damp air was already cold enough, but the sides of the cave offered no purchase. Eldred jumped.

CAVE

The cave was neither especially deep nor high, rising only fifteen feet above the water and going only fifty feet back to a wall that was pounded by each crashing wave. Up ahead, Sammanus made his way to a jutting rock in the center of the cave; everything else was underwater.

Sammanus panted as he pulled himself up onto the rock. Eldred followed and clambered up after him. After a brief respite where Sammanus just stood and breathed, he pointed at a spot along the wall.

"You have to go through there."

"Through where?"

Sammanus shivered. "A passage opens up, or at least it used to. You have to wade over by the back wall and then dive under. The Maldavians said it was sixty feet back to the chamber."

"They all made it though? Right?"

"Yes, the dragon killed them. It is freezing. Do not dawdle."

Eldred edged back into the cold water and found his way up on a knee-deep underwater ledge along the back wall. As he splashed around in frustration, he looked up to see Sammanus motioning him to the side. He couldn't hear Sammanus over the noise of the surf. As he walked on, the shelf dropped sharply into a pool that was partly sheltered by the ledge.

Eldred stood hip deep in the water, taking deep breaths and studying the darkness below him. The passage was there, wide enough for the dragon. Sixty feet back. Eldred grimaced. He was not the strongest swimmer, but if forty Maldavians had made it, he could too.

One final breath, and he went, diving deep and swimming as fast as he could. The ceiling of the passage spurred him onward. Almost immediately, the ground sloped up. After a few more strokes, Eldred was standing up in a long narrow cavern. The chamber was not sixty feet down the passage; it was more like fifteen feet.

Eldred smiled. "They lied."

The ceiling rose forty feet above the cavern floor, which extended a few hundred feet from the pool where Eldred stood. The walls and floor were damp. In the center of the chamber lay the remains of the dragon, surrounded by piles of debris.

Not much remained of the Maldavians; just fragments of skull and hip bones. Everything else had dissolved into slight discolorations on the wet stones. Rusted swords and helmets crumbled at the touch of Eldred's finger.

The dragon's carcass had withstood the rigors of time much better. Forty feet long, covered in green scales, it looked fresh, except for its enormous head that rested on its side, mouth agape. The eyes had rotted out and the tongue had the look of old leather. Eldred sniffed. There was a rancid odor, not unbearable, but not pleasant either.

Eldred ran his hand over the scales on the dragon's left shoulder. They were smooth to the touch. Eldred crinkled up his face and squeezed the dragon's left front leg, but he could not shift it. After several failed attempts to budge the leg, Eldred scouted across the cave floor till he found a loose rock. He pounded the leg a dozen times until the rock disintegrated. The scales showed not the merest scratch.

Eldred walked the length of the body, vainly searching for a gap in its scaly armor or a sign of damage. Even the tip of the tail was covered in a mosaic of green scales. He found a jagged stone, knelt down by the tail and struck it repeatedly, but the scales were impervious.

Eldred approached the top of the dragon's head. After examining the blackened residue in the left eye socket, he struck the left eye socket with the stone. The dragon's head rocked under the impact, but the socket remained undamaged. Eldred furiously beat the socket. After his blows, Eldred scraped out the dried mess with his fingers, only to find smooth unbroken bone.

Eldred issued an annoyed grunt. "How did you die?"

The dragon's head was on its side with the mouth open, a two-foot gap between its upper and lower fangs. The upper fangs were more than a foot long.

Eldred set down his pack and dug out the rods that Sir Aemilanus had given him, which he used to widen the gap between its jaws. Taking a scoop, some sample bags and a pick, he carefully stepped into the dragon's mouth where the concentrated stench made him gag. He dug a wet cloth out of his pocket and covered his nose and mouth. While it helped, each minute in the rotted mouth took an act of will.

The dragon's gums were dry and blackened. Traces of metal and bone lodged between its teeth marked the fate of unfortunate warriors. A small dagger dug in between two fangs caught Eldred's eye. Its pristine appearance suggested a blessed weapon. Eldred tried to work it free with the pick, but the position of the dragon's teeth hampered his efforts and the blade was stuck in the bone. Disappointed, Eldred set to the work at hand.

Eldred hunched over and started picking at the dragon's palate. Progress was slow. If he struck too hard, the head rocked and set the teeth in dangerous motion. With patient effort, he worked through the leathery flesh and dug through the bone that encased the underside of its skull. At last, a foul smelling liquid oozed out, running down the pick handle onto his fingers. Eldred shuddered, but persevered and turned the drip into a steady stream, splashing down on the floor.

Eldred filled a sample bag until the discharge slowed to a trickle. He sealed the bag tightly, then used the pick to hook the skull and tilt it up, pouring out more of the dragon's watery remains. After filling three bags, nothing more came. He scraped up the slop on the ground with the scoop, filling the last bag a quarter full before stepping out of the dragon's mouth. The comparatively fresh air of the cavern brought a smile of relief to his face. Eldred packed his samples and walked back to the pool.

As he rinsed his hands and face, he kept looking back at the dragon. It lay there motionless, a weak guardian. Setting the pack down, he pulled out the pick and returned to the dragon's mouth. The rods still held the jaws apart.

Back inside the mouth, hunched over the dagger, it seemed to glow faintly, just a trace of light. It had to be blessed, a gift from some long dead Maldavian. Tiny, careful taps with the pick failed to dislodge it. The dagger was stuck. He could not grab it; the fangs prevented him. It would take something more. Eldred struck harder and harder. Finally, a wild swing knocked the dagger loose but struck a fang.

Eldred watched as the dagger slid across the ground, revealing a broken blade, mired with rust. Not blessed! Absent-mindedly, he wiped a drop of wetness on his right cheek with the back of his left hand. He was still staring at the dagger when he realized something was wrong. The skin on his hand was burning. His cheek felt like fire.

Eldred screamed and ran for the pool. He splashed his face and thrashed his hand under the water, but he could not bring himself to examine the skin. He felt a lurching sensation in his gut. His feet were slipping out from under him.

Eldred grabbed the pack and dove into the pool, swimming erratically, bumping the sides of the channel, choking on water, before erupting from the surface in the sea cave. His vision narrowed as he staggered up onto the underwater shelf and sank down against the wall, water halfway up his chest, clutching the pack in front of him.

Sammanus was yelling something, but Eldred could not understand the words. Sammanus paddled over. What a funny way to swim. The waves rocked Eldred, knocking his shoulders against the rock. The water felt warm as he shut his eyes.

SURVIVAL

Eldred became aware of pain, a white-hot pain lancing through the back of his left hand. He lay in agony, unable to shift or bend or twist or speak. He suffered. As he endured, he heard voices.

A man's voice, an older man. "The powder should be having some effect now. Odd to be using it like this."

A younger woman's voice. "It looks terrible. The bones are showing."

The man chuckled. "Now that I applied the powder, you can just lay the graft on top; no stitching necessary. I do not care for the expense, but this is a most interesting case. Help me turn him over."

After some grunting and bumping sounds, Eldred felt a knife dig in, cutting into his rear. Fresh pain.

The man's voice. "Not so deep; we need a thin layer. We will practice on the hand first, before you try the face."

"His skin is tough."

"Tougher than deer hide with the same thickness. I discovered as much when I cut away the dead flesh, a surprising deviation from the Mercians I dissected in the past. We should perform a thorough analysis, but I believe we will find the answer in the dermis. I examined a sample with my lenses and found unusual knots of collagen distributed in a grid-like pattern."

"How could he develop an improvement if Regula is gone?" asked the woman.

"It can happen naturally, but do not discount his three fatum lapides. He is not your typical stupid Mercian. He is blessed with an abundance of wasted potential. Still, it is a surprising development. Perhaps someone down south has some meager knowledge regarding the art of shaping."

Pain radiated as Eldred felt the skin on his rear peeling back.

"Go further and take extra material. He has plenty to spare, and we need a single unbroken piece."

"Of course."

"Now, help me flip him back."

There was more grunting.

"You would think he would lose everything from the elbow down with these injuries," said the woman.

"Yes, so it appears, but we can save this Mercian's hand. It only requires half a packet of the powder of Balaur. A triumph for medicine, considering the circumstances, but I am not convinced of the benefits. He keeps his hand to what end? To steal? To strike someone in the face? Choking? Definitely choking. Any Mercian with a strong grip will seize the opportunity to squeeze the life out of someone."

The woman tittered.

"Well placed," said the man. "That is exactly right. Now smooth the skin while it forms a bond with the paste."

A vision swam in front of Eldred of the back of someone's hand, smeared with blood, covered with a flap of pale skin. A finger traced the edges of the flap, keeping it taut.

"Should I bandage his buttocks?"

"No need. The sheets are already a mess. You did fine work today. We will work on his face tomorrow."

Eldred caught sight of the woman. She was young for a citizen, and thin even for the Sun People. Her arms were like rails. There was someone behind her on a table, wrapped in sheets. A heavy man, lying still. The pain in his hand faded and his sight dissolved into black squares.

·)̣·

Sir Aemilanus stood next to Sammanus. They were talking; at least, their mouths were moving, but Eldred heard nothing. Eldred was looking down at them from above. As Eldred focused, their words came through.

Sammanus shook his head. "By your own description, the surgery was not a success."

"Well, you need to bear in mind that he is alive, which is altogether improbable. The man I received into my care had but the narrowest chance of survival." Sir Aemilanus pointed to something in front of him. "He will live."

Sammanus raised his hands. "And I am certain the outcome is spectacular in that regard. But she sent me over because she has other uses for him. Her plans depend on him having a certain degree of charisma. You must concede that his current appearance poses a serious obstacle in this regard."

Sir Aemilanus sighed. "And I have explained, as I will explain again, that I have already spent two of our packets getting him to this state. Given what we are dealing with, nothing short of the powder is going to make a substantial difference at this point. Is she suggesting I use more? Are any citizens so worried about his facial features that they would willingly give up their own treatments in order to make him less repugnant?"

"I am merely passing on her request. She has it in her mind he is the key to the short way."

"Huh, all of that is a mistake. The long way is the only way. We all fail, but they will fail sooner. We can depend on that."

"She desires to return, as do many of us," said Sammanus.

"Regillium has its charm, but so does Turicum. And we are the fortunate ones, in case anyone has forgotten."

Sammanus crossed his arms. "You always know best, but on this occasion she has not sent me here to debate you—a fool's errand at the best of times. I am merely passing on her request. He must have a passable appearance. How you accomplish this, by whatever miraculous invention or brilliant discovery, is for you to work out. We all appreciate your effort on this matter, which is of the utmost importance. If, in the end, you determine you need to use more powder, you will have the full support of the council."

Sir Aemilanus seethed as he glared at the floor. "This is madness." As Sir Aemilanus started to curse, the men faded into the distance.

·)·

A man was climbing stairs, passing through shadows and muttering. Eldred could not catch his words. He paused on a landing and grabbed the banister, waiting to catch his breath. He waited, and waited and waited. Very dull. The borders of space around the man started to fade and dim, Eldred was turning away. But then the man set forward again and tugged Eldred's attention after him, like a bird tied on a string.

Up the man went, climbing the next flight of stairs, grabbing the railing with each step. His muttering grew louder as he walked out into a vast room, full of shelves and tables. The man did not look up. He turned to the left, and walked down a narrow aisle of shelves stuffed with half-full glass jars and small wooden boxes. At the end of the shelf, he reached up into a potted green fern and sifted through the dry leaves covering the dirt. He pulled something out.

Walking on, he knelt by a black iron box that came up chest high. He inserted a key—he had found a key in the pot—and turned it to the left, before spinning a silver lever three times around. The iron box opened. There, on a small shelf, sat a black square plate with six square woven packets.

The man huffed as he selected a packet and shut the door. Eldred's vision faded away into the blackness of the door.

·)⁖

A statue of a golden lion adorned a table by the window. The light in the room made it glow, showing every detail down to its finely wrought teeth. As Eldred focused on the statue, he became aware of a thin man standing in the room with his back turned. The man seemed frail, unimportant. The man alternated gazing at the lion, or out the window, or sometimes at his feet.

Then she arrived. Her gray eyes radiated power.

"It's done," said the man.

The woman's voice was soft but commanding. "Properly done?"

The man nodded. "Satisfactory, given what I had to work with. We just need to wait."

"For how long?"

"Perhaps a few days. We can move him from the Hall. I do not need him there, nor do I want him."

"Very well, Gaius can monitor him."

"You are making a mistake. You want it too much."

The woman laughed softly. "If you want nothing, you may as well not exist."

The man held out his hands. "We should wait. Nobody can wait longer than you can."

"Sound council, as always, I am sure. But this is not a matter of natural order. There will never come a time when we can easily assert our rights. We have foes we have not yet met, enemies whose abilities we might never guess. We cannot wait indefinitely."

"If we move too soon—"

"I choose the short way!"

Her words knocked Eldred away.

AWAKENING

Eldred cracked his eyes open. Gaius sat across the room from him reading a book. Eldred scanned the room. He was in Turicum, in his bed. He was alive! Reluctantly, his eyes moved to his left hand, which lay across his chest. A discolored patch of skin covered the back of his hand. Eldred's eyes grew wet as he moved his fingers. His hand was hideous. Cautiously, Eldred reached up to touch his right cheek. There was skin. It felt like rough, dry skin. But how did it look?

"You are awake, sir," said Gaius.

"Yes," said Eldred weakly. The movement of his lips and tongue felt strange.

"Do you understand me?"

"I do."

"That was a concern for everyone, especially for Sir Aemilanus. We were not certain how the dragon venom would impact your ability to think."

Eldred stared blankly at Gaius.

"How do you feel, sir? Are you hungry? It is late, but I can ask Marcia to make you a batch of cakes."

"Cakes—cakes are good. Where is Opimia?"

"Opimia? She has not been here."

"I heard her speaking," insisted Eldred in a wispy voice.

Gaius paused. "I do not think you would have, sir. Although she has asked after you, she has not come to see you."

"Sir Aemilanus?"

"Yes, Sir Aemilanus has been by repeatedly. He has managed your treatment. He will be quite pleased to learn of your progress."

Eldred blinked. "He was arguing with Opimia, or was he arguing with Sammanus?"

"What? I do not think he would, sir. What makes you say that?"

"I saw it. I heard them," said Eldred, getting louder. "She wanted him to use more powder. He said—it was a waste."

"A dream, sir?" suggested Gaius. "You just woke up now for the first time, did you not?"

Eldred yawned. His mouth tasted sour. "I saw something."

"Regarding Sir Aemilanus, he saved you. It was quite amazing. He journeyed out of the town for the first time in many years. He treated you right at the top of the cliffs. Valens and Avitus carried you up, no easy feat considering your girth. And Sammanus wrestled you out of the water onto a rock. He rode back to town, while I watched you in the cave. So we all lent our assistance, sir."

Eldred placed his hand back on his cheek. It felt scaly. "Thank you," he muttered.

"You are most welcome, sir. But, above all others, it is Sir Aemilanus you must thank. He has been treating you for twelve days."

Eldred turned away.

"Should I see about the cakes, sir?"

"Yes, thank you."

Once Gaius had been gone for a few minutes, Eldred slowly slid to the edge of the bed and placed his feet on the floor. As he reached for his robe, Eldred once again found himself examining his left hand. It looked like dead dried up skin. Eldred grimaced and walked unsteadily to a chair at the table near the window.

After some time, Gaius returned carrying a plate of flat cakes. "You moved, sir. You really must be feeling better. I sent Longinus to fetch Sir Aemilanus."

Eldred nodded and started to clumsily slather the cakes with jam.

"Will you be wanting more, sir?"

Eldred studied the morsel on his fork. "I don't know. I don't know if I can eat."

"Very well, sir."

Eldred was finishing the plate of flat cakes when Sir Aemilanus and Longinus arrived.

"So how is our patient this evening?" asked Sir Aemilanus jovially.

Eldred frowned.

"Are you feeling unwell?" said Sir Aemilanus.

"Can you get me a hand mirror?" asked Eldred.

"A mirror, of course. Gaius, does Eldred have a mirror in his residence?"

"I have one at my lodgings across the alley. I will fetch it right away."

They waited in silence for Gaius's return. He handed a finely crafted silver mirror to Eldred, who grasped it tentatively.

Sir Aemilanus walked behind Eldred as Eldred gazed silently at his reflection, lips pressed tightly together. A layer of unnaturally pale skin covered much of his right cheek.

Sir Aemilanus pointed over Eldred's shoulder. "The pale patch, that is where I had to replace your skin. Dragon's venom kills whatever it touches. When I first saw you by the cliffs, I thought you were too far gone, a rare error on my part. You pulled through in robust fashion."

"What's on my face?" whispered Eldred.

"Your skin; it came from you. It is pale, but perfectly serviceable. Addressing the damage to your face accounted for much of the time we spent in my surgical parlor. You were fortunate, just a trifle more venom and there would have been nothing I could do."

Eldred's hand shook as he studied his reflection. "This is how it will remain?"

"Yes, this is your face. In my view, you look much the same as you did before. In time, the coloring should match better, though I expect you will always have this outline on your cheek. Fortunately, you are not overly dependent on your appearance. In any case, how did you get venom on your face? I have been wondering since I treated you at the cliffs."

Eldred thought about the dagger as he set down the mirror. "I don't recall. What about the samples? Did you make the powder for me?"

"A work in progress. I have been focused on your care. They might produce a small portion of Balaur powder, but—unfortunately—I needed far more than you provided to heal you to your present state."

"More powder could finish the healing and could help me get the Bond."

"You should regard yourself as already healed. On the matter of the Bond, consider our effort complete. You have already consumed many years worth of our supplies."

Eldred clasped his hands together and looked up at the ceiling. "You first used up two packets, leaving you with six. Then, you used more. That's what I saw."

Sir Aemilanus stepped back. "That is an odd thing to say."

"You used more because Opimia ordered you to."

"What a strange conjecture."

Gaius stepped closer. "He had dreams. He told me he dreamt you and Opimia were arguing."

"Did he?" said Sir Aemilanus.

Eldred shook his head. "No. I wasn't dreaming. Did she order it?"

"Nobody orders me about. I am a member of the council."

Eldred frowned. "What about a Maldavian lining you up for the count?"

Sir Aemilanus jerked upright and glowered at Eldred. "I stand corrected. That is an occasion where every citizen of Turicum is obliged to do as they are directed. Well, you seem to have fully regained your wits, such as they are. I am beyond grateful my ministrations have brought you back to such an excellent state of health. You have clearly completed your recovery and no longer warrant my care. Farewell."

Gaius reached for Sir Aemilanus's arm. "I am sure Eldred—"

Sir Aemilanus waved him off. "No, I am quite through. What a senseless waste." He stormed out of the room with Longinus trailing after him.

Gaius shook his head. "What are you doing, sir? You must know by now the citizens of Turicum do not care to discuss the counts."

"I was merely making a point—and I can end those counts once I am king," said Eldred tiredly. "Opimia ordered him to use the packets."

"I do not understand, sir. That was quite rude. Elders on the council should be treated with respect. Of all people, I would have thought you would have more gratitude, considering what he did for you. I wonder if anyone— anywhere—could have healed you to such an apparently functional state."

Eldred glared back through half-lidded eyes. "I'm grateful, but I do not care for lies."

ATTACK

Eldred woke the next day to the distant roar of the dragon. He stirred from the bed and lurched to the window. The sun was high in the sky, almost midday. After a moment, another cry came from the direction of the harbor, on the other side of the city. Eldred held onto the window sill and glanced back at his bed.

Longinus came out to his door across the alley and waved to Eldred, then disappeared back inside his house. A moment later, Longinus ran across the street carrying a basket. Eldred was still standing at the window when Longinus knocked on the bedroom door.

Eldred settled at the table by the window. "Come in."

Longinus burst through the door, holding out the basket in front of him. "Marcia left this for you."

Eldred peeled back the cloth covering the basket to find a plate of slightly warm cakes along with a jar of jam.

Longinus smiled. "Your favorite."

Eldred gestured towards the window. "The dragon is here."

"Quite far away. We are safe."

"But it's come to eat someone. Who's down there? Who's still living by the harbor?"

"We will see what happens. Eat your breakfast, or lunch, rather. We can see what has happened once the dragon goes. I can send for your horse, if you need."

"Don't bother Hobbie," said Eldred, taking a breath. "I can walk."

Longinus fidgeted as Eldred ate. The roar of the dragon subsided. An occasional crashing noise echoed through the city.

After a few moments of silence, Longinus tossed some clothes on the bed. "It must be done. You should come and check. The count will be higher now."

Eldred trailed after Longinus as they made their way across Turicum. Thirty minutes had passed since Eldred had heard anything. A few people were out. Eldred ignored them and focused on his steps, keeping his balance. He didn't feel weak, just unsteady. He felt like his body was the wrong size, as if more was stuffed inside his skin than belonged.

The scene was familiar—a destroyed house across from the water with a crowd of citizens sifting through the ruins. The same pungent scent hung in the air. Eldred sat on a rock wall across the street and watched them search for their precious notes. When someone found them, they scattered to deliver them.

Gaius came across the street with Longinus. "Good afternoon, sir."

Eldred gestured at the destruction across the way. "Is it?"

"No, of course not," said Gaius. "But a disaster is no excuse to abandon courtesy."

"Whose turn was it this time?" asked Eldred.

Gaius clasped his hands behind his back. "Several people lived in the house. We need to confirm, since some could have been out, given the time of day, but judging from the notes, it seems that no fewer than six citizens perished, bringing the total count to thirteen."

"What were their names?"

"Cassian, Titiana, Porcia, Aelia, Domita and Ahenobarbus," said Longinus.

Eldred narrowed his brows. "Ahenobarbus, the sprinter?"

Gaius nodded.

"He should've run," said Eldred. "They all lived there, in the same house?"

"Yes," said Gaius.

"They were a family?"

"They were related," said Gaius.

"And they didn't spread out? They stayed in the same house by the harbor? They didn't have any other houses?"

"Unfortunately, that is the case. The count is thirteen," said Gaius.

Eldred shook his head. Across the street, the citizens piled up rocks. Eldred stood up and looked out to sea.

"They were out again," muttered Eldred.

Gaius raised an eyebrow. "What, sir?"

"Your boats. All of your boats are out, far out, some miles out. I don't see any of them."

"Yes, quite observant of you."

The brothers followed Eldred as he crossed the street and carefully made his way through the milling citizens. The scent was strongest in the center of the ruin. Streaks of blood ran across the stones. Eldred stiffly stooped down and sniffed the ground. Hortensius and another young man came up and started mopping up the blood.

Gaius came alongside Eldred. "Are you looking for something, sir?"

Eldred shook his head.

"If you are ready for lunch, Longinus can escort you back. But only if you are done checking. Are you done, sir?" said Gaius.

Eldred glanced up towards Galla's Mound. "I should ride up and speak with the lords."

"They are not there, sir. Calvus spotted them riding north ten days ago. Nobody has seen them since."

"Do they know I was injured?"

"No, sir," said Gaius. "We planned to wait until you were better. We were concerned regarding how they—how they might take the news."

Longinus smiled his normal smile, but something in his eyes suggested a hint of menace. "You are on your own, sir."

Eldred gazed blankly at Longinus. His left leg trembled slightly as he straightened up. "Just lunch, then."

THE DEAD

The next morning, Eldred rose late and took a leisurely breakfast. After a bath, he set out for a walk accompanied by Longinus.

After a meandering stroll through the city, he ended up at the Hall of Ages, standing for an hour in front of the exhibit of his people. They made a mournful sight, their bones trapped in a timeless world, barely stirred by Eldred's passage. Bugs had stripped the flesh from the Maldavian maiden. She could be Eldred's relative. A table next to the Deiran boy displayed a small knife and two wooden dice, his belongings. Did he put up a fight? The Mercian skeleton topped Eldred by three inches. Eldred gazed approvingly at the rusted sword lying by his feet. Longinus stood meekly across the hall by the door.

Everything else on display was an animal. Even the celebrated Balbina was a mere animal. They were a woman, a boy and a man. Whatever else had happened, they had not volunteered to stand in the Mother forsaken hall for eternity. They were not birds, or dogs or cats. They were people, people as dear and private as anyone.

Eldred turned and marched towards Longinus through the pack of skeletons. "I'm going to the Hall of the Dead."

"I am not sure—"

"I am!"

Longinus hung back thirty feet as Eldred strode through the streets. Eldred tried a new route, one which he thought would lead right to the hall.

On the way, he came across a squat single-story building with a pair of crossed swords inscribed above the door. He stopped, envisioning racks of ancient blades blessed by the Night Mother.

Past an unlocked door, he entered an empty room with worn flagstones. A few crates and chairs circled a practice area. Some wide shelves held what appeared to be the wooden swords and shields used when he sparred with the citizens. Two swords and a shield had been tossed on the floor in a corner, apart from the others. One of the swords was of a darker hue.

Eldred cast an irritated look at Longinus, who lingered by the door. "Are these my weapons?"

"You are not allowed arms in the city, sir. The agreement is quite clear."

"I'm not taking them. I'm asking if these are the weapons I used."

Longinus shrugged. "I do not know, sir. Does it matter if they are?"

Eldred huffed. "Well, I find it odd you would throw these on the floor when your armory is so barren." Eldred pointed at the darker sword. "That might be the best sword in Turicum. It certainly is the winningest."

"If you say so, sir."

Eldred bent over and picked up the arms.

"Sir, you must leave those."

Eldred glared. "I'm moving them to the shelves."

Eldred dumped the arms on the shelves and stalked towards the exit, kicking an empty crate out of the way as he passed. Longinus flinched as it shattered against the wall.

Longinus hung even further back as they continued on.

THE HALL OF THE DEAD

Inside, Eldred gazed up and down the long procession of statues lining the walls of the hall. Some were painted gaudy colors—pink, red and purple—others were the color of plain stone. Brass plaques or stone tablets hung near each of them.

Down the wide floor of the hall stood a series of twelve massive monuments, paired two by two. Each consisted of a stone tower—decorated with statues of men and women—rising thirty feet above the floor. Each was surrounded by a wide stone moat.

Eldred went to the nearest monument and peered down. A sheer wall covered by uniformly spaced bronze plaques descended thirty feet to a circular paved floor. From the center of the floor rose the tower, set with statues standing in alcoves and on ledges along its entire length.

Eldred shook his head. "I've never seen anything like this."

Longinus shushed him. "You cannot be loud here."

"Why not?"

Longinus pointed to a solitary woman midway down the hall. "You will disturb her."

The woman sat in front of a statue some hundred feet away. She kept glancing at the two of them.

"Very well," said Eldred softly. He pointed into the moat. "Is this where you will put Sir Aemilanus?"

"Oh, he would not be placed down there. When he dies, he will stand over there."

Longinus pointed at the fifth monument down on the left.

Eldred started towards it, examining the statues on the towers as he went.

Each tower had a different theme. On one tower, the figures were set against a motif of wheat, grain and barley. On its pair, the people stood among the beast of the field. Another featured hunters stalking ferocious cats, wolves and even—at the top of their tower—a black scaled dragon with shining fangs. Warriors exchanged blows and rode chariots on the next tower. Musicians played harps and flutes. Poets, bakers, chefs, dancers and athletes each had their place.

As he passed the woman, she rose to her feet and hurried past to the entrance.

When he reached Sir Aemilanus's future resting place, he regarded the statues it housed. The figures held books, pens and scales. "I see why this is his tower."

"Yes. The Pillar of the Mind."

"Where will he be placed?"

"I expect near the top, but it's hard to be certain, given the circumstances."

"What circumstances?"

"In former days, Regula would decide. She would choose whom to honor and set their relative elevation. Mind you, being on the tower at any height, even right at the base, is quite an honor."

Eldred frowned at the tower. "We don't have anything like this."

"Of course not. Botrus was a farming town. In Regillium, there stands the Great Hall of the Dead. That is where Sir Aemilanus should properly rest. These souls here, they are honorable enough, but the truly venerated mark the years in Regillium."

Women and men holding rods, standing on pedestals, occupied the paired tower. Eldred gestured at them. "Your leaders?"

"Not ours. The woman near the top, with the black cowl and the golden crown, Terentia, she was the mayor of Turicum."

"But this is Turicum?"

"Correct, but we—all the current inhabitants—are from Regillium."

The last two towers were different.

"Why are these segregated by gender?" asked Eldred.

"Her favorites. Statues of her closest friends of either sex. Some of the men were her consorts."

Eldred studied the status of the men. "Which ones?"

"The man near the top, Viridius. He enjoyed her favor some five hundred years ago. But as I mentioned, her true favorites rest in the capital."

The statue of Viridius had long golden hair flowing down over his shoulders. His eyes were set with light gray crystals and looked out from a friendly, pleasing face. A stone tablet below him gave his epitaph:

Viridius, beautiful in life and mourned in death. He amused me for a century with poems and gossip. B. MLXVI D. MCCXIII.

Eldred stared at the tablet. "Is that correct?"
"Hmm, which part? The gossip or the poems?"
"It states he entertained her for a hundred years."
"An exaggeration."
"But the dates! He lived for—one hundred forty-seven years."
Eldred spied Terentia's plaque.

A humble and generous soul, with warmth enough to fill a city and wisdom enough to govern it. DXXXIV - DCCLI

Eldred's eyes grew wide. "She lived for, for two hundred years, a bit more than two hundred years!"
"Quiet. You cannot be loud here."
"I don't know of anyone who lived even fifty years. Few Deirans reach their fortieth year. Mercians rarely last to thirty-five."
Longinus sighed. "Gaius said you could read. Nobody mentioned you could do arithmetic."
Eldred raced around the monuments, checking the tablets. "He's two hundred. She's around one hundred eighty. Two hundred twenty! Is that the most? Who is the oldest? Wait, these're the lesser ones. Who's in Regillium? Who's the oldest still alive? How old is Sir Aemilanus?"
Longinus crossed his arms. "I have nothing more to say."

QUESTIONS

Eldred sat alone at the kitchen table on his ground floor, eating a veal sandwich. A large carafe of blueberry juice sat near his glass.

Gaius entered the room and nodded to Eldred. "Longinus tells me you visited the hall. You read the epitaphs."

"Of course I did," said Eldred with an edge in his voice.

Gaius took a breath. "This is a delicate matter."

"Is it?" asked Eldred. "In what way is it delicate?"

"Well, our burial customs are a private matter, sir."

"I see. It's a private matter when your people die—a private matter, private, but grand. You have statues, monuments, plaques, even the words of Regula herself. When my people die, we go on display. We get posed with animals. We feed the bugs. If I had died—if I had succumbed to the venom—I would be there too. Wouldn't I?"

Gaius shifted his feet. "I am certain that would not be the case, sir. We all worked together to ensure your survival. Everyone contributed. We used our most valuable resources. If we had failed, which I am so pleased we did not, we would certainly have returned your remains to your friends with the expedition."

"Do you think they didn't have friends?" asked Eldred.

"I do not know, sir. We are discussing a display from quite some time ago. No disrespect is intended. It is for science. Sir Aemilanus himself might contribute his remains to the hall, as he told you."

"No, he won't. He lied. Your brother showed me where Sir Aemilanus is destined."

"Nobody lied about anything. Nor could anyone have lied on this matter while Sir Aemilanus still lives."

Eldred's face grew tight. "You lie all the time. You lie about your age. You lie about my people. You lie about Sir Aemilanus. What don't you lie about?"

Gaius sighed. "You seem upset, sir. Perhaps the walk today taxed you?"

Eldred sipped his juice. "What taxes me is your deceit."

"I protest, sir."

"You protest? I protest. You summoned us here under a false pretense. You had trouble with a dragon? You manufactured trouble with a dragon. The scent, that's from you. That's you showing the mastery you boast about. You got the dragon to come here so you could pull us along after. It's the short path. The path she wanted. And none of you care, even if you kill a few of your own as you sell your deception."

"I do not understand you, sir. I do not know about this 'short' path."

Eldred scoffed. "I told you, I saw it. And I saw Sir Aemilanus say it would be a waste to use the powder to heal me—a waste. And you say I should thank him—that he is the one who saved me."

"He did save you. You are confused by your dreams."

Eldred stood up and hurled the carafe across the room, shattering it on the wall behind Gaius, who ducked away. "Stop calling them dreams!"

The juice sprayed over a white linen couch. Glass shards scattered across the floor.

Gaius rose, a dark expression on his face. "A mess. Can you not control yourself?"

Eldred slammed his fist on the table, making it jump. "Stop lying!"

Gaius stared coldly at Eldred. "I have had enough of your abuse, sir. Can you regain control of yourself? Will you even make the effort?"

"Then get out. Sammanus said I could switch minders. I want one with at least a trace of honesty."

"I will see what I can do, sir. But you should know that the citizens are not lining up for the honor of spending time with you."

Eldred frowned as Gaius left the house.

ROYAL VISIT

Eldred sat by the window in his bedroom, watching the alley below. An hour after Gaius left, armed visitors started to arrive at Longinus's house. The first pair to arrive was Sebine and Phabia, contestants from the arena. Next came Decima and Naevia. Finally, Valens arrived with Hortensius in tow. Eldred surveyed his room. He could pull a post off of the bed to use as a club. There were knives in the pantry on the ground floor.

They had been inside, plotting with Longinus and Gaius for an hour, when Opimia arrived. Ten minutes after she arrived, the visitors streamed out. Decima, Naevia, Sebine and Phabia headed down the alley in the direction of the harbor. Hortensius set off towards the stables. Opimia, Valens, Longinus and Gaius remained inside the house.

Shortly after, Opimia came across the alley, carrying a basket, and knocked on Eldred's door. Eldred went down to meet her.

Opimia handed Eldred the basket. "I thought you might like some fruit."

"Fruit?" said Eldred.

"And I feel we should speak."

"Come inside. Mind the glass on the floor."

Eldred led her up to the middle floor and placed the fruit basket on a side table. After they sat, Eldred ate a grape from the basket. "Very sweet."

"You are welcome. I understand you have a grievance with Gaius. You feel he was untruthful. Is that so?"

Eldred took another grape as he considered his response. "I'm not happy with Gaius. I'm not happy with the gathering across the street, either."

Opimia smiled. "Some foolishness I put to rest. Your behavior unsettled Gaius. He did not appreciate your display when you smashed the bottle."

"Valens is still there."

"He merely waits to learn the outcome of our meeting. As I told you before, you do not frighten me. Now, if you have concerns, please share them."

"What would be the result if I did?" asked Eldred. "Who are you? You live in the grandest house in the city. I heard you order Sir Aemilanus about, and it wasn't a dream. I heard it."

"I do not claim to understand what you experienced, but I do have influence on the council and I do live in a fine house, though many citizens keep exquisite homes."

"There you go again. You avoid my meaning just like Gaius, dodging my words. I don't care for Longinus, but at least he is not as skilled at escaping the truth."

Opimia laughed. "No, Longinus is good-hearted, but not the diplomat Gaius is."

"That's not diplomacy. That's deceit."

"The two can be intertwined."

"For you and the Sun People, maybe. But not for me."

"You demand honesty from me?" asked Opimia as her gaze intensified.

"I do," said Eldred.

Opimia straightened in her chair. "Your people kill mine, take our lands, confine us in our last city and limit our population. What do you wish to complain about?"

Eldred raised his palms. "That's her edict. Your precious Regula. Oh, and you're not weak. I have witnessed the footspeed of your old citizens, the strength of your women in combat. And you have knowledge, far more than we do."

"I did not say we were weak."

Eldred's voice softened. "And you live. You live so much longer than we do. I saw the plaques in your Hall of the Dead. You live for hundreds of years."

Opimia gave the slightest of shrugs. "Now, you are taking issue with the actions of Regula. She had the power to grant you a long life, but she chose other gifts for you, such as the Bond."

Eldred sighed. "The Bond."

Opimia pressed the tips of her fingers together. "You might develop the Bond. Sir Aemilanus used more powder of Balaur in your care than he ever has on anyone. You are the only person I know of who survived contact with dragon venom."

Eldred grunted and looked down at the basket.

"What troubles you? Are you not treated well? Do you not have fine clothes and good food? A comfortable house?" asked Opimia.

Eldred tapped his index fingers together.

"Perhaps you were just weary from your injuries," suggested Opimia.

"No," said Eldred, his voice firm. "I heard you talking with Sir Aemilanus. It wasn't a dream."

"What did you hear? Perhaps I can confirm whether it happened."

"You were speaking of the short way. Sir Aemilanus wanted the long way."

"I see," said Opimia.

"The long way is something about we will all fail, but your people will fail more slowly. I have a clearer sense of what you mean by the short way."

"Which is?"

"The dragon," said Eldred. "First, you want it to kill the lords. Then you want me to bring more people from the south to feed it. You're even willing to sacrifice your own precious citizens for this farce."

Opimia nodded serenely. "I do not dispute that I wish to see your lords dead. If your people had suffered as mine have, would you not want to see your enemies eliminated?"

Eldred frowned. "I would."

"And when the lords die, I would like more men from the south to spend their blood, but not all men, and not you."

Eldred looked into her dark gray eyes. "Why not?"

"You remind me of what you are, where your people came from. The fall of Regillium—I was there. I helped to negotiate the covenant with Regula. She sent a thousand of us here to Turicum. A thousand stock of people for her to keep on hand, should she have some fancy, or need us for one of her experiments. But thousands more were turned, changed, some to Maldavians, some to Mercian, some to Deirans."

Eldred shook his head. "No, no. She made us new. We're our own people."

"I knew Regula," said Opimia in a commanding voice. "She never wasted effort. We, the Sun People, the people she had shaped for more than a thousand years, were putty in her hands. All of your people, even the disastrous Torvid, came from us. The First Born came from barbarians we captured for her, but all the rest of you, both before and after the fall of Regillium, originated from our flesh. You are one of us. You could be my great-great-great-great-grand nephew."

Eldred grimaced. "That's not true."

Opimia's face softened. "She is gone now. Her whims no longer sweep our peoples to destruction. My people need to grow in strength and numbers. We will live once again in Regillium, my home. But your people must live too. You could be our partner, Eldred. You are unique. You could rule the three tribes."

Eldred glanced at his scarred left hand. "I can't even rule the Deirans."

"We helped you before; we saved your life. Now, we can strengthen you. We can arm you. We can train you. I do not fully understand your ways, but to rule the Mercians, am I correct in thinking you need only kill one person?"

Eldred raised his finger. "That's true. You only have to kill the king in a duel."

"Do you not agree that such a thing is possible?"

"It is."

"Will you work with me?" asked Opimia.

Eldred paused. "I won't kill anyone. I won't kill the lords."

"You need not. When the lords cease their dallying and face their end, we will start our work. We will drain the strength of the Deirans and Maldavians with the dragon. We will make you king of the Mercians. The short way."

"I don't know," said Eldred quietly.

"You have to decide. Now that you know the truth, the truth you demanded, you could do us great harm. We are hanging on by a finger's grip. An army from the south could crush us while our numbers remain low. Will you keep our secrets?" asked Opimia.

Eldred nodded slowly.

"I need to hear your agreement," demanded Opimia.

"I will. You have my word."

RECOVERY

The week passed quickly for Eldred. During the day, he rose and spent his time outside the city with Hobbie, his investigations complete. In the evening, he sat and read books Opimia lent him. He slept well, without visions or strange dreams.

The routine quickly restored Eldred's health. On the eighth day, he went on a lengthy run outside the city walls with his greatsword strapped to his back. He was walking the last mile back to Turicum when he spotted Lord Kenelm in the distance, riding towards the city.

Eldred raced towards him, waving his hand in the air. Lord Kenelm saw Eldred and kicked his horse into a trot.

As Lord Kenelm drew close, he pulled up his horse and wrinkled his brow. "What happened to your face?"

"Nothing," said Eldred. "Oh, I know. You mean my cheek."

Lord Kenelm glanced towards Turicum. "What happened to you?"

"It's nothing they did. I got these marks from dragon venom."

"The dragon attacked you?"

"No, not that dragon. I have this from the dragon the Maldavians killed."

"Why were you messing with that?" asked Lord Kenelm.

"For no good reason, it appears," said Eldred. "The venom almost killed me, but the citizens of Turicum worked hard to save me."

Lord Kenelm narrowed his eyes. "Did they?"

"Yes. They did. Can you—can you tell anything different about me?"

Lord Kenelm looked Eldred over. "Well, there's your face. Your hand looks injured, too."

"Not that. I mean the Bond. Do you sense the Bond in me? Do you see a glimmer?"

Lord Kenelm frowned and shook his head. "No. Did something change?"

"Perhaps not. Perhaps not yet." Eldred paused and wet his lips. "What brings you to the city? Were you looking for me?"

"I was," said Lord Kenelm. "I came to ask for your help."

Eldred pointed to his chest. "For my help? I'm surprised Lord Vance wants my help."

"It remains for me to convince him he does, but I'm sure he will come around."

Eldred gave a short laugh. "You won't have an easy time doing that."

"In any case, we have a plan."

Eldred grinned. "And you need my sword."

"Well, no, not your sword. We require your footspeed. Mance once told me you were the fastest squire by no small measure. Given that he was not inclined to sing your praises, I believe he was telling the truth."

"He was," confirmed Eldred.

"Good, because our current plan depends on someone outrunning the dragon."

Eldred's eyes grew wide. "What? I don't know if anyone is that fast. I've seen it move. It's very quick."

"You would not be running across open ground. You would be in a footrace through tunnels. We need the fastest man we can find. And you can see in the dark."

Eldred grunted. "How does the race end?"

"Lord Thom directed us in building a trap at one of the less traveled entrances to its lair. If we can get the dragon to run in blindly, we can bury it under a pile of rocks."

Eldred laughed. "Is that how the great Lord Vance is going to kill the dragon, with a pile of rocks? Where's the honor in that?"

Lord Kenelm frowned. "It's a necessity. We're too few in number to kill the dragon by any other means. We all agree. It's time to be done and return home."

"I'll let the citizens know your intentions."

"No; tell them nothing."

"Why?" asked Eldred.

"Suppose the dragon leaves a few weakened survivors. The Wretched may well finish them off."

Eldred shook his head. "They're not evil, Lord Kenelm."

"Yes, they are. They're our enemies. They're the enemies of the Night Mother."

Eldred glanced back at Turicum. "I see. So you came back to ask me to lead the dragon into your trap?"

Lord Kenelm nodded. "That's right."

Eldred sighed. "And if I outrun the dragon, I win the honor of being a steward?"

"You can be a steward in any case. Your uncle offered you a position. I also offer you a position. My estates are not as grand as his, but I would be honored to have you serve me."

Eldred raised his eyebrows. "I'm not sure, Lord Kenelm. This adventure seems more exciting than digging a latrine, but I'm not finding it sensible. Do you truly know how fast the dragon can run? Can you count on it standing still while you drop rocks on it? Your plan sounds desperate."

"We are desperate. We can't fight it in the open field. This is the only way."

"No. No. You can walk away. You don't have to fight the dragon. I—I can find another way to protect the citizens. I'm sure I can."

Lord Kenelm raised his fist. "This was never about them. This is about our honor. We're bonded warriors. We gave our oath, and we will see this through."

Eldrd took a deep breath. "Then, I'm sorry for you. I'm sorry my father tricked you. But this is foolish. If your plan made any sense, one of you would already have lured the dragon out. You would have gone, or Lord Osbert, or perhaps Lord Vance. One of you would already have teased the dragon. You wouldn't be here asking help from a man who isn't even a squire. You took my swords away, Lord Kenelm. When we faced the wolves, you took my swords."

Lord Kenelm shifted on his horse and looked up at Galla's mound. "They said many things in camp. Some spoke of you in unflattering terms. There were allegations about how you left the Academy."

Eldred made a fist at his side. "What of it?"

"I think some of their claims are true. But I have met you, spoken with you. I believe you're an honorable man. I think you have had no opportunity to demonstrate your honor. You'll never be a warrior, a real warrior. You can join up with the Maldavians, or the Mercians, but this is your chance, your only chance—ever—to show your honor as a Deiran. I don't want you to throw this opportunity away."

Eldred looked at the ground. "I don't know."

"You're only bound by honor. Nothing more. There's no reward. You can already be your uncle's steward, or mine. I don't know if there is anyone but me who thinks you would do it."

"Well, you're wrong. Send Lord Ferris down the tunnel, or Lord Vance. Just kill the Motherless beast in the tunnel. You're the real warriors."

Lord Kenelm nodded. "It may come to that. I leave an hour after sunrise tomorrow. Come with me. We need you."

THE NIGHT

Eldred chewed the roasted pork, sweet and spicy in the same bite. Marcia had drizzled on more lark sauce, per his request, drowning the food, as Gaius put it. But it was better this way. The extra sauce flowed onto the potatoes. Eldred absentmindedly built a small dam of potato to contain his reserve. It was delicious, better than anything he had ever eaten at the Academy, far better even than those rare banquets at Boar's Tusk. Certainly better than whatever Lord Kenelm was eating that evening.

Eldred glanced up from his plate. Longinus was speaking.

"Sorry, Longinus. What were you saying?"

Longinus hung back by the door. He was never far from the door if he could help it. "I said it is done, sir."

"What's done?"

"What you asked for, the burial. Your three comrades, from the Hall of Ages."

Eldred nodded. "Oh, good. That's excellent."

Longinus smiled.

"Where did you bury them?"

"I do not have the details, but I understand it's somewhere outside the city walls, a neutral location, not one with some other purpose. The graves are marked simply but with dignity, sir."

"I'm glad to hear it," said Eldred. "Probably a century overdue, but progress."

"Very good, sir," said Longinus. "I heard something else as well, sir. Calvus saw one of the men from the expedition with you today."

"That's right. Lord Kenelm came to see me."

"For some specific reason, sir? Where have they been?"

"They have been up north, along the coast. He said they were working on a plan."

"Is something happening?" asked Longinus.

Eldred shrugged. "I can't say. They have a plan of some sort. It doesn't change anything for us."

"Lady Opimia will be pleased if they finally step up. She desires to move on to the next stage of our enterprise."

Eldred smiled. "I do as well. I'll finally get the honor of sparring with the mighty Valens."

"I hear he is equally enthusiastic, sir. He sees tremendous potential in you. He said you have real skill, that you can do much more than just take punishment."

Eldred frowned. "I like to think so."

"Absolutely, sir," said Longinus.

When Eldred retired to his bedroom in the evening, he took a book of folktales Opimia had lent him. As he leafed through the pages, he recognized some of the stories as Deiran tales. Sometimes the Deiran version had switched the names, Pete for Petrus and Henry for Henricus, but in a number of cases, the Deiran tales had the same name. Marcus tricked the wolf. Lucilla lived on an island and was raised by barbarians.

Eldred sighed. "We're the same."

It was late when Eldred set down the book and tried to sleep. The bed was soft and warm. The fire was fading in the fireplace, casting a pleasant light over the room. Despite these comforts, Eldred could not sleep. He kept imagining Lord Kenelm stumbling down a dark tunnel. They would definitely send him. Who else would be so agreeable when asked to throw away his life? Eldred turned on his side. He lay on his back. He rolled to his chest and pushed his face into the pillow.

When the predawn glow showed through the window, Eldred tiredly sat up. "The old fool is too slow."

MORNING

Eldred rose and dressed in his Deiran clothes. Peering out his window into the darkness, Eldred spied Longinus asleep, propped up in a chair by his front window. Eldred shook his head and headed downstairs to gather some food.

Crossing the street, Eldred knocked on the glass and stirred Longinus awake.

"What is it, good sir?" mumbled Longinus.

"I'm meeting with the expedition, and I need supplies."

Longinus glanced around his house with bleary eyes. "I do not have any cakes, sir."

"Not cakes," said Eldred impatiently. "Come with me."

The streets were empty as they made their way to the Hall of Ages.

Longinus paused as he went to open the door of the hall. "You are sure you need these?"

"Not entirely," said Eldred.

"You could come back for them later if it turns out you do need them. Then I could get them at a more decent hour."

"You would waste its potency. Sir Aemilanus was quite clear that you should always harvest it as soon as possible."

Longinus sighed. "Wait here. I will get his assistant."

"Fine."

Longinus returned a few minutes later with a frail looking young woman. Eldred stared at her as she peered around the door.

"What is it you need, sir?" she said.

Eldred leaned forward. "Who are you? I recognize you."

"My name is Fausta. I attended the contests, sir."

"No, no. You worked on me. You worked on this." Eldred pointed to the back of his hand.

"But how do you know that? You were unconscious," said Fausta.

"It only seemed like I was."

Fausta stepped back. "Oh."

Eldred huffed. "I need sample bags. All the sample bags you have, or at least a large bag full of them."

"I would like to help, but Sir Aemilanus still slumbers. Have you discussed this with him?"

"No," said Eldred. "I'm just now headed to visit the expedition. If they have somehow contrived to kill the dragon, I need to harvest its brain before it deteriorates."

"Oh, that is true. Your last samples were entirely unusable. We dumped them in the bay."

Eldred raised his hand to his cheek. "Unusable? All of it—unusable?"

Fausta nodded.

Eldred took a deep breath. "Well, if the opportunity presents itself, I must be prepared."

"Very sensible," said Fausta. "I wish you had discussed this with him. I cannot wake him at this hour. Can you come back after lunch?"

"I'm leaving now. I could leave the brains to spoil, I suppose. It would be a missed opportunity."

Fauta tilted her head from side to side. "No. That cannot be allowed. Come in, but please be quiet on the stairs."

They followed Fausta up the stairs of the tower. Eldred hands turned clammy as they passed the open door of the surgical room. He had almost died on that cold stone table. They climbed the stairs in silence, save for Longinus's panting. The morning light greeted them as they reached the study at the top of the tower, illuminating the *Somnium ferrum* by the window.

"Will two sacks full of sample bags suffice?" asked Fausta.

Eldred shrugged. "You have some sense of the dragon. I leave it to you."

Fausta nodded and headed off through the maze of shelves, leaving Eldred and Longinus by the stairs. As Longinus leaned on a shelf and recovered, Eldred looked off to the left and noticed a narrow aisle, an aisle stocked with glass jars and a few small boxes. At the end, on the left, a potted fern rested on a shelf. Eldred stared at the plant, fixated.

"Are you well, sir?" asked Longinus.

Eldred grunted. "I need to check."

"We should wait here, sir."

Eldred walked to the fern and lifted down the pot. He pushed aside the fronds. There was a key. Eldred peered at it, both surprised and not surprised.

"That might be a valuable plant, sir. A wonder. Best you put it back."

Eldred took the key and set the pot on the shelf.

"That's better, sir. Oh, wait. Come back here, sir."

Eldred continued past the aisle. The black iron chest was exactly where he had seen it in the vision. Eldred knelt down and inserted the key. A turn to the left, three rotations of the lever, the chest eased open. Inside there were papers, a few daggers, stacks of coins and a black square plate with four small woven packets.

Longinus hurried over, turning red in the face. "Oh, no, sir. What are you doing? Why are you doing this?"

"I told your brother they were not dreams. I saw him. I saw him!" said Eldred, raising his voice.

Fausta returned with two sacks stuffed with sample bags. "What is this? How did you get in there?"

"He said they were dreams. This proves they weren't. This proves all of it," ranted Eldred.

"You need to shut that. Give me the key," demanded Fausta.

Eldred lightly shoved her back as she grabbed at the key, and stood up, holding the plate in one hand and rubbing his forehead with the other. "No, it's not as simple as that. Lord Kenelm made a point. I'm honor bound to help them. My obligations didn't end just because I left."

Eldred set the plate on a table and stared at the four packets. "What would be the fair thing? What's fair? This medicine can cure wounds inflicted by a dragon's venom, and so has value to the expedition. It also has value to you, the Sun People."

Fausta dropped the bags and stood with her hands on her hips. "The powder is ours. You have already taken more than your share—more than anyone's share."

Sir Aemilanus appeared in his night clothes down the aisle behind Fausta. "By Regula, what is happening? What is he doing here?"

Fausta turned to Sir Aemilanus on the verge of tears. "He tricked me. He has our powder of Balaur."

"You thieving scoundrel!" Sir Aemilanus plucked a glass jar, half filled with a silvery liquid, off the shelf and hurled it at Eldred, who caught it.

Eldred set the surprisingly heavy jar on the table next to the plate. "I'm trying to be fair!"

"You are stealing from us. From all of us! From every citizen in the city!" yelled Sir Aemilanus.

"That's not true. I would only be borrowing some packets."

Sir Aemilanus fished a thin bladed knife out of a box on the shelves. Fausta and Longinus retreated in alarm.

Sir Aemilanus pointed the knife at Eldred. "If you had asked, it might be borrowing."

"It is borrowing. I'll keep the packets in one of the sample bags. If we die, you can recover them. If we live, the dragon is defeated and you get all these bags full of brains, yielding more powder of Balaur than you ever had, even if I have to use one packet to save a lord or myself."

"You will take none. Leave now and never return," said Sir Aemilanus.

"One of the lords could die. I could die."

"You will all die," exclaimed Sir Aemilanus. "The powder is a powerful medicine in skilled hands. It is worthless in the hands of an idiot."

"I'll take two packets," said Eldred.

"I will kill you on the spot," said Sir Aemilanus.

Eldred held up his hands in front of him. "Longinus, speak some sense to him. Fausta, do something. I don't want to hurt him."

Sir Aemilanus charged at Eldred with surprising quickness, thrusting the knife at Eldred's neck. Eldred stepped to the side and slapped Sir Aemilanus in the face. As Sir Aemilanus recoiled, Eldred grabbed his hand and made him drop the knife. When Eldred released him, Sir Aemilanus sank down against the shelves.

Fausta came forward to hold Sir Aemilanus. "Do not just stand there, Longinus. Do something."

Longinus looked back and forth between Eldred and Fausta. "Sir, this is beyond improper."

Eldred picked up the sacks of sample bags and fished one out. "I'm leaving."

From down on the floor, Sir Aemilanus groaned. "I will add a new exhibit downstairs with your bones. It will be the first of many."

Eldred frowned and selected two packets.

"To think I saved your life," said Sir Aemilanus. "I should have let you die, fool that you are. What a missed opportunity to cast your worthless corpse into the sea. I will right that wrong."

Eldred sealed the packets in the sample bag and shook his head. "You can't have it both ways."

Eldred took the sacks Fausta had dropped and stepped around Sir Aemilanus as he made his way down the stairs.

·)

As Eldred rode up the hill towards Galla's Mound, he glanced back towards Turicum. They wouldn't be pleased, but it likely wouldn't matter. They would find the packets if they bothered to come looking. Out past the city, the islands became visible as he gained altitude. The air was unusually clear and the sea was dead calm. Eldred noticed them, mere flecks in the distance, three small boats coming around the side of Imbros and sailing towards the city.

Eldred pulled up Hobbie and stared at them. "Lucilla…"

LORD KENELM

Lord Kenelm led the way north, following a faint track through fields and over low rolling hills on an inland route some way from the coast. As they rode, Lord Kenelm kept glancing at Eldred's face.

"It's just a minor injury," said Eldred finally.

Lord Kenelm grunted.

Eldred ran his finger over the bottom edge of the patch, feeling the edge. "The skin is paler. Sir Aemilanus said it might match eventually."

Lord Kenelm nodded. "I've seen worse."

"Then why do you keep staring?"

"I was just thinking about how to explain your injury when we return south. We won't want people associating you with the Wretcheds. Chatter like that could make for a bad start as a steward."

"As your steward?" asked Eldred.

"If you agree."

Eldred tilted his head. "I might manifest the Bond. I might even already have done so."

Lord Kenelm raised his eyebrows. "I don't see it in you. Besides, warriors get the Bond from the Night Mother, not by mixing with Wretcheds."

Eldred glanced at the back of his left hand. "My treatment included many applications of the powder of Balaur."

Lord Kenelm shrugged.

"That's a medicine, a powerful treatment of the Sun People. It brings new life."

"Who are the Sun People?"

"The Wretcheds. That's what they call themselves."

Lord Kenelm shook his head. "You should never have gone into that Motherless city. And I don't just mean because of your injuries."

"We might find out today. I could manifest the Bond. The powder made my insides young again."

"You were never old," said Lord Kenelm.

"They say I'm the first person ever to survive dragon venom. They gave me more powder of Balaur than they have ever given anyone."

Lord Kenelm sighed. "I wouldn't talk about that with the others."

"I'm not ashamed," said Eldred. "I feel stronger. I can run faster. I was out running when you met me yesterday."

"That might be the one good thing," said Lord Kenelm.

REUNION

When Lord Kenelm and Eldred rode into the expedition's forward camp, the four lords were sitting around a fire, eating a roasted bird of some sort. The two tied their horses and walked over to the others.

Lord Ferris glanced up. "So you found our rabbit."

"I wouldn't put it that way," said Lord Kenelm.

Lord Vance studied Eldred while chewing on a piece of meat. "What happened to your face?"

"I encountered a dragon."

Lord Vance looked Eldred in the eye. "You fought it?"

"No, another dragon, a dead one," said Eldred.

Lord Ferris snorted. "You should reconsider being our rabbit."

Eldred straightened his back. "I haven't agreed to help you as yet."

Lord Vance narrowed his eyes. "Then why're you here?"

"I might tease the dragon, but first, I need to examine this trap of Lord Thom's."

"We will drop half the hillside on the creature," said Lord Thom.

"You had best be sure you do. The—citizens say it runs faster than a horse. As for a pitched fight, you couldn't hurt it."

Lord Vance grunted. "How would you know? Did you read that in your book?"

"No, I examined the corpse of the other dragon, the one the Maldavians fought. Its scales didn't have a scratch."

Lord Ferris raised his eyebrow. "Yet they killed the monster."

"I didn't see how," said Eldred.

Lord Ferris grinned. "Well, you know more than I do about the capabilities of Maldavians, since that is more or less what you are. But they did kill it. They stabbed it in the eye or slit its throat. They did something you didn't notice when you poked around its bones."

"I pounded its eye sockets and scales with far more strength than you have, Lord Ferris. I couldn't damage either."

Lord Vance scratched his chin. "We have a plan. We drop a mountain of rocks. If the beast survives, we give it the sword. If you need to examine Thom's trap to settle your nerves, I'll allow it."

"I have another condition," said Eldred.

Lord Vance groaned. "Do you? Do you truly?"

"If the dragon evades the boulders, I stand with you in battle."

Lord Ferris laughed.

Lord Vance stared at Eldred with his mouth open. "How many times must we revisit this matter?"

"These are my demands. Agree or pick another rabbit. Who's faster, Lord Osbert or Lord Ferris? Is either fast enough?"

The two lords exchanged glances.

Lord Vance turned to Lord Kenelm. "How do we know he's quick?"

"He has the footspeed of a Mercian. You know he can see in the dark."

Lord Vance scowled at the dirt.

As Eldred started to speak, Lord Kenelm cut him off. "He won't be in our way. The creature is wide enough. Eldred can fight off to the side."

Lord Vance glared at Eldred. "You're as selfish and arrogant as your father. Wave your sword around for all the good it will do, but stay clear of us. Do you understand!"

Eldred nodded.

Lord Vance rose to his feet. "Let's put this to an end."

THE TRAP

They rode in silence through the trees. Lord Vance took the lead. Behind him followed Lord Osbert, pulling a pack horse loaded with spears. Lord Thom was next, towing a horse carrying picks and shovels. Lord Ferris shepherded a pack horse bearing supplies. Lord Kenelm and Eldred brought up the rear.

As they headed north, the trees grew shorter and sparser. The ground became rockier, and the soil turned red and sandy. Massive outcroppings of bare rock covered the hills rising before them.

Eldred surveyed their surroundings as they started up a hill. They were riding out in the open, with only low-lying bushes for cover. "Are we safe here?"

Lord Kenelm scanned the area. "We have traveled this path many times. If the Mother favors us, this will be the last."

Eventually, they came to the entrance to a narrow canyon set between two sheer walls of rock. Lord Vance dismounted to the left of the entrance, and tethered his horse to a stunted tree. As the others followed suit, Eldred hopped down and stood by himself, rubbing Hobbie's neck.

"Best tie him," said Lord Kenelm.

"No. He knows to wait." Eldred glanced at the canyon entrance. "I wouldn't want him tied here."

Hobbie nudged Eldred and rested his neck on Eldred's shoulder. Eldred ruffled Hobbie's ear and whispered. "When Sir Aemilanus said the dragon is faster than a horse, I'm sure he didn't mean you."

The men set to unloading the pack animals and parceling out the equipment. Eldred joined in, looking to carry his share.

When Eldred reached for a spear, Lord Ferris snatched it away. "We only have five."

Eldred stifled a yawn. "They won't hurt the dragon, in any case."

Eldred ended up carrying four shovels and several containers of water. He stood with the others while Lord Vance crept to the edge to scout the canyon. The sun was high and the day was warming. Eldred leaned back against the rock, his eyes nearly shut. His sleepless night was catching up to him.

Hobbie kept looking at him. The trap might not be right. What would even slow a dragon that could demolish the stone houses of Turicum? What choice would he have then? Eldred scowled at the patch of skin on his hand.

Lord Osbert smacked Eldred on the shoulder. "Wake up. We're going."

They hiked a quarter mile down the sand strewn passage. Sheer cliffs penned them in. When they neared a turn, Lord Vance continued on while the other lords stopped. Lord Vance crawled through the red sand for the final twenty feet on his hands and knees. He stopped at the turn and peered into the space beyond. After several minutes, Lord Vance scooted backward and rejoined the group.

Lord Thom tapped Eldred on the shoulder and motioned for him to follow. Eldred set down his gear, taking nothing but his swords. The cool sand dusted Eldred's hands as he crossed the last stretch. Eldred sidled up next to Lord Thom and gazed into a canyon that opened up around the turn. The rounded red walls offered purchase, with many routes up the sides. One approach on the left appeared easy enough that you might walk up.

Lord Thom wagged a finger in Eldred's face and gestured at the rock wall on the far side of the canyon. At the bottom, shaded from the sun, was a cave. Lord Thom pointed at Eldred and nodded emphatically.

Eldred sighed.

"Look up top," whispered Lord Thom.

A short slope connected the sheer rock face with the plateau above the cave entrance. An array of stones in a triangle formation stretched down to the edge. A tangle of ropes held the stones in place.

Lord Thom patted Eldred on the shoulder and pointed to a flat shelf, halfway up the left wall of the canyon. Several piles of round boulders were stacked, ready for action.

Finally, Lord Thom directed Eldred's attention to an enormous rock high up the right wall of the canyon. The rock stretched sixty feet high and looked like a mushroom. It balanced on an edge scarcely larger than two hand widths.

Eldred looked back and forth at the rock and the cave entrance below. It would be a devastating blow if only it would land.

When Eldred returned, the men were drinking water. Lord Kenelm offered Eldred a flask. As Eldred drank the cool water, Lord Vance pointed at Eldred and raised his eyebrow. Eldred nodded.

Lord Vance approached close enough for Eldred to smell his sour breath and motioned for Eldred to bend down. "Isn't she a beauty?"

Eldred gave a short laugh.

Lord Vance's eyes narrowed. "Are you up for this? We get but one try."

Eldred glanced back to where Lord Thom was lying on the ground. "Yes."

Lord Vance licked his lips. "Are you certain? You don't look your best."

Eldred frowned. "My legs are fine."

"Very well," said Lord Vance. "Go in there and bring it out at speed."

Lord Vance stepped away.

Lord Kenelm came forward and clasped Eldred's shoulder. "You can do it. This is your moment."

Eldred felt his heartbeat accelerate. "I know."

"Don't let it get close. The dragon is fast, but you'll be quicker around the turns. That's your advantage."

"I know."

"Good. I'll take you up."

When they approached the final stretch, Eldred unbuckled his swords and handed them to Lord Kenelm. "Keep these for me here. They'll only slow me down."

Lord Kenelm patted his chest over his heart. "Count on it."

Eldred reached inside his tunic and pulled out a sample bag. "This is the powder of Balaur. Return it to the Sun People if I don't make it out."

Lord Kenelm wrinkled his nose. "As you wish."

NEW CAVE

The stone floor of the cave was smooth and dry. The walls looked like baked clay and matched the reddish colors of the canyon, with colored bands running parallel to the ground. The ceiling flowed gracefully into curves that formed an arch sixty feet overhead.

Cool air invited Eldred inside. As the light faded, his dark vision engaged, revealing the path ahead, stretching off into the distance. He advanced well into the cave before he encountered a junction wide enough for the dragon to navigate. The passage on the left descended and continued deeper into the rock plateau. The one on the right rose up and doubled back in the direction Eldred had entered.

Eldred paused and bit his lip. If the creature got behind him, he would have no choice but to flee blindly through the tunnels. After some hesitation, he turned right.

As he wound up, he came across tiny crannies where he could peer down on his earlier route. Some were so narrow that he couldn't even squeeze his arm through. Other gaps were large enough to stick his head out and look straight down on the floor of the tunnel below.

Just before the passage veered off, he came to a wider opening that invited him out on a ledge, thirty feet above the hard clay. He studied the way down, mostly smooth with narrow ridges in a few spots. A difficult climb but doable.

Eldred hunched down and listened, occasionally shifting to switch his gaze between the passage behind and the tunnel below. But nothing came, and he only heard the distant drip of water droplets. After a few minutes, Eldred took a deep breath and pressed onward.

Eldred crept along the passage as it straightened and ascended through layers of earth. After a time, he felt a light draft on his face. The air smelled fresher. He had reached an exit. Eldred kept low against the cave wall as he made his way out.

Once his eyes adjusted to sunlight, he found himself inside a circular crater a quarter of a mile across ringed with sheer red cliffs. In the center was a lake filled with coppery green water. Natural stone pillars, some more than twenty feet high, jutted out from the water. Beyond the lake, on the opposite side of the crater, were two cave entrances set some hundred feet apart.

Eldred padded quickly across the dried mud to the edge of the water, where he remained crouched behind a boulder as he surveyed the caves, waiting. As the moments dragged on, he gazed up at the white clouds blown on the winds. They flew swiftly overhead, but the air in the crater was still. Eldred leaned on the warm rock, smooth against his belly. Had the dragon chosen this day to visit Turicum? Didn't the citizens know the farce was almost at an end?

After an hour, Eldred sprawled across the rock, resting his head on his hands, facing the cave entrances. More and more, his neck drooped down and he gazed at the racing clouds reflected in the mirror surface of the lake.

He was staring in the water when a ripple crossed his view. He lifted his head. There was no breeze. The wave found its way around the boulder and lapped up against his toes. As the disturbance faded, Eldred tiredly lay his head back down on his hands.

But shortly, another ripple passed by. The waves were coming from behind a massive tower two hundred feet out in the water to Eldred's right. Eldred pushed himself off the warm rock and headed along the shore, checking the cave entrances every few seconds.

As he advanced, the source of the ripples came into view. Out in the water, seventy feet past the rock tower, the water bulged. Not constantly, but from time to time a circle of water would rise up and race to the shore in an expanding series of rings.

Eldred observed several sets of waves over a period of five minutes. Then, on one set, something black flashed just below the surface. Eldred frowned, waiting for disturbance to repeat. As he waited, a movement at the base of the rock tower caught his attention—the dragon!

The dragon shifted its head and observed Eldred with its enormous blue right eye; the left remained closed. The beast lay still on a narrow sandbar, its black scales glistening in the sun. Only its head and neck showed; the rest of its body remained submerged, except for the tip of its tail, which now rose up to the surface and slowly stirred the water.

Eldred held his breath as he stared back at the creature. The dragon thrust out its forked tongue and blinked. After a few slow blinks, the right eye shut. The creature had fallen asleep.

Eldred took a shuddering breath—heart racing—as he stood, studying the slumbering beast. It seemed so huge, so close. He glanced back at the cave entrance where he had come in. He wanted to sneak off. If he wanted to live, that's what he should surely do. The dragon would kill them all.

Eldred frowned. If he snuck off, the lords wouldn't quit. One by one, they would end up in the crater, or maybe they would all come at once. Either way, they would die. The trap, the mushroom rock high up on the wall, did not offer much chance, but they offered some hope. Eldred picked up a rock. He would have to decide. There would be no going back. He stared at the rock, squeezing it in his hand.

With a sigh, he flung the rock out in the lake, where it splashed fifty feet short of the creature. "Wake, dragon!"

The creature opened its right eye a crack, but promptly shut it.

Eldred grabbed a small egg-shaped stone and hurled it. The stone hit the red sand ten feet from the creature's head and bounced.

The dragon heaved itself up on its feet—lifting its shoulders out of the water—and stood, staring at Eldred. Eldred stared back. When the creature didn't move, Eldred picked up another stone and let it fly. The dragon watched it splash in the lake a few feet in front of it, then slid into the water and started swimming. Eldred dashed towards the entrance from which he had come, glancing back over his shoulder. When the dragon reached the shallows, it rose up above the surface, sending water cascading off of its back. Eldred ran for all he was worth into the cave.

As Eldred raced through the passage, the pounding footsteps behind him grew louder. A strange whirring sound filled the tunnel. The dragon's breath or its heart? As the sound closed in, Eldred labored on, running for his life.

When Eldred reached the overlook, he jumped without hesitation. Behind him, he heard the snap of the dragon's jaws, seemingly only inches away. Eldred hurtled down and smashed into hard clay, rolling into the opposite wall, where he lay, stunned. He laid there for a moment before getting up on his hands and knees and struggling up to his feet. His left arm and side were scraped and oozing blood.

As he stood breathing, he glanced up at the overlook. The dragon was gone. A thumping noise sounded in the distance, growing fainter until it faded away. Eldred licked his lips. He could not leave without it. He made a fist and took an unsteady step towards the depths of the cave.

After ten steps, he heard a faint noise and stopped. The thumping had returned in front of him. Eldred crinkled up his face and listened. The sound was growing louder. It was coming for him! It had just gone up to the junction. Eldred turned around and trotted towards the cave entrance. As the whirring closed in, he sped up into a gimpy run. The light was just ahead.

BATTLE

"It's coming! It's coming!" shouted Eldred as he ran through the opening. Boulders roared down the walls of the canyon, chasing Eldred. Behind him, the dragon screamed in a high-pitched wail.

When Eldred reached the turn, he spun around to see a landslide sweep down and bury the hind legs of the dragon. On the right wall of the canyon, Lord Vance toppled the giant mushroom rock, sending it crashing down, cracking the screaming dragon on its side. From the shelf on the left wall, Lord Osbert rolled one boulder after another down on the creature. Some skittered away harmlessly, but others struck true. One lucky strike caught the dragon in the head, and it flopped to the ground with its claws curled up.

As the dragon lay motionless, the lords continued to unleash their fury. Lord Osbert's missiles hammered its head and neck. The other lords hurled down rocks from their perch above the cave mouth. A giant mound of dirt and rock, twenty feet high, covered half the dragon's length.

Eldred pulled his eyes away from the spectacle to retrieve his weapons and his sample bag of Balaur powder. Coughing on the thick dust filling in the canyon and wiping his eyes, Eldred waited for the onslaught to peter out. Finally, after they threw their last boulder, the lords made their way down, carrying their spears.

Lord Kenelm jogged over to Eldred. "You're bleeding."

Eldred coughed in his hand. "I fell."

"But you're well?"

"Well enough."

The others advanced to the dragon's head and struck it with their swords, though not to any apparent effect.

Lord Kenelm nodded. "It's dead."

Eldred followed him to the dragon.

Lord Osbert leaned his spear against a rock beside the dragon and climbed up on the snout of the beast with his sword in hand. He tried to wedge his blade into the dragon's right eye, but he could not get past its eyelid. Cursing, he switched to his dagger. After straining to push its eye open a crack, he plunged his knife into its eyeball.

"I got its eye!"

As he shouted, the immense blue eyes of the dragon flicked open, freezing Lord Osbert in surprise. In a flash, the dragon grabbed him and slammed him to the ground in a crushing blow. The dragon reached out with its left paw and scattered the lords, who ducked away, stabbing at the creature with their spears. Lord Osbert screamed, thrashing on the ground in the dragon's scaly grip.

The lords harried the pinned creature from outside its reach, striking at its grasping paw and snout. Choosing his moment, Eldred darted forward and grabbed Lord Osbert's spear. Standing off to the left, Eldred joined the attack, stabbing the dragon repeatedly. But each time, the spear tip glanced harmlessly off the scales.

As the fight dragged on, Lord Osbert's voice grew fainter and the eyes of the dragon grew more focused. It strained forward in tiny spurts.

Eldred stuck the dragon for the twentieth time. "It's getting free!"

The lords drew their swords and charged. The men were quick and their blades quicker, but the beast would not release the now silent Lord Osbert.

The dragon swatted Lord Kenelm away, sending him flying into a rock. He lay stunned, feebly feeling for his sword on the ground, next to him. The dragon raked Lord Thom with its claws, ripping through his torso and dropping him to the ground in a bloody pile. Lord Vance and Lord Ferris retreated out of reach. Eldred clutched his spear and watched in horror. If the creature released Lord Osbert, it could grab Lord Kenelm. He was right there.

The dragon wiggled and stretched for the corpse of Lord Thom. It bit his leg and dragged his limp body closer. Once the body was close enough, the dragon stuffed the remains in its mouth and chewed slowly while looking over the remaining warriors.

Lord Vance raised his sword over his head. "Curse you, you Motherless dragon!"

The dragon swallowed and focused on Lord Vance. It opened its mouth and unleashed an ear-splitting roar that blasted the canyon. Lord Ferris covered his ears and stepped back. After a moment of hesitation, Eldred darted forward and dragged Lord Kenelm from the dragon's reach. The creature's scream went on for several seconds, showing off the inside of its cavernous mouth.

Lord Vance stood his ground. "Die, you abomination!"

The dragon glared at Lord Vance and stretched out to dig into the ground with its front claws, releasing Lord Osbert, who lay still. The creature strained, chest on the ground, locking its shoulders. It started inching its way out from the heap of stone and dirt, some of which tumbled down to the side in a fresh cloud of dust. It made an odd noise as it worked itself free. It seemed to Eldred it was laughing. Opimia had said they could laugh.

Eldred clutched his spear so tightly that his hands hurt. His mind raced. The passage. It was time to go. If he could reach Hobbie, he could ride away. The thought came again and again, but Eldred just stood and watched the dragon worm its way free.

Once the dragon slithered a few feet forward, Lord Vance and Lord Ferris hurled their spears, which bounced harmlessly off its head. Eldred threw his spear at the dragon's neck to similar effect.

Eldred grabbed Lord Kenelm's shoulder. "We have to go."

Lord Kenelm brushed him off.

Eldred grabbed both of Lord Kenelm's shoulders. "We have to go now!"

Lord Kenelm turned and looked Eldred in the eye. "It has to breathe. Stay here."

He took off running towards the dragon. Lord Vance and Lord Ferris were charging too. Lord Kenelm and Lord Ferris ran side by side between the dragon's outstretched paws with Lord Vance in pursuit, a dagger in each hand. Eldred stared in disbelief, then jogged after them. The dragon paused its efforts and opened its mouth to scream once again.

As the dragon screamed, its chin ten feet up in the air, Lord Kenelm and Lord Ferris stopped, grabbed hands and vaulted Lord Vance up into the dragon's mouth just as it slammed shut.

"No!" cried Eldred.

The dragon erupted in motion and made a guttural sound, thrashing its neck with growing intensity.

Lord Kenelm and Lord Ferris darted around the flailing beast and grabbed Lord Osbert. Eldred chased after them as they carried Lord Osbert to the entrance of the canyon, laying him down on his back in the dirt. He joined them as they turned to face the dragon with swords raised.

The dragon slid free of the piled stones and started pushing up on its front legs and smacking its head on the ground. It repeated the action several times in rapid succession, kicking up a cloud of red dust and rattling the nearby rocks. Then it convulsed and pawed at its chest, its motions growing weaker. Finally, it collapsed.

"He did it!" cried Lord Ferris.

AFTERMATH

Lord Kenelm pointed at the motionless creature. "We need to get him out of there."

Eldred shook his head. "They're gone. We should attend to Lord Osbert."

"Osbert's dead. Vance still lives," said Lord Ferris.

The two lords ran to the dragon's head and struggled to raise its upper jaw. Eldred trailed after them, picking up discarded spears.

"Leave those! We need your strength," said Lord Kenelm.

Eldred tossed each of the lords a spear. "If you want to look in there, we need to turn its head."

Eldred walked to the dragon's right side and worked his spear under the dragon's jaw. After watching Eldred, the lords followed suit. On Eldred's signal, they heaved. At first, the dragon's head barely moved, but once it reached the tipping point, it rolled smoothly onto its side, and the dragon's mouth opened slightly.

Lord Kenelm and Lord Ferris dropped their spears and raced around to the front of the dragon.

"Don't go near its teeth! We need to pry its jaws open!" shouted Eldred.

Eldred retrieved the dropped spears. Working together, they wedged its mouth open, leaving a narrow gap between the upper and lower fangs. Lord Kenelm hurriedly stepped through the opening.

Eldred pointed at the rows of teeth. "Be careful. A drop of venom can kill you."

Lord Kenelm pulled the tongue away from the floor of the dragon's mouth and searched through the exposed crannies.

"What are you doing?" asked Eldred.

"Here!" cried Lord Kenelm. He pulled down on a flap of skin and reached into the revealed orifice.

"He's fading!" shouted Lord Ferris.

Lord Kenelm drew his arm out and stepped back. "Eldred, get in here. We need your reach."

"Go!" screamed Lord Ferris.

Eldred cautiously stepped between the fangs and approached the tubelike opening. Peering inside, Eldred was surprised to see a boot. "It's him. He's here."

"We know. Get him out," said Lord Kenelm.

Eldred reached in and grabbed the boot by the toe. He pulled Lord Vance a few inches closer, but the narrow passage held Lord Vance tight and sucked him back when Eldred released to get a better hold.

"Hurry," said Lord Kenelm.

Eldred jammed his arm in as far as he could and gripped the ankle of the boot. He set his feet and worked Lord Vance up the passage inch by inch until he slithered out and dropped to the ground.

"Watch that," said Lord Ferris.

Eldred blocked Lord Kenelm's hand as he reached for Lord Vance. "Don't. There's venom."

Ignoring Lord Ferris's protests, Eldred slowly backed out of the dragon's mouth, dragging Lord Vance behind him. Out in the sun, the damage was clear. Blackened cuts ran down Lord Vance's forehead. His sword hand had an ugly, open wound. A pool of blood formed by his left shoulder. He took small gasping breaths and rolled his head slightly side to side.

Tears streaked down Lord Ferris's face. "Your father, that false king, did this. He may as well have stabbed Vance himself."

Eldred shuffled back. The patches on his hand and cheek seemed to itch this close to the dying man.

"What about your medicine?" asked Lord Kenelm.

Eldred nodded. "Yes, the powder. If we heat some water, I can make a paste."

Lord Vance stirred and spoke with slurred speech. "No. Keep him away."

Eldred looked Lord Kenelm in the eye. "Should I make the paste?"

Lord Kenelm glanced up at the sky. "Just get the horses."

Eldred surveyed the canyon. Nothing remained of Lord Thom; just a slight discoloration in the sand. Lord Osbert lay intact but crushed, taken in his moment of glory. The dragon, the most amazing of the Night Mother's creations, must have been shocked. Could it even have imagined suffering a violent death? It would surely make its way to the Hall of Ages piece by piece, crowding out the other exhibits. And Lord Vance, not dead yet, but soon to be. A small man even by Deiran standards—small, but graced with the speed and power of the Bond. He had faced an indomitable foe and yet found a means to prevail—the most dangerous of the Night Mother's creations, excepting one.

Eldred sighed and headed out to fetch the horses, the sound of the dragon's cry still echoing in his head. The most dangerous creation would be the winners—the victors of the day—who were likely just sitting down to tea. The Sun People had added four victims to their tally.

Outside the passage, Hobbie trotted over to Eldred. Eldred hugged his neck, holding on for several minutes, relaxing to the sound of Hobbie's heartbeat. They would ride away. It seemed unbelievable, but it was true. They would ride away.

When Eldred returned, leading the horses, Lord Vance lay still, his head in Lord Ferris's lap. Lord Ferris was washing Lord Vance's face with a wet cloth.

"Is he alive?" asked Eldred.

Lord Kenelm nodded from where he sat on a nearby rock, working his lower back with his knuckles.

Eldred looked over at the dragon. "Did Lord Vance know what he was doing?"

"Of course," snapped Lord Ferris.

Lord Kenelm sighed. "There was no other means to kill the dragon. Vance almost made it past the teeth." Lord Kenelm wiped his eyes. "So very close."

Eldred stood quietly at attention, occasionally checking the scrapes on his left arm and side. Fifteen minutes later, Lord Vance died. The lords wrapped him in blankets. Eldred gathered the sample bags and entered the dragon's mouth, cutting at the palate with his knife.

After some time, Lord Kenelm looked in on him. "We're headed out."

Eldred continued chipping into the bone. "Good."

"I don't see a change. Did you feel anything?"

"No. Nothing."

Lord Kenelm watched Eldred work. "This is valuable to them?"

"They use it to make the powder I was telling you about."

"So you are staying with the Wretcheds?"

Eldred paused. "I suppose so."

"I don't expect we will leave before noon tomorrow."

"The snow doesn't worry you?"

"It won't be easy, but we can't afford to wait," said Lord Kenelm. "Your father has already had time enough to set his treachery in motion."

"I'm sorry."

"I don't blame you."

Eldred gave a quick nod and resumed his work.

"I'll check down the hill before we ride out," said Lord Kenelm.

"Good luck to you, Lord Kenelm."

"And to you, Eldred. Bond or no Bond, you showed honor today."

VISITOR AT THE GATE

The afternoon slid into evening before Eldred finished collecting the dragon's brains. Eldred carried the last bags out of the dragon's mouth and packed them on Hobbie. The dragon appeared at peace. It could have just been sleeping.

Eldred set off, leading Hobbie through the canyon. He smiled as they made their way through the darkness. The night air was pleasantly cool and had an earthy scent. As he walked, he kept counting the specimen bags.

Beyond the canyon, the crescent moon gave enough light for Hobbie to walk unaided. Eldred mounted up and ate a snack. With some food in his stomach and the gentle rocking of the saddle, Eldred soon fell into a state of partial slumber, but Hobbie kept to the trail.

It was after midnight when they approached the gate. The sound of a muffled bell roused Eldred. Eldred patted Hobbie's neck. "Open the gate, Calvus. I'm tired."

There was no answer. Eldred stared at the window above the gate, pressing his lips together. "The gate, Calvus! Open the gate!"

Nothing stirred. Eldred sighed and glanced to the far side of the gate. Someone had set up a table covered with goods. Eldred dismounted and walked over to investigate. There were a variety of foods, including loaves of bread and smoked sausages. Eldred picked up a small loaf of white bread and ate it as he fished through a stack of clothes next to the food.

He stopped when he found a worn green hat with purple feathers mixed in the pile. "What's this? Why is my hat here?"

"Because you are leaving," said Valens, looking down from the window above the gate.

"Valens! What's happening?"

"I am here to see you off."

"What do you mean?" asked Eldred.

"In addition to your possessions, you will find winter clothes and food on the table. Our parting gifts to you."

Eldred gestured towards Hobbie. "I don't think you understand. Those bags are overflowing with dragon brains."

"Yes, we know. Sammanus spoke with your Lord Kenelm this evening. We heard about your heroic efforts."

Eldred rubbed his forehead. "I see. Let's talk tomorrow. I need rest. I need to get to my house."

Valens shook his head. "Would that such were possible, Eldred. You left us rather a mess. Sir Aemilanus is quite unhappy."

"He tried to kill me!" said Eldred.

"As he would tell it, he tried to prevent you from stealing."

"I borrowed the packets. Now I have returned them and brought the brains as well. The dragon's dead, but that's not my fault."

"Interesting. Lord Kenelm gave you credit enough. According to him, you were indispensable to their efforts."

Eldred sighed and leaned on the table. "No. No. It just wasn't the champion you hoped for."

"Neither of you were."

Eldred looked Valens in the eye. "I'm still the key to the short way."

"Perhaps you could be," said Valens.

"You must live up to your part," demanded Eldred.

"Our part, Eldred? You nullified the agreement when you killed the dragon. Our part is done. You are strengthened by our previous treatments. You possess two packets, which you are free to keep. Build your strength with them if you like."

"What about my training? And what about a named blade? You're supposed to help me kill the Mercian king!"

"Since you like to borrow from people, why not take your father's sword? Capito has a worthy reputation and a long history with my people. For your training, go out in the world and learn. The world is vast and full of lessons. But you must move on from Turicum. Our gates are closed to you."

"You're banning me because I defended myself from a crazy old man. Does Opimia agree?"

"We speak with one voice," said Valens. "Return when you end the count. Then, we will take the next step."

Eldred clasped his hands on his head.

Valens gestured to the table. "But let us part on an amicable note. On the table, you will find your gifts, presents of the sort that friends might exchange. Sammanus provided a warm jacket he is certain will fit you. Opimia has offered forth a cloak that will keep you dry in any storm. From Sebine, fur lined boots, for comfort on your ride south. Lady Agrippa has long since granted you the finest of horses. And Marcia has cooked many of your favorite dishes, including the cakes."

"The cakes," muttered Eldred.

Eldred beckoned Hobbie and started unloading the sample bags next to the table. "Don't forget my present to you—enough brains to make a mound of Balaur powder. That's worth far more than two packets and a few flat cakes!"

"A princely gift, indeed. The first of your two great gifts."

Eldred jerked around to look up at Valens. "You want something more?"

"The count. You must let them know the count is thirteen."

Eldred resumed unloading. "Hmm, thirteen."

"A report to your Uncle Julian, thirteen citizens killed and eaten by the dragon."

Eldred paused and put his hands on his hips. "The true count is three warriors, all killed today."

"What do you mean?" asked Valens.

"I never witnessed the dragon kill your citizens. I only saw the notes. Mastery—Sun People mastery. You led me around by the nose the same as you did for the dragon, the same as you did for the expedition. None of your citizens perished. You're simply becoming island barbarians, like in the tale."

"Is this another speculation based on some dream, Eldred?"

"No. I'm not blind. Shall I gather Julian's men and have them sail out to Imbros and Sarnia, like your boats do almost every day?"

Valens pursed his lips. "Very well. What do you want?"

Eldred wearily placed the last bag down by the table. "You saved my life, Valens. I would have died, or at least been disfigured—more disfigured." Eldred's eyes wandered to Galla's Mound, which showed clearly in the moonlight. "I'll keep your secret, just as a friend might. I would find no joy in the destruction of Turicum or the slaughter of your people for breaking the covenant."

Valens nodded slowly.

"I can present the count as thirteen, or any number you like," said Eldred. "You need not destroy another house or write more flowery notes. Just tell me the count directly and I'll share it with my uncle."

"A worthy gift." Valens considered. "Forty-three then. I ask you to give the count as forty-three."

"Fine. Thirty more to make their way to the islands. I'll make your count known."

Eldred took the clothing and most of the food. His stomach growled with interest when he found a batch of Marcia's flat cakes rolled in a cloth.

After Eldred packed the last item, he turned to Valens. "My path seems so long."

"You are a strong man, Eldred, with many years."

Eldred held his face tight. "Mother's blessings, Valens."

"Farewell, Eldred."

The hour was late when Eldred arrived at the lodge. He unpacked his supplies as quietly as he could and opened the door.

Lord Kenelm sat up. "Oh, it's you, Eldred."

Lord Ferris briefly glared at Eldred, then turned away and settled into his blankets.

Lord Kenelm yawned loudly. "You decided to join us?"

"I did."

"Good. Get some rest. Tomorrow we start for home."

HOMEWARD BOUND

Eldred examined the line of swords stuck in the side of the hill, gleaming dully in the pale light of morning. Three new swords joined the memorial. Lord Thom's practice sword was stuck in the ground off to the side; there had been nothing to bury. Lord Osbert's swords marked both graves, since Lord Vance's blade had proved unrecoverable. Eldred wondered which contained the corpse of Lord Vance, a thorny man, an ignorant man, but a hero.

Lord Kenelm walked up behind Eldred. "Will your friends, the Wretcheds, come up here to steal these swords?"

Eldred shook his head. "No. They prefer things that they make themselves."

"I hope you're right."

Lord Kenelm gazed down the side of the hill towards Turicum. "I thought you were going to stay."

Eldred shrugged. "I never committed to staying. I repaid them. That's done."

"You should never have gone to their Wretched city."

"They're more like us than you think. They might surprise you."

Lord Kenelm theatrically gripped the hilt of his sword. "Best that they don't."

Eldred smiled and turned south, looking at the mountains. "Now we just head back. My father will be waiting."

Lord Kenelm furrowed his brow. "He'll be surprised."

They set off an hour later with Lord Kenelm and Lord Ferris sharing the lead, riding abreast of each other. To Eldred's annoyance, Lord Ferris kept

Thunder and took Lord Vance's horse as an additional mount. Lord Kenelm took Lord Thom's horse as his spare. Eldred took Lord Osbert's horse, which had originally been Yeowars. In addition, they each pulled a lightly loaded pack horse.

Lord Kenelm and Lord Ferris constantly took the measure of the other. Every time Eldred checked, they were scowling as they stared into each other's eyes.

"What're you doing?" asked Eldred.

Lord Ferris frowned. "Nothing. Nothing that pertains to you in any way."

"You've been staring at each other for hours. Have you gone mad?"

Lord Kenelm turned stiffly to face Eldred. "It's not your concern. This is just a consequence of our—changed situation."

"I don't understand."

"That will always be your problem," said Lord Ferris.

The behavior continued as they set camp that evening. The lords were locked in visual combat from the moment they sat down to their supper of dried meat.

Eldred enjoyed a helping of pork in lark's sauce from the supplies the Sun People had provided. "You can eat my food. You don't have enough for the crossing."

Lord Ferris glanced towards Eldred. "I would sooner eat dirt than the offal that the Wretcheds packed for you."

Lord Kenelm sighed. "We have enough, Eldred. If we must, we can butcher the pack horses. They're no longer essential."

Eldred grimaced. "Kill a pack horse? They carried our gear across half the world. I rode one for days. Can't you simply eat the food provided by the citizens of Turicum. It's delicious. They didn't poison it."

The lords returned to their contest without comment.

The wind grew colder the next day as the trail wound higher up into the mountains. When they paused to switch mounts, Eldred dug out the jacket Sammanus had given him and put it on. As was the case for much of the clothing in Turicum, it was very colorful, dark blue and gray and sewn through with red and purple lines. He donned the cloak from Opimia and the boots from Sebine.

Lord Ferris laughed. "Are you dressing up for our amusement?"

Lord Kenelm set down his canteen and shook his head. "You won't want to be wearing that later."

Eldred adjusted the cloak. "I'm dressing for the weather."

Throughout the day, with its occasional bouts of freezing rain, Eldred found himself joining in their behavior out of boredom. First, he would follow behind Lord Kenelm and stare at Lord Ferris's face. Then, he would drift behind Lord Ferris and direct his gaze towards Lord Kenelm. Whenever the lords noticed his behavior, Eldred turned away and studied the scenery.

They made camp that night at a spot they had stayed at on the way out. It was at the top of a bluff against a stand of trees. The view was directed back to the north, towards Turicum, but the mountains had long since concealed any sign of either the city or the sea. Eldred collected wood and built a fire as the lords sat and stared into each other's eyes.

Eldred settled with his blankets next to the fire. "It's getting colder."

"How observant," said Lord Ferris.

"What if the trail is covered in snow ahead? What if it gets too deep for the horses?" asked Eldred.

"Then we go around," said Lord Kenelm.

"Around what? Around all of it?" said Eldred.

Lord Kenelm shrugged. "We survived the dragon. A bit of cold won't kill us."

"If the horses die, we'll die," said Eldred.

"The horses are fine," said Lord Kenelm tiredly. "Your horse seems to enjoy the cold."

"Fret about it if you must. Just don't bother us with it," said Lord Ferris.

Eldred frowned, shifting to find some comfort on the rocky ground. The lords sat up for another hour, engaged in their silent debate.

The following day favored them with better weather. The sun came out and the breeze was light, though brisk. Snow capped mountains rose in a wall before them. Patches of snow lay beside the path wherever there was shade. Eldred remained snug in his Turicum provided gear and marveled at the scenery at the start of the day, but after a while, he found himself joining in the contest.

He was riding behind Lord Kenelm, looking blankly at Lord Ferris, when Lord Ferris turned to him and barked. "Stop it."

It took a moment before Eldred was aware that Lord Ferris was speaking to him. "What?"

"Stop it. Stop staring," snarled Lord Ferris.

"I'm not meaning to," said Eldred.

Lord Ferris fingered his sword hilt. "I don't care. Restrain yourself or I'll deal with you."

Eldred shrugged and focused on the distant mountains.

After an hour, Eldred drifted behind Lord Ferris and began gazing at Lord Kenelm. With the gentle swaying of Hobbie and the monotony of the long ride, Eldred's mind wandered. When he came to his senses, he found both lords staring at him.

"What is it?" asked Eldred.

Neither lord answered Eldred. Lord Ferris shook his head and muttered something under his breath.

They paused by a stream to water the horses at midday. The lords searched through their saddlebags for something to eat while Eldred helped himself to a meat pie. Eventually, the lords settled on some turnips that Lord Kenelm pulled out of his pack. The three were standing and eating while the horses drank from the stream.

"What was that about?" asked Eldred.

The lords showed no reaction.

"Earlier today, you were both staring at me," continued Eldred.

"You were looking at us," corrected Lord Ferris.

"I was. But today you stared back. You both acted strangely—more strangely than usual."

Lord Kenelm pressed his lips together. "There was a bit of noise about you."

"What does that mean?" asked Eldred.

"Sometimes, with a squire or—someone young, they might show a trace of the Bond," said Lord Kenelm. "It seemed like that."

"You sensed the Bond in me? You both did?"

Lord Ferris scoffed. "No, most definitely not. Kenelm is calling it noise. I don't agree. Noise of the sort he mentioned is pleasant. You touch the edge of the Bond with someone who is not fully present. What you have is diabolical. It tugs. It annoys. I heard of a boy who had something like this. He lived out by Bert, near the Vindius Mountains."

"And?" said Eldred.

"They killed him," said Lord Ferris.

Eldred crossed his arms. "Maybe someone else dies this time."

Lord Kenelm raised his palms. "Now, let's be reasonable, both of you. Eldred, I expect you find this news encouraging, but hold your hopes in check. Lord Ferris is right that there is something odd in this noise."

Lord Ferris narrowed his eyes. "Did the Wretcheds do something to you? You said they were treating your wounds, which is why your face is so ugly."

Eldred sighed. "I have a Deiran stone. Perhaps transference triggered it during the battle with the dragon."

Lord Ferris shook his head. "Well, you had best hope your condition fades quickly. If you are as aggravating as this when you reach Boar's Tusk, it will not be long before someone puts you out of your misery. That is, if I can't restrain myself with the headache you are giving me."

"The noise does distract," said Lord Kenelm, glancing at Eldred's jacket.

Eldred rode well out in front for the rest of the day at Lord Ferris's insistence. It was twilight when they reached the next campsite they had used on their trip out.

Eldred searched for wood in the dark. When he returned with an armful of branches, he found Lord Kenelm butchering the smallest pack horse.

"Oh," said Eldred.

"Get a fire going," said Lord Ferris from his seat by the darkened fire pit.

Eldred grunted and started arranging the wood.

"You should build a separate fire for yourself. Your noise is growing more insufferable."

"Find your own wood, then," snapped Eldred.

Lord Ferris moved to another log and massaged his temples. Lord Kenelm sliced open the horse's hide and carved out chunks of flesh. He set the meat on a small patch of snow. Once he had a good amount piled up, he started cutting thin strips and rubbing them down with snow.

Lord Kenelm glanced over his shoulder as he worked. "We'll make jerky."

"How long will it keep?" asked Lord Ferris.

"About a week."

Lord Ferris nodded. "We can butcher Eldred's fancy mount after that."

Lord Kenelm continued slicing the horsemeat. "Your games grow tiresome, Ferris. Vance is gone. Best you adapt to the changed circumstances."

Lord Ferris scowled.

With Eldred's help, Lord Kenelm gathered some long thin branches and built a lattice over the fire, where he draped strips of meat. After the last strip was hung, he fished a small iron pan out of a saddlebag. "We'll cook some steaks tonight. You should eat some, Eldred. It's more hearty than whatever the Wretcheds packed for you."

Eldred made a face. "You're eating horsemeat."

"Horsemeat is meat," said Lord Kenelm.

Lord Kenelm and Lord Ferris ate with terrific hunger. Eldred contented himself with sliced sausage and pickled cabbage from the stores the Sun People had provided.

Lord Ferris rose in the predawn darkness. He took most of Lord Kenelm's meat strips and rode off on Thunder, leading his spare mount and pack horse.

Once he was gone, Eldred reached over to nudge Lord Kenelm.

Lord Kenelm kept his eyes shut. "What?"

"Lord Ferris left."

"I know."

"Should we follow him?"

Lord Kenelm edged further away from Eldred. "If he heads south."

"He took most of your food."

"It's fine, Eldred. It's all fine. I need rest and I can't think while you're here. Why don't you go? I'll follow later."

"Very well," said Eldred.

"Just stay alert."

Eldred felt slightly chilled as he set out on foot, leading Hobbie and Yeowars's mount. He could see Lord Ferris's tracks occasionally, as the road was about half dirt and half stone over that stretch. Freezing gusts blew down from the peaks above, but Eldred warmed up as he walked.

When dawn finally arrived, Eldred mounted Hobbie and helped himself to some soft cheese spread on hard bread. The bread was hard, not stale. He scanned the distance ahead and behind for the lords, but saw no sign of them. He pulled back on Hobbie, slowing the pace. Was Lord Kenelm able to follow? He had looked tired and cold.

Eldred reached a fork he recalled from the outward trip, a smaller track going east-west while the main road went north-south. Ten minutes further on, he came to a patch of fresh snow bereft of hoofprints covering the route. Shaking his head, Eldred returned to the crossroad to investigate. The tracks were clear; Lord Ferris had ridden west.

"That idiot," muttered Eldred.

Eldred waited at the fork for an hour, pacing back and forth to stay warm, before spotting Lord Kenelm in the distance. When Lord Kenelm finally reached the crossroads, Eldred pointed west.

"He went on the wrong road!"

Lord Kenelm kept moving. "Then we ride without him."

Eldred mounted up and chased after him. "You knew he was going to leave?"

"He was no friend to either of us."

"He could die out there on his own."

"It would be best if he did," said Lord Kenelm. "Now, please either ride ahead or behind. It must be a good distance. The noise wears on me."

"Will he double back?" continued Eldred.

Lord Kenelm drew up his horse. "We have seen the last of him. Why don't you go ahead?"

Eldred rode on.

FINAL STEPS

Every day was an exercise in solitude. Eldred rode ahead, stopping each evening to build a fire to guide Lord Kenelm. Each night, Lord Kenelm arrived later and later.

On the eleventh night after Lord Ferris had slipped away, Eldred sat by the fire and gazed at Regillium. A half moon illuminated the empty city. From time to time, Eldred glanced down the trail for Lord Kenelm.

Lord Kenelm did not arrive until two hours after sundown. He was shivering as he climbed down from his saddle and settled in by the fire. Eldred set the horses for the night and dug out horsemeat strips from a saddlebag.

Eldred handed the strips to Lord Kenelm. "Are you well?"

"I'm just tired, Eldred. I still feel that blow from the dragon, but I'm alive, thank the Mother. After we pass through Hobart Gap tomorrow, I'll be only three days from home."

"You're not returning to Boar's Tusk?" asked Eldred.

"No. Arriving at Boar's Tusk without allies is not in my plans."

"What do you think he's done?"

"I'm not sure. The other lords had seats closer to your father. I expect that helps my cause. Still, I have neighbors of questionable temperament. I'm not certain of what I'll find."

"Then we part after Hobart Gap," said Eldred.

"Are you certain?"

"We killed the dragon. I have a glimmer of the Bond. The circumstances are promising."

Lord Kenelm sighed. "The noise, Eldred. Ferris is right about its nature. People will object. And it's growing stronger. Or perhaps I grow more weary. You should be careful. You should come to Evenwood with me."

"To be your steward?"

Lord Kenelm smiled. "You have no interest in being anyone's steward. Do you?".

"No, I don't. There isn't time enough with all my plans. I must ask though, do you need a steward?"

Lord Kenelm raised his palms. "You have me confused now. What do you want?"

"There's a boy, a young man, who lives in the village of Mamble on the banks of the River Stour. Do you know it?"

Lord Kenelm nodded. "Yes, that's not far from my lands."

Eldred crinkled up his face. "He's not the most polished young man. He can be a bit rough. But take all the squires at the Academy, you won't find anyone smarter. That should matter for a steward."

"I take it he did not pass the trial."

Eldred shook his head. "No. His name is Dreven. He was the one thrown out with me."

Lord Kenelm raised his eyebrows. "Oh."

They stared at the fire in silence for a spell.

Lord Kenelm cleared his throat. "So, despite Dreven's troubled past, you wish me to take this young man as my steward in your place?"

"I would," said Eldred. "I very much would."

"I suppose I could try it. But I'm a strong believer in character. His actions would reflect on me if he were in my service."

"You won't be disappointed. And he is clever." Eldred gave a short laugh. "Perhaps too clever. But that should be a good trait in a steward."

Lord Kenelm smiled. "So you keep assuring me."

"Thank you," said Eldred.

"What of you? What are these plans you spoke of?"

Eldred shrugged. "I'm still thinking them through. With this Mercian frame, I probably only have fifteen or sixteen years left."

Lord Kenelm narrowed his eyes. "That's a lot of time. That's half your life."

Eldred rubbed his chin. "It's not much. It's hardly any time at all—not for all I mean to do."

Lord Kenelm laughed. "By your thinking, I should be in great fear of dying in ten years. What has put all these dreadful thoughts in your mind? It's the Wretcheds. Am I right?"

Eldred studied the city on the hill. "They showed me things. They have mastery."

Lord Kenelm waved his hand dismissively. "Forget their nonsense. Come with me. You don't have to be a steward. We will leave that honor for your friend. Some of my vassals lack the Bond. I expect you won't bother them. Your condition could even be helpful if we end up fighting other Deirans."

"I'll think on it," said Eldred. "What about Lord Ferris? Do you think he'll make it back?"

"He might. If you meet him, be careful."

Eldred clapped his hands. "He should take care."

Lord Kenelm laughed. "Calm yourself. You should sleep. Your noise tugs less when you sleep."

It was an easy ride toward Hobart Gap the next morning. The weather was brisk but not freezing now that they were at lower altitude. Eldred rode in front, keeping about a quarter mile ahead of Lord Kenelm.

They passed through the gap before noon. A few miles on, Eldred reached the ridge trail that led to Evenwood. He traced it as it stretched out for miles on a rocky trek, winding off to the west. Eldred's road banked to the south, heading down a series of switchbacks to the valley below.

Eldred turned to watch Lord Kenelm approach. At two hundred yards, Lord Kenelm set his jaw. At a hundred feet, Lord Kenelm rubbed his temples and his face grew taut.

Lord Kenelm stopped forty feet away. "Did you make your decision?"

Eldred nodded. "I'll continue on to Boar's Tusk."

"Your mind is fixed?"

"Yes. I need to settle things."

"You're not worried about what they might do?"

Eldred shrugged. "They're my family."

"If you change your mind, make your way to Evenwood."

"We will meet again, Lord Kenelm."

Lord Kenelm smiled. "We should have died, Eldred. Everything now is only by the grace of the Night Mother. Don't forget that. Go on. I'll stop holding you back. May the Son walk beside you."

"Mother's blessings, Lord Kenelm!"

THANKS

Thanks for taking the time to read The Dragon of Turicum. I hope you enjoyed your stay in Gauraci and sharing the adventures of Eldred. For those who are interested to learn what happens next—does Eldred have the Bond, will the Deirans welcome him home with open arms—please continue on with the second book in the series, **The Crooked Ladder.** These matters and a great many more are played out, and we see the return of many familiar characters.

For my part, I really enjoyed writing the book and love getting feedback. If you can spare the time, then—unlike Sammanus who showed greater reserve when stating his requests—I am begging you to leave feedback. A rating for the book would be most appreciated. For the more loquacious among you, a review consisting of a few sentences would capture my attention.

Best wishes to all of you as you battle your dragons!

ACKNOWLEDGMENTS

My deepest thanks to my friends and family who entertained my long running ruminations regarding what would make sense and what ought to happen in the land of Guaraci. They suffered through very rough drafts of the book and provided great feedback and inspiration. These long suffering individuals include, among others: A. Bracher, J.S. Bracher, R. Bracher, J. Etow, J. Kintner, M. Liinamaa, M. Miller, K. Roberts, B. Shreve, J. Velsy.

This book benefitted from great professional contributions, including the cover art, illustrations, editing and beta reading. My thanks and appreciation to each of these individuals.

Cover by Jeff Brown, jeffbrowngraphics.com

Map Illustration by FictiveDesigns

Line Editing/Proofreading by Kit Duncan

Interior Book Design by Lorna Reid

Guerilla Marketing by C. Schelstraete

Beta Readers: Sarah Sutton, SJ Davison, M.D. DeCillis, Ellie Race, Pul Parmer

.

Printed in Great Britain
by Amazon